MOSES

(For the love of Jane book 3)

GRACE WILLIAMS

J

The journey ends.

With love

x Grace Williams
xxx

Moses

Disclaimer

This is a work of fiction. Names characters, places and incidents either are the product of the author's imagination or are used fictitiously, and are no resemblance to actual persons, living or dead business establishments, events or locales is entirely coincidental.

Contents

Dedication

In memory of two very special people who have sadly left us, my Step Dad John, you were part of my life for over 50 years, I will hold onto those special memories.

My beautiful friend Darlene who gave me so much love and believed in me. I will read this book too aloud for you to hear in heaven.

My Brother Ian and Sister Colette, I love you both very much, thank you for being as excited as me about these books and wanting to tell the world.

Acknowledgments

To my family and friends, thank you for your support and love, your patience and most of all believing in me. I have some very special people in my life who without you I couldn't have written this trilogy.

Thank you to my lovely friend Greg Anderson who allowed me to use him as Jasper, I hope I described you well and to my Best friend Phil who is my Moses, thank you for keeping my secret. My gorgeous girls Laura and Carianne I love you and hope you approve. Denise, Dark Desires, thank you for allowing me to share your wonderful things and collaborating with Laura's FM and me.

Tempo O'Neil thank you for your beautiful piece of music, I love it.

Lerin Gaines thank you for showcasing me on your shows, it is a delight and so much fun. Looking forward to working with you on Dorian in my next series and joining you in September for Reading Between the Wines.

Playlist

Feeling Good – Nina Simone

My Little Girl – Tim McGraw

Just the Way you are – Bruno Mars

You're the First the Last my Everything – Barry White

At Last – Etta James

Jealous of the Angels – Donna Taggart

Goodbye – Kenney Rogers

Chapter 1

Bad News

Moses was sat rubbing his hands together, his palms were sweating, he felt like Princess and the Pea in the chair, he was moving about unable to get comfortable, leaning back, his arms across his body to leaning forward, his legs open, rubbing his hands together, he felt like his t-shirt was stuck to his back, he was getting anxious waiting for Mr Guthrie to come into the consulting room, he had put this off for too long but Jane always came first. There was no way he would leave her until he knew she was okay, regardless of what was coming for him or moreso what was wrong, so here he was finally waiting for the bad news.

Mr Guthrie walked in with a half smile, Moses stood and shook his hand.
"Christian, it's good to finally see you back, I understand you have been out of the country?"
"Yes I was helping my friend Jane, she had an accident and needed support."
"This is your close friend Jane, we spoke about when you came to me before you went away, she is your next of kin?" He asked moving around to his desk, flicking to the details page of Moses file.
"Yes that's right she is." Moses moved further to the edge of the chair, pushing his hands down his legs trying to wipe the sweat off. He wanted to just shout out *for fuck sake tell me get it over with.* But he knew he couldn't. His heart was pounding, his mouth dry, he knew it was going to be bad.

"Okay, well I have reviewed your scan and test results, it is as we thought Christian."
"Please Doc call me Moses, only my Mum or the Police call me Christian it makes it easier to take in."
"Okay Moses as you wish, as you know you have a lump in your testicals, how do they feel at the moment?"
"Heavy, painful, I do tend to feel it alot, maybe it's because I know something is there that shouldn't be. You mentioned something else last time too Doc, Meta something?"

"Yes that's right Moses, Metatstatic Cancer, we have found it has spread to your lymph nodes in your stomach, it's not just your testical. We only did a lower scan I think it maybe wise to do a further scan of the whole body now as it has been some time since we saw you last. We know it has spread so we need to see if it is in your lungs or not. We need to be realisitic, you have left this along time, so a new full body scan will help us determine how bad it is and if it has spread anywhere else. Then we can decide how we are going to progress."

Moses listened his head was full, he wasn't sure if he heard right. He felt physically sick.

"Excuse me Doc," he lept out of his chair, his hand across his mouth. He rushed out of the door knocking into the nurse as he rushed to the toilet, he ran into the cubicle and slid onto his knees as he emptied his stomach into the bowl. Mr Guthrie followed him in, the door to the toilet was open, the nurse was behind him stopping anyone else coming in behind him. He handed him his hankerchief, Moses took it and wiped his face, his legs were trembling as he stood, tears staining his face.

"How are you feeling Moses?, I know it's a lot to take in, I was hoping you would bring someone with you, it's not something you should hear alone."

"It's fine Doc, the only one I could bring is Jane but I wouldn't put her through this."

"Christi...Moses sorry, this isn't going away anytime soon and you will need support."

"I know Doc, I told you, I'm fine, can we just get back to it?" He motioned to Mr Guthrie to leave the toilet and go back to the consulting room while he washed his face.

He returned to the room sitting down, he put his head in his hands the heels pushed into his eyes, he sighed heavily.

"Okay Doc, what's next?"

"We will get you back in a few days for your scan, further blood tests today, the nurse is waiting for you after this and will take you through to get them done. Once we have the scan results back I will give you a call and get you back in and we can discuss where we go from here. You need to understand Moses this is not going to be easy, you need support. I don't mean just from charities here but from friends and family."

"I understand, thank you, anything else Doc?"

"No, that's it with me for today, I think that is enough to take in for one day." He smiled and stood up shaking Moses hand.

"Thanks Doc, I will see you in a week or so then."

"Yes you will. Take care."

"Little late for that now", he snapped walking out.

The nurse was waiting for him, she gave him a sad smile and led him towards the Phlebotomist who was waiting for him.

"Hi Mr Abbott, would you like to take a seat here?" She showed him to the seat and placed a cushion on the arm of the chair. Moses was in a daze and just nodded and did as he was asked.

He was done, he walked out of the door in a daze, not sure of where he was going. He finally found an entrance and headed for the nearest bench. He slumped down into it leaning back putting his arm across the back, he took his phone out of his pocket and turned it back on, it lit up with missed calls and texts from various people including Jane. She had been ringing daily using all the skills she had to find out what was going on, but Moses wasn't giving away anything. She would be the last person he would tell at the moment, he would wait until he knew more and speak with Jasper first, depending on the situation. He dialled G.

"Hey Brother, where have you been? You never turn your phone off?" G said softly full of concern.

"Well today I needed too. We need to talk, can you meet me at my place?"

"What's going on Moses, you never go to your place?" G knew straight away this wasn't going to be an easy conversation whatever it was.

"Just get there when you can, I will be back there in about 15 minutes."

"Will meet you there." G left the bike he was working on and headed out.

Gwen caught him as he left. "Where are you going in such a hurry?"

"Out Gwen, I will be back later!!" he yelled at her.

"Woo there Mr, no need to rip my head off!" Gwen stood with her hands on her hips staring at him.

G strode back towards her getting into her face his nose almost touching hers.

"Gwen there are times when you don't need to know everything and now is one of those." He glared at her, their eyes not moving.

"Well there is no harm in being civil, whatever has crawled up your arse and annoyed you today you don't get to speak to me like that, when all I did was ask out of caring about you."

G softened. "Gwen love, I am sorry, but right now I need to be somewhere, if I can talk about it later I will." He put his hand on her shoulder and pulled her into his chest, he kissed the top of her head hugging her tight.

"See wasn't difficult was it?" she looked up at him and smiled. He shook his head, let her go and walked away.

"See you later Gwen."

"Okay love, here if you need to talk." She waved as he reached his bike and started it up.

Pulling on his crash helmet and gloves he screeched out of the car park and sped off down the road. Within 20 minutes he reached Moses house. He took a deep breath as he turned off the bike and got off. He felt sick to the stomach, really unsure of what he was going to hear but he had that feeling this wasn't good.

Chapter 2

Perfecting the lies

Jane had been up early she still felt something was wrong, but she was trying to distract herself, she had called Moses earlier but his phone was off, she paced around waiting for him to call, Jasper didn't say a word he just watched her. She chewed the inside of her mouth when she was nervous, he could tell she was doing it again as the side of her cheek was sucked in. She walked into the shower room pulling her hair up on top of her head clipping it up. She was still naked but felt comfortable with her body finally, now they were alone she was happy to walk around like it.

She headed to the kitchen and made a drink for them both as she walked back in her phone rang. She pounced on it as she put the cups down and squeezed onto the edge of the bed pushing Jasper over. He laughed shaking his head at her, whatever was his space always became hers when she wanted it.

"Hi love, sorry I didn't realise my phone had died I hadn't plugged the charger in last night."
Jane raised her eyebrow not sure whether to believe him or not, she looked around at Jasper and scowled, he couldn't help but smile at her. He wondered how many times she did that to him.
"Oh okay, well you know how to worry someone. Did you see the Doctor about your back?"
"Yes, as promised I did, he said I had pulled a muscle, so not sure how I did it, but it will be fine in a week or two."
"Okay well just rest please, don't go overdoing it at work or anything."
"Yes boss." He laughed.
Jane tutted. "Okay go and do what you need to and we will catch up tomorrow. Love you."
"Okay babe. love you too. Say Hi to Jay for me."
"Thanks, I will." Jane hung up sighing, looking at Jasper. She climbed onto the bed sitting in front of him crossing her legs.

She huffed "Apparently he pulled a muscle in his back and he will be fine in a couple of weeks."

"Well, that's good news Belle, not as bad as you thought." Jasper wasn't convinced either and would get to speak to him when Jane was out of the way. He saw how grey he looked when he went home.

Jasper took a mouthful of tea "Right then your last day at home, what are we going to do today?"

"That's easy." she giggled pulling his hand, bringing him towards her, she rubbed noses with him whispering. "I want you all day long."

Jasper smiled. "Well, if that's what my lady wants that's what my lady will get."

He climbed off the bed and walked into the main bathroom turning the taps on to fill the bath, squeezed some bubbles in and went back to the bedroom, Jane looked at him as he came back in raising her eyebrows.

"What are you doing?"

"Running a bath, why?"

"I said I wanted you all day long and you moved off the bed and went into the bathroom!"

Jasper smiled, gulped down his tea, picked her up and threw her over his shoulder slapping her bottom, Jane was giggling as he walked quickly with her. As they got to the bathroom the bubbles were almost at the top of the bath. Jasper turned the taps off put Jane on the floor, putting his foot in testing the temperature, he nodded happy it wasn't too hot for them both, he climbed in and sat down against the end, he put his hand up for her to join him, as she climbed in he turned her around so she was facing away from him, she sat down between his legs sinking back into his chest with a deep sigh. The bubbles covered her to her chin giving her a beard, she laughed trying to move them away.

Feeling good– Nina Simone

"Mmmmmm, this feels good, we don't do this often enough." Jane mewled. Jasper put his hands on her shoulders, bending to kiss the back of her neck. He worked his thumbs up and down as she bent forward groaning softly. He moved out onto her shoulders in circles, Jane whimpered, feeling the tension leave her. She brought her knees up against her chest, as Jasper worked down her back, He moved closer and licked up her spine that was out of the water. Jane felt a gentle tremor move through her body, she was relaxing, the warmth of the water and Jaspers touch were perfect. He gently pulled her into him, Jane went willingly, his hands moving over her shoulders onto her breasts. She slid down a little more on his body, the water lapping at her skin teasing her, she could feel Jaspers cock growing hard pushing into her back, her nipples responded under his touch, he followed the line of her areola as her nipples grew harder, he smiled kissing her shoulder, biting gently, kissing her again, she tilted her head, as he moved up with teasing licks and kisses until he reached her ear, his tongue teased around the outside, Jane tingled as he blew gently, his tongue teased a little more dipping into the shell, as he licked, he blew, the hotness of his tongue turning cool as he blew on her, Jane shuddered completely lost in his touch. Jasper moved his arms from over her shoulder, lifting her arms so his were underneath, he moved his hand along her right thigh pulling her leg open, his hand moved back up to her tummy. Moving his left hand back to her right breast, cupping it from underneath. His right hand moving down her body, to the top of her pussy, Jasper pulled on her nipple making Jane gasp. He moved his hand down slowly enjoying the feel of her smoothness, she opened her legs wider for him, her left leg hanging over the edge of the bath. He moved his fingers down to feel her folds, it was slightly open, he slid a finger inside as Jane moaned, his other fingers opened her pussy allowing the water to tease her more, he flicked her clitoris, Jane groaned deeply pushing her bottom into him. His cock now rock hard for her, Jane turned her head, Jasper moved around so he could catch her lip in his teeth, his finger moving deeper inside her, another joining it, Jane arched her back as he bit down on her lip again, he cupped her chin kissing her hard, their breathing getting deep. Jane let go, her orgasm about to take her. Jasper stopped, lifting her up, she knew without words what he wanted, he opened his legs as Jane held onto the bath, she slid her pussy slowly onto his waiting cock, they both moaned loudly as he filled her. Jane used the edge of the bath to give her leverage to move up and down on him. He grabbed her thighs underneath, helping her slowly move up and down. Hissing through his teeth whispered. "Fuck why haven't we done this before?"

Jane groaned in response. Her breathing getting faster.

"Don't come Belle." He whispered. She nodded slowing down.

Jane lifted herself off standing up, she bent holding onto the bath about to turn around as Jasper grabbed her bottom opening her cheeks, burying his face in her, the water was dripping off her, Jasper licked her making her giggle, he bit her bottom and spanked her before turning her around. She bent and kissed him catching his bottom lip in her teeth. She bit gently making him pull away, he caught her wet bottom again, spanking her leaving a red mark making her let go of his tongue. He pulled her down to him.

"I want to wash you Belle then take you back to bed and lick you dry."

Jane smiled grinding herself against him.

"If you don't want another spank lady you better stop that now."

Jane grinned at him lowering her eyes, giving him her little girl look.

"That doesn't work either." He laughed kissing her.

Jasper turned and grabbed the bath cream, squeezing some on his hand, he put the bottle back and rubbed his hands together grinning at her, putting his hands on her shoulders covering her in more bubbles circling across her neck and chest, he moved onto her breasts moaning, Jane watched him intently as he circled her nipples again, moving to the bottom cupping them, he pushed them together making Jane laugh, he moved his face down rubbing his nose back and forth against her nipples. Covering his face and beard in bubbles, Jane rubbed it in, washing his face as he worked down her body. He lifted her up and washed her stomach.

"Open wide Belle." Jane looked down smiling at him.

"I think if you do mine then I will do yours?"

Jasper pushed his cock up above the water, "I'm game, ready when you are."

Jane laughed, she couldn't help it, he was like a little boy. She opened her legs for him as he slid his soapy hand between them, washing her. He moved down her legs finishing her feet.

"Turn Belle and sit." She did as he asked and knelt in front of him so he could wash her back. "Come and lay back and wash it off love." She did and moved down the bath turning over moving back up the bath towards him with a naughty look in her eye.

"On your knees Mr." she beckoned.

Jasper did, she moved in closer, she began washing him down, creating more bubbles, she moved down his chest, circling his nipples making them both laugh, she tweaked his making him wince.

"Oh, you want to play games do you?"

Jane shook her head and continued down his body, over his stomach, they both stared at each other as she reached the start of his cock, Jane poured more bath crème into her hands rubbing them together. She moved one hand down his stomach onto his thigh and across onto his balls, cupping them. Jasper gasped, her other hand moved down to the start of his cock and her fingers walked to the tip, she wrapped her hand around it, twisting as she moved down to the base. She moved her other hand onto his cock, both lathered up sliding up and down twisting either way. Jaspers eye's opened wide, glazing over, he was lost to her touch. She began to move up and down faster, she could see Jaspers breathing getting deeper.

"Belle please." He whispered begging her.

She moved into his lips, licking the bottom one. He opened his mouth, his tongue meeting hers, his breathing getting deeper, he groaned. Jane stopped, moving her hands to his face, Jasper exhaling deeply coming back to her. Jane stood moving out of his way, so he could lay down and rinse off. He smiled at her as he came out of the water.

Jane got out grabbing towels for them both. He wrapped Jane in her towel putting his round his waist, as she turned away he grabbed her lifting her into his arms. She squealed and laughed as he dashed to the bedroom with her. He stood at the foot of the bed and dropped her onto her back, grabbing her towel opening it as he bent over her. He pulled his towel off letting it drop to the floor, his cock standing proud. He pulled her legs down the bed, kissing her stomach, moving up to her breasts, Jane cupped them pushing them together as he had in the bath as he licked back and forth across them, Jane giggled.

He moved back down her stomach climbing on the bed.

"On your stomach Belle."

Jane did. He knelt over her, pulling her face around to meet his kissing her. He pushed her legs open.

"Bottom up." Jane pushed her bottom up, leaning on her arms, he put his hands either side of her, his legs straight out putting his weight on his toes, his cock ready to enter her, Jane looked back trying to watch him as he entered her, she pushed her bottom up higher, she groaned as he filled her.

"Fuck Belle you are so wet." He groaned, sliding back in easily. Slowly pushing in and out. Jane pushed herself back onto him, meeting his thrusts. He stopped, he knew she was desperate to cum. He pulled her up onto her knees kneeling behind her, pushing her head down into the bed, kissing down her back, his tongue teasing down to her bottom, he pulled her cheeks apart again, spreading her legs further apart. Jane could feel her pussy tingling she knew what he was going to do and the wait was killing her, she moved her hand between her legs and began to tease her clit. Jasper smiled watching her.

"Is my baby desperate?" He smiled. Jane moaned in response. "Show me Belle, turn over and play for me."

Jane turned over, moving up to the pillow, Jasper sat back on his feet, his hand wrapped around his cock, waiting for the show to start. Jane smiled at him. She turned to open her drawer and took out her vibrator. Jaspers eyes grew wide along with his smile, he slid his hand up and down his cock slowly. Jane settled back onto the bed, opening her legs, she sucked on her toy making it wet, turning it onto a gentle vibrate, she pressed it onto her pubic bone, enjoying the vibration before moving it down slowly catching her clit, she jumped as the first vibration hit her, she sucked her fingers, moving them down to her pussy pushing them inside her as she left the vibrator on her clit, she was instantly wet, she could feel her body growing warm. She moved it down, not wanting to cum too soon, she slid it inside, arching off the bed as the vibration teased her. Jasper was transfixed, his cock fit to burst watching her lost in her own pleasure. He was desperate to join her but didn't want to spoil what he was watching. He moved his hand down to his balls, squeezing, wanting the vibration against him too.

"Fuck it, I need you Belle." he moved up the bed, taking the vibrator from her, sliding it in and out of her himself, he laid onto his stomach, moving his head in close. He opened her lips, her juices glistening from playing, he slid his finger down from her clit to her bottom, Jane moaned softly, her body tingling. Jasper moved closer, his tongue at the bottom of her pussy, he flicked his tongue across the opening of her licking her clit. He moved the vibrator back into her placing it on her clit as his tongue moved down, he opened her lips further, dipping his tongue into her, Jane lifted her bottom off the bed, her fingers digging into the sheets.

"Oh Jesus Jasper, please let me cum." Jasper smiled. Continuing, he felt Jane clench around him, he pressed the vibrator harder into her clit. Jane screamed as the vibration and Jaspers tongue hit her hard. She clenched her thighs around Jasper, her fingers dragging the sheet further up the bed.

"Oh fuck, oh fuuuuck!" she screamed. Jasper didn't stop. He continued licking and slid his fingers inside her, her bottom lifted again, she squeezed harder around him as her orgasm peaked, she grabbed his head letting go of the bedding as her body became sensitive, she pushed at him to stop, Jasper continued. Jane was giggling.

"Please baby stop, stop, I can't………," she giggled more, as the vibrator continued teasing her making her body more sensitive. She felt like she was losing her mind.

Jasper looked up. "Something wrong Belle?" he laughed.

Jane was gasping her body tingling. Jasper crawled up the bed between her legs, taking his cock he ran it up and down her pussy teasing them both before sliding it inside hard, Jane gasped pushing into him. He wrapped his arm around her back, holding her, as he pushed deeper. He put his head against her, kissing her nose as he slowly moved in and out of her, making love to her slowly. Their bodies in perfect sync as his orgasm built. Jane began to clench around him, he moaned as he pushed harder his orgasm taking him.

"ohhhhhh, fuuuuuuuck Belle…." He yelled, his body rigid. Still pushing into her as he emptied himself. He panted as it slowed down, falling down next to her. He pulled her into him her back against his chest. Nuzzling into her closing his eyes.

Chapter 3

Trusting you

G rode out to Moses, he was dreading arriving even though he was breaking most of the speed limits to get there, he pulled up on the drive, slipped his gloves and helmet off and swung his leg off the bike. Moses opened the door as soon as he got off the bike.

"Thanks for coming G." Both men hugged, patting each other on the back.

"Well it didn't sound good, even though you didn't tell me anything, come on brother talk to me." G stepped inside the door and followed Moses into the house.

Moses made coffee handing one to G and they both went into the lounge and sat. G was getting anxious, for once he really looked at his best friend and saw how tired he was, he had lost a lot of weight from working out, he wasn't so sure now, seeing how drawn he was. He took a deep breath.

"Ok talk please, my gut can't take any more of this." G complained.

"Before I tell you anything this stays between us, do you hear me? You are not to tell anyone, and most certainly not Jane."

"Fuck sake Moses, just fucking tell me Brother, I won't tell anyone, you have my word!"

Moses rubbed his hands up his face sighing. "Okay, before we went to the US to see Jane I found a lump in my balls, I went to the Doctors and they got me an appointment to see a specialist, I saw him and he told me he was sure it was Testicular Cancer. They did a scan and more tests then we left to see Jane, when she was taken there was no way I was coming back until she was ready. I rang my consultant a few days before I left Jane, he told me he needed to see me urgently as I had missed his appointments. So when I got to the airport I rang and I saw him this morning."

G put his head in his hands, "Jesus fucking christ Moses, why did you wait? I would have stayed with Jane."

"I didn't want to leave her, she was in a bad way, I knew this cancer was bad and if it goes south then at least I know I had that time with her."

"Fuck!, so what now?"

"They are doing a full body scan now, it has spread into my lymph nodes in my stomach, so it's now Metatstatic Cancer, not just my balls, it all depends how far it's gone and what stage it is at. I'm waiting on a call for my scan this week, had blood tests this morning, they need to check my lungs too. Once we have a fuller picture they can decide how to proceed. I have to be realistic it may be too late."

G just sat staring into space, shaking his head, he wiped his eyes roughly with his hands, he didn't want Moses to see he was crying. His throat was hurting holding it back.

"Okay well I will be with you every step of the way."

"You don't need to, I'm a big boy I can handle it."

"Fuck you Moses, this isn't up for discussion, I will be there regardless." He slammed his hand down on the table, pushing up off the sofa, he started to pace the room screwing his fist into the palm of his hand.

"Fine if that's what you want." Moses sighed heavily and laid back into his chair.

"How do you feel Brother, I mean in yourself?"

"Fucking balls ache, they feel heavy. I'm tired, my back aches, I told Jane I had back issues, it wasn't a lie. I pulled one off whilst in the shower months ago and noticed blood in my semen, didn't think anything of it until I found the lump, that on it's own is okay, but now it's spread it's not so good."

"I'm sorry Brother I don't know what to say, I'm kind of lost for words, I'm fucking mad with you for waiting, did you think it was just going to go away?"

"It's ok, I understand, yes, maybe I was stupid to stay so long and Jane would be as mad as hell if she knew, but I did it for good reason, she knows something is wrong I don't think I can get away with my back being an issue for long. I will call Jasper and have a chat with him when Jane is back at work tomorrow."

"Good idea, what about the wedding? You know she will cancel it if she knows."

"That's why she isn't going to know, I will make it to the wedding, we will just have to play it by ear."

"You really do think she is stupid don't you, let me tell you Brother she will sniff that fucking rat out as soon as she sets eyes on you again, you can't fucking lie to her, none of us can."

"That's why I left so soon after they came back from the cottage. I struggled to look at her."

Moses phone rang in his pocket, he pulled it out answering quickly. G looked at him as he answered it.
"Yes?"
"Hi, Mr Abbott, this is Mr Guthrie's secretary, I have a slot for your scan tomorrow if that's okay, it's 11.30am here?"
"That's fine, thank you for letting me know, I will see you tomorrow." He hung up pushing his phone into his pocket.
"Tomorrow then?" G asked.
"Yes it is, 11.30am."
"Okay, I will bring the truck over and drive you down."
"Sure, whatever you like." Moses stood up, rubbing his head back and forth.
"Do you want me to stick around for the rest of the day?"
"No, it's fine I need to make some calls anyway, sort a few things out, you go back to work, I will see you tomorrow."
"Okay Brother, call if you need anything okay?" they hugged again as G left, he stood outside next to his bike. He heard the door close as Moses went back into the house.

"Fuck, Fuck, Fuck, Fuck!!" He yelled punching his seat over and over, he couldn't hold back his tears, he held his head down pretending to do something on his bike in case anyone was watching, he pushed his finger and thumb into the corners of his eyes to stop the tears but it was no use. He pulled his crash helmet and gloves on, fired up the bike and wheel span off the driveway, he didn't know where he was going, he just headed to the motorway. He rode for a while and found himself at the beach, he knew the area well, it was where he went to talk to his Mum. He pulled into a car park and climbed off the bike. He walked up the slope and found a spot and sat down on the pebbles. He pulled out his phone and began flicking through the pictures they took in Connecticut before Jane was taken, he smiled to himself.
"Good times." he sighed as he swiped to one of him and Moses.

They had been best friends since they joined up at 17, they had been through some shit together, saving each-others' lives more than once. He smiled again finding the folder of them both in the army. They both played the fool, never taking life seriously. Moses was G's sergeant, they fell out a few times when G put himself up for tough jobs, he would say he didn't have a family so it would be better for him to take the risk rather than others. G put his phone away, rubbed his hand through his hair and sighed heavily.

"Hey Mum, yes it's been a while I know, I never stop thinking of you though. I need your help please, I know you will be on good terms with the big guy, please Mum tell him not to take Moses, he's a good guy, give him a break please, I will do anything for him. I can't lose him Mum, he's the Brother I never had. He has taken care of Jane all these years and all of us, this isn't fair. I know he's hiding his pain, I won't let him down though, I will be by his side every step of the way. Tell the big guy I will go back to church and pray every night if I have to. Just don't take him please?"

He picked up a handful of stones, sorted through them for the flat ones, discarding the others. He pushed himself up and walked down to the waters edge. He loved skimming stones across the water with his Dad, they challenged each other since he was old enough to throw a stone. He threw the first, he counted as his Dad used to with him. 1,2,3…. He tried again, 1,2,3….

"Shit, come on!" he scolded himself. He tried again, he felt the wind blow behind him and his Mum's voice in his head *Duck, Drake Lardy cake*, the stone bounced 4 times. He smiled remembering his parents love of Lardy cake, he stopped eating it when he realised it had real lard in it. A real heart attack waiting to happen in each one. He laughed to himself walking back up the beach, he looked up at the sky and blew a kiss.

"Love you both." He walked back to his bike and climbed on pulling his helmet on before firing the bike up. He rode out of Gosport and headed back to the garage.

Chapter 4

Back to work

Jasper rolled over to find the bed empty, he looked at the clock, it was 4.30am, he kicked the covers back pulled on his shorts and went in search of Jane. She was nowhere to be found in the house, he noticed the door on the latch, he pushed it open putting his slippers and jacket on, it was getting light, he walked down the garden to the rose bed, he could see her inside the Rattan seat. He smiled knowing she would be asleep. He walked up to her and climbed in, she had pulled the blanket up over herself, she was sat up with the little lights on. He got underneath the blanket with her and snuggled in, she moaned softly and wrapped herself around him. Jasper pulled her into him and laid looking up at the sky. This was a big day for her going back to work. He didn't want to fall asleep and find they were late getting in.

It was 5.45am, Jasper bent over Jane kissing her eyes, she smiled, but didn't move, he kissed her again on the nose, she twitched and smiled again.
"Playing hard to get are we? well we will see about that." Jasper laughed, grabbing her face smothering her with tiny butterfly kisses all over her face as fast as he could. Jane couldn't move away, she started to squeal. Jasper laughed and stopped as she opened her eyes.

"Good Morning Belle, what happened?"
"I was hot and restless, so I came out here to sit for a while, I must have fallen asleep."
"You know you could have woken me, I would have sat with you?"
Jane pulled his face down and kissed him. "I didn't want to wake you up."
"Well, you know it's not an issue, we better get you back in and showered, big day today."
Jane groaned, pretending to be disappointed to be going back, in reality she just wanted to get back to normal. They walked back into the house

hand in hand, made tea and headed to the shower. Within the hour they were both ready to leave.

They arrived quite early and Jane commented how quiet it was as they walked through the turnstile. Jasper walked her to her office helping her to get settled before he left. A knock came to the door, she called out and Chicca popped her head in.

"Moooooorning beautiful!" she squealed, running in, grabbing Jane, squeezing the air out of her.

"God, I have missed you here Jane."

Jane laughed "You saw me 2 days ago at home."

"That's different, anyway don't spoil my excitement." She let Jane go and sat on the edge of the desk.

"As you are back, fancy being dropped in the deep end, I have 30 guys starting today and could do with some help before you do your bit."

"Of course, it will be good to do something."

"Great!" Chicca jumped off the desk, kissed Jane on the cheek and headed for the door, she turned "See you at 8am sharp, don't be late."

Jane laughed and shouted after her "Get out cheeky." Chicca waved laughing and left.

Jane texted Jasper to let him know she would be with Chicca, she didn't want to worry him if he came looking. Jasper read the text and smiled, turned the phone and showed Chicca.

"Well done Chicca, now let me help, what do you need me to do?"

"Not much left to do, the canteen will deliver the food just before 8am, the guys are about to put the banner up, you could escort Jane in if you like, I'm sure you can find a reason. I will call your phone once, so you know we are ready. Kiss her face off or something until you hear from me."

Jasper laughed and left the induction room heading to Janes office. He walked into her office just before 8am.

"What are you doing here, I told you I was going to help Chicca?"

"I just thought my lady would like to be escorted?" he grinned at her as he walked to her desk taking her hand to help her up, he pulled her into him kissing her hard.

"Wow what did I do to deserve that?"

"Does there have to be a reason to kiss my girl?"

Jane shook her head. Kissing Jasper. "No there doesn't." She grinned back.

"Well, my lady may I escort you to the Induction room?" he put his hand across his waist and bowed.

Jane giggled. "Yes of course you may." Jane grabbed her pen pushing into her pocket and picked up her laptop ready for her session after the inductions.

Jasper took her laptop from her and took her hand, he lifted it and kissed it.

"Jasper please never change." She beamed.

"I promise Belle." He smiled lifting her hand again blowing a raspberry on it.

They walked down to the induction room together, a couple of guys nodded as they walked on ahead. Jasper slowed down giving everyone time to be ready, he turned Jane to face him as his phone rang once.

"I love you Belle." He kissed her nose smiling down at her and began walking again. Jane smiled holding his hand with both of hers. Jasper stopped at the door, put his hand on the handle and pushed the door open for Jane to walk in first, she looked up at Jasper to kiss him, before she had chance she heard the cheers coming from the room. Her head shot around confused as to what was going on, she turned to see the banners, the smiling faces, everyone was clapping and cheering.

"Oh my god! What is this for?" She laughed looking around the room at everyone, she turned to look at Jasper and scanned the room for Chicca. They both smiled at her. She pointed her finger at them.

"You buggers!" she giggled. Holding her face with her hands hiding her tears.

The guys all moved towards her, hugging her. She wiped her eyes laughing at herself, overwhelmed by the welcome. Chicca came up behind her hugging her. Jane turned. Chicca grabbed her hugging her hard. Both of them crying.

"Oh Chicca, this is amazing, I don't know what to say. Thank you so much."

"You know you scared the crap out of us all, we were scared for a while that you wouldn't be back, everyone just wanted to give you a good welcome back and to show you how much we all love you. Don't do that that again you daft cow." Chicca laughed hugging Jane again continuing to cry.

Jane turned looking at everyone as the room fell silent.

"For once I am lost for words, I am still in shock that you guys would do this for me." She wiped her eyes again. "Thank you all so very, very much, I can't tell you how good it feels to be back. This just tops it for me. You are all so wonderful."

Everyone clapped again. "Can we eat now Chicca, I'm bloody starving?" a voice came from the back making everyone laugh.

"Christ, you greedy lot, tuck in."

Andy walked up to Jane with a cup of tea, handing it to her he smiled.

"Here if you need a chat Jane." She wiped her eyes looking up to him.

Thank you Andy, I may take you up on that. How are you doing, have the family stopped panicking every time you are alone yet?"

"Yes, they have, I know it's not easy to deal with for them, but I am in a much better place and I am glad to still be here."

"I'm so glad to hear that. You know I am always here for you." Jasper came to her side putting his hand on her shoulder bending to kiss her head.

"Thanks Jane, it's good to have you back. I think someone wants you." He laughed touching her hand walking back to his work mates.

"I think we better grab something to eat before this hungry lot finish it off Belle?"

Jane nodded and walked to the table grabbing a bacon roll from the tray sitting down with some of the guys to eat. They sat chatting while they ate, most of the guys left waving as they walked out. The room fell quiet as Jane looked around at the banners and pictures of her and the team. It hit her suddenly that this almost didn't happen, she fell quiet looking down to the floor. Chicca wrapped her arm around her shoulder as Jane turned into her holding her tight as she cried.

"Hey, you okay love?"

"Yes thank you, just realised how things change so quickly. Thankfully the nightmare is over and I can get on with my life." They hugged hard again, Chicca stood taking Janes hand.

"We better get this show on the road, we have work to do lady, don't think you can sit here all day."

"Cheeky cow, just tell me what you want and let's do this."

Jasper smiled walking out of the room with the others leaving Chicca and Jane to do their Inductions knowing she was finally getting back to being herself.

Chapter 5

Time to put things in place.

Moses woke up feeling pretty rubbish, he kicked the covers off himself and sat up. He grabbed his phone and turned off the alarm, he needed to get back to work but needed to do a few things first, one being his scan.

He walked into the shower sighing heavily, it was all becoming very real, he had tried to hide long enough. He stood under the water, his hands against the wall the water cascading down his body, he turned the heat up more, it was helping his aching bones. He washed himself off, looking down at his cock grabbing it.
"I suppose you are going to be of no use shortly I better do something about that." He laughed to himself. "I should have listened to you and took Susan out. Susan! I wonder how she is?"

He finished washing himself, getting out of the shower, drying his face, wrapping the towel around his waist. He cleaned his teeth staring in the mirror, pulling the bottom of his eye down to see if there were any changes. He sighed again finishing, walking back to his bedroom to get dressed.

"Right then, let's do this, he grabbed his video camera out of the draw and two memory sticks. He set it up on its stand making sure it was in the right place to capture him and sat down on the bed.
He pressed record on the remote looking at the camera.

"Hi babe, well what is it they say on these kind of videos? if you are watching this I am no longer around, so I guess that's why you are watching this. I'm sorry I lied to you, I was just trying to protect you, today I have decided whichever way this goes I need to do this anyway. I love you Half-pint, you are my best friend, I will never be far away even if I am gone, I will be watching over you, but I promise never to enter your bedroom when you are in there, not something I want to see." He smiled, pulling a face and continued. When he had finished he turned it off, put his head in his hands and began to cry.

The doorbell went, he jumped up off the bed wiping his eyes. The second video would have to wait.

He reached the door as G pounded on it. He opened it. G stood scowling at him.

"What took you so long?"

"Morning to you too G!"

"Yeah sorry, morning. You took your time I was worried."

"I'm not dead yet you know!"

"Don't even joke Brother, this is serious!" G scolded him, screwing up his face.

"I wasn't G, stop worrying, I promise you will be around for that." Moses stood back letting G in.

"I just need my keys and my pack of papers. I have made an appointment with my solicitor too, do you mind if you take me there too after the scan?"

"Stupid bloody question Moses, of course I don't mind." G knew he needed to get his anger under control, but he was scared and he couldn't shake off his temper.

"Right let's go then, I need to get this over with and know what I am dealing with. I just want everything in place too incase it isn't good."

"I understand that. Right, hospital first."

They both fell silent on the short drive to the hospital. Moses was making notes on his phone for when he got to the Solicitor, he wanted to deal with today so he could concentrate on whatever the results would be, his paperwork at home was always in order, that was left from being in the army. He just needed a few things changing now he was out. He knew his military pension would die with him as he wasn't married.

G pulled into a parking space outside the hospital. "Do you want me to come with you?"

"Yes please Brother." G nodded getting out.

They walked in together looking at the signs for instructions on where to go, G spotted it first, they walked down to the MRI unit. Moses felt sick. He didn't like small spaces, he just hoped it was a big unit, he didn't fancy having a panic attack in there. He felt stupid thinking about it, he knew Jane would understand how he was feeling, they had talked about it a lot, from his time in Bosnia. He had been down some dark holes in his time, even digging out the toilet blocks he hated.

They arrived at the check in desk. The receptionist gave Moses a locker key and directed him to the changing rooms. G patted him on the back and took a seat. Moses got himself changed and sat waiting for the radiographer to come and collect him.

"Christian?" a quiet voice questioned him.
"Uh yeah that's me, call me Moses please?"
"Moses, are you not Christian then?"
"Yes I am, but nobody calls me that, Moses is my nickname."
"Oh I see, should I ask?"
"It's a long story but basically I make things happen, having a name like Christian Abbot my army mates decided I should be Moses and it stuck."
"Clever, Moses suits you." She smiled leading him into the scanner room.

"Right then, you will be inside this for around 45 minutes, it does get noisy so you need to wear these headphones, we can play music for you, do you have a preference? We have classic, 60's country, Radio 2, 4 or local radio."
"Radio 2 will be fine. Thanks."
"Okay if you can lay down on here for me, your head to this end here."
Moses felt his stomach sink, he was sweating, just looking at the small tunnel wasn't helping him.
He sat on the bed, swinging his legs up, laying flat on the bed, he sighed.
"Are you okay Moses?"
"Yeah, yeah, just don't like small spaces."
"Okay we will take it slowly, if at any time you feel anxious just let me know and we will stop, you can close your eyes if it helps. You will reach here so you won't go completely into the lower part." She put her hand onto the high part of the scanner to show him. Moses just nodded. The nurse put his headphones on, squeezed his arm and walked towards the controls, Moses looked up to the ceiling, concentrating on his breathing trying to slow it down.

"Okay Moses are you ready?"

"Yes." He nodded. The bed began moving into the tunnel, he closed his eyes, his heart was racing. He concentrated hard on his breathing, screwing his eyes together.

"Okay you are in, please stay completely still, if you need us to stop just speak we can hear you."

Moses nodded again as the nurse left him. The noise began, he remembered it from the last time so he knew what to expect, but he didn't like it any better. He laid still thinking of Jane, concentrating on her face, seeing her smile and the two of them being silly, he forgot about his breathing and began to relax.

He was thinking about the day he met her and how he felt when she turned and smiled at him. He was captivated, she was with a few others chatting, he had just got back from a tour in the middle east. He was on two weeks R&R with G, their first stop was the club to collect their bikes.

G had tapped him on the shoulder, he was staring at Jane, he laughed to himself, when G asked him what had caught his attention, he had followed his eyes and found Jane too. She introduced herself to them both, it was a very rare occasion she was on her own, her husband was with his friends so she could relax. She simply introduced herself as Jane, Gwen followed her over and explained who she was. Both men nodded listening intently. When she walked away Gwen explained who her husband was. Moses and G had heard of him, they knew he had a bad temper.

Over the weeks and months that followed they saw more of Jane and got to know her properly. They saw the change in her when Mark was about, Moses grew concerned about how quiet she became, the day he hit her in the club he knew then she was special and he had to do something to help her. He was due to go away again to Afghan, he had spoken to Jane about it and she offered to write to him which he loved, over the 6 months he was away they grew close, Jane was able to be honest with him and confided in him. She had her letters sent to work so Mark never knew. Moses offered his home to her on more than one occasion as a way out, but Jane continued to make excuses for Mark.

"Moses?" The radiographer spoke softly to him so not to alarm him.

"Uh, oh sorry I must have drifted off."

"Well, whatever it was it certainly helped you to relax."

Moses smiled and said nothing. He sat up for a few minutes before getting off the bed.

"Right your consultant will get your results in a day or two, I assume you have another appointment with him?"

"Yes, I do thanks."

"Okay, well take care."

Moses nodded. "Thank you and you." He walked back to the changing area put his clothes on and walked back to G.

"All done?"

"Yes, that's it now until Thursday when I see the Doc again."

"Okay, do you want me there with you? I can write things down if you like at least then we both hear it in case you forget something."

"Sure, if you like. Thanks."

They reached G's truck within a few minutes and drove to the Solicitors office.

"Shall I wait out here?"

"You may as well hear it all, so come in, I will need you to work with Jane anyway once I'm gone."

"Shit Brother, please stop talking like that!"

"I'm being realistic, that's all. If this thing takes me then you have to work with Jane, I'm not planning on going anywhere believe me, but you know we always put our affairs in order and that's all I am doing just in case, you may as well know everything now anyway as it's all for you and Jane."

G put his head down, pushed his thumb and forefinger into the corners of his eyes, he sniffed as quietly as he could as they entered the office trying to clear his tears.

They sat in the waiting room, G looked around, it was an old building that once was a house but it had been converted to an office, the windows were all odd, none of them straight, he looked at the floor it was floorboards, he looked towards the other window wondering what the family were like who had lived there when it was first built. Everything had been painted white except for the open beams. They were black, the old fireplace had long gone, it was just an empty space.

"Mr Abbott, Mr Harris will see you now", the receptionist led the way to the office. G followed him in.

Mr Harris stood as they entered offering them a chair each. They all sat down. Moses pulled his papers out and put them onto the desk.

"It's good to see you Christian, how can I help today?"

"Moses please?"

"Yes, I'm sorry Moses. How can I help?"

"I have cancer, I don't know how bad things are, I have had another scan today which I get the results for in a few days, I wanted to get things in order today so regardless of what happens it's sorted."

"I'm so sorry to hear that, I hope things go in your favour. I have your file here we have most things covered from when you went away last time. What do you need to change?"

Moses took a deep breath and looked at G. "This is G he is already down as my executer I would like to add Jane too." He looked back at G who looked shocked, he didn't know he was already written in.

"We can do that, anything else, what have you got there?"

"This is my savings account that my army pension goes into, I haven't touched it so there is a nice amount in there. That goes to G." He raised his hand using his thumb to point at him.

G opened his mouth to speak, Moses just raised his hand to stop him.

My life pension document has been updated too, that goes to both Jane and G. split 50/50. I believe the total on that at present is £120k.

G gulped not enjoying this conversation at all.

"My house goes to Jane, I would like it sold. I'm never there, it doesn't mean anything to me, but that's her decision, I know she is emotional about shit like that. My bikes are to go to G, I know you have that already, except for the original one I brought for Jane, her and Jasper will enjoy that. I want that to go to her. I also have another two properties that I rent out, he looked back at G, he looked down to the floor. They are to be sold only when the tenants move out. The monthly income goes into this account. The mortgages are paid off, this is also for G and Jane."

G put his hand onto Moses shoulder, not wanting to hear anymore. Moses continued.

"My medals I want to go to Jane, I know she will want those, there are also all the letters we wrote to each other I want her to have too. The few bits of jewelry go to her, I know I said to sell them before so please change that." He sighed sitting back in his chair. He looked at G, "My tools go to G, and everything else in the garages. Sorry mate there is a lot of shit in there. Oh, and I want to be cremated my ashes scattered, I don't want them going in the ground. You know the rest, I have probably said more than you need as most of it you have already but anyway I wanted to get it updated."

"No problem at all, I will get this updated and let you know when to pop back and sign it."

"Thanks very much." they all stood and shook hands before G and Moses left.

They reached the truck and got in. G thumped the steering wheel in frustration.

"What the fuck are you playing at Brother, leaving all this shit to me?"

Moses turned to look at him. "Who else do I have apart from you and Jane? You are the closest thing to family I have, if you don't want it just fucking say so and I will send it to a fucking dog charity!"

"I don't want it because that means you will have gone and that I cannot cope with, you are my Brother, we are supposed to be grumpy old fuckers together moving to the coast to terrorise the place. I'm sorry but I am not dealing with this well." He put his head in his hands and cried openly. Moses bent across to him, putting his hand on his shoulder.

"Listen to me I have no intention of going anywhere soon, I am just making sure that things are in place that's all. I am going to fight this no matter how tough it gets. I just need to know you are here for me, I don't want to tell Jane until I know more, she is going to roast my balls when she finds out and probably be on the next flight out. I really cannot deal with that. It will break her and I'm sorry I am putting this on your shoulders Brother, as soon as Jane knows we will tell the club, but I don't want the women crying and all the shit."

"Oh, you want wailing women, you're not some Adonis you know." They both started laughing. Moses pushed G.

"Cheeky fucker, you know what I mean." He laughed back at G, hugging him.

"Now for fucks sake take us somewhere for food and a beer and let's change the subject."

G nodded smiling pulling out of the car park heading for a local pub.

"Thanks Brother, I mean it, thanks for being here for me, I don't know anyone else I would want by my side."

G smiled. "You're welcome. Just don't tell Half-pint I knew all this time, she can roast your nuts but not mine, I kind of like mine how they are and I intend on using them pretty soon."

"Wishful thinking, unless you got someone you haven't let on about?"

"No. I haven't but you never know who will walk in the door. I need to be ready."

Moses laughed again. "Whatever you say Brother."

Chapter 6

Dress Day

"Jane!" Jasper grumbled, "how many more magazines are you going to leave laying around the house?" he picked up yet another, open on another dress that she liked, he knew what she was trying to do and he wasn't going to give in about a style, it was her decision. He smiled as he picked up the magazine, she had folded down a page with a knee length fifties style dress, he knew she would look good in anything and he thought how cute she would look in this one, he closed it up putting it into the rack on her side of the sofa, on top of a dozen more. He smirked and walked towards the garden.

Jane came into the house with her hair piled high on her head a smear of dirt across her face, her cheeks rosy red grinning from ear to ear.
"I take it I am in trouble, you never call me Jane?" she grinned at Jasper knowing what he was going to say.
"Belle, how many more magazines can you buy with wedding dresses in, surely you have run out of choices?" he was trying to be serious but failing.
Jane grabbed a piece of her hair and started to twirl it like a little girl. "You want me to be happy in my dress, don't you?"
"Belle, don't try that on with me lady, or I will put you across my knee!"
"Ohhhhh, I like the sound of that." she teased, smiling.
"It's supposed to be a punishment not enjoyment!" he laughed looking away, still trying to be serious.
"I'm game if you are?" she laughed bending over sticking her bottom out.
"Belle I think you have been reading too much of that smut in your books. I need to take your Kindle away for a while."
"I don't need those books, it's you who has done this to me, I just can't get enough of you, are you telling me I am too much for you?" she smiled putting her hand on her hip pushing it out, puckering her lips at him.
Jasper laughed, grabbed her, pulling her into him kissing her hard. "I love you Belle, but please stop with the magazines." He patted her on

the bottom. "Now go and finish what you were doing and get in here for a shower, you don't want to be late for Chicca."

"Oh shit, what time is it?" she asked rushing at Jaspers watch, grabbing his hand to look smearing dirt up his arm. He tutted looking down.

"It's only 8.30, you have a couple of hours." He laughed watching her dash down the garden to clear up, he got his shoes on and went out to help her.

"Go Belle, let me finish off out here, I don't mind." Jasper said bending down kissing her on the top of the head. Jane grabbed him by the neck of his t-shirt pulling him in, kissing him before running off into the house. As she reached the step she was about to run into the patio door her boots full of mud.

"Boots Belle!" Jasper shouted after her. She skidded to a halt, put her hand in the air turning towards the garage. She kicked her boots off ran through the house to the bathroom stripping off as she went in leaving a trial of clothes behind her, as she got to the bed she had her jeans around her ankles as she tried to pull her foot out she fell over falling flat onto the bed, she laid giggling at herself as Lady came dashing into the room diving on the bed licking her face. Jasper walked into the house picking up her clothes as he went towards the bedroom, he was shaking his head as he reached the room, Jane was hanging off the bed, her jeans around her ankles, Lady licking her face while Jane giggled at her. Jasper called Lady stopping her.

"Come her girl, or your Mum will never get ready." Lady jumped off the bed running to Jasper with her tail wagging. He patted her while Jane composed herself. He bent and pulled her jeans from her ankles, Jane rolled over onto her back, her hair half out of her grip spread over her face, Jasper laughed sitting her up.

"Come on you silly girl, shower!" Jane composed herself wiping her hair from her face still giggling. Jasper stood her pulling her knickers down sat her back on the bed before taking her feet out of them, he scooped her up in his arms and carried her into the bathroom. He leaned in turning the shower on before standing her up, she turned pointing at her grip that was knotted in her hair, Jasper started pulling hair out of it to try and unwrap it without hurting her. She was squeaking as he pulled at her. "Sorry Belle, it's all knotted up. He said sighing shaking his head at her. Jane covered her face gritting her teeth as he continued tugging. He finished leaving the grip on the side as she stepped into the shower, he grabbed her towels, as he turned he could see Jane giggling again. "Now what Belle?" He laughed with her not knowing what he was laughing at.

"Oh my god Jasper you should have seen me, I slam dunked myself onto the bed, it was so funny." She giggled at herself again, bending in the shower trying to breath, she began coughing trying to catch her breath. Jasper dashed into the shower rubbing her back, turning the shower off, patting her gently not wanting to hurt her, he didn't know what to do for the best.

"Jane please breath love, slowly." Jane was gasping for air, going red in the face. He picked her up taking her into the bedroom where it was cooler. She began to breath and stopped gasping, Jasper sighed in relief. He rubbed her back a little more, he sat her on the bed grabbing some water from the bathroom, Jane sipped it slowly regaining her composure.

"You ok Belle?"

She nodded, "Yes thank you."

"Christ woman you scared the hell out of me."

"I'm sorry love, I couldn't stop myself, I just kept seeing myself all over again and it made me laugh", she began to giggle again, taking deep breaths to stop herself. Jasper shook his head laughing at her.

"Come on you better finish your shower, or you will definitely be late for Chicca." He went back into the bathroom with her to make sure she was okay and chatted to her to stop her from giggling again. Jane finished her shower cleaned her teeth and sat on the bed while Jasper dried her hair. Lady sat at her feet, while Jane rubbed her feet into her fur making her go silly.

An hour later Chicca knocked on the door as Jane was finishing getting herself ready. Jasper went down to let her in.

"Hey JDubz." Chicca bounced in kissing Jasper on the cheek and bending down to fuss lady.

"You might want to go up, she has changed her underwear a dozen times, her hair has been up, down and platted. I have no idea what to do with her."

Chicca laughed, "leave her to me I will sort her out." She dashed off to the bedroom, "Princess, get your arse sorted girl or we will be late." She walked into the bedroom Jane was applying her mascara. "Are you going looking like that?" she teased.

Jane turned, "Oh no, shall I change?"

"No silly, you look gorgeous, grab your bag love we are out of here." She grabbed Jane pulling her out of the door.

Jane laughed, "Give me a chance woman, I need my bag." She stopped and grabbed her bag as they left the room.

Jasper looked down at Lady, "Don't worry Lady it will go quiet soon, the baby elephant will be gone for a while we can have some peace and quiet."

The girls came into the lounge laughing. "Told you I would sort her out, I will bring her back later. Don't wait up." Chicca laughed kissing him on the cheek.

"Look after each other please girls, call if you need anything."

"Thanks love, enjoy your peace and quiet." Jane laughed patting and kissing Lady on the head.

"The dog comes first every time, I know my place." He winked at Jane as she kissed him. "Have fun love." He spanked her on the bottom as they left. Jane waved as they walked out getting into Chicca's car.

"Buckle up love, let's do this", she turned the engine on, the music blasted out. Jane put her fingers into her ears. "Jesus woman, when are you getting your ears checked?"

"Nah, no need for that, I just like it loud." She turned it down singing the song. "If it's too loud you're too old."

"Cheeky mare!" Chicca pulled out of the drive and drove off at speed into town. She parked in the car park with minutes to spare for their appointment.

They walked into the shop, the old lady greeted Chicca first, "Darlingggg, how wonderful to see you both again", she kissed Chicca on both cheeks and moved to Jane.

"So, I was right then! He wants to marry you?" She smiled.

Jane grinned, "Yes you were right, it has been a whirlwind to be honest."

"Then it must be right then, I hope you don't mind my Niece is with me today, she is doing her final studies and will be taking the shop over from me so has decided to spend time with me to help."

"Of course we don't mind, the more the merrier, I hope you don't mind my friend can't be here due to travelling so I said I would ask if we could video call her once I start trying dresses on, she asked me to give this to you as well. I haven't opened it yet?"

"Yes Darling of course, you won't need anyone's opinion though as you will look beautiful in all the gowns. Oh, there you are Sasha, this is Chicca and Jane, the ladies I told you about." Sasha nodded her head, she was elegant looking very tall with black hair, cut into a bob.

"Can I get you a drink ladies?" Sasha asked. "We have champagne if you would like some?"

"Oh that would be nice, thank you." Chicca grinned. "One won't hurt me and we are eating after this anyway." Jane nodded in agreement, as Sasha walked away.

"Come, come, let me show you what I have for you", she walked past the door and put the lock on, turning the sign to closed.

"We don't need anyone else coming in today, so now you can relax knowing you are alone.

"That's very kind, thank you." Jane grinned looking at Chicca raising her eyebrows. Chicca grinned back following behind the old lady. Sasha came out with the champagne putting it down on the small table, showing Chicca and Jane where to sit.

Sasha walked over to the curtain pulling it back, her aunt stood behind it sorting dresses out pulling them out of their bags. "These dresses are not in magazines, they are basic that I have put together from fine silk and lace, we can make any adjustments for you. If there is nothing you like, then we can do some drawings and Sasha and I can make it for you." Jane nodded, not sure what to expect.

Sasha grinned beckoning her in for the first dress. Jane got up looking back at Chicca. Pulling a silly face trying to look nervous. Chicca laughed smacking her backside.

"Undress", the old lady beckoned, Jane began undressing feeling their eyes on her.

"You have lost weight! What happened to you?"

"We will tell you later." Chicca spoke up not wanting Jane to get emotional.

Jane stood in her bra and knickers in the changing area, it was a huge room, she didn't remember seeing it the last time she came, she couldn't believe the amount of dresses that were hanging up, she couldn't really see them just so much lace, silk and netting and different shades of white and cream. Sasha stood in front of her. "Lift your arms up, keep them up until I tell you to move them down." Jane nodded, she felt the silk touch her body. It was a tight bodice and a full skirt.

"This sits just below your knee, I don't think it will be right as you are small, but I wanted to show you anyway. The skirt can be changed if you want a long one." She held the dress up, it was a tule and satin white dress, no straps just the tule with no sleeves with a sweetheart neckline. It tapered at the waist, the skirt was A line, with a ribbon around the waist. It had tiny jewels stitched into it. Jane touched it feeling the soft tule.

"It's pretty, let's try it, I have no idea what I want so I am game for anything." They got her changed and Sasha pulled back the curtain, Chicca sat with her hands under her chin leaning on her knees chatting to Lily. "Oh hang on, here she comes." Chicca turned the phone around. "It's pretty, but it's not you Jane." Jane turned to the mirror, swayed her hips feeling the fabric move smiling, "I agree. Lily what do you think?"

"I agree I think it's wrong too."

"As I thought, Sasha, help Jane out of this one I will get the next one." Sasha unzipped Jane and lifted the dress over her head and took it away. Jane waited for the next one.

"Remember dear these are basic and can be changed to anything you wish, it's just trying to give you an idea of what you would like." She smiled as Jane lifted her arms up waiting for the next one.

The second was very simple it was a glossy fabric, off the shoulder v neck with wrap sleeves with an A line over skirt, that fell to the floor in a long train. Jane smiled feeling the fabric, like she had stepped out of a 50's movie, imagining Audrey Hepburn wearing it. She turned to look at herself in the mirror and gasped, Sasha came behind her holding her hair up pinning it. Leaving a few loose long curls. Sasha opened the curtain for Chicca and Lily to see.

"Oh my fucking god!!, Jesus woman you look like a million fucking dollars, I love it! Lil look, it's amazing." Jane stood with a huge grin on her face.

Lil wiped her face. "Oh, Jane you look absolutely stunning. But you don't look comfortable?"

"I love it, but I don't feel like it is my wedding dress." She screwed her nose up, Chicca laughed. "I would wear it to a black-tie event in red or something, I just feel it's too much, oh I don't know what I mean, help me girls. Pleaseeeeee."

Chicca walked over to her, "Turn please." Jane did as she was asked looking over her shoulder at Chicca. "Jane you look gorgeous, but you need to be comfortable, if you don't feel it's right then we will keep going, leave that to one side and we can come back to it." Jane nodded turning to Sasha.

"Am I pain? I am sorry."

"No, you are not a pain, this is important, we have plenty more and the one I think is right you haven't tried yet." The old lady was undoing another bag already.

Jane looked at Lily, "what do you think really?"

"I agree, I think it's perfect for one of your events, but not for your wedding. Get Jasper to buy it for your honeymoon." She giggled.

"I don't think there will be need for clothes do you?"

"Well, it depends what he has planned, does anyone know yet?" Lily asked.

"No idea, we hoped you would have a clue."

"Sorry no, my hubby will keep his lips sealed if he knows though, he knows I get too excited so never tells me anything."

"Join the club." They all laughed.

Sasha came back across to Jane. She smiled at her. "My aunt is never wrong Jane, trust her." Jane nodded again lifting her arms for the next. She turned away from the mirror again, she felt the lace slide down her body, instantly feeling at home, she screwed her eyes up tight not wanting to cheat and peak, she smiled widely.

"Are you trying to hold your wind in or something Jane? You look like a baby doing that."

Jane burst into a fit of giggles desperate to keep her eyes closed. "No! I'm not, you cheeky cow, I was smiling, I love the feel of this lace, it's amazing, it's so soft." Chicca giggled under her breath, she knew that but loved teasing her. She looked down at Lily, they both nodded when they saw the fabric. Jane was turned to the mirror as the zip was pulled up. She opened her eyes slowly and felt the tears welling up. She looked behind her and nodded. Chicca looked up. She fell silent looking down at the floor, took a mouthful or her champagne and walked towards Jane, she hugged her gently. Lily was already crying knowing what was in the box would be perfect.

"JDubz is going to cry when he sees you in this and the rest of them. You look absolutely beautiful, like an angel. Leave your hair down Jane please." She sniffed, pulling away.

"I'm with Chicca Jane, you look incredible and more beautiful in the flesh I would imagine."

Jane stood looking in the mirror, gently feeling every inch with her fingertips, the dress was pure lace, the straps made of lace applique flowers, joining at the bust into a deep sweetheart neckline but saving her modesty. It had boning and lining to perfect the flawless look. The back was an open oval, it fell to the floor in a fit and flare shape. Continuing into a small train. The others looked at each other nodding and began chatting. Jane was lost in thought looking in the mirror.

My Little Girl – Tim McGraw

She closed her eyes tight, the tears stuck in her throat, she cleared the lump, fighting the tears thinking of her Dad, she felt a soft hand on her shoulder, she caught her breath smiling to herself, placing her hand in the same place, as if he was there. "Dad?", she whispered softly. "I wish you were here, I miss you so much", she let out a small sob. squeezing her eyes even tighter, drifting into her favorite memories.
"Sweetheart, I know you are hiding behind the sofa, if you come out, we can talk about this." Her Dad said with a giggle in his voice, Jane blocked her ears and began singing. George their Labrador had been locked in his cage, looking confused.
"La la la la la la." Her Dad picked her up while she continued, sitting on the sofa with her. Jane began to open her eyes and stopped singing.
"Buttercup, talk to me, did George really ask you to paint his toenails?"
Jane nodded, pouting, her big blue eyes looking up to her Dad. He felt his heart melt looking down at her. "How did he ask you darling, tell me please?" Jane's Mum entered the room her hands on her hips looking upset, Jane turned in her Dads lap, she thought she couldn't be seen if she couldn't see someone.
"George came to watch me playing Daddy."
"Okay......, then what happened?" He spoke softly to her, slowly shaking his head at her Mum who was still stood in the doorway.
Jane pulled a curl from the side of her head twisting it nervously in her fingers. She took a deep breath and sighed, putting her index finger onto her bottom lip.
"Well......." She started to twist side to side thinking of what to say next.
"I was colouring Mummies mirror and I dropped the bottle, George put

his foot on it, so I asked him if he wanted his nails painted, he just looked at me, so I did it."

Her Dad was trying desperately not to laugh, her Mum huffed and walked away. "Okay darling, so did you paint the bottom of his paws too?"

Jane nodded frantically, her finger still on her lips. "Yes Daddy." She grinned.

"Okay, now you know that was Mummies favourite mirror, so do you think we should go and say sorry?"

"I was trying to make it pretty for her, doesn't she like it?" Jane frowned at her Dad confused.

Jane got down onto the floor holding her Dads hand going in search of her Mum. As they left the lounge her Dad looked down at the floor, George had left a trail of footprints of red nail polish into the carpet, they followed it up stairs and into their bedroom. Jane's Mum was sat on the bed with nail polish remover scrubbing the mirror trying to remove the polish as they walked in. Jane stopped looking up at her Dad, he nodded letting go of her hand pointing at her Mum. Jane walked over to her Mum with her head down.

"Mummy, don't you like it? I was trying to make it pretty for you." Her mum turned to look at her.

"Jane come here." She took her hand and sat her on the bed next to her. "Mummy does like the colour but it isn't for the dog, or the mirror or the floor, it's for Mummies nails."

"But George wanted it too Mummy." Jane looked up at her mum confused.

"You have to promise me Jane you will never touch Mummies make up again. Can you see what you have done to George and Mummies mirror? That can be dangerous for George."

Jane nodded tears forming in her eyes. "I'm sorry Mummy." She sniffed. As her tears began to escape and fall onto her cheeks. Her mum pulled her into her chest holding her close to her. Her Dad came to join them cuddling them both. He looked down at the white bedroom carpet, he was trying not to laugh, George had left footprints in the spilt nail polish and walked it through the house.

Jane jumped off the bed and ran to her bedroom grabbing her piggy bank off the side and rushing back into her parents room, she pulled the plug off the bottom and emptied the contents onto the bed. "Mummy this is for you to buy a new mirror and a new colour. I am sorry Mummy.

I won't touch it again I promise." She began to cry again, sniffing, her nose running, she wiped her nose with the back of her arm. Her Dad picked her up carrying her to the bathroom, sitting her onto the toilet lid, he grabbed the toilet paper placing it over her nose.

"Blow buttercup." Jane nodded and blew as hard as she could. "Now let's wipe those tears and hear no more about it. Go and play and I will help Mummy clean up."

"Okay Daddy, I'm sorry." He kissed her head as he lifted her off the toilet, he patted her bottom as she ran into her bedroom to play.

"Jane, are you okay love?" Jane jumped as she felt Chicca touch her hand. She brushed the tear from her eyes.

"Yes sorry, I was just thinking of my Mum and Dad." She half smiled at Chicca.

"Sorry love, I can't imagine how hard it is. They will be watching over you though." Jane nodded.

"They are both here with you Jane, don't forget that love." Lily wiped her tears again.

"Well, I think we can clearly say you have found the dress, don't you?"

"God yes, it's so beautiful and feels amazing too." Sasha came over to her.

"Would you like a vail too?"

"I don't think I do to be honest, I have my Mum's tiara and I will get Moses to bring it with him."

"Darlingggg there is one more thing. please close your eyes again." Jane looked confused and closed her eyes. Lily had her hand over her mouth, waiting patiently hoping Jane would be happy.

Jane felt her hair being messed with and a tiara being put in place. She felt the lace fall down her back. She was confused for a second.

"Open your eyes now." Sasha asked.

Jane opened her eyes and looked in the mirror, her hand shot to her mouth. "Oh my god, where did that come from, it's amazing! It looks perfect." Her head shot around to look at Chicca and Lily, then she remembered the box. "Oh Lily, it's so beautiful!!, I don't know what to say." She wiped her eyes gently. She pulled the veil gently around her, the soft fabric matching her dress perfectly.

"You don't need to say anything unless you are sure you want to wear it then say yes."

"Oh my god yes, yes, yes." Everyone smiled nodding in agreement. "It matches my Mum's tiara too."

"It looks perfect. Let's get you measured in this properly and we can finish it off for you, we will keep it here until you are ready for it, we just need you to come back in a couple of weeks-time for a final fitting."
"Perfect thank you, Jasper won't believe I have found something so quickly."
"We haven't finished yet, you need shoes and underwear remember."
"Come and see our shoes Jane we have some beautiful ones, I think we might have the perfect pair for you. They haven't been on display, Auntie likes to keep one offs for that special bride.

They walked into another area of the shop that Jane didn't even realise existed. Sasha pulled some boxes off the shelf and beckoned Jane to sit down. She pulled the dress up to her knees as Sasha knelt in front of her, she pulled the sandals out of the box, Jane slid her foot inside frowning, she wasn't sure what to make of them. The heels were three inches high, around the heel were laces flowers like the dress, they carried on over the shoe, part of it was clear and just the rigid lace flowers, they were delicately placed across the toes and the top of the foot, continuing up the ankle wrapping around the leg up to the knee. As Sasha finished tying them up Jane gasped. Her hands covering her mouth again. "Oh my god they are amazing Sasha!" she turned her foot looking down her leg to her ankle, grinning widely.
"Do they fit okay, we do have the next size up?"
"No, they are perfect and so comfortable too, I can't believe how beautiful they are, I feel like a princess." She grinned again looking up at Chicca and Lily who were wiping their tears.
"You are a Princess Jane. You look so beautiful. I can't wait to see you all dressed and finished off, Jasper will be amazed." She bent down and kissed Jane on the head.
"Now all we have to do is decide on your hair and the underwear."
"I will definitely be there for the next fitting Jane." Lily said smiling wiping her eyes. "I will leave you girls to finish off, enjoy the rest of the day and see you in a few weeks." She blew kisses at Jane and Chicca and hung up.

"Can I get you to come back to the dressing room in them Jane so we can measure the length of the dress so we get it right and finish off the rest so you can get out of it?"

"Yes of course." Sasha helped Jane up and she walked with her head up sashaying to the changing room holding the front of her dress up. Chicca smiled, she looked so confident.

"You walk like that down the aisle Jane and the men will be dropping at their feet at you wiggling your bum." The girls all giggled as they reached the changing room.

"Well you all sound happy, I assume we have found the right shoes." The old lady said sternly.

"Yes Auntie we have." She looked down at Janes legs as she pulled the dress up showing her legs bound in lace. The old lady nodded in agreement.

"Help her up please Chicca onto the step so we can get the length right." Chicca nodded supporting Jane as she climbed on, both ladies got down onto their knees working around the dress pinning it up. Sasha stood, "arms up Jane please and straighten them out in front of you", Jane did as she was asked. Sasha was checking the fit. "okay up as if you were doing your hair, Jane did again, Sasha looked under her arms making sure the dress didn't drop to low showing her breast.

"Okay that's it, the rest looks perfect Jane, you can get changed now, but we need to be careful not to dislodge the pins. Chicca helped her off the step and held the dress up as they moved into the changing room. They slowly slipped her out of the dress and took it away allowing Jane to dress alone.

"Okay I'm dressed", she came out from behind the curtain.

"Great, so leave it with us, we will call you when we are done so you can come and have another fitting, try not to lose any more weight or put any on."

"Damn that's your cream cake down the drain today then." Chicca laughed.

"Oh I beg to differ, I have been waiting for that!" Sasha and her aunt came and kissed both girls as they left. Chicca and Jane waved as they walked out of the door, another girl was looking in the window.

"Are they open, I thought they were closed?" she frowned.

"Yes, they are now, you won't be sorry once you step inside. Enjoy it." Jane grinned at the girl as she stepped inside.

"Come on let's go and eat I'm starving", Chicca moaned pulling Jane with her. They both ran down the street giggling like young teenagers. They stopped outside a beautiful tea shop. Staring at the menu.

"Oh wow look they some yummy cakes Jane, shall we try it out?"

"Silly question, come on." Jane grabbed Chicca's hand. They walked inside, the smell of sweet treats teasing their noses. Jane looked at Chicca they were both grinning like little girls. A waitress greeted them dressed in a white crisp blouse and pinny. She looked like she stepped out of the Victorian era.

"Table for two?" Chicca nodded. "Follow me." She showed them to a table in the window, gave them a menu each and asked what drinks they would like, she took their order and left.

"oh my god Jane look at the size of that cake, its enormous, do you think we need to share one?"

"I don't bloody think so! Even if I make myself feel sick, I will have one of my own, but feel free to share yours with me." Jane laughed.

"Cheeky cow, I was being kind, thinking of your waistline. I aint sharing nothing!" they giggled again going back to the menu as their drinks arrived. They looked up as the waitress stood patiently waiting for their orders.

"Can I have Devils food cake with cream please?" Jane asked.

"Can I have the Veruca Salt please?" the waitress nodded at them both and walked away.

"So where to next? I need to decide what I want to wear underneath my dress?"

"Well, funny enough Gwen sent us a friends FB page, she said you may want to check it out, there are some seriously gorgeous things on there. Gwen said she would bring them across for you. I was looking at it when you were getting dressed."

Jane pulled her phone out to check. "Dark Desires, oooohh like the sound of that." She opened the link and saw the first few pictures of delicate lacey fabrics, she scrolled further, "oh wow, have you seen this, I want this." She turned her phone to show Chicca, it was a sheer white lace halter teddy, fringed with eyelash lace. The back open, tied around the neck high with a snap crutch.

"No way you can wear that under your dress love, it's far too high, you have a low neck on the dress, there must be something else."

"Hmm you're right, I will keep looking, we have plenty of time." They both kept scrolling giggling at what they found.

"Oh, oh, oh, you need one of these for JDubz when he goes away again", she turned the phone laughing. "It's a male chastity device." Jane burst into a fit of giggles.

"Can you imagine his face if I give it to him." Jane was trying to stop herself giggling too loud.

"You need to drop his pants the morning he is heading out and snap it on him." She banged the table, in fits of laughter.

"Stop I can't breath." Jane was holding her stomach. Mascara sticking to her eyelids as she cried laughing. The waitress came over with their cakes, they were still laughing trying to compose themselves.

"How much cream would you like?" the waitress asked. Both girls fell into hysterics. The waitress looked at them both smiling.

"Sorrrry." Jane tried to compose herself, clearing her throat. "Forgive us, we are just being silly."

"it's ok I did catch a glimpse when I came to the table, I get it. You must tell me though where you are seeing these pictures I gotta get one of these for my husband too." All the girls began howling together. Jane put her finger up to her pursed lips.

"Shhhhhhh, we don't want to get kicked out of her, everyone is looking at us." She was trying to smother her own laughter.

"You won't get kicked out believe me, this is my families place, my Dad will be pleased to see some fun and laughter in here, it gets too serious."

"Pull up a chair and join us."

"No, it's okay honestly, I need to keep the customers fed and watered, but don't go without leaving your number, I will definitely be interesting in this stuff. My husband is part of the Skulls MC and likes to think he is a ladies man, he flirts with all the club girls so they are always hanging around him. I will put this on him next time they go away."

"Oh, are you a club member too, do you know Shadow?

"Yes, I do, he's lovely, but soooo big, not being funny, but how does a girl cope with that?" Chicca snorted, gagging herself. Trying not to laugh too loud.

"I better go, look I go to the club on Wednesday and Saturday, I work the bar sometimes too, we should have a girls night, there?"

"Well, we have a hen night to set up, Jane is getting married so what a great place to start."

"You're Jane, from the UK?", she pointed.

Jane smiled. "Yes, I am, this is Chicca."

"Oh my god, we definitely need to do something, look, write your number on here we can catch up at the club and get the girls involved, maybe we can have some fun, ask your friend to come over with her kit. We can make some sales for her."

"She's in the UK, but she is a good friend of Gwen's so we could ask her to bring it with her, maybe we can video call her too."

"Perfect, I will see you at the club and we can set a date."

"Sounds good to me, Gwen is coming over early anyway so we can sort the date with her too."

"I can't wait now." Jane grinned.

"Enjoy your cakes, I will leave the cream with you and bring some fresh drinks over."

"We didn't get your name?" Chicca asked.

"It's Violet, but my friends call me V."

"Good to meet you V, we will see you at the club this weekend all being well, Jane can you make it?"

"We don't have any plans so yes sounds good to me."

"Great look forward to it. See you both then. Food and drink is on the house, if you need anything more give me a shout."

"Thanks V, that's really kind."

They finished eating and said goodbye to Violet. Laughing and joking about what they found on Dark Desires page.

"Any news on where you are going for your honeymoon Jane?"

"No idea, you know Jasper loves surprising me, so I'm leaving it to him. I don't mind where we go as long as it's just the two of us relaxing. No phones, internet or TV."

"Oh, my kind of holiday, but with lots of sun, laying on the beach all day."

"Sounds nice, but I like to explore too, Jasper gets bored quickly, so I'm sure it will be a bit of both."

"Hang on there girl, bored on your honeymoon!!? I bloody hope not."

"Oh Chicca, I didn't mean that, I meant he can't lay on the beach for too long, we do have a great sex life, so that won't be a problem, I have plans too." She grinned raising one eyebrow.

"Well, they say the quiet ones are the worst and I wouldn't put it past you lady to be very naughty. We will have to get you drunk so you give up all your secrets."

"Quiet, I'm not quiet, but you won't get it out of me either."

"We will see." Chicca grinned making a mental note to tell the girls.

Chapter 7

Reality check

Moses was sat up all night thinking about what would come of the appointment with the Doctor and what his chances were. He knew Jane was going out with Chicca for the day, so he had the time to call Jasper while she was out. He knew it was wrong not to tell her, but he couldn't be there to tell her himself and wanted Jasper to know first before he had his video call with her.

He looked at the clock, it was 3am, he picked up his phone, scrolled through the names and stopped at Susan's number. He opened up his WhatsApp and started a message.

Hi Susan, how are you? I was awake so thought at as it's evening there I would see how you were doing. I'm sorry I didn't get chance to speak to you before I left but I needed to get back, it was a bit last thing. x

He sent the message and stared at the screen, within seconds he saw her appear online, he sat up straighter in bed.

Susan. Hi stranger, I'm doing good, how are you, what was so important that you left like a bride running from the alter, am I that scary? x

Moses. Oh funny, just some stuff I had to deal with back here. I'm okay love. x

Susan. Why don't I believe that? It's what 3am there and you are texting me, do you think I am stupid Moses? How bad is it? x

Moses. What are you talking about? x

Susan. I know you are not well Moses, I worked on a Cancer unit long enough to know the signs. x

Moses. Oh. Can I call you? x

Susan. Of course x

Moses took a deep breath and dialed her number, purposely leaving his camera off.

"Hi Susan."

"Hi love, so come on then, talk to me."

"To be honest I don't know much, its testicular and possibly stomach but until today I don't know, I have an appointment and hopefully it's not as bad as I think it is."

"I'm sorry love. Why didn't you call me before this?"

"You know I am a private person but laying here awake I thought I could distract myself by talking to you and flirting a little."

"No change there then. Does Jane know?"

"No, she doesn't, I want to keep it that way. I am calling Jasper once I know, to talk to him first, I want him to be there when I tell her."

"Good idea, when is the wedding, will you still be coming across for it."

"Of course, wild horses wouldn't stop me being there. Will you like to be my plus 1?"

"You can be mine if you like, I have a verbal offer from when I saw her last at the hospital."

"Deal! That means I get the first dance then."

"Isn't that the Fathers dance?"

"Cheeky bitch, I'm not that old." Moses smiled, he was feeling better for talking to Susan.

"That's better, I like it when you smile, now turn the damn camera on and let me see your ugly face old timer." Susan was shocked at herself for being so flirty. Moses did as he was told, he was sat in bed naked, smiling at Susan.

"Good to see you Moses, wish it was under better circumstances. I do hope you are not naked below the camera?"

"Well as you asked, yes I am, would you like to see in a purely professional capacity of course?"

"Oh, that cheekiness certainly hasn't stopped. I will let the Doctors do that for you, just keep your hands where I can see them."

"Here was me thinking my luck was in tonight, damn you woman, take pity on a sick man."

"So damn cheeky, no Moses. Not this time, you have a big day today, let's talk later and we can go from there."

"Ohhhh, you didn't say no, I must be in with a chance then."

"Moses….."

"Okay, okay, I will stop." Moses laughed at the firmness of Susan's voice.

"Right, so rest up, tell me later once you speak to the Doctor. I will do all I can to help you."

"Thanks love, I will be in touch later."

Moses moved down the bed putting his phone on the side, he tossed and turned for a while before falling asleep for a few hours.

He woke with a pounding headache, he laid on his back rubbing his head. He looked at the clock it was 7.10am, he stayed there for a few minutes, his mind racing. He finally sat up in bed, stretching and yawning, he pushed himself off the bed and walked into the bathroom. He stood in the mirror putting his hands onto the sink looking at himself. He closed his eyes sighing heavily. He could see Jane stood in front of him, she was sat on her trike the day she picked it up with a huge smile on her face. He took his phone out of his pocket and took some pictures of her, it was the first time he had seen her so relaxed.

"Moses put that damn phone away and come here and see, isn't she beautiful?"

"She? Next you will be giving it a name."

"Yes of course, my Red Robin."

"Oh lord help me." He laughed. Jane slipped off the seat running across to Moses. She jumped into his arms squealing like a child. He caught her as she wrapped her arms and legs around him, grabbing his face kissing him all over. He couldn't stop laughing, "stop, you silly mare."

"If it wasn't for you this would never have happened, I am forever saying thank you and I mean it every time I say it."

"I know you do Half-pint and you don't need to. I will always be here for you no matter what."

Jane slid down from his body. "Come on, come and see Red Robin, we can go out on a ride out now, you can be my pillion."

"Not on your life, the only time I will be on a bike is when I ride it myself, I will take you out on it though happily."

Jane laughed at him. "That is never going to happen either."

"Well, a ride out on our own bikes then it is." They reached the trike, Moses was really happy with it. It glistened under the lights of the garage, he couldn't wait to see her on it. She was desperate for a private plate, but he had argued with her that it was too obvious and could get her identified if her ex saw her, so she accepted it but sulked for a while.

He opened his eyes, sighing, feeling sick to the stomach. "I will fight this for you Jane, I promise."
He walked into the shower, looking down at his body, he liked the look of himself, he was almost back to where he was when he was in the army, he didn't think the weight loss had anything to do with the cancer, he assumed it was the hard work he put in, but realistically he was protecting himself and trying to push it to the back of his mind. He showered knowing G would be with him soon. He dressed and went downstairs to get another coffee, he couldn't stomach anything to eat and a coffee would fill him up enough.

He heard G pull up in the truck, he got up out of the sofa and walked to the door to meet him.
"Morning Brother, come in." They hugged each other as G came in.
"How are you feeling, nervous I would imagine?"
"Yes, I am, not slept much, but it is what it is, I left it too long so hope to Christ it's not as bad, or it's treatable. Or Half-pint will kill me anyway."
They both laughed with the image of Jane losing her temper at them.
"Well let's see what the Doc has to say today, I'm right here for you." G put his hand on Moses shoulder patting him.
"Thank you, I know, I am grateful you have kept this to yourself and I know how hard it must be I promise once I tell Half-pint you can tell the gang, I just don't want any of that pity shit, or tears from the girls."
"Wishful thinking Brother." G teased him, trying to lighten the conversation.
Moses rinsed his cup out and left it on the side, "Let's get this shit over with then." He grabbed his jacket, slipped his boots on and walked out the door to G's truck. They drove in silence, G kept quiet he didn't know what to say and felt this was the time to keep quiet. They parked up and walked into the hospital. Moses was sweating now, struggling to take a deep breath, he just wanted to know now, so he knew what to do. They were sat for a few minutes when the Consultant called them in.

"Moses, come on in, take a seat, how are you feeling?" He shook hands with Moses and G smiling at him, pleased someone was here with him.

"Anxious to be honest. This is G, he will be around for anything and he is my contact here in the UK so if anything happens you call him first. I would like him to know everything too."

"Pleased to meet you G. okay I won't waste time with small talk, I have looked at your scan and blood work, it is as we thought, the cancer has spread into your stomach, so to start we will need to run a course of Radiotherapy which will hopefully shrink the tumour and then carry out a Gastrectomy and all being well remove all of the cancerous tissues. There is no guarantee this will work, the odds of complete cure are low, but we can manage it, you may need Chemotherapy after but we will know more once you have had Radiotherapy, it will hopefully kill off what is in your Testicles too."

G was holding back his tears. He put his hand on Moses shoulder.

Moses wiped his face with his hands, covering his mouth, his mind running at 100 miles an hour.

"If you can't get it all what does that mean?"

"The outlook for stomach cancer depends on your age, diet, your general health and wellbeing, and what you put in and what stage you are at."

"Okay so worst-case scenario is what Doc?"

"Half of those diagnosed die within the first year. But we are going to fight this and do all we can Moses. So, let's get you booked in to see the team and start your radiotherapy for four weeks then we can do another scan and see how much it has shrunk. Then we know where we go next."

G sat quiet, he squeezed Moses shoulder harder. He felt sick himself, not knowing what he was going to say to his friend. The room fell quiet.

Moses cleared his throat and wiped his eyes. "Tell me what you want me to do Doc, I don't intend on going anywhere yet. I don't want to hear any more about if I had come in sooner, if Jane hears that she will start blaming herself", he looked back at G, "as far as anyone knows I found a lump and came home to get it sorted."

"You can count on me Moses you know that." He half smiled at Moses and nodded.

"Right then, the team are waiting for you if you go with the nurse now, they will talk you through it and get you ready for your first session, any questions at all ask, it might be worth writing things down too as you think of them."

"Good idea Doc, thanks, we will." Moses and G stood, shook hands with the Doctor and followed the nurse out into another clinic.

A team were waiting for them when they arrived. They had decided external therapy would be the best option, 5 days a week for 4 weeks. Moses and G sat and listened, G took notes on his phone. Moses just sat nodding trying to take it all in.

"Okay Moses, have a think and chat to your friend here and let us know tomorrow if you have any questions, I know it is a lot to take in, we do need to get you started as soon as possible, we will need to give you a few tattoo dots on your body but looking at you I can see that won't be an issue, we will do those tomorrow for you and start your treatment on Monday. Do you have any questions for me?"
"I don't think so at this moment."
"Okay, Clare will take care of you now and talk you through self-care etc, she will be your nurse throughout the treatment." The Doctor stood, shook hands with the men and left the room.
"Thanks Doc." They said in unison as Clare sat down in the Doctors chair.

"Hi Moses, is it?" she frowned at his name.
"Yes, only my Mum calls me Christian so please don't call me that."
"Whatever makes you happy Moses, okay then, there is a lot for you to take in and I don't want to overload you, a couple of things though. One of the biggest side effects of treatment especially around the stomach is sickness, we will give you an anti-sickness if needed. Eat little and often, try and stay as healthy as you can, not processed food and no alcohol either. Your skin will feel like it is sunburnt, some people say it feels like it inside too. You will need this lotion to rub onto your body to keep your skin moistened. You will lose hair around that area too, it will grow back once treatment is over. Its hidden so it shouldn't be an issue. You will get very tired as your treatment progresses, rest as much as you can, you may notice weight loss too, but I understand you have already lost a lot of weight so try and keep eating, if not we can give you some liquid food. Which will help. I know your head must be full right now, I am here for you whenever you need to talk. Just give me a call, here is my card. Can I just confirm your details, and your friends?"
"Umm yeah sure", he looked down at the paper and nodded at the information, "That's correct nurse."
"Clare please."

"Sure, sorry Clare." Moses dropped his head. He didn't know how to feel or what to think, he was half listening and so glad G was with him.

"Right then, that is all for today, if you come back tomorrow we can get you marked up and it will give us a couple of days to be ready for you on Monday. Any questions?"

Moses looked at G, they both shook their heads. "No thanks Clare."

"Okay I will see you tomorrow at 10am. Take all the time you need here, leave when you are ready." She stood, shook hands with them both, smiling and left the room.

"Get me out of here G please?"

"Sure Brother, come on." They walked out in silence back to G's truck, they both climbed in and Moses sat silent, the tears he had been holding back started to fall, his head hung low, he sniffed, wiping his face, his throat hurt from holding back.

"Drive G, I don't care where but not home. I need some air." G pulled out of the car park and headed for the beach, it worked for him and he hoped it would help Moses. He had no idea what to say, his best friend was the one who held everyone else together and now he needed them. He wasn't letting him down he just didn't know where to start.

G pulled up at the kerb, they were in Gosport. The beach was quiet, Moses got out of the car, turning to G. "Give me a few minutes please?"

"Whatever you need Brother."

Moses walked up onto the beach, the stones making it harder to walk under foot, the breeze was blowing straight at him, the air waking him up, he could smell the sea, the tide was in, he walked down to the edge and sat down on the stones. Pulled his phone out, his and Jane's picture was his background, he smiled at the memory and felt sick knowing he had to tell her. He knew she would be frantic with worry and it scared him putting her through it. But he needed her strength too.

He dialed Jasper. "Moses, how are you brother, everything okay, it's not like you to call this early in the day. Jane will kick herself."

"Hi J, sorry I know she is out which is why I called, I hate to put this on your shoulders Brother, but I need your help."

"Talk to me, whatever you need."

"Okay, I left you early because I found a lump in my balls, I knew it wasn't good, just had that feeling so came straight home and saw the Doctor, I have testicular cancer and it has gone into my stomach. I am starting Radiotherapy Monday for 4 weeks then I need surgery, they hope to remove it all, but if not, then who knows. I am not expecting you to tell Half-Pint but I wanted you to be ready when she hears it from me. I just need to get my head round it first, so if the weekend is good, I will call you then? I know she is wedding dress shopping today and I am not ruining that for her."

"Fuck Moses! It spread that fast, how long have you had the lump for Brother?"

Moses sighed. "A while, but you needed me, Half-Pint needed me and I needed to be there, so I stayed, you have to promise me you will never fucking tell her, I don't want her blaming herself for this."

"It's safe with me, but you better get your story straight, you know she is going to dig deep over this."

"Yeah, yeah I fucking know it, she can be a pain in the fucking arse at times. I will be ready for her. Just please work with me on this. I won't tell her you knew either, I just wanted you to be ready."

"I appreciate that Moses, she will have my balls on a plate if she found that out anyway. Just text me when you are ready to call. I imagine your mind is all over the place right now, promise me if you need anything at all you will call, you know she will want to be on the next plane out too."

"Yeah don't I, that's where we have to be cruel to be kind and stop her. Give me a few weeks to get used to it then she can come out for a few days."

"Whatever you want buddy. We will be guided by you."

"Thanks Brother. Speak to you later. I will explain all of it with you both at the weekend."

"Take care of yourself, I assume G is with you?"

"Yes, he is."

"Great okay. Talk soon." They both hung up. Moses dropped his phone onto the stones, putting his head into his hands, he began to cry, he pushed the heels of his hands into his eyes, wiping his face roughly, sniffing trying to stop any further tears. He had opened the flood gates, his body shook as he sobbed openly. He hugged his knees wiping his face across his jeans at the knee.

He heard footsteps on the stones and turned to the side, a dog cautiously walked towards him. Moses smiled thinking of Lady and the pups. He put his hand out to the dog. He looked up to see if there was an owner about but he was alone. The dog came closer, sniffing his hand, Moses touched his head, the dog sniffed again and moved in closer, sitting down looking up at him. Moses smiled.

"Hello fella, where did you come from?" The dog stood wagging his tail getting closer, putting his head on Moses shoulder and licked his ear. He smiled again.

"You are a friendly little guy. He turned his head and the dog slobbered up his face. licking his tears away. Moses laughed at him, grabbing the bottom of his t-shirt wiping the slobber off his face.

"Thanks for that, where is your owner?" He took his collar, he had a disc on it, just a name no number. "Well Hello Mr Bojangles, do you dance?" He heard whistling as a man came towards them.

"Mr Bojangles will you come here please!" he scolded the dog. "I'm so sorry he has disturbed you. he seems to think everyone is there for him to talk to."

"He's no bother honestly, he actually was just what I needed, he's a beautiful dog. I just asked him if he was a dancer?"

"Oh you know of Bojangles Robinson then?"

"Yes I do, as soon as I saw the name I smiled. Does he dance then or sing?

"Does he ever, we changed his name when he found his voice. He doesn't shut up. If the wife sings that's it, he joins in. He loves people and seems to know when someone needs a hug."

"Well. he certainly made me feel better. Just what I needed", he rubbed the dogs head who came back closer and licked him again.

"I'm glad he wasn't bothering you. are you ok? Do you need to talk? Sometimes strangers are easier to talk to."

"Thank you, I have just been diagnosed with Cancer, well I say just I have had it for sometime but a friend needed me more so I have only just dealt with it seriously."

"Wow, this friend must be something special?"

"Yes, she is, have you ever looked at someone and fallen head over heels in love with them? well I did, I have messed about for years and then she came into my life."

"Did you marry her?"

"No, she had a complicated life, she needed a friend more and that's how we still are, all these years later, she is about to marry someone else so that boat has sailed."

"Are you crazy?! If you are that in love with her you need to tell her, fight for her. Jesus that doesn't happen twice in a lifetime, tell her."

"I can't, she is so happy, this new guy is everything I wanted to be, he is perfect for her. I would hate to lose her by telling her, so I will accept her as my best friend instead."

"I know we don't know each other so forgive me for saying mate but you are a bloody fool."

They both laughed together as G came across the beach. "Looks like you have company." He nodded up towards G.

"Yes that's G."

"I will leave you too it, Mr Bojangles come on leave this fella alone. I'm Scott by the way, nice to meet you."

"Moses, nice to meet you too, thanks for the chat." They shook hands and Scott and the dog walked away. Moses stood up as G reached him. "You okay?"

"Yeah, the dog decided to make friends."

"Oh nice. How are you doing?"

"I'm okay, I rang J, I knew Half-pint was out shopping today, I am going to call her at the weekend. I don't fancy being him once we hang up."

"Christ no, she is going to suspect so much and poor Jasper is going to get both barrels, he will certainly know who he's marrying." They both smiled and walked back up the beach to the car.

"Where do you want to go, home or somewhere else?"

"Well I am actually hungry now, so let's go and get something to eat, I could do with a juicy steak.

"Big O's it is then." They both nodded. G pulled out and drove in the direction of their friends steak house.

Chapter 8

Pleasing you

Chicca dropped Jane at home, they were still giggling after the conversation in the tea shop.

"Saturday it is then you better tell JDubz we are going down there. Talk to Gwen too let her know what the plans are."

"Will do." She leant over and kissed her cheek before getting out of the car, she opened the back door pulling out her bags and waved goodbye.

She walked into the house, Lady came running at her, smiling, her tail going around in a circle. She got onto her knees fussing her as Jasper walked out of the office.

"Hey gorgeous, did you have fun?"

"Oh my God we had such a good laugh, we went into a tea shop and met a girl from the club too, her Dad is a member, we have made plans for my Hen night already."

"Christ that was quick."

Jasper put his hand out to help her off the floor, "It's all Gwen's fault."

"Why Gwen? She wasn't there?"

"She sent us a link over for naughty underwear and toys, we were looking at it in the tea shop, we couldn't stop giggling and the waitress came across chatting to us making us worse, that's how we met her, she wants to introduce us to the girls and her hubby and Dad. We said we would go Saturday if you're up for it?"

"Sounds like a plan, yeah why not." He turned away heading into the kitchen he had been cooking since he spoke to Moses, he needed to keep busy, so decided to cook something nice for when Jane got home. She followed him into the kitchen and sat on the stool watching him, she loved how he moved so easily.

"What you cooking?" she put her elbows on the worktop leaning her chin on her hands.

"What would you like it to be?"

"Anything you cook is perfect, so I don't mind, but if you are offering? I would say you naked on this worktop." Jane pouted as Jasper turned to look at her, he laughed seeing how funny she looked.

He leant onto the worktop bending into her kissing her puckered lips. Jane opened her eyes.

"Is that the best you can do?" she moved further onto the worktop, Jasper leaned in again and kissed her while she had her eyes closed. He grabbed her arms pulling her across the top into his arms kissing her with tiny butterfly kisses all over her face, Jane began squealing and giggling. Trying to push him away. He grabbed her legs putting them either side of him and walked her into the lounge laying her down onto the sofa, getting down on his knees he pulled up her top and began blowing raspberries on her stomach. Jane was screaming to be set free, Jasper was laughing as she tried to push his head away, he took her hands and put them over the top of her head. She wriggled as much as she could trying to get away but was failing badly.

"Pleaseeeeee stop." She begged, over and over, through her giggles and coughs. Jasper continued, his lips were going numb after blowing so many raspberries on her. He loved seeing her laugh it never failed to make him melt and fall in love with her more. Jane wriggled free. She began calling Lady for help, she came bounding into the room and jumped on top of them both licking them. They both began to giggle. Jasper stopped and sat back on his heels, giving Jane a chance to breath.

"I thought you were supposed to protect me not join in Lady?" She laughed at the dog.

"What you forgot Belle is I was home with her, we had it all planned out."

"Yeah, yeah right." She giggled straightening herself up and sitting up. Jasper got up and sat next to Jane, Lady joined them at their feet.

"Tell me more about this naughty stuff then Gwen told you about, are you going to let me see this website?"

I'm not sure about that, you might get frisky on me."

"Frisky? I'm not a dog or cat!" he laughed at Jane she was shaking her head.

"You haven't seen this stuff, it's amazing."

"Okay come on then test me, let me see it."

Jane grabbed her phone out of her bag, she had the knowing look on her face. She found the link and opened the page. She sat down next to Jasper. He laid his chin on her shoulder.

"Dark Desires? I like the sound of that…. Hang on why is there a car tyre on the page? Is it from a model." He pointed.

Jane looked down and began giggling. "You are a wally, look what is says."

"The Cox's Cog? Gentleman's C ring?" Jasper began laughing. "That's one of those things you put on me after the black tie event?"

"That thing, is a cock ring Jasper and yes, it is love." She looked back at him, his eyes were wide.

She began scrolling.

 "Stop, stop, stop, wow!! look at those boots, we gotta get you some of those! Can you imagine you being on the bike wearing those?"

"So, are you feeling frisky then?"

"No, keep going, but save those please. I think I need a new camera, we could take some sexy pictures of you on the bike in this stuff."

"No? I think you are telling me lies Mr M, care to look down?" Jasper began laughing.

"I don't know what you mean." He looked down at his cock, "You let me down again. Why do you do that to me? now she's going to think I'm frisky!" He whispered to himself.

"Umm, I can hear you darling." He screwed his face up at his cock as it began pushing at his jeans.

"Damn you woman." He grinned kissing her. "You should be happy me wanting to see you in all this."

"Oh I am." She grinned.

"Keep scrolling then, no, no, no, keep going. Boring, boring, ooooohhhh, stop, stop, stop, wow, now those are perfect for you!"

"Jasper, these are not boring they are very naughty, we are talking crutchless knickers, suspenders, lace etc."

"I know Belle, but I just don't like some of them. But these I like very much!"

"I am sure you have a boot fetish."

"With you in them, yes I do."

"Can you see how many lace holes there are?"

"Yes, but I wouldn't be taking them off you, they are worth leaving on all night. The killer heels, the leather up your thigh, Jesus, I wouldn't leave you alone!"

"You don't now."

"Well yeah true, but this could be lots of fun. How long will it take to get it here?"

"Gwen said she would bring it with her."

"Oh no, we don't want to wait for Gwen, get this lady Dee's number and we can give her an order and I will pay for it to be shipped across."

"You are funny Jasper." Jane laughed covering her face. "You are like a school boy looking into a games catalogue."

"Yes, but big boys toys for his love."

"There are plenty for men too you know, maybe I should be choosing plenty then! I will let the girls know you want to ship it across, we are having a virtual party soon with Dee at the club, let's make it worthwhile."

"I don't need to be thinking of Chicca and James thank you very much, that's just not a nice thought."

"Are you sure about that?" she teased, brushing his cock with her hand.

"Yes, I am sure, cheeky, if you don't want spanking then you better stop that. Unless you want to be put across my knee, maybe we should order a paddle for your arse too?"

"Or yours, don't think I am the only one you will be dressing up." Jasper spun to look at Jane, she sat laughing. "There is no way you are getting me in any of this stuff."

"Stuff? you mean naughty underwear love, you want me to wear it then you can too, in fact you could wear these under your jeans and nobody but me would know. Imagine that! I could tease you all day. Yummy." She began giggling again looking at the pants.

"Gold or silver shorts? I don't think so Belle." He laughed nervously.

"How about these Christmas boxers? With a bow around your neck, that could be your Christmas day outfit." Jane was laughing at him screwing his face up.

"Give me that!", he took the phone from her hand, "well then you have to wear these. I think you will look gorgeous in red fish net stockings, with this lacey little number, my Belle in red, just perfect. You can leave the G string out though."

"Why, it's part of the set?"

"Easier access when you bend over to look in the oven, I can slide my fingers in easier." He grinned as Jane looked at him.

"You need to take a cold shower Mr, you are getting yourself all hot and bothered."

"Cold shower? I don't think so."

He grabbed Jane pushing her flat on the sofa, climbing on top of her, he moved her hair from her neck and began nibbling at her, Jane stretched leaning her head to the left to give him more access. She laid moaning as his hand moved up to her breast. She opened her legs wanting to be touched. Jasper smiled moving his hand down her thigh, Jane wriggled beneath him trying to move his hand.

"My girl frisky?" he whispered into her ear.

"I want you." she groaned.

Jasper moved down biting her through her clothes, nuzzling her. He undid her jeans standing so he could pull them down her legs. Jane was kicking trying to get them off, he pulled his t-shirt off and got back down on his knees, he pulled her closer to him her legs either side of his head. He bit her pussy gentle making Jane squeal, he smiled doing it again. Jane pushed her pussy into his face.

"Oh, my girl is hungry for me." He teased her rubbing his finger up and down the outside of her knickers, he could feel her wetness on them, he smiled sliding a finger inside, making Jane arch.

"Mmmmmmm you're so wet Belle." He leant into her moving her knickers out of the way blowing on her pussy, Jane grabbed his head pushing him in further. Jasper grinned loving it. He flicked his tongue quickly against her warm wet skin, teasing her, she groaned under him. He did it again. Jane pushed his head again trying to force his lips onto her. He sat back on his knees lifting her legs pulling at her knickers, he threw them onto the floor, then moved back to her legs, kissing and licking down her thigh. Jane groaned with every bite and kiss, his fingers walked down her legs to her pussy, slipping his finger in Jasper groaned, he loved seeing her so wet, he moved his finger up and down making her completely wet, he moved closer, the scent of her making his mouth water. He moved his middle finger in turning his hand, slowly moving in and out of her, his tongue going into her hood licking her gently, Jane grabbed the cushion behind her head screwing it up. Trying not to scream out, she didn't want Lady jumping on them again. Jasper pulled his finger out opening her up, her pussy glistening he laid his tongue flat against her slowly licking every inch of her pussy, he felt her clit swell under his tongue. Jane grabbed the cushion putting over her head muffling her sounds. He circled her clit, licking hard, making her groan and push into him. He pushed his finger back into her feeling the wetness around it, Jane clenched as he licked harder. She moved the cushion breathing deeply, gasping as he continued. He pushed another finger inside her tight pussy, Jane grabbed his head. Her breathing erratic, she dug her fingers into his hair gripping tight, Jasper pushed harder into her. Teasing her clit more. His beard rubbing her was driving her nuts, her moans were deep, her breathing completely erratic. She felt her orgasm building her body getting hot, tingling, Jasper picked up the pace, licking faster, his fingers getting deeper pushing against her. He was breathing heavy, her juices warm as she got wetter waiting for her orgasm, Jasper kissed her clit, slowing down, teasing her, Jane pushed up again, she was on the brink, she moved her hand down, touching herself, Jasper smiled watching her, he sat back pulling his fingers out, as her finger slid inside. Her thumb laying on her clit as her finger slid in. She bucked into her finger desperate to reach her orgasm, Jasper got closer, wanting to see close up, Jane continued her small fingers getting faster as she brought herself to orgasm, her body convulsing, as she reached it Jasper moved her hand pushing his tongue to her clit, sucking her juices as she squeezed his head between her legs, gritting her teeth stopping her moans. She was desperate to stop Jasper, but he knew he could make her cum again. He continued to lap at her juices as Jane shook, he felt her reach her second, she clenched harder around his head, trying to force him away, he continued licking and sucking drinking every drop of her. Jane was exhausted her hand relaxing, her body on fire, tingling from head to toe. He moved up to her laying between her legs. Jane smiled pulling him to her, his beard wet with her juices, Jane kissed him smelling herself on him. She reached down to his jeans trying to undo him.

"No Belle. This is about you. I just wanted to please you." he smiled kissing her again.

"But you are rock hard baby, don't you want me?"

"Oh Belle, of course I do, but sometimes it's nice to want to do something for you and not expect anything in return."

Jane grabbed his face squeezing his cheeks so he pouted like a fish. She kissed him hard. "God I love you so much, you are wonderful." Jasper sat back lifting Jane up, passing her knickers and jeans to her.

"I think I will get changed into my shorts and be comfortable." She got up carrying her clothes heading for the bedroom. Jasper grabbed her phone looking through the naughty underwear ear marking lots of it, Jane came down minutes later she stopped watching Jasper as he turned her phone frowning at something on the screen, she crept up behind him.

"Did you find something you like the look of?" she whispered making him jump.

"Jesus Belle, you made me jump. Have you seen this?" he turned the phone to her.

Jane laughed "Yes that's the alternative for our vibrators, just slide into it and it will feel like a pussy."

"You can't lick it though."

"Well, you could if you really wanted, but I don't think it's for that." Jane was giggling. "We could get you one if you like, you know when you go away for work?"

"Could you imagine me going through customs! They would have a field day, no thank you Belle, I would rather use my hand if I am without you."

"Sometimes I think you are a little prudish Jasper." She laughed taking the phone from him.

"No, I just don't see the point and anyway I would rather have toys and naughty clothes we can both enjoy!" Jane added it to her wish list, she knew they could have some fun with it.

"Well don't think I will be a nun while you're away again, a girl has needs and you have flicked my switch and I will be playing while you are away. If you are not available whilst entertaining and can't call, then I will be using other things." Jasper laughed turning to look at her.

"You horny little girl of mine. Come here." Jane walked around the sofa, Jasper pulled her onto his knee, she cuddled into him as he kissed her cheek. "I'm glad I flicked your switch, you certainly flicked mine too. I have never wanted to devour someone the way I do with you." He kissed her hard sighing, he knew Moses was due to call and was dreading the fallout from it.

"Come on beautiful let's get some dinner going then we can chill out in front of the TV, you can pick the movie." He sat forward Jane still on his knee standing carrying her to the kitchen.

"I miss you carrying me, is that bad, does that make me a princess and needy?"

"Yes." He giggled, Jane slapped his shoulder. "No Belle, I miss that closeness too. It's not about carrying you, it brought us together, quicker than we would have I think, it brings back wonderful memories and you know I will carry you anywhere you want to go." He kissed her nose sitting her on the stool. "Your throne Princess." He grinned teasing her. Jane spun in her seat slapping him as he tried to move. He laughed walking away. He lifted the lid off the slow cooker, prodding the chicken. "Think it's ready Belle", she jumped off the stool grabbing the bowls from the cupboard. Jasper pulled out the ladle. They stood together getting the casserole out, Jane split the bread putting on their plates, they moved to the table to eat. Jaspers phone beeped on the side. He felt sick, he stood to grab it, it was Moses.

Moses. Hi Brother, I'm not calling today, I won't spoil her day from picking her wedding dress, I will call tomorrow, sorry buddy I didn't want to spoil your evening."

Jasper. Thanks Moses, really appreciate that, she is on a high and I was dreading you calling.

Moses, talk tomorrow, it will be early, so I don't keep you on pins all day.

Jasper, thanks, appreciate that. Talk to you tomorrow.

"It's not like you to get up and answer your phone, what's wrong love?"
"Nothing Belle, I am expecting a call and thought that might be it."
"Something I need to know about?" she frowned looking at him.
"No Belle, don't be nosey." He was trying to think on his feet. "it's a surprise so leave it there."
"Oooooh I like surprises, will you give me a clue?"
Jasper laughed relaxing. "No Belle I won't it's a surprise, you know what that means don't you?" Jane pouted like a little girl.
"You're not playing fair now."
"If I tell you, it will spoil it and I won't do that, so you can pout and sulk all you like. You will never forgive yourself if I tell you." Jane huffed finishing her dinner in silence. Jasper smiled at her.
They finished dinner, loaded the dishwasher together taking their drinks to the lounge. They cuddled up on the sofa, Lady joined them both squeezing down below Jane's feet. Jane was searching for a film to watch, she was huffing and puffing, Jasper knew she was sulking still, but he couldn't tell her anything. He did have a surprise for her and there was no way he was giving in. It was too big to spoil. Finally she found a new series to watch.
"That will do."
"This looks a bit blood thirsty Belle?"
"I just fancy something different that's all, let's try it see how we get on."

"If you're sure." She nodded and curled into him as the programme started.

Chapter 9

Being honest

Moses was walking around the house trying to decide how to talk to Jane and what to say to her, he was glad Jasper was with her. He spent the evening talking to Susan, he regretted not taking her out when he was with Jane in the US. But he had never been bothered. He had enough one-night stands or casual girlfriends, he had slept with a few of the girls at the club too.

Suddenly getting older and losing Jane to the US and Jasper he realized how alone he was. Susan was a great distraction, he enjoyed the flirting and the fun they had and wished they were closer. He stopped pacing and looked out of the window, his phone beeped.

Susan. Morning love, how are you? Have you spoken to Jane yet? x

Moses. Not yet no, I was going to wait until 9am your time. x

Susan. Good idea. You ok? Figured out what you are going to say yet? x

Moses. Not yet no, I keep pacing the damn house. x

Susan. if you want a chat after give me a call, I don't mind. Instead of all this back and forth on texts. x

Moses. Thanks Susan, I would be lost without you being there and talking sense into me. G hates seeing me at the moment he doesn't know what to say and that is the hardest thing going. Once I tell Jane I will tell the club too. I know Gwen will beat the shit out of me for not talking to her and getting sorted sooner but I would rather that than be ignored. x

Susan. You're welcome love, don't think you will get off lightly with me though. Lol x

Moses. Don't I know it. Right, I will make a drink then make that call. Talk later love x

Moses smiled as he put his phone down and went into the kitchen to make a drink. His stomach was in knots. He went back to the lounge and turned the TV on ready to dial Jane. He swiped his phone onto the screen and sat back, Jasper answered.

"Hey buddy how are you? Let me just give her a call."

"Belle it's Moses." Jasper called from the lounge, she was in the kitchen making a drink.

"Terrified of talking to her if I'm honest, I've been talking to Susan a lot about it, she used to be a Cancer nurse so knows everything and it kind of helps. She has offered to come and talk to Half-Pint too."

"That's great, you need someone who isn't too close." Moses smiled as he saw Jane walk into the room with two cups of tea.

"Where's mine?" he teased her.

"Well get your arse back here and I will make you one." Jane grinned.

"Any way why are you calling so early it's not like you?"

"You never miss a damn thing do you", he mumbled under his breath.

"I heard that."

Jasper motioned for Jane to sit down and cuddled her into him. Moses watched as she got comfortable.

"Wow it seems ages since I saw your place, surprised you are not at the club. Something must be wrong, you feeling okay?"

"Jane listen to me love, I need you to let me talk then you can ask anything you need to."

"You never call me Jane." Her voice trembled she knew this wasn't going to be good. The tears were already building behind her eyes, she swallowed hard. Jasper squeezed her hand.

"Half-pint, I'm sorry. I'm going to start from the beginning and I need you to listen." She nodded.

He took a deep breath. "Okay, I left you earlier than I had planned because I found a lump in my testicles, I know that's not a nice thought but just listen. I went to the specialist and I have testicular cancer, and it has spread to my stomach, it's one of the reasons for my weight loss and back ache. It is serious, I had a scan and they are going to do all they can for me. They think they have caught it early but depending on the next set of results I will know the extent, I am going in next week to start my Radiotherapy every day for 28 days, they are hoping this will shrink it."

He stopped and looked at Jasper not sure whether to continue. Jasper nodded. Jane was squeezing his hand so tight it was going white, the tears began to fall silently. Her throat hurt from holding back. She just wanted to scream.

"G knows, he came with me to the hospital, I also took him to the Solicitor with me to put everything in order." Jane took a deep breath to speak but shut up. She had promised to be quiet. "If anything happens to me then you and G are in charge of everything, I know you don't want to hear this, but you need to. Everything is sorted, basically it's all yours and G's. I will also be signing a DNR, I don't want to fight with you over it and I am asking you to honour that if ever the time comes. I don't know what the future holds but I will promise you one thing I am going to fight this." He wiped his eye as a stray tear escaped. He didn't realise how hard this would be. "Okay love you can ask anything now."

Jane took a deep breath, wiped her eyes with her t-shirt and looked at Moses, she moved off the sofa and got down on her knees touching the screen on his face, chocking on her tears.

"I don't know what to say to be honest, I'm sad you couldn't tell me. But I understand why, who else knows?"

Jasper moved behind Jane and shook his head gently. She didn't need to know he knew.

"G obviously, and Susan."

"Susan? Who is she?"

"Your nurse love."

Jane felt herself get jealous. Her skin prickled. "Why are you talking to her, what has she got to do with it." Her face was getting red in annoyance.

"I had her number from when you were ill. I needed to talk to a stranger, I messaged her and she knew straight away. We have been chatting a week now. She has offered to come and explain it all to you, she was a Cancer nurse before she moved across."

"I don't need someone else to explain it to me thank you." she snapped, feeling annoyed.

"Half-pint I know you are angry with me, but please don't be, I couldn't tell you, don't you understand that? You are the most important person in my life. I knew this was going to hurt you, that's the last thing I wanted to do. But I promise you from here on in you will know everything."

"How can I trust you, you have lied already when I told you I knew something was wrong, how do I know you won't lie again to protect me. I'm not a child Moses, I'm a big girl I can look after myself."

"Not too much emphasis on the big Half-Pint", he laughed trying to lighten the situation.

"You're not funny", she pouted poking her tongue out at him. "I just wish I was there, so I could give you a hug. I need to see you properly, I'm coming home."

"No Jane, not yet, please. Let me get my head sorted first. G is here, I don't want you dropping everything, you have a wedding to plan remember."

"I know that, but you are also important too. I know how this goes remember." Jane began to sob, her tears no longer at bay, Jasper got onto the floor behind her, grabbing her, he passed her the tissues from the table beside him. She was wiping her eyes and nose trying to be strong.

"I need you to be strong and pray for me love, I will be there soon enough for the wedding, let me get this treatment over with first. I promise you I am not going anywhere, I won't give up."

Jane nodded her face smudging her mascara, she was crying ugly as she called it, her nose was running like a tap, she was sobbing again.

"Promise me again you won't leave me." Moses looked at Jasper. He took a deep breath.

"I promise Half-Pint." Jane nodded wiping her eyes, she grabbed Jaspers hand holding against her face. "Anything else you want to know love?"

"Have they told you what stage you are at?" He knew she was aware about cancer it had affected her family so much and she wouldn't be fooled.

"No love, he said it was the lymph nodes in my stomach and my balls.

"So it's Metastatic then?"

"Yes babe. I found the lumps when you were away and called straight away."

Jane nodded again. "Okay, so you start 4 weeks of Radiotherapy then what?"

"They do another scan and we go from there, I really don't know love, I think they are banking on it shrinking with the treatment if needs be I will have to have more. I know I might be sick, but I have to look after myself, eat properly etc, so I will. I'm sure Gwen will see to that once she knows."

Jane nodded again. "Okay, thank you for telling me, I'm sorry I got angry. I just worry about you that's all." She touched his face again on the screen.

"I know love, I said to G you can read my like a book and I couldn't keep it from you for much longer."

"Just promise me if you wake up in the middle of the night you will call me? I know you have Susan too."

"Half-Pint, she isn't replacing you."

"I know that." She huffed. "I just worry about how this is going to affect you mentally, I know what you are like remember, how many sleepless nights have you had?"

"Point taken, and enough, but now you know it will be easier."

"Heard that shit before Moses, I know it's not that easy, stop protecting me please!"

Moses smiled. "Yes boss."

"I'm still angry with you, so don't try and make me laugh because I don't want too." She was chewing her bottom lip trying not to smile.

"Yes, you do, we have been through a lot together and we will fight this too, just don't stay angry with me too long."

"I'm scared Moses, that's all. You know that." She wiped her eyes again, Jasper squeezed her shoulder and kissed the back of her head. She grabbed his hand holding onto it.

"I know love, so am I. I don't intend on going anywhere I have a lot of years left in me yet."

Jane sniffed. "Okay, so will you call me daily even for a minute after your treatment so I know how you are doing?"

"Yes love, I will. G is taking me every day as I don't fancy driving or riding as I don't know how I am going to feel."

"If you need anything Moses please let us know, we can fly out anytime." Jasper said. Jane looked back at him and smiled.

"Thanks Brother, I will. I appreciate your support. Right. I am going to get it over with and tell the guys, I will speak to you later Half-pint. I would rather get this over and done with in one."

"Of course, keep in touch and I will speak to you Monday, love you Moses."

"Love you too Half-pint, look after each other."

"Thanks Moses we will."

Moses hung up and sank back into the sofa. His emotions all over the place. He knew he had enough time to call Susan before he went to the club. He texted her to check it was ok to call.

Moses. Hi love, are you free, I could do with a chat? x
Susan. Of course. x

Susan picked up straight away. "Hi love, how did it go with Jane?"
"Bloody awful, I could see it all over her face, it destroyed her."
"Moses this isn't your fault, you cannot be responsible for how she feels. I know you love her and want to protect her, but she is a big girl, stop wrapping her in cotton wool."
"It is my fault though, I have had this a while, I knew before I came over there, I just kept putting it off. When I first met Jane she was like a tiny meak mouse, she was scared of her own shadow, she flinched every time anyone came near her for what her husband did to her. She has grown so much but still needs that protection, yes you know how much I love her and I always will but I won't destroy what we have. We have relied on each other for so long, I wouldn't have got through my PTSD without her, when I came back from Afghan I was a mess, it was a buildup of everything I had seen over many years of being in war zones. She thinks I helped her but in reality she helped me more, having her live with me for a few years was the best medicine for me, I miss that. I love her like nothing else. I would give my life for her." Moses squeezed his eyes with his thumb and forefinger, desperate not to cry.
"I understand that Moses and it is very obvious, I saw you and Jasper in hospital remember, I can tell you adore her. But you have to stop blaming yourself, she would tell you that too. Many of us don't act on lumps and bumps, it's the fear of the unknown, you found an excuse to hide from it and she was the reason. What made you go back so quickly though?"

He sighed heavily. "I was playing in the shower and squeezed my balls, I felt the lump, it had grown more, my backache wasn't going away, I knew I was feeling pretty rough so decided to bite the bullet and deal with it, so when I saw how good she looked whilst at the cottage I booked the flight home. I am scared, I won't deny that, I miss someone being here that I can talk too in the middle of the night when I wake up.

Half-pint was a light sleeper for years so always knew when I was awake, she would come in and sit with me in the dark and let me talk."

"I am always here for you too, I am due some leave, I would happily jump on a plane and be there for you. Just say the word. It would purely be friends, just having someone there. Have a think about it, just give me a weeks notice."

"Thanks Susan, that means a lot. I will think about it. Let's see how the treatment goes."

"Right, now I am going to shower and get sorted for the day, are you going to the club this afternoon?"

"Yes I'm waiting for G to come and get me, then we will tell everyone, I think you will hear Gwen from here."

"I don't doubt that for a minute, just remember they do it out of love."

"I know, she can be a pain in the arse at times, but she has a heart of gold."

"Right text when you like, or just call, no need to ask."

"Thank love, will do."

They hung up, Moses sat with his head in his hands, he slumped back into the sofa, the heels of his hands in his eyes pushing back the tears.

"Shit just got fucking real. Arghhhh. Wish you were here Mum, I'm fucking scared shitless. Anyone tells me they are taking it in their stride is a fucking liar." He punched the sofa next to him pushing himself up out of it. He heard G pull up.

"Thank fuck for that, I really don't like this silence. It's too fucking easy to think."

He walked to the door opening it. G walked in looking questioningly at him.

"Well?"

Moses nodded. "Wasn't easy, it broke her. If the worst happens you fucking promise me you will tell her in person, you get on the first flight out and tell her."

"I promise you I will. but nothing is going to fucking happen, the old man up there only takes the good ones, and sorry to say Brother but you aint no angel, so you have a lot longer here with us."

"Fuck off arseole." Moses laughed at G.

"Made you fucking smile anyway. Come on let's get this over with."

Moses grabbed his jacket and keys walking out with G.

G pulled into the parking spot right outside the doors, he looked over at Moses, he could see he was finding this hard, the more people he told the harder and realer it got for him. He put his hand on his shoulder. "You ready Brother?"

"As I will ever be." He opened the door and got out, sighing heavily, his stomach turning, his mouth going dry. He hated attention and this was going to put him front and centre, but he had to be honest with the club and his job.

They walked in, the bar was quite busy, the usual crowd were in, Steve and Matt were playing pool, the girls were sat at the bar chatting. Music was booming out. They walked to the bar, Moses put his arms around the girls shoulders kissing both of them on the head.

"Hello ladies." They both turned smiling kissing him in return.

"Hi sweetie, how are you, not seen you in a few days, you been hiding?"

"Something like that. Do me a favour Jax, get G and me a beer and turn the music off please, I need to talk to everyone." He walked over to the big table in the middle of the room and sat down with G.

"What's going on Moses?" Gwen followed him with her glass. "Matt, Steve, come over here please."

"Can't it wait, we are in the middle of a game here?"

"Do as you are fucking told. Moses wants to talk to us all." She screamed at them both scowling. Matt knew not to push her when she had that face on. They put their cues down walking to the table. Linda grabbed a few others and they all joined them at the table. The girls sat together at the end of the table, knowing something big was coming.

"Thanks all, I only wanted to say this once, I don't want rumours or hearsay so if you want to know anything you come to me or G." Everyone nodded looking around the table, completely confused.

Moses took a deep breath, G stood behind him. "Okay in short I have cancer, it's in my balls and my stomach." He went on to tell them everything he knew. The girls wiped their eyes keeping quiet. Waiting for him to finish, he went onto to tell them about his treatment plan and lied about when he had found it. Only G and Susan knew that, he didn't want anyone else knowing. He finished and sat back in the chair. G squeezed his shoulder.

Steve was first to speak. "Fuck Brother I'm sorry, this is a shock for us all of course. What can we do to help?" Everyone nodded in agreement.

"Thanks Steve, nothing anyone can do at the moment, like I said G is taking me to my appointments and until I know anything else then it's life as usual."

The girls got out of their chairs moving around to Moses as he stood up. Gwen hugged him hard. Not wanting to let go. "Oh Moses, I'm sorry I don't mean to cry, please promise you won't push us away, let us help you, even with practical things, you need to eat properly so me and the girls will do your dinners every day." Moses smiled. Not wanting the attention but knowing he had to give in a little. He nodded. "Thanks Gwen. Sounds good to me."

Linda and Jax joined them hugging him, all fighting the tears. They were a close knit group, they were all feeling the same. The boys came to hug him, all saying the same thing, they all wanted to do their part in helping him. It quietened down, Moses and G sat with Steve and Matt.

"Did you tell Jane?" Steve asked.

"Yes, this morning, she was ready to jump on a plane and come home but there isn't any point, she's just scared like I am."

"As we all are for you Brother, just tell us what you need anytime, don't try and be brave."

Moses laughed. "Already doing that Brother. Thanks though, I know you're right. I just hate being the centre of attention."

"I understand that, but you better get used to it, look behind you, the girls are already planning loads of shit I'm sure." They all laughed knowing what was going on.

"They can do what they like but they won't be doing my ironing. I will have to be at deaths door before that happens." He laughed, the others didn't. "Lighten up guys I need to be able to take the piss out of myself."

"Just a bit too early to expect us to do that Brother, you and G have had time to think about this."

"Tomorrow then, that enough time for ya?" they all smiled and nodded. "Right well get me another beer then, you can stop sitting there with sad faces, you're supposed to be cheering me up."

"Coming up", Matt stood, "You can cheer me up by letting me whoop your arse on the pool table then."

"Fuck off, you know I will wipe the floor with you." Moses stood walking towards the table.

"Yeah, yeah, put your fucking money where your mouth is Brother." They all began to relax a little and joined Moses at the pool table, within 10 minutes they were laughing and teasing each other. G stood back watching his best friend. Relieved everyone knew but still scared of the chance of losing him.

Chapter 10

Good memories

Jane hung up. Sitting down on her knees still facing the TV. Jasper waited, he knew she would turn soon. He wrapped his arms around her, feeling her body tremble as she began to cry again. He moved closer to her, resting his head on hers, kissing her.

"Jasper he can't die. Promise me he won't die?" Her body wracked with sobs Jane turned into Jaspers arms, her face buried in his chest. He could feel the wet of her tears soaking into his t-shirt. He had been dreading this moment, he just wanted to protect her from everything, he knew this was going to hit her hard.

"Belle, you heard what Moses said, he will fight this with everything he has, I can't promise you anything, I wish I could, he is seeing the right people and his treatment starts Monday. We just have to be positive and keep him upbeat. Jasper bent and kissed her head. Jane nodded, sniffing rubbing her face into his t-shirt. He laid back against the sofa pulling Jane onto his lap, she curled into him further, her tears slowing down, she sighed heavily, quieting, Jasper held her, his thumb rubbing her back gently, he heard her breathing slow down. Her sniffing stopped. She looked up at him, her nose red from crying her eyes red, she looked like a little girl, he kissed her forehead. Brushing her hair from her face that had become stuck with tears and sweat. Mascara had smudged under her eyes.

"Hey panda eyes." He kissed her nose softly rubbing the mascara from her face, sucking his thumb making it wet to help with getting rid of the smears, he didn't want to move her just to get a face cloth. He bent and kissed her lips, her big eyes looking lost and sad.

"I'm sorry I cried so much."

"Belle, don't be silly, you have nothing to be sorry for. He is your best friend. It's a scary time. You cry as much as you need to just don't hide it from me." Jane nodded again.

"How did I get so lucky to find you, you are my everything Jasper. I love you so much."

"I love you too Belle. I'm the lucky one." He smiled down at her, kissing her nose again as she cuddled back into him. Lady came over her head down, she knew something was wrong. Jane put her hand out to her stroking her head. She cuddled up to them both. Jasper smiled looking down at the two ladies in his life, thinking how lucky he was.

Jasper's legs were going to sleep, he was getting pins and needles, he was trying to move his toes without disturbing Jane. She felt his leg muscles contracting underneath her.

"What's wrong love," she asked looking up at him.

"Nothing Belle, just a dead leg, I was just trying to move it about to get rid of the pins and needles."

"Why didn't you say?" she slapped him on the chest moving off him. Lady got up and moved away.

"I didn't want to disturb you love. We were comfortable, I needed you close to me too."

"You are funny, but I love you for it. Come on, let's get a drink, I think I need some fresh air, I need to digest all this. Can we sit outside?"

"You don't need to ask woman, of course we can, go out with Lady I will make the tea and bring it out." Jane smiled as she walked out with Lady. She walked round to the rose bed and got onto the swing, her heart was heavy, she sat down sighing looking at the ground. She swang back pushing herself a little higher, closing her eyes as she swang back and forth. Drifting off into thoughts of Moses and happier times.

"Half-pint are you getting up today? there is a cup of tea out here for you." Jane stretched in her tent, she felt like Princess and the pea, every little lump in the night had disturbed her, she did have quite a bit to drink the night before and her head was pounding. She knew they were away for a couple of days so had a couple of bottles with the girls.

"urghhh, my head hurts, please be quiet."

"Someone's hung over, did you have too many glasses last night, have you got lots of hammers in your head?" G stuck his head into her tent.

"Piss off." She threw her boot at him as he backed away laughing. He closed the tent flap going back to the guys.

"Oh, she looks like she had a hard night. I hope she does something with that hair she nearly scared the hell out of me." He laughed as he got slapped around the head. "Ouchh, what was that for?" he looked behind him to see Jane stood looking at him. Everyone laughed.

"Hey how you feeling?" Moses laughed looking at her. She pulled her sunglasses down to look at him quickly putting them back on. "Shit girl, you got it bad. Gwen give her some paracetamol and a greasy breakfast roll. You might need to prize those eyes open too, they look like piss holes in the snow!" Jane slapped him hard on the back of the head as she walked towards Gwen, "Fuck woman you got a hard hand." He grabbed her as she walked past pulling her down onto the ground sitting on top of her. "Now say sorry or the tickling will begin." Jane was struggling beneath him to get away.

"No, let me go, my head hurts, please Moses." She whined.

"Oh no, say sorry first." He started to tickle her at the waist, knowing she couldn't cope with it, she was screeching struggling to get away. He covered her mouth laughing. "Say sorry and I will let you go."

"I will say it to you but not to G, little shit."

"That'll do it for me."

"okay, I'm sorry." He tickled her quickly.

"See that was easy wasn't it?" He laughed kissing her on the head before he climbed off her legs. She sat up straightening herself and readjusting her hair. G was laughing at her, she stuck her middle finger up at him, making him laugh more. She got up and went over to Gwen for tea and sympathy.

"Jesus woman how many did you have last night? I have never seen you let your hair down like that before." She brushed Jane's fringe away from her face trying to tidy the mess of hair. "For God sake sit let me sort this for you." she huffed looking at the mess Jane had made.

"You better take those glasses off too, I can't get the comb in there otherwise." Jane pulled her glasses of squinting. "Jesus Christ woman you ever heard of a mirror, those bloody panda eyes are not a good look on you!" she grabbed her make up bag off the table, pulling out her wipes handing them to Jane, "do something with them love, here take the mirror, look for yourself."

"Oh shit, how many did I have?"

"I have no idea, but it was going down rather quickly, do you remember what you were doing?"

"What do you mean what I was doing?" She frowned looking up at Gwen while she was trying to pull the knots out of her hair.

"Oh shit you don't remember then, hang on I will show you." Gwen got her phone out and gave it to Jane, "take a look." She pressed play on the screen, Motorheads Ace of Spades screamed out, Jane promptly got onto the table and began to air guitar and head bang to the song. Her long hair swinging from side to side as she played her air guitar. She gawped at the screen, mortified at what she was seeing, a crowd formed around her as she continued, Gwen began to laugh behind her as Jane covered her face, peeking through her fingers, she watched herself fall into the crowd and be passed across to where G and Moses were stood with their hands on their hips.

"Oh my God, the shame of it, who else has seen this?" she passed Gwen her phone back.

"Well, most of the gang were here so don't need to see this, but you can bet your bottom dollar this will come back to haunt you at some stage."

"Great! Not my finest moment."

"It was good to see you let your hair down love, it's about time. At least you didn't go off and shag someone in full view of everyone."

"Why who did?"

"Not one of us, but another club bitch did, she was spit roasted by two of the big guys from Oxford."

"Christ, is she known for it?"

"Well not as bad as that normally, she does flirt with everyone but never seen her doing anything so stupid, she had a crowd around her too, they were all loving it, she is known for being a bike. So, no change there I suppose."

"Silly girl, I don't feel so stupid now. I do remember seeing a lot of drugs being passed around, must have been coke there was a lot of snorting going on."

"Sounds about right yes. Glad none of ours do that. I'm sure some of the Outlaws do but that's up to them. I know Moses wouldn't tolerate it in the club."

"Well, he has seen what it can do to someone first-hand hasn't he."

"Yeah, very sad, Johnno was only 24 when he died, he had cleaned himself up too, just a stupid party gone wrong. I don't think Moses ever recovered from it. Talk of the devil." Moses came walking towards them.

"Feeling better Half pint?"

"A little yes, feeling stupid about what I did though." He pushed his hands into his pockets.

"It was a little stupid we don't know these guys, anything could have happened, but thankfully they all just enjoyed watching you and joining in. No wonder your hair is in knots, you certainly shook it well." He began laughing.

"No need to remind me." Jane covered her face.

"Are you coming out on the ride out, we are going up to Corfe castle. We're meeting some of the Outlaws up there, they have been out at Studland."

"No thanks, I had too much to drink last night, I will stay here."

"You can come on the back of me if you like?"

"It's ok thanks Moses."

"You're not staying on your own though? Are you going out Gwen?"

"No love, staying her, don't worry she won't get into any trouble."

"I am a big girl now, I don't need looking after. You can go Gwen."

"No, I would rather stay Jane, honestly. Give Matt a break anyway."

"Okay, well call if you need anything. Corfe is small so we will probably get moved on and ride back down here into Swanage anyway."

"See you later then, enjoy!" Jane waved as he walked away. "I love that guy but he does panic so much."

"Yeah, he is very protective of you. It's nice though. Right let me finish this hair of yours."

Jasper came out with the drinks, he stopped, watching Jane on the swing with a huge smile on her face. She hadn't heard him come up to her so he sat on the seat and just enjoyed watching her, he knew she loved to drift off into daydreams. Lady stood up to speak to Jasper and nudge Jane, it made her jump and open her eyes. She suddenly realised where she was.

"Nice dream Belle?"

She smiled. "Just a funny memory about Moses on a weekend away that's all." She didn't want to share it, purely because he would want to see the video and as far as she was aware it had gone long ago but she didn't want to remind anyone either. She stopped the swing and got off walking to the seat to join Jasper.

"How are you feeling love?"

"I'm ok, just a shock really, not what I expected to hear." She climbed onto the seat properly and snuggled into Jasper.

"I do love this garden and seat, I love snuggling up to you even more." She smiled up at Jasper. He bent and kissed her head.

"Me too Belle." He moved his arm around her properly pulling her into him. "When you're ready to talk about it let me know, I know you will want to go home soon I will come with you if you want, but that's up to you."

"Thank you, I will wait and see how he gets on, I won't smother him, Gwen will do enough of that for us all. I need to be realistic, what can I do there that G and the others aren't already doing, he will call me every day when he feels like it. I will know when the time is right."

"Good, well whatever you need Belle we can make it work." He lifted her chin with his forefinger, staring into her eyes and gently kissed her lips. "I love you Belle."

"I love you too. Thank you for putting up with me. I know I can be hard work."

"You're not hard work Belle, you just care a lot, certainly about others, sometimes not yourself though. That makes you who you are. That's who I fell in love with, that crazy funny stubborn loving woman."

"Less of the crazy please." She frowned making Jasper laugh. He grabbed her face kissing her hard.

"Okay boss. What would you like to do for the rest of the day?"

"Can we go out for a ride? Fancy getting out for a bit. Not had the bike out for a while?"

"Of course. Lady will be okay for a while."

"Oh, my beautiful girl, we need a side car or trailer for her. She has to be able to come with us."

"Crazy woman, come on, get those leathers on, let's get some air. I will pull the bikes out, so don't rush." Jasper tried to casually walk into the house desperate to beat Jane to the garage not wanting to spoil his surprise, he wasn't going to do it today in the light of Moses call, but maybe it was the right day.

He dashed into the bedroom pulling his leathers on and went out into the garage, pulled his bike out and then Janes. He kept the door closed until she was ready, he took Lady with him. He heard Jane coming, he came back into the house.

"Ready Belle?"

"Yes love, are you?"

"Yep, everything's ready, your jacket and lid are outside with mine, just need your gorgeous arse out there now so we can go." He grinned at her.

"Did you put Lady out for a wee?"

"Yes love." He nodded, knowing he wasn't lying. Just extending the truth. "Right your chariot awaits my lady." He opened the door, Jane stopped in shock. Her hand covering her mouth.

"Oh my god!! When did you do that, where did you get it from!" She began to cry not sure whether to run over to the bike or back at Jasper, she turned running at him jumping into his waiting arms.

"I love you so bloody much, you are a big softy Jasper. Look at her sat there like the queen." They both looked over at Lady, she was sat in her own trailer, it had side windows and a little sun-roof she could put her head out of when they stopped.

"How, when?" she looked back at Jasper.

"I was chatting to Shadow and mentioned it to him, he put me in touch with a guy that builds them, he came over and matched the colour, the top window is automatic, so as you pull away it will close, we just need to remind Lady to lay down before we move away, there is plenty of room inside for her and she is strapped in. I brought her a new bed its really comfortable and it won't slip around. I was worried you might not be happy to be honest."

"Why wouldn't I? I bloody love it, she can come away all the time now, you really know how my brain works."

"Something like that love yes." He grinned, knowing he got it right again made him happy. The guys had told him he was a soft touch, but he didn't care, he just wanted to make her happy every day.

They both climbed on their bikes, Lady laid down and they pulled away, Jane was grinning like a Cheshire cat.

Chapter 11

"Start as we mean to go on"

Moses and Susan spent hours on the phone, it was early hours for him, Susan could tell he was getting tired and she was well aware he had his first treatment in the morning but didn't want to push him to hang up.

"So, if you do come out here where will you sleep?" Moses chuckled knowing he was pushing his luck.

"You have a spare room don't you, that will do me fine." Moses slapped his head, he realised she already knew about his house from an earlier conversation. He was laid in bed he decided to have a little fun.

"Fancy a video call, my ear is burning holding the phone to it."

"You do know there is a speaker button on your phone don't you?"

"Yes, thank you, clever arse, I do." He pressed the camera button and waited grinning to himself.

"I didn't say yes." Susan smiled at Moses as she appeared on the screen.

"Well, aint you a sight for sore eyes." Moses grinned. His bodied tingled looking at her.

"Smooth talker." Susan blushed.

"I aim to please Susan, and if you come out here then I certainly will..... oooops did I say that out loud?"

Susan couldn't help but giggle. "I think you meant to. Are you feeling brave because we are so far away from each other?"

"I don't know what you mean!" he was laughing but knew she was right. He was enjoying flirting with her though.

"I think you do Moses. Anyway if you are a good boy who knows what will happen..... Ooops did I just say that out loud." She teased. Moses banged the bed laughing, he loved her sense of humour.

"Cheeky cow."

"Moo." Susan laughed at herself making a stupid noise sounding like a donkey. Moses couldn't breath, listening to her he was laughing so much.

"God you're beautiful when you laugh." He whispered to himself.

"Sorry love you went quiet then, I didn't hear you."

"Nothing I just said you make me laugh, you are so funny." Susan just smiled at him.

"I don't want to be a party pooper but I do think it's time you got some sleep, it must be 2am there?"

"Spoil sport, how can I sleep now you have been making me laugh?" he pouted making Susan laugh.

"You can stop that pouting, it won't get you anywhere." He pretended to sulk. "Tomorrow we will talk about you taking more care of yourself."

"What's your name Jane?"

"Don't let her hear you say that."

"She will laugh and say good if I did tell her. Well, if you are going to get all serious on me then I will try and sleep." He smiled.

"Okay love, you can call anytime you know that. Talk tomorrow."

"Goodnight love. Thanks again. I've had a lot of fun tonight."

"Me too Moses. Thanks."

Moses hung up, he was now wide awake, he sighed putting his phone down. He tossed and turned for a couple of hours, he finally dropped off.

The alarm went off at 8am, he woke with a thick head, he suddenly remembered what today was about. He felt sick and a little anxious. He threw back the bedclothes walking into the shower.

His morning glory was stood proud. "Well, they say this stuff can stop me getting hard, so let's make the most of it." He wrapped his hand around his cock, closing his eyes. His mind wondering to Susan, her smile lit up her face, he remembered her in her uniform when Jane was in hospital and how it hid her curves until she bent over. He desperately wanted to spank her when she bent in front of him. He imagined grabbing her hips pulling her into him. He slipped his hand up and down the shaft with his left hand, his right grabbing his balls, he groaned squeezing his cock as the water ran down his body hitting his cock lubricating it for him. He let go of his balls and began running his hand across his body, pinching his nipples hard, he hadn't had it rough in a long time, he wondered if Susan was up for it. The thought of her being tied up and spanked made him groan louder, his balls aching. He kept his eyes closed, imagining her in cuffs, on her knees unable to move. Attached to the bedhead, him moving up on his back so his head would be between her legs, pulling her pussy down onto him. He hoped she wasn't shaved, he loved the feel of the soft hair tickle his face. He would pull her down onto his face plunging his tongue deep inside her, keeping his arms wrapped around her thighs so he could tease her pussy. Her juices covering his face as he sucked and licked her. He pumped his cock harder wanting the release, he teased the very tip of his cock, imagining Susan's tongue gently flicking it, her lips like butterfly kisses teasing him. "Fuck Susan, I want you so bad!" he growled, "I want you here to fuck me hard. Tired or not I will have you. Fuuuuckkk." He groaned as he squeezed his cock harder, pumping it faster until he couldn't take anymore and his knees buckled as he came hard, his body convulsing as he continued rubbing himself, panting he stopped looking up into the shower laughing.

"Stupid bastard, you think she wants you? we will see." He rinsed himself off grabbing the shower gel, the seriousness of today sinking in again. He finished his shower stepping out, he grabbed his towel heading to the sink, stopping suddenly as he heard a noise downstairs.

The hairs on the back of his neck stood on end, he crept slowly to the door opening it, someone was definitely downstairs. He walked to the stairs listening hard, his heart pounding, anger building.

"Whoever you are you will be sorry you picked on the wrong house." He whispered. His fists balling as he slowly crept downstairs, he caught his towel on the rail as he rounded the stairs, he brushed it off in frustration leaving it behind him. Whoever was there they were in the kitchen, he grabbed his crash helmet off the side table and slowly moved towards the door. He could hear his heart beating in his ears. He stopped trying to catch his breath, his mouth dry, he pushed the door open hitting the person in the back, raising the crash helmet in the air moving behind the door to lunge at the person behind it. He stopped suddenly before he cracked the thief over the head.

"Fucking hell Brother what the hell are you trying to do?" G was bent over the bottom cupboard looking for something.

"What do you mean what the hell am I doing?"

"Why didn't you fucking shout up the stairs you were here, I was about to cave your fucking head in?"

"You were in the shower, I didn't hear you finish."

"Well why are you nosing around my fucking kitchen anyway?"

"I was looking for the blender, start as we mean to go on, I am making you a vegetable and fruit smoothie, I found it online last night."

"You can fuck right off, you are not getting me to drink no green shit like that. I'm not some kind of hippy." He groaned putting his crash helmet behind him. G grabbed the tea towel, passing it to him.

"For Christ sake it's not hippy shit, you will thank me for this week's down the line when you needed all these vitamins and minerals, do us both a favour cover that shit up please, I really don't need your old man pointing at me. We are not in Afghan now."

Moses huffed. "Fuck you." He span and walked back upstairs to get dressed. G found the blender and continued to prepare the smoothie for him regardless of what he'd said, he was prepared to force it down him if needed. He chopped up the fruit and veg dropping it into the blender with a pot of live yoghurt, he could hear Moses complaining upstairs he laughed and continued, he poured them both a glass full and sat waiting for him to come down.

"Right then we will drink this together, it's not green look." He held the glass out to Moses.

"What's in it?" he asked screwing his face up sniffing it.

"Carrot, mango, orange and celery. Just fucking drink it or I will hold your nose and force it down."

"Fuck you." Moses spat at G, he ignored him and continued to drink his.

"It's nice actually, give it a chance." Moses closed his eyes taking a gulp and swallowed it quickly pulling faces like a child.

"You are such a child Brother, get used to it, they are not going anywhere." He took his glass to the sink washing it out folding his arms waiting for Moses to finish.

"You are such a fucking arseole G."

"Yep, sure am, you think this is bad, I haven't even started yet, so get used to it."

"I should have let Half-Pint come home she would have been softer on me."

G laughed. "In your dreams mate, you ever heard of phones? Well, we talk remember."

"Fuck I should have known better." Moses smiled. He shook his head and took the last mouthful of the smoothie shaking his head as he swallowed it. "Happy now?" he handed the glass to G sulking.

"I am now yes, get your jacket let's go."

They walked out getting into G's truck heading to the hospital, they got caught up in traffic. G's phone rang.

"Hi beautiful, you okay?"

"Yes thank you, just checking in, are you with Moses yet, how did the smoothie go?"

"I am here you know, I'm not a child." G looked across at him smiling.

"He's sulking love, just ignore him, he was streaking through the house threating me with his old man hanging out earlier."

"Good God, have you no respect Moses?"

"Hang on, get the fucking story straight G, I didn't know he was in the house, he was in the kitchen in and out of my cupboards, what was I supposed to think?"

"If you had looked out of the window you would have known." Jane laughed.

"Smart arse, well I didn't, did I? and I lost my towel on the stairs." Jane giggled.

"Yeah, yeah whatever, we've heard it all before."

"Fuck off the pair of you." Moses grumbled.

"We will check in with you later love, once he has been cooked."

"Thanks G, love you both, talk to you later."

"Talk later Half-pint." Both men replied.

Chapter 12

More secrets

Jasper was in the office at home, he told Jane he needed some space to do some work on a separate project. She never questioned it just went in on the trike leaving him to get on. He pulled out some drawings from his bag unfolding them on the desk. He picked the phone and called Henry.

"Hello Lily, how are you love?"

"Hi sweetheart, how lovely to hear from you. We're okay, how are you both doing, Is Jane still driving you crazy with wedding preparations?"

"Now that's a silly question." He laughed. "She is panicking more now though with the news of Moses. She wants to make sure everything is okay if he isn't well, putting a lot of her ideas to one side."

"She's just worried love and that is understandable. Remember the wedding is about you both, it doesn't matter about all the extras, it's you two coming together as husband and wife that matters."

"You're right, I couldn't do this without you both, it's not easy keeping secrets from her and this is the biggest ever, she is going to go nuts, but I promise after this I will rein it in."

"You think we believe you? I know Jane won't either. Have you told Moses what is going on?"

"Yes, I wanted him to feel relaxed about it. I just hope she won't be disappointed."

"Well, I don't know her as well as you do but I am sure she will love every minute of it."

"Are you sure you haven't taken too much on Lily? You need to enjoy it too remember."

"Oh my darling this is an honour, we are both excited, I have a couple of people helping me out too."

"As long as you are sure?"

"A hundred percent love. I will hand you over to Henry, give me a call if you think of anything else."

"Thanks Lily I will love."

"Hello Son, how are you? have you made a decision?"

"Hi Henry, I'm good thank you, hiding at home so Jane doesn't get to hear anything. Yes, I have, I think I would like to go with your plan, it looks incredible. It's perfect in fact, you really read my mind. I can't thank you enough, are you really sure about this?"

"Yes, we are, you have no idea how happy you have made us."

"Thank you so much, I just don't want to put too much pressure on you, call me if you need anything else, I will email the other details across now so you have it all."

"Sounds good to me. I promise you, it is an absolute pleasure, I do have a young lad working with me too, it's nice to have someone interested. Look forward to hearing from you, take care of each other."

"Thanks Henry, you too." Jasper put the phone down grinning from ear to ear, this was the biggest risk he has taken on a surprise for Jane and he knew this had to be the last, he just couldn't help himself, he loved to see her smile and he lived for it. He looked at the clock, it was almost lunchtime, he picked up his phone and called Jane.

"Hi honey, you okay?"

"Yes love, I got done earlier than I thought I would, so I wondered if you had any plans for lunch, if not I will come in with something if you have time."

"That would be lovely, of course I have time. How long will you be?"

"I would say 30 minutes, anything you fancy?"

"Just you." she grinned.

"I thought I was afters?"

"Hmmmmm, that's true. Well, I have time for that too."

"Naughty girl, you're supposed to be working."

"You didn't complain the last time!"

He laughed. "That's true and I never would."

"Right answer, Mr M, see you shortly. I love you."

"Love you too Belle." Jasper grabbed his things and headed out to work, he stopped at the local bakery grabbing sandwiches for them both before heading into the office.

He knocked on Janes door before walking in just in case someone was there.

"Come in, it's open." Jane called out. Jasper smiled as he walked in. He flipped the lock behind him.

"Hi, are you ready to eat?"

"My god yes, I'm ravenous, I was ok until you called. What did you get for us this time?"

"BLT for you, and beef for me, unless you want to share?"

No, no that's fine with me, thank you." She kissed Jasper as he handed the sandwich to her.

"Anything from Moses or G?" Jasper asked as he took a mouthful of sandwich.

"No nothing, but I didn't expect it to be honest. I will call him later. I don't want to crowd him."

"What have you done with Jane? Who are you?" He started laughing.

"What do you mean?" Jane frowned at him.

"You said you didn't want to crowd him. Who are you, the Belle I know will be on the phone every hour."

"Oh, ha, ha, you're not funny." She poked her tongue out at Jasper as he sat grinning at her. "I am trying to give him space, I know I can be a pain in the arse, but he needs time to think this through and if Susan is there for him then hopefully, she can help, after all she has the knowledge."

"I am really proud of you love. I know you want to be on the next plane out and you are worried about him. But promise me if you are struggling you will talk to me."

"I promise I will love. I will chat to Susan at some stage too. But to be honest there is nothing I can do, except get in the way and he can be quite grumpy when he's not well and I don't want to be the cause of his frustration, he will want time alone too." Jasper bent into Jane kissing her nose.

"I love you so much Belle. You are just incredible; every day is another day I find more reasons to fall in love with you even more." Jane blushed a little leaning into Jasper as he put his arm out to her pulling her in for a cuddle.

"Have you got a busy afternoon, or do you have time to come onto site for a walk around?"

"I definitely have time for that. Yes, please I haven't been out there since I came back." Jane clapped her hands together excited to go out.

"Right then get your kit on and we will go out. I will go and grab my stuff, see you in a few minutes."

Jasper was back within minutes with his PPE, he locked the door as he came back in so Jane could get changed into her jeans without being disturbed. He stood watching her, she turned away bending over slightly as she pulled her trousers down over her bottom giving Jasper a glimpse of her tattoo and the top of her lace knickers. She heard him groan, making her smile. She bit her lip feeling naughty, pulling her trousers further down she purposefully caught the elastic from her knickers pulling them down too. Jasper groaned louder making Jane tingle. He stepped towards her, placing his hands on her hips gently pulling her bottom towards him, his cock twitching in his jeans. He sucked through his teeth looking down at her soft perfect skin. Bending he kissed her tattoo.

"This is what I wanted to do the first day I saw you bend over, I was mesmerized by you then, now I can touch you it turns me on even more." He teased her skin with the back of his fingers grazing them up and down her bottom slowly. Jane mewled softly. She bit her knuckle stopping herself from screaming at him to take her. She pushed back onto him, needing to feel him more, Jasper smiled.

"My naughty Belle, don't do this to me, you're killing me." He moved his hand across to the centre of her bottom and spanked her hard. Jane jumped making a muffled squeal with her hand still in her mouth. He ran his finger across to the base of her spine and down between her cheeks, his cock getting harder. "Fuck I want you." He whispered, his finger travelling further down the middle of her cheeks. Jane opened her legs wider, desperate to be touched, she could feel herself getting wetter. Jasper knew what she wanted and so did he, he slipped his finger further round feeling the moistness before his finger slid inside her, Jane being mewling, her hand now free from her mouth, she held onto the table as Jaspers finger plunged deeper inside her.

"Belle I have to have you now." Jane nodded, he fought to undo his jeans, if anyone were to knock or walk past the end window they could be seen. He unzipped himself pushing his jeans down, his pants following. "Turn baby, I want to look at you." Jane turned, he lifted her, she wrapped her legs around him, he moved them over to the desk, sitting her, he spread her legs bringing her closer to him his cock rock hard waiting desperately to take her. He groaned looking at her glistening pussy waiting for him, he teased her, with the tip of his cock. Slowly he moved closer easing himself into her, moaning at every small movement he made getting deeper inside her. Jane's head fell back her hair falling onto the desk. She supported herself on her elbows desperate to watch him fill her. He slowly moved in and out of her.

"Fuck me Jasper please, make it quick." Jasper raised his eyebrows, smiling he pulled her legs closer to him. He slid out of her, pounding back in harder, pulling out completely and ramming back in harder over and over, making her feel every thrust. His fingers moved to her clit, rubbing her, she wanted it fast so he was determined to give it to her, Jane was moaning louder as the heat intensified between them and she could feel her orgasm growing. She began to push against him, needing the extra pressure, she came hard, Jasper kept rubbing her making it last not stopping as she begged him too. He knew he was about to cum he grabbed her legs wanting to be deeper inside her.

"Cum for me baby please." Jane begged. "I want to feel you."

"Oh, Fuuuuck yessssss." Jasper moaned as his body tingled, he pushed hard as he came too. He panted hard, laughing. Jane sat up as he moved towards her kissing her.

"You never fail to surprise me Belle." He grinned kissing her again. "We better clean up before anyone comes in." He moved back pulling his pants and jeans up, grabbing the tissues helping Jane off the desk. She quickly cleaned up pulling on her jeans sitting down on the chair to put her boots on. Jasper grabbed her leg helping to tie her laces while she put her hair up.

Within a few minutes they were laughing with each other ready to go out onto site. Jasper led the way locking the cabin behind them as they walked towards the site entrance. She felt flushed and was sure she had that *just fucked* look on her face. She smiled up at Jasper grabbing his arm walking into the first building.

"Well, I'll be buggered. I didn't expect to see you out here today, you should have said you were coming." Chicca came up behind Jane grabbing her from behind digging her fingers into her hips. Whispering "Ummm, I could be wrong, but I never am, you've just had sex you lucky bitch!"

Jane laughed, "I don't know what you mean."

"You fucking do, look at those rosey cheeks, you can't kid me lady. I'm fucking jealous." She laughed loudly as Jasper finished talking to one of the guys.

"What are you two giggling about?"

"Girly stuff JDubz, nothing for you to worry about." Both girls burst into a fit of giggles.

"I am so glad I won't be around on your hen night, I think it will be far worse than mine ever could be!"

"You're damn right there. Even Jane doesn't know the half of it yet." She winked at Jane. "Not long now though and all will be revealed."

"Oh God, I think I'm going to regret this." Chicca giggled walking away. "Catcha later love birds."

"What was that all about?"

"I wish I knew, now I'm worried, between Chicca and Gwen there is no hope. They are definitely cooking something up."

"I'm sure it will be fine." Jasper smiled knowing a little of what was going on, Chicca wanted to make sure Jasper was okay with a few things before they went ahead with it. She had the greatest respect for them both and didn't want to go too far. She knew now that she wouldn't be.

Jasper continued to show Jane in and out of several of the houses and apartments that had been built already, they stopped and chatted to a few people as they made their way to the new school building.

"This is incredible." Jane exclaimed as she looked up to the roof of the new school hall.

"It will be when it's finished Jane. How are you doing now, I haven't seen you in a while." One of the young labourers asked.

"I'm doing really well thank you, no permanent damage."

"That's great, are you all set for the wedding, you must be really excited?" Jane frowned.

"Yes. I am thank you, I didn't realise everyone knew?" She questioned. Jasper glared at the young lad. Shaking his head behind Jane.

"Oh yeah, Chicca talks about it all the time, you know what she can be like." Jane smiled.

"Of course, I forgot what she's like. Jasper smiled giving him the thumbs up.

"Come on love, let's head back." Jane nodded and said cheerio to the young guy, heading back to the cabins.

"That was a surprise, does Chicca always talk about the wedding, I didn't think it was that important to anyone else."

"Well, he is a friend of the club too so it's not surprising, you said you wanted a BBQ there after the wedding so they can join in to remember, he probably heard it mentioned there.

"I suppose." Jane's mind was working overtime. She knew she was very well respected but was surprised to hear another guy talking about the wedding. She decided to ask Chicca about it. There was no secret about the wedding at all, she wasn't sure why she was bothered.

They got back to the cabin at almost home time. Jasper gave Jane her keys and stepped inside to collect his things.

"I just have to pop and see a few of the guys, give me fifteen minutes and I will follow you home."

"Sure love." Jane put her hard hat and glasses down before taking her jacket off, Jasper kissed her before walking out. He hurried back to the drying rooms to find the guys getting ready to go home.

"Hello Jasper, what brings you in here?"

Hey Tea bag, I just wanted a quick word, the cat was almost out of the bag a few minutes ago about the wedding, could you guys remember this is a huge surprise, Jane has no idea and I need to keep it that way or my balls will be on a plate in the canteen for lunch."

"Jesus Brother of course. Sorry about that."

"No harm done, just a gentle reminder, or all the hard work you've done to make it happen will go to waste."

"I will have a word, leave it with me, I will mention it at the morning meeting. I know a few of the guys have some stuff to do for it this weekend."

"Thanks, really appreciate it."

"I hope this doesn't mean Jane will have our balls on a plate after?" Jasper laughed.

"No Teabag, just mine, but once the wedding is in full swing, she will have forgotten about it."

"Phew, I kind of like mine where they are." Jasper patted him on the back and left.

He arrived back with Jane as she was getting into her boots ready for the ride home.

"Christ woman, are you trying to kill me today?" he spanked her hard as she pulled the zip up on her boots. The leather trousers going tight across her bottom.

"You couldn't cope." Jane smiled patting Jasper on the cheek.

"Are you challenging me?" He teased.

"Ohhhh, Jane is it, someone's feeling threatened?" Jane giggled.

"If you don't want putting over my shoulder and carrying out of the gate you better run lady." He spanked her again as Jane ran around her desk.

"Okay, okay I'm sorry." She giggled putting her hands up as he followed her. He grabbed her, kissed her nose and walked towards the door.

"Crap, I think I'm in trouble now." She whispered following him out of the door. She knew Jasper well enough to know he would do it. They got to the trike Jane started it up.

"Be careful love please, I will follow you."

"I will love, you should know that." She blew him a kiss as she climbed on. He walked away unlocking the car climbing in. He followed her out, he was always nervous when she was alone. He trusted her riding ability completely it was the other idiots on the road he didn't. He knew he was overprotective but couldn't help it. They were both home in no time, Lady greeted them at the door when they came out of the garage. Jane got down onto the floor to save being knocked over when Lady charged at her excited to finally see her home. Jasper shook his head at them both smiling. Jane was talking to Lady like a baby as she ran around in circles making odd noises at her.

Jane got up off the floor brushing herself down after being licked to death by Lady.

"I swear she thinks I have been gone for weeks." Jane laughed brushing herself down, rubbing her nose to remove fur.

"That's how it must feel to her though. It would be interesting to film her and see what she gets up to during the day."

"Oh no I couldn't, it would break my heart seeing her looking sad."

"I'm sure she has a party when we are gone, she will be sniffing at everything and anything, laying on the sofa and I wouldn't be surprised if she has slept on the bed most of the day."

"She wouldn't do that."

"Yeah right, little madam would." Lady sat looking up at them both, her head tilting side to side listening to them both. "Yes, we are talking about you, Madam." Lady wagged her tail walking over to Jasper for a fuss. "My turn is it now, you had enough of Mum for now?" Jane laughed walking away to get her leathers off.

"Going to get these off and call Moses love."

"Sure, say Hi for me, I will take Lady out for a walk down the garden and feed her."

Jane got changed into her favourite shorts and t-shirt, she climbed onto the bed and called Moses. It was bedtime but she knew he would still be awake.

"Hi love, how was your first day?"

"Hi Half-pint, we were just talking about you", he turned the phone to face G.

"Hey G, all good I hope, should I be worried? Jasper said Hi too."

"No love, just talking about the wedding and our plans that's all. Say Hi."

"Great, so tell me."

"We plan to be there two weeks before the wedding, the warmth will do me good apparently and I will rest too."

"Yay fantastic, I will get the beds ready for you both."

"No love, we are staying in the apartment, you two will need your space, we will see you every day."

Jane pouted.

"Don't do that lady!" G scolded her.

"We want you here though, please."

"Gwen can stay with you a few days before when Jasper moves in with us or his mates. You will need the time, you are still working remember."

"I know, I know, but I want you around me too."

"We will be, I promise." Jane nodded in agreement.

"So how did it go?"

"It was okay love, it will be a week or two until I feel any real affects. Once it's done it will give me a month before we come over, then I should know more about how it's going."

"Can't wait to see you both."

"Same here love, and to think our girl is getting married. Never thought that would happen, did you?"

"Never in my wildest dreams, I was quite happy as I was. I had you two looking after me, then whoosh in walks Jasper." Jane grinned widely.

"Certainly a whirlwind love. At least we know he looks after you."

"A little too much, she's becoming a Princess!" G laughed as Moses shot him a look.

Jane frowned, what does that mean G. I'm no Princess? Yes, Jasper loves me and takes care of me just the way you did."

"I was teasing love." He stared back at Moses knowing he had opened his mouth to much.

"Ignore him love, he's just jealous he hasn't found his Prince yet." Moses began laughing at G as he threw a cushion across the room at him.

"I will leave you two girls to fight, I'm going to help with dinner. Take care and I will text tomorrow. Love you both."

"We love you too Half-pint." Moses hung up first, Jane climbed off the bed heading to the kitchen.

"Hello love, how is he?" Jasper kissed Jane as she walked into the kitchen, Lady had gone to her bed with a full stomach.
"He's okay, they were just talking about the wedding and their plans, they are coming two weeks before the wedding."
"Oh great."
"They are not staying her though. They are going to the apartment."
"That's ok love, I thought you wanted Gwen here anyway."
"I would love everyone here if we had the space."
"I know, you can always have them camp in the garden." Jasper laughed pulling Jane between his legs.
"I don't think so." She laughed putting her arms around his neck. "Do you know this is the only time I am almost the same height as you?"
"Almost love yes."
"Well, if I put my heels on, I will be taller." Jasper laughed loudly.
"Oh Belle, you are funny, I do love you so much."
"What? It's true, shall I show you?" she dashed off to the bedroom coming back with her heels that she could barely stand in. She put them on and walked back into Jaspers open legs. She put her hand on her head and moved it towards Jaspers measuring the difference.
"Like I said Belle, almost. However, I have to say you look pretty damn hot in those shorts and heels, turn around." He turned her from her hips, her shorts were short, barely reaching the end of her bottom. He spanked her making her jump. He soothed her cheek sliding his hand under her shorts, caressing her. Jane bent slightly as she had earlier with her leathers on, she wiggled from side to side, Jasper slid off the stool, pulling her into him, his cock hardening, she was just the perfect height, his cock was level with her bottom. She looked over her shoulder smiling.
"You are such a tease my naughty Belle." Jane smiled bending over slightly more opening her legs. "Jesus Christ woman, so fucking gorgeous." He got down onto his knees pulling Jane's shorts to one side burying his tongue into her. Jane groaned as she bent over the stool. Opening her legs wider. He slid his fingers inside coating them, pulling them out, sucking them clean.

"I swear you taste better and better." He bit her bottom playfully spanking her again. He got up off his knees turning her back around to face him. "We better do some dinner love before I take you to bed and eat you up."

"I'm not good enough for dinner then anymore?" She asked putting her hand on her hips.

"Oh no, you are definitely dessert, my most favourite." He slipped his hands into her hair pulling her closer, his tongue licking her bottom lip gently, he pushed his tongue into her mouth, crushing his lips onto hers. Jane felt her legs go weak, her eyes fogging over. She followed Jasper putting her hands in his hair, her nails caressing the back of his neck. Jasper moaned. "Mmmmmmm, you can keep doing that all over my body if you like. You know I love your massages."

"Play your cards right and I might just do that later." Jasper smiled kissing her again, biting her lip gently.

"See, now you're teasing me again." He smiled letting go of her moving to the fridge to get the dinner ready.

Chapter 13

Old friends

Moses got into bed, he felt relieved the first session was over, he laid down in bed pulling the duvet up over his body, his head sinking into the pillow.

"Ohhhh, that feels good." He sighed, turning onto his left side, his hand moving under the pillow, his legs slightly apart. He fell into a deep sleep almost immediately.

He woke the next morning with a headache and a dry throat, he sat up in bed rubbing his face. "Okay body, day 2 we can do this." He headed to the shower turning the water on, he heard G arrive, he got out of the car and headed towards the door, Moses walked to the top of the stairs. "Jesus Brother, you may as well move in for God's sake. How much earlier do you want to be?"

"Just being prepared that's all." Moses grumbled under his breath knowing what he meant. He walked into the shower.

G was downstairs preparing the smoothie of the day for Moses and himself as Moses walked in.

"I hope this tastes better than yesterday?"

"You are one miserable fucker, here I am slaving over this fruit and veg and all you can do is whine. I'm drinking it too you know." He handed Moses his glass.

"I have an excuse, I'm allowed to be miserable." He pulled a face and sniffed it.

"I beg to differ, let's see what the girls have to say later shall we, or shall I call Jane?"

"Fuck off aresole." He grumbled. G laughed passing Moses his vitamins. Moses grumbled taking them from him, walking into the lounge he sat down swallowing the tablets and slowly drinking.

"Okay seriously how are you feeling?"

"I'm ok, just a headache that's it."

"Good, not anxious about today or anything?"

"Jesus what's your name Jane?"

"I am trying to help here."

"Yeah, yeah I know."

"You better get used to the questions too, you think I'm bad, just wait and see later. The girls are driving me fucking nuts and we are only on day two."

"Maybe we can forget going today, make up some excuse?"

"No fucking way, unless you want them taking over the house and your life?"

"Fine, whatever."

"Listen Brother, talk to me, is there something you are not telling me? I know you are a miserable fucker normally, but this isn't like you."

"To be honest I don't know. I am positive about this, I don't want to be ill and I do appreciate everything you are doing."

"But?"

"I'm shit scared you know that." Moses put his head into his hands sighing heavily.

"Doesn't mean you have to shut us out. Let us help. Being happy doesn't mean you are not struggling remember."

"I know, I just need to get this out of the way. I know it's going to be a long arsed month."

"Yes, it will and we are all here for you. Have you told Susan how you feel, she's the expert?"

"We do talk about it, but I don't want to bog her down with my feelings, it's nice just to have a laugh with her, it helps me forget about it. I can flirt and it's nice."

"Fair play. So, talk to Jane, or someone else. You need to be honest Brother. We don't want you going down that dark hole again."

"I hear you Brother, I will I promise. Come on, let's get this over with and go in and see everyone.

G washed the glasses and wiped down the kitchen before they left, Moses stood watching him shaking his head smiling. He knew how lucky he was to have good friends but was struggling with it now.

They finished at the hospital and went straight to the club. The garage was full as was the shop with customers, most of them G and Moses knew. The girls came out squealing from the café as they walked in, all asking questions at the same time.

"Jesus you would think I have been on tour."

"We just want to know how you are feeling, is there anything we can do for you?" Gwen was in his face fussing over him."

"Gwen, stop, I'm fine, it's only day two love."

I know, I know, but I just worry that's all. Would you like me to come over and do some cleaning, you know you will get tired right?"

Moses laughed, "Yeah I know love."

"So, let me and the girls go over while you are out of the house then, I can do your washing and ironing if you like."

G laughed shaking his head. "Now that I would like to see."

"Nobody is touching my ironing, you hear me?"

"Told ya." G laughed again.

"Well, we can do everything else."

"We will see, I'm fine at the moment, so let's leave it there shall we."

"Please Moses, if nothing else let us cook your meals for you, I know G is doing smoothies for you, we can cook nice meals and at least you don't have to cook then?"

"You're not giving up, are you?"

"Nope." The girls grinned.

"If it keeps you quiet then okay. But no fussing over me okay?"

"Deal", the girls ran off clapping chatting at speed about what they were going to cook. Moses shook his head smiling.

Moses continued to walk into the garage to see some of the other guys and spent the next hour chatting to his friends. He had had enough of standing around and began feeling tired, he wanted to go. He nodded to G who came across and joined in the conversation with him and a few others.

"Sorry buddy it's time to go, you have another appointment in an hour we need to get across town."

"Of course, thanks all, it's great to see you, will come back in a few days for a beer." He hugged everyone and left, sighing heavily as they walked out.

"You ok Brother?" G frowned looking at him.

"Yeah, just tired of standing, just feel tired, not slept so good in a few days."

"I will drop you home and leave you to it, let you get some rest."

"Thanks G, I appreciate it." Moses walked into the house, flopped down onto the sofa and fell asleep instantly.

He woke up with a start, the house was in darkness, he squinted at the screen. Struggling to see it still half asleep. He wasn't sure he was reading the screen right but still spoke.

"Dorian J Blaize, Jesus Christ, where were you when I was in the states a few months back?"

"Hey Brother, well I was a bit busy to be honest, if you hadn't noticed I have been touring for a year. Not been out on the bike for some time but I hope to put that right for the next few weeks. I saw Shadow the other day, he told me you were sick, what's going on, can I do anything?"

"Well, you will go and get famous, you should take the bike with you. I'm okay, just a bit of the big C, but just started treatment so hopefully it will sort it out for me. I'm glad you called I was thinking about you a few weeks ago."

"Now that is music to my ears, are you going to give in to me after all these years?"

"Fuck off, I'm not your type."

"Damn, you can't knock a guy for trying. What can I do for you, it must be something good?"

"You remember Jane don't you?"

"Little Lady Jane, yeah of course, gorgeous girl. How is she?"

"She's good, that's the reason I wanted to speak to you, she is getting married in two months, I wondered how you felt about surprising her and doing a song or two for her?"

"Of course, just let me know when and I will fly out for a few days, it will be good to see everyone."

"It's there in the US, she moved 6 months ago, met Jasper and fell in love."

"Jesus, never saw that coming. I better keep a low profile then, so she doesn't know I'm in town. I'm heading out of town for a while, need some down time. Heading off to the Maldives."

"Oh yeah, who is he?" Moses laughed.

"Nobody you know, we hooked up on the tour, it's not serious just fooling around but who knows."

"You would never settle down, for as long as I have known you, nobody has ever made you want to do that."

"Well, if you were to say yes to me then maybe I would." Moses laughed.

"In your dreams Dorian, in your fucking dreams."

"Well yes you are, that's what I'm saying." He started to laugh knowing it wound Moses up.

"Fuck off." Moses laughed. "I will send you the details of the wedding, I will let Jasper know too and give you his details. I will make sure we book you into the hotel we are in too. Just make sure you are not next to me, I don't want to hear your antics all night." Moses teased him.

"Yeah, yeah, I know secretly you do." He grinned, enjoying chatting to Moses again.

"In all seriousness if you need anything you call me, I can fly out, I have my own jet on call now so it's easier for me to get about."

"Thanks Brother, really appreciate that, I will see you before the wedding if your back from your holiday, I'm in town a couple of weeks before the wedding with G and Gwen anyway."

"Fantastic, let me know when you are here, we can get together. I have a nice place outside of town, come and stay with me, if you like, unless Jane has plans to visit. Anyway, have a think about it, the place is huge and has a separate bungalow. I will let you go for now Brother, take care of yourself and talk to you soon."

"Sounds great. Look forward to that. It's good to talk to you Dorian, the guys are going to be thrilled to see you." They hung up, Moses was smiling, Dorian was a great friend, he knew he would make something of himself but never realised how big he would be.

Dorian dialed Gwen, he put her on video call. He had already spoke to her so knew what was going on with Moses.

"Hi love. How did it go?"

"It was great, he sounded tired. He said you are coming out here before the wedding, which you didn't tell me about."

"Sorry love I forgot to mention it. Yes, we are, four of us are going out. The kids are staying home with my Mum."

"Right, I am coming to collect you all then, that poor bastard is going to be knackered after his treatment, he doesn't need to be on a huge fucking plane with screaming kids, he can sleep on mine instead."

"Dorian what the hell are you talking about?"

"Duh, I have a jet of my own, so I am coming out to collect you all, then we can fly back together."

"Get lost, no you haven't."

"Yes I have, cheeky cow. Do you actually know how famous I am?"

"Of course I do. Just never thought you would have your own jet."

"Well how else am I going to get any peace with my latest, out of the way of prying eyes." Gwen began laughing at him.

"True I suppose. Who is it this time and will we get to meet him?"

"Weeeell, his name is Rafik, he's 26." Dorian was grinning.

"26, wow! Cradle snatcher! Tell me more." Gwen clapped her hands together.

"He's 6ft, from Morocco. He has this smile that lights up his face and these eyes that drink you in. He has very little body hair, which isn't normally my type, but when I heard his voice the first time, my pants twitched, you know what I mean, well, I knew I was going to have him before the night was out. I did and he blew my mind. It was amazing!"

"Oh my god I cannot wait to meet him. Is he a keeper?"

"Don't know love, we will see, he is here with me so you will see him when I come to get you."

"I can't believe you are doing that for us."

"Why wouldn't I? I love you guys, if I can't share my wealth with you then who can I?"

"We love you too Dor, can't wait to see you."

"Me too love, don't tell Moses though, will you?"

"Of course not. Mums the word."

"Great, right Chick I am going to go, I will see you in about 6 weeks, keep in touch though, let me know how Moses is doing. I don't want to disturb him. Love ya."

"Thanks darling. Love you loads." They both hung up smiling. Gwen was ecstatic. She walked into her bedroom and flopped on the bed, giggling throwing her arms and legs around in excitement. She had loved Dorian from the moment she first met him, he was great at dressing a woman, he loved good clothes and was picky about his men.

Chapter 14

Hurting

Gwen had been pacing all morning, she was so nervous about seeing Moses, not knowing what to say to him. She was feeling tearful and didn't want to make him uncomfortable, they had known each other more years than she could remember, he had always been the strong one in the group. What she hadn't known was how he suffered with PTSD after coming home from his tours away. Linda came up behind her, putting her arms around her and her head on her shoulder.

"I know you are worried love, he's going to be okay."

"You don't know that. I don't want to cry like an idiot in front of him."

"Look at me Gwen." She turned her to face her, grabbing her face in her hands. "How many times as he gone away and we all cried? Then when he came home and we cried?"

"This is different though, he could be dying." She sniffed wiping her eyes.

"Could, yes, but all the signs are good, so stop with the negative thoughts, get into the bathroom and sort those panda eyes out, you tell everyone else about it, now do it yourself."

"Okay, okay. God you can be a nag at times."

"Well, someone has to be with you, nobody else is brave enough or stupid enough to cross you, except me." She hugged Gwen kissing her head and sent her off to the ladies to sort herself out.

Gwen walked into the bathroom wiping her eyes, she hadn't called Jane she didn't know what to say, G had told her he was just tired, but she saw how much weight he had lost and how pale he was looking. She had rang Dorian the night before to update him, he had offered to fly out but Gwen knew he would get mobbed if he turned up in town. She wiped her face and sorted herself out, she straightened her shoulders and walked out back into the café. Linda met her linking her arm as Moses and G pulled in. She took a deep breath mumbling under her breath as Moses walked in. She didn't speak just walked up to him hugging him gently.

"Hi sweetheart, how are you feeling?"

"I'm ok love." He half smiled.

She knew he was lying but he wasn't well enough for conflict, she let him get away with it. They all took a seat together.

"What can I get you love?" she asked already knowing the answer.

"Unless you have a bottle of after sun I can drink to stop this burning then just a bottle of water please love." Gwen felt the tears at the back of her throat she was desperate not to cry, she got up quickly dashing behind the counter. The guys all sat around him. G had his hand on his shoulder.

"Here you go love, what can I get you G?"

"Coffee please Gwen. I'm not hungry." She nodded. She saw the strain on his face, he suddenly began looking old with the strain, she knew this was hurting him.

"So how is the treatment going? Any updated yet Moses?

"I'm knackered, my insides feel like they are sun burnt. I just have to keep going, 5 more to go then hopefully it will be easier. I'm due a scan two weeks after the last session and get the results before we leave for Half-pints. I need to sort my suit out too. But that can wait a few more days. I don't have the energy to go out shopping."

"We can help love, just rest." Gwen pulled her chair closer squeezing his hand. She had an idea, she was going to speak to Dorian later and see if he could make it happen.

"Yes, we can, let us in more love. You are allowed to say yes, that's what friends are for. No I'm not nagging but Gwen is right." Linda moved to his other side.

"The girls are right Brother", Steve appeared behind him squeezing his shoulders gently. "Yes I know it's hard to believe I agree with them. If you want to be well enough to fly out to the Doc's wedding then you will let us help and relax more."

"Okay, okay, I hear you. There is no way I am missing her wedding so do what you have to do but stay away from my ironing you hear me?"

"Don't worry I will do that." G smiled looking at him.

"If you don't mind guys, I'm pretty knackered and want to go and sleep." He stood up, his shoulders slumped with exhaustion.

"Don't be silly of course we don't mind. It's been good to see you. we will drop off some stuff later and Linda and I will pop in tomorrow while you're at the hospital to do the cleaning.

"Thanks girls." They all hugged each other, Linda stood behind Gwen when they left, her legs buckled as she began to cry.

"I know I am being a whimp I just can't help it."

"No you're not, it's good to let it out love. I'm just not the crying type or I would join you, come on, let's see what we can make for Moses, try and get something into him. I don't think those meal replacements are good enough."

"Agreed, he has lost so much weight. When is he going to tell Jane, he seems to manage to get through her video calls quite well G said."

"Yeah I know, he knows he has to I suppose, he's trying to protect her, I understand that, she is a long way away. It can't be easy, their relationship is like nothing else, I just hope to God he gets through this, I hate to think what it would do to Jane if anything happens to him."

"Don't Linda, I can't even think about that. Let's put some good music on and stop this negative shit." Gwen walked over to the radio, selecting an 80s music channel. It boomed out lifting their spirits as they swayed their hips as they moved around the kitchen.

Chapter 15

Fun times

Jane was buzzing, Moses, G, Matt and Gwen were on their way, Jasper had told Jane he organized a car for them from the airport so she didn't know Dorian had flown them over on his jet, he couldn't believe Dorian was actually going to sing at their wedding, he knew they were friends but was still shocked. He knew Jane would be thrilled to see him.

"Hey Belle, you okay?"
"Yes of course, I just want to get Lady ready, she is going to love seeing Moses again."
"Sweetheart he won't be here until this afternoon. It's 8am!" Jane pouted.
"I know that, but we need to be ready, have we got enough milk, what about his meal drinks?"
"Stop love, please, slow down. Susan has that sorted, she is bringing them over tonight." He put his hands up to stop her. "I know you are scared and nervous about seeing him, it's going to be okay, just slow down, catch your breath and we can be ready in plenty of time. He is going to be tired so don't expect too much out of him and remember don't fuss." Jane put her head down. Jasper pulled her into his chest. She wrapped her arms around him holding him tight.
"I'm sorry I can't help it. I just don't want to cry and upset him, I know Gwen has sent me pictures but it is so different in real life. It is going to be odd seeing him and Susan together too, but I am happy he has someone else."
"I know Belle, I understand, I can't imagine how you are feeling, the only person I have ever been that close to is you and you know how I reacted when you were in hospital. But this is different. Let's get some breakfast then we can go and shower." Jane nodded heading into the kitchen.
They sat and had breakfast before heading to the shower. Jane was doing silly dances around the bedroom, Jasper stood against the door frame smiling watching her. She began stripping, her t-shirt came off first, she swang it around her head singing to Bob Marley.

"I wonna love ya, I wonna love ya, every day and every night." Her hips were moving in circles backwards and forwards, Jasper was mesmerized now. She had her short shorts on, giving him full view of her cheeks peaking out of the bottom, he felt his cock getting hard. He slipped his hand down over his shorts, his thumb rubbing his cock as he got harder. He wanted her, but wanted to watch her too. She was still facing away from him. She bent over still swinging her hips.

"Fuck yes." He groaned, his cock now paying full attention, he slipped his hand inside releasing it over the top of his shorts. He began rubbing slowly, enjoying the feeling and the show in front of him, he slipped his hand around his balls squeezing them, pushing his shorts down, he stepped out of them, opening his legs wider. He continued to rub his cock. Jane had no idea he was watching her, she grabbed the brush using it as a microphone as another song started. "Oh, oh, oh sweet love of mine", She took her hair clip out swinging her hair, she bent down and began head banging slowly. Jasper loved seeing her so relaxed. Music transported her to a good place. The song drew to an end, Jane stood up fluffing her hair turning towards the door.

She caught sight of Jasper stood in the doorway with a huge smile on his face his cock in his hand rubbing it. She walked towards him pushing her shorts off, stepping out of them as she reached him. She took his cock in her hand tiptoeing up to reach his lips. She kissed him, their tongues meeting, darting in and out of each others mouths, she bit his lip pulling it out smiling at him. Both moaning softly, Jasper grabbed her around the bottom lifting her, she wrapped her legs around him as he walked them to the bed their tongues still dualling. Hi cock laying just on the edge of her pussy, he could feel her warm juices against the tip. He turned laying on the bed, Jane was on top of him, she slid down to his cock, placing her pussy over it as it laid against his body, she smiled sitting up, she rubbed her now soaking pussy up and down it, her clit reaching the tip teasing herself she continued, she moved her hand lifting his cock giving her the pressure she needed. Jasper laid watching, his cock getting harder as she rubbed herself against it. Jane stopped herself sitting back on her knees.

"Come here Belle, sit on my face. I want to eat you." he smiled giving her his hand. Jane bit the side of her lip groaning as she stood, moving herself up the bed, she crouched over his face, sitting up on her knees, Jaspers nose touched her clit, she trembled in pleasure lowering herself more. His tongue teasing her lips. Jane put her hands on his chest to hold herself up, teasing her pussy as she moved back and forth over his tongue, gasping as he caught her clit. Jasper held onto her bottom moving with her as he lapped at her pussy, he pushed his tongue deep inside, Jane grabbed her hair scrunching under her hands on the top of her head, her head falling back as she moaned loudly.

"Oh Jesus, yes baby fuck me with your tongue, oh God, this is heaven." She groaned louder. She grabbed the top of his head grinding herself on his face, Jasper was sucking hard, his tongue darting in and out of her, her juices covering his beard. She felt her orgasm build, she wanted to cum but wanted to stop. She didn't want this to end, she moved herself back looking down at him, catching her breath.

"What Belle?"

"Nothing, just stopping myself cumming that's all."

"Why?"

"I'm enjoying it that's all." She grinned pushing her fingers into her pussy coating them, she pulled them out sucking them off. Smiling at Jasper, he lifted her off, sat up against the bed.

"Come sit between my legs love." He patted the bed between his legs. Jane grinned, turning, sitting down with her back to him. He opened his legs wide, Jane followed placing hers on top of his. He moved her hair from her shoulder, freeing up her neck, he pushed her head to the side, licking her down to her shoulder blade, his left hand moving around to her breast, he cupped it from underneath pinching her nipple in his fingers. Jane bucked her hips, feeling her juices in her pussy making her wet again. She moved her hand down, teasing herself. She pushed in slowly her thumb teasing her clit, she slipped a second in, gasping, closing her eyes. Biting down on her lips. Jasper stroked down the inside of her arm with his fingertips, Jane could feel the deep sensation in her arm, almost like a tickle but deeper, her nipples hardened under his touch, he reached her wrist, moving his fingers between hers, pushing his middle finger into her pussy with hers. Jane groaned again pushing back into him. He bent kissing her shoulder, biting gently back and forth. She moved one of her fingers out as Jasper pushed both his middle fingers in, still holding onto Jane's hand, both penetrating her pussy, her sensitiveness heightening as they grew faster pushing harder. Jane moved her thumb back to her clit. She grabbed Jaspers leg, squeezing, her breath deepening. Her orgasm close. Jasper slowed down pulling out of her. Jane turned looking shocked.

"You said you wanted the feeling to last!" Jane laughed as he got up, pulling her down to the edge of the bed, he got onto his knees on the floor. Opening her legs wide, he slid two fingers inside her slowly, his hand completely flat, her pussy glistened with her juices, he pushed her leg flat, opening her up further. He bent flicking his tongue across the hood, making Jane lift of the bed. He slid in and out of her making her groan more, he sucked her pussy pushing his tongue in with his fingers. She grabbed her breasts, squeezing them, pushing them together, bending to lick her nipples, biting them hard, she was going out of her mind. She moved from one to the other sucking and licking. Jasper stopped licking, getting off the floor he bent to join her sucking her nipples. Their tongues jostling on them. Jane fed him her breast, he covered her nipple with his mouth sucking hard making silly slurping noises. Jane laughed as he pulled away making a pop sound. He pulled her further to the end of the bed, taking his cock in his hand, he rubbed her pussy back and forth, Jane got up onto her elbows watching him. He held the tip as he pushed slowly as far as he could, Jane watched intently, her eyes closing as she felt herself fill with him. He pushed her legs open flat against the bed. Pushing hard into her, looking deep into her eyes. The intensity building. He moved his thumb across the tip of her clit, Jane flinched, she was so sensitive, her clit throbbing under his touch. He grew faster pushing hard, rubbing her clit, Jane grabbed the bed sheets screwing them up, this time he wasn't allowing her to stop, he wanted to feel her cum, to feel her cover his cock in her juices. Her skin tingling, she felt the heat flood her body.

"Jaaasssssperrrrrrr", she screamed, as her orgasm took over, her body convulsing as she came hard. Jasper felt her cover his cock, he pushed hard chasing his own orgasm, as she clenched around him.

"Arghhhhhhh, fucking hell", he yelled, bending backwards pushing into her. Jane squeezed again milking him. He began laughing, feeling so sensitive. Jane was determined to tease him more, she clenched hard holding him inside her. Pushing her hips back and forth. Jasper was laughing trying to stop her. "Please baby stop, I can't cope", he giggled. She slowed down laughing with him. He pulled out of her, groaning. Bending over her, he caught her lip in his teeth biting gently.

"I love you Belle. My naughty lady." He brushed his lips against hers, his tongue licking gently. She put her arms around his neck, as he stood up she wrapped her legs around him as he walked them both into the shower room.

Chapter 16

Surprise

The minibus arrived at the airport, Matt paid the driver, they all climbed out. G grabbed Moses bags, shaking his head at him defying him to argue with him. Moses was relieved. They walked in the door and Gwen walked to the information centre, they were directed to the business centre, Moses frowned. "What's going on guys?"

"Nothing love, we have been upgraded that's all."

"You can't do that from here."

"Well, it's a good job your buddy is here to make it happen then, isn't it?" Dorian put his arms around Moses from behind, kissing him on the side of the head.

"Where the hell did you come from, what are you doing here Dor?" Moses turned looking at him.

"I thought you might prefer a decent flight away from squealing kids for the day, come on before anyone else sees me, I am trying to keep a low profile. I have already signed my life away a few dozen times for the staff. Give me a bag or two G, let me help." Moses passed the bags to him and they walked towards the business centre. They walked in the door as they were met by 3 stewards who took their bags away.

"We can go straight onto the jet unless you want to have a drink out here?"

"No let's go, you don't need any more attention, I think you have been spotted we better be quick." G stood behind Moses walking with him out of the door onto the carpet at the foot of the jet stairs.

"You okay Brother?" G put his hand on his shoulder. Moses nodded looking up at the jet in front of him. Even though it was small it still looked huge. They climbed the stairs slowly, Matt and G ducked as they went onto the jet.

"Jesus Dor, this is incredible, how the hell do you get used to this?"

"You don't, it still amazes me every day, I'm still the goofy, gay Dorian you all know. I just sing for a living." His face lit up as Rafiq headed towards him. He placed his hand onto his chest as Rafiq bent, his hand going onto the back of Dorians head pulling him into his lips, mouths open their lips met, Rafiq teased Dorian's lip with his tongue, his thumb rubbing the side of Dorians head. They smiled as they pulled apart. "Guys, can I introduce you all to Rafiq. This is Moses, G, Matt and one of my favourite girls, Gwen." They all shook hands except for Gwen, she walked into him.

"Well, if you're good enough for Dor, then you're good enough for me", she hugged him hard making everyone else laugh.

"Sit everyone please so we can take off. Moses you can lay down in the bed at the back if you like or the sofa, it's up to you."

"I'm ok here for now thanks Dorian." They all took a seat looking around the jet. Everything inside was cream. The chairs were huge soft leather, two sets of two with a table in between, at the other end were two rows of three facing a huge TV screen. Beyond that was the kitchen, bedroom and bathroom. At the other end was a space for the two stewards and their bar area, just in front of the cock pit. They all fastened up their belts as the plane taxied onto the runway, before long they were in the air. Moses had fallen asleep in his chair. One of the stewards covered him with a blanket, G was sat opposite him, he smiled nodding at the steward, she smiled back. Dorian had explained the situation and wanted them all to be looked after.

Moses slept most of the flight, Dorian and the others sat around chatting quietly. Gwen was watching how tactile Dorian and Rafiq were, she remembered back to when Dorian was pretending to be straight, she saw the pain in his eyes every time someone asked him when he was going to meet a nice girl, his parents were strict church goers, he knew it would break them to tell them he was gay so he took a few girls home but never had the urge to sleep with any of them. He was a good-looking man, his skin was perfect, not a blemish, he still had the goaty beard he'd had from years before. He had a cheeky smile when he talked, the edge of his lips always smiling. He found a lot of his friends disowned him when he came out, being black and gay was tough for him, but he finally wanted to be himself, they guys in the club all stood by him. They never judged anyone. A few had been in prison and had fucked around with other men, apparently to them it didn't count if you took someone else as long as they didn't take your arse. Gwen smiled not listening to the men, she went back to her book. It was a new one she was trying to get into.

"Anyone want some food, do you think we should wake Moses?"

"No let him sleep, he hasn't eaten much for a few weeks, were hoping this week around us all he might have a little."

"Did you stay with him G?"

Yes, I did, I went in from the end of the first week, when he started to get really tired. He hasn't done too bad to be honest. The sickness was stopped with some good anti sickness, but as you can see the weight has dropped off him."

"Well, he has two weeks to feel better before the wedding. Let's hope he improves a bit more. Did he get his results yet?"

"No, the consultant is calling him tomorrow."

Dorian nodded, "if needed we can get him in to see someone in the states."

"Thanks Dor, hopefully that won't be needed. Are you really sure about us staying with you? I know we still struggle to keep Jane away, but we can get Gwen to do that. Especially as she is staying with her next week."

"Of course, I don't mind, the house is huge, Moses and G are in the bungalow. Matt and Gwen you are in the south wing, Rafiq and I are in the centre."

"Sounds great, thank you Brother."

"Anytime, so what's the plan for the wedding, tell me about Jasper?"

They told Dorian and Rafiq about Jasper, how he cared about Jane, what happened when she was taken. Dorian felt like he had been away too long. He missed the gang more and more. Being on tour was a lonely time, he had his fair share of men. He hoped him and Rafiq would be different.

Gwen laughed. "I think you might like Jasper, he is rather hot."

"Ohhh, tell us more."

"Well, he is as tall as you Rafiq, he has the most incredible body, not big though, just right, he has these eyes that could melt the hardest of people, you can see women dropping their knickers when he walks in a door." Matt stared at Gwen. "Oh, you can stop that nonsense Matt. You know I think he is sexy, I have never hidden it." The guys laughed at Matt, he shrugged and sat listening as they continued. The stewards came across with food platters for them all to share, they were full of continental meats and fish, with all kinds of accompaniments, they all tucked in laughing and joking. G reminded Dorian of some of the antics in Afghan when they first met. They had become firm friends since then.

"So, what am I singing at the wedding, have they decided yet?"

"Jasper wants Etta James, At last."

"Ohh, beautiful, happily do that for them, that man has taste."

"Jane loves Barry White. You're the first my last my everything."

"Very sexy song, I can do that justice too. Even if I say so myself. I don't mind doing a few songs, especially if everyone is going to be there."

"That would be amazing, but you have done enough already."

"I don't think so G, you two saved my life, I owe you more than you could ever imagine, if it wasn't for the club I wouldn't be where I am today, you are my family you know that. What I have is yours."

Gwen moved seats to cuddle into Dorian. "You are one special man, shame you weren't straight or I would have stood him up for you." Matt pouted making everyone laugh.

"Oh, that was an awesome night helping you get ready. You were a bag of nerves."

"Shhh, don't tell him that, I'm supposed to be the hard one."

"Matt you ever want this girls secrets you can ask me anything you like." Gwen slapped Dorian playfully as they all teased Matt. G heard a murmur behind him. Moses had woken up.

He moved across to sit opposite him. "Hi Brother, how are you doing?

"I'm ok thanks G, feel better for that sleep. How long have we been flying?"

"I think we have around an hour or so before we land, do you want a drink or anything?"

"Please just water thank you. Gwen packed you a few of your meal drinks if you want one?"

"No thanks, water is fine."

Dorian came across sitting on the sofa to the side of them, Moses swiveled in his chair.

"How are you feeling Moses?" he put his hand on his leg.

"I'm ok thank you, I just said to G I feel a little better for that sleep."

"Good news, let's hope tomorrow you get some good news."

"Thanks Brother, fingers crossed for sure. I don't fancy any more of that radiation."

"So, tell me, I thought you and Jane were as thick as thieves what happened, why didn't you tell her how you felt? It's clear to see how much she loves you."

"There is a big difference, she isn't in love with me, the way I am with her, don't you say a damn word Dor."

"Cross my heart Brother, I wouldn't do anything to hurt either of you. Do you really rate this Jasper?"

"Damn right I do, he puts up with her silliness like we do, he absolutely adores her, you wait until you see them together, it makes me happy knowing she is happy, I couldn't make her as happy as he does."

"One of these days you will stop knocking yourself, any woman will be bloody lucky to have you."

"Thanks Dor. I do have a friend out here, she was Jane's nurse, she was actually a Cancer nurse once, she has been great to have as a friend, she does things to me too, so who knows. Nobody else knows. I don't know why I am telling you though." He laughed nervously.

"Because you know I will understand, I promise, I won't say a word."

"Now what can I get you? anything you need, do you want to shower and freshen up, I can help if you like?"

Moses laughed. He never stopped teasing him. "That would be good if you don't mind?"

"Come with me." Moses stood up and followed Dorian into the bedroom, he looked around in awe at the amazing room, it was like a state room on ship.

"Jesus Dor, this room is fucking amazing!"

"It's my favourite place on the plane, I love it. Right in here is the shower, I will turn it on ready for you, just turn it to the right to turn it off. Towels are there, shampoo and body wash are in there too. Take your time. We land in around an hour so no hurry."

Dorian left, leaving Moses alone, he stood looking around the room. It was cream with dark wood panels, the bed was white Egyptian linen, he ran his hand across it thinking of Susan being there with him. He smiled, turning to the shower. He expected a small caravan like shower, this was full on plush, glass screens surrounded it. There was room enough for two. He felt like he was stepping into a jewel and not just glass, the lights were bouncing off the pristine glass, the shower gel and shampoo were in crystal pump containers. He showered slowly turning the temperature to cold before he got out to wake himself up. he stepped out onto the mat, grabbing a towel which was pure luxury, he felt like he was wrapping himself in cotton wool. He turned to the sink and looked in the mirror, he caught sight of the dark rings under his eyes and the gaunt look on his face. He was dreading the Doctors report. He just hoped and prayed it was going to be okay. He finished up, got dressed and headed back to the group. The steward met him with a fresh glass of water as he sat down. Gwen squeezed his leg.

"You ok babe?"

"Yes love, I'm ok, I feel better for that."

"Good, can we get you anything to eat, I have your drinks with me?"

"I'm ok love, maybe later." Gwen nodded smiling, sitting back in her seat.

"Ladies and gentleman, please take your seats we will soon be making our decent into the airport. The weather in Connecticut is dry and sunny, currently 70 degrees. We hope you have enjoyed your flight and look forward to welcoming you back on board for your return flight."

They all turned to look at Dorian with their mouths open.

"What don't look at me like that. I told you what I have is yours, I only have little old me to spend it on, why would you want to fly back home cattle class when you can use this jet."

Moses felt quite tearful, Gwen jumped into Dorians lap hugging him tight.

"You are so kind Dor, thank you." She kissed him quickly before returning to her own seat and buckling up. They landed within 15 minutes, they exited the plan onto the tarmac they were met by a limousine big enough for them all.

"We will go to mine first to drop me off and your bags, then you will be taken to Jane and Jaspers. When you are ready to come back just text me and I will send the car back."

"It seems so unfair you can't come too." Gwen looked sadly at Dorian.

"Don't worry I am part of the big surprise, I will get plenty of time to catch up later, I am not going far for some time anyway. Apart from our break next week in the Maldives, that's if we get there."

"You have no idea how much this means love, we really do all appreciate it, we know how busy you are so getting this time with you is priceless, if we get on your nerves feel free to kick us out."

"Don't be daft, it's been too long, if I wasn't mobbed so much, I would have been back sooner. It's good for me to feel grounded too being back with the crew. Can we get a ride out some time, even after the wedding?"

"Sounds like a plan, we can get some bikes from Shadow."

"No need I have a garage full, take your pick." He grinned feeling pleased with himself, he loved sharing things with his friends. "Right here we are. We will see you later. Have fun with Jane, for Gods sake don't let the cat out of the bag. Tell her you had a shit journey." He laughed as he got out of the car, Rafiq and the security guard helped the driver with the bags, as they waved the car off.

They sat talking about the flight and how incredible it was, they planned their answers to all the questions they knew Jane would ask, they were ready as they pulled outside the house. Jane wasn't surprised when she saw the limousine as Jasper had said he sent one for them. She squealed as they arrived. Jumping up and down like a little girl. Gwen jumped out first. She ran over to Jane squeezing her tight. "Hi beautiful, you look incredible, it's so good to see you on your feet again."

"Thanks Gwen, you look tired, was it a bad journey?"

"Yeah, it was, lots of kids on the flight, you know me I don't tolerate them anymore after having mine." They both laughed as the others got out. Matt kissed Jane and hugged Jasper, G helped Moses out of the car. As he walked into view Jane felt her legs go weak, she hadn't expected him to look so thin. Jasper was right behind her holding onto her like he was hugging her from behind.

"Hey Half-pint." Moses smiled as he reached Jane, the others moved away as she hugged him, her throat was hurting holding back the tears.

"Don't hold them back on my account silly. I knew it was going to happen, you promised you would be you, no hiding anything." Jane let go of her tears, her body trembling as she sobbed, G came behind her holding them both. He laid his head onto Jane's, soothing her, Moses began crying too, G was struggling with his tears. But was desperate to be strong for them both. Gwen grabbed Jaspers hand with both of hers, she had a few tears, Jasper pulled her in to his chest.

"You need to let go to Gwen, I can see you are struggling with it, maybe time with Jane on your own will be good for you. I will move into the spare room so you can share." Gwen looked up at him eyes full of tears. "Do you know how amazing you are?" She has her lover and soul mate wrapped up all in one."

"I'm not Gwen, I just love her like no other. She completes me."

"Awww, now you made me go all mushy, stop that." She smiled up at Jasper, he kissed her on the head as G moved away from Jane allowing her to talk to Moses.

Moses lifted her head. "You ok Half-pint", Jane nodded at him sniffing.

"Yes, I'm supposed to be saying that to you." He smiled, kissing her forehead.

"Let's not change the habit of a lifetime." She hit him gently taking his hand leading him to Jasper.

Jasper hugged him gently, "Good to see you Moses."

"Same Brother. Thanks for everything. They walked into the house.

"Get settled and I will let Lady in to see you. We won't let her jump up though."

"Let her out now, let me see her." Jane opened the door, Lady came bounding out, her tail going crazy, she wasn't sure where to go first, she suddenly stopped when she spotted Moses, she wasn't sure at first, her nose was twitching as she was sniffing the air, Moses called her, she stopped in front of him, he put his hand out to her, she sniffed at him closer and suddenly realised it was him, she lept up onto his lap, whining and lapping at his face, he put his head down laughing, she licked his ear his head and his face, everyone was laughing, it lightened the mood.

"Someone is definitely happy to see you!" Jasper said laughing.

"Good to know." He smiled, Jasper picked her up putting her onto the floor he could see Moses was wincing, he knew he wanted to play with her, but he wasn't well enough just yet.

"I know you wouldn't want too many people around tonight so the others we can see tomorrow if you like?"

"Sounds like a good idea. Thanks love, I appreciate that." He smiled at Jane, grateful to her for understanding.

"G you can take the Range Rover, it will help you all get around, we can use the bikes or the car."

"Thanks J, that would be great." The others nodded, knowing it would make it easier than trying to explain the limousine every time.

They were sat chatting when the doorbell went. Jane got up heading to the door she knew it would be Susan, she was still unsure about her feelings and seeing them together was going to be hard for her. She didn't want Moses, but she had mixed emotions about their relationship.

"Hi Susan, come in." Jane stood back allowing Susan to step in. they hugged each other.

"Thanks Jane, how are you?"

"I'm great thank you, it's good to have him here, I was a bit shocked at how much weight he has lost to be honest."

"That's understandable, once he starts eating again he will put it all back on, but we need to tempt him now, food will smell different for him and taste odd. That won't help him either. He did mention he can smell himself he said it smells like burning, or chlorine. It's not an unusual thing, it doesn't help though that he has sores around his lower stomach. Once they heal it will go away."

Jane put her hand onto Susan's. "Thank you so much for being here for us all, I can't thank you enough for being there for him too, that's the most important thing."

"He's a great guy, we are good friends and we actually help each other."

"That's lovely, anyway let's get you in there to meet the guys again and see Moses."

"Have to say I am a bit embarrassed, we have had some lovely evenings chatting and stuff and now seeing him face to face I know I am going to blush."

"Wait here then, I will go and get him, you can see each other in private." Jane smiled walking into the lounge.

"Moses love, can I borrow you for a few minutes please?"

"Sure love, everything okay?" He pushed himself out of the chair wincing, Lady was laid on his feet, she didn't move when he stood. Jasper called her over laughing.

"Sorry Moses, you know she has a thing for you."

"It's lovely honestly." He followed Jane into the kitchen, he saw Susan sat at the dining table, he looked back at Jane smiling.

"Thanks love", he hugged her kissing her cheek, Jane smiled and walked away closing the doors behind her. She felt a small knot in her stomach of jealousy but tried hard to dismiss it.

Chapter 17

Getting to know each other

Susan stood up as Moses walked in, her hands sweating as he walked over to her. She had no idea what to do, Moses put his hands on her shoulder pulling her to him, his head tilting to one side as he gently brushed his lips across hers.

"Is this okay?" he whispered. Susan nodded. Her hands moving to his waist, Moses pulled her in closer, his hands moving to her face, he looked down at her, Susan was blushing a little, he smiled lifting her chin up.

"Hi." He smiled almost laughing.

"Hi." Susan laughed. He pulled her head in hard, his lips crashing down onto hers. Susan's hands moved up his back, she tugged on his t-shirt as they kissed hungrily. Moses pushed his tongue gently into her mouth, he wanted to taste her, their breathing erratic, needy. Moses stopped.

"We better stop, or heaven knows where this will end."

"I think we do know where." Susan laughed. She teased her hair back into place, wiping the side of her mouth. Moses wiped her across her lips and licked his thumb. Susan blushed again.

"Come on before I eat you up." They both laughed as Moses led them both into the lounge.

"Well now I know why you were gone so long." Matt teased.

Jane felt flushed with jealousy, she smiled and joined in, but couldn't help feeling a loss.

Everyone stood up and hugged Susan. G moved off the sofa to let Susan and Moses sit together.

They all sat chatting and laughing for an hour, Susan noticed Moses became quiet she knew he was feeling tired, she squeezed his hand. "I think you should head off love." Moses nodded in agreement.

"Time to go I think Moses, you're looking pretty wiped out." G stood up, pulling him out of the sofa. Everyone stood agreeing it had been a long day for them all.

"We will stay at the apartment tomorrow if that's ok?" Moses asked looking at Jane.

"Of course it is, you need to rest as much as you can. Just call when you want to come over, or we can come to you."

"No, we will come here." Jasper passed the keys to G for the Range Rover, they all hugged and walked out. Susan walked with Moses to her car. She was smiling feeling like a little girl.

"Let me know how you feel tomorrow, I can pop over and see you if you like, but no pressure." He nodded.

"I would like that."

"Great, get some rest and we will talk tomorrow." He kissed her gently before she got into her car, he closed the door as she started the engine, they waved at each other as she pulled away. Jane was watching his every move, the knot still in her stomach. Moses turned and waved blowing Jane a kiss, she returned it pretending to catch it. She smiled remembering him doing it when he went on tour.

Jasper hugged Jane as they went back into the house. "You ok Belle?"

"I think so. How does he look to you?"

"Very tired, yes he has lost a lot of weight but that's normal, I'm sure by the wedding he will feel much better and have lots more energy."

"I'm not bothered about how he looks for the wedding, I meant in himself, please don't think this is all about me and the wedding."

"Hey, hey, where did that come from, why are you snapping? I didn't mean for one minute this was about you, I meant it as a milestone, they told him after a couple of weeks of treatment he would start to feel better, I meant it for him." He pulled her into his chest. Kissing her head "Talk to me love."

"I'm sorry I don't know why I snapped." She bent backwards looking up at Jasper. "Is it bad that I am jealous of Susan, I don't love Moses like that, I don't fancy him, but I just feel this knot in my stomach. I don't want to feel like this, Susan is a lovely lady, but it hurts." Jasper took Jane by the hand and sat her on his knee on the sofa.

"Belle, think about it, you have been the closest thing to a wife, sister, best friend that he has ever had, it is no wonder you are feeling like this, you're probably feeling like you're not needed anymore, your mind goes into overdrive too. I can imagine you think she is going to take over and you won't be needed anymore. I can guarantee that will never happen, that kind of love is hard to find, nobody can take that away from you both. If Susan is the lady for him then great, but she will never replace you as his best friend."

Jane nodded. "You're probably right, I really want him to be happy, I would love to see him married and have children, yes I know that won't happen now, the children anyway. I suppose I am scared of losing him."

"How do you think he feels, you leave him after 10 years of protecting you, within days you are with another man and now you are marrying him. Don't you think he may feel that way too?"

"No I don't, he loves you Jasper, like everyone does."

"That doesn't matter", Jasper scooted them both back into the sofa, he thought it was about time she knew a few things. "When you were taken, Moses went into meltdown, he was down the garden in front of the roses, he cried Belle, he was mad at himself because you moved here and he wasn't here to look after you, that man couldn't love you anymore than he does now. There is no woman on this earth that could ever come close. When you were in hospital he wouldn't leave, I am glad he does feel that way about you, he is an incredible man. I suppose at times I get jealous of your relationship with him, but that has been years of a huge amount of good and bad situations that brought you to the relationship that it is today. G is the same, don't ever think he doesn't feel the same way, he just stands back and allows Moses to take control. They would both give their lives for you. There is nothing they wouldn't do. They proved it when you were taken. I'm glad you told me how you feel, if you had hidden it then it would be a cause for concern, that maybe you felt more than love for him. Does that make sense?"

Jane sat listening, she still felt there was so much she didn't know about the time she was gone, she only knew her side of things which she wanted to share with them all but she wasn't sure. Tears welled up in her eyes, she wiped them away with her sleeve, sniffing she looked at Jasper.

"You are the most incredible man I have ever known, you make complete sense, I look at you sometimes and wonder why and how I got so lucky, what did I do to deserve you in my life. I never thought anyone could love me the way you do, or that I could love anyone the way I do you. The thought of losing you feels me with dread, I know if anything happened, I would die of a broken heart. You are my world." She sniffed again, Jaspers hand went automatically to her face, his thumb wiping her tears away. She smiled bending to kiss his fingers. He slid his left hand into her hair, pulling her into him. He rubbed noses with her, kissed the end of it and looked her in the eyes.

"Jane Kirkpatrick, you are the most beautiful woman I have ever known. Now can you move off my legs please as you are giving me pins and needles." He laughed waiting for the slap. He wasn't disappointed, Jane punched him into the stomach, he doubled over as she climbed off. He kicked his legs in the air rubbing them like crazy, he jumped up hopping around the room as one began going numb, he fell onto the sofa laughing at himself.

"Oh, you were serious?" she laughed.

"Yes love, I didn't mean you were heavy, you must have been sat wrong on me." He was still rubbing his leg trying to get it to come back to life, Jane knelt next to him, Lady joined them, Jane began rubbing up and down his leg. They both laughed as Jasper was yelling at the feeling in his leg.

"You are such a child Jasper."

"Oh thanks, remind me to say that to you when you have it next time." Jane just grinned at him giving him her best silly smile.

"Any better?"

"Yes love, thank you, He sat up properly still rubbing his leg, Lady was sat with Jane thinking it was playtime with her being sat on the floor, Jasper joined her, Lady laid down in the middle of them on her back, they both laughed.

"I swear she is saying come and get me boys when she lays down like that." Jane began giggling.

"Oh my god yes, that's so funny. Look at that silly face. She has us both at her beck and call." They both continued to rub her tummy, Jasper moved across to Jane kissing her smiling.

"Two doting parents I think they call it." Jane nodded.

"I agree. Stupid parents I think."

Chapter 18

All for Moses

The guys arrived back at Dorians, they hadn't noticed the house when they pulled in earlier due to the small dark windows on the limousine. As G pulled into the drive they all gasped. The gates were closed, the Security guard came out. G wound the window down.

"Hi there, we are Dorians friends from early in the limo?" The guard looked at his tablet.

"Can you confirm your names please?"

"Moses, G, Matt and Gwen. Don't you dare ask me my full name or you will get a punch", he continued under his breath.

"That's correct, please go ahead. You just follow the road around and you will arrive outside the main house. You will be met at the door by the housekeeper." G nodded.

"Thank you." They pulled in through the white gates. The whole grounds that they could see were a mass of trees and grass, there were shrubs in large flower beds. They followed the road around.

"Jesus Christ, this singing career lark certainly does make some sweet money." G laughed whistling.

"You're telling me Brother, Matt leant through the seats to get a look at the house as they went up the drive.

"It's like a park, it's incredible." Gwen gasped.

They arrived at the front of the house. In front of them was a large square, they drove around it, inside was a maze of bushes, the house looked almost colonial. It didn't look so big from the front but they could see more off to the sides. As they arrived at the front door it opened. An older lady came to the door, she stood smiling as they all got out of the car.

"You can leave your car there, Dorian's cars are in the garage. Come on in, Dorian will be down shortly, he was in the studio." They all walked into the main house, their mouths dropping open. They were met by a huge staircase that swept around the left-hand side of the hall. The floors were marble. The wallpaper was yellow with exotic birds on it, it was on the top half of the walls going up the stairs, the bottom was wood panelling. There were huge plants and ornaments everywhere including the staircase.

"Your first visit I take it?" asked the housekeeper smiling. They all nodded.

"Yes, we normally see Dorian in the UK, the house there is much smaller than this."

"So I understand. Well, this is the main house entrance, we all normally use the kitchen entrance. There is another staircase round the corner that takes you up to the centre of the house. There is another leading to where you will be staying, it's all very private. Your bags have been taken care of. Come let's go into the kitchen and I will make some tea, I baked some cookies earlier too."

They followed her into the kitchen, which was bigger than most homes total footprint. It was a huge expanse of white. A central island sat 6 people, in front of them was a bay window, it looked out into the middle of the lawned area. Behind them was a smaller lounge area, with huge leather sofas and a dining table.

"Go into the breakfast area, I will bring the tea over." They went as directed and sat at the table. Dorian came into the kitchen kissing Kitty on the cheek.

"So you have all had the pleasure of meeting Kitty she has been with me for 10 years now, she has kept me on the straight and narrow. Haven't you?" She blushed.

"Well yes I suppose I have. But you are a good lad, you don't really need to much looking after, not when you are here anyway. I dread to think what goes on when you are away, in fact I don't want to know." They all laughed.

"Come on Kitty I am good boy", he winked at his friends who shook their heads. "Right then tuck in, these cookies are amazing. Are you still cooking Gwen?"

"Yes love, I still run the kitchen, I do a few things on the side too like weddings and funer…, she choked back her tears. Not wanting to look across at Moses. It was too close to home. The room fell quiet. Kitty knew all about Moses so changed the subject quickly.

"Well maybe Gwen you and I could spend some time swapping recipes, I do love to be challenged to new stuff."

"I would love to."

"Great, I am sure the boys will be off doing crazy things outside or fishing tomorrow, so if you don't want to go with them we can do some cooking if you don't think it's too much like a busman's holiday?"

"No that would be amazing, I definitely don't like fishing so leave the boys to themselves. We are not seeing Jane tomorrow anyway so it will be nice to have another girl about to chat too."

"Oh how wonderful, I will look forward to that. Right now, here we go, help yourself." She placed the pots on the table.

"Kitty join us please?", Moses asked.

"I don't want to get in the way of friends catching up."

"Don't be silly, you know him as well as we do so it's nice to meet someone else who is close to him."

"Thank you, that's kind of you." Kitty joined them, she helped Gwen to pour the tea and hand out the cookies.

"Won't your friend Jane like to come here before the wedding, I mean once she finds out where you have been staying?"

"I was thinking the same too Kitty, I kind of feel guilty, if it was only a couple of days it wouldn't be so bad, but two weeks is a long time." Gwen said looking around at the men.

"We will need to speak to Jasper, he is the one arranging this surprise." Moses added. "But I would want them to be here too, I hate to think we are taking up your time and she doesn't get to spend any of it with you. Are you still going away Dor?"

"No, I have decided to stay home as you guys are here."

"Are you sure, we don't want you to feel like you have to keep us entertained."

"Don't be stupid, I would much prefer to be here with you."

"Excellent, news."

"Forgive the intrusion I know a little about the wedding plans, I just had an idea if you would still like to surprise Jane. How about arranging a pre Wedding meal, you can say you have been invited here, she doesn't need to know who by, I am sure you can get Jasper to say something, then when you are all sat in the lounge waiting for dinner you could walk in Dorian, I would love to cook for you all, it's been a long time since anyone has been here for anything special."

"Oh yes Dorian we must, I can help too, do you think you would be up to eating next week Moses?"

"I can give it a good go, yes for sure."

"Sorted then." Dorian clapped. "Ladies you are responsible for the menu, we will talk to Jasper and he can plan the night, maybe he can say it's a clients house or something?"

"Great idea." G smiled looking over at Moses he saw how his face lit up. "You have to invite Susan too Brother." Moses nodded.

They continued to sit and plan the evening surprise. Gwen was excited to be part of planning the meal. She didn't want Jane missing out on this time with Dorian either.

"Right let me show you to your rooms, Moses you and G are in the bungalow I will take you out there. Gwen, Matt, Kitty will take you to your end of the house. Let's get back together later once you have all had a rest."

Moses and G followed Dorian outside to his bungalow it was a short walk around the side of the house, they walked across a red bridge and came out onto the lawn of the bungalow. It had cream boards on the outside, double aspect bay windows at the front. They walked in through the front door, it was a huge double heavy door painted in dark grey with a glass panel in the middle. The whole place was light and airy, it was a spacious 4 bedroom bungalow with cathedral ceilings allowing light to pour in. The day room had two huge sofas opposite each other, at the end of them was a huge TV above an old stone fireplace, which had been converted to gas with a glass front. They walked down the large hallway into bedroom one. It had its own private entrance onto its own patio, Moses nodded liking what he was seeing. All windows were replica sash windows. Each bedroom had its own full bathroom with a double shower and bath. Everything was white except for hints of another colour in each room.

"This is yours Moses, if you push those doors open there is a patio with a covered area, in the middle is a gas fire and sofas around it, a lovely place to entertain if you get my meaning."

"Thanks Brother, it's beautiful. Jasper and Jane are going to love this place."

"G come on yours is next door, its identical just the other way round. Your patio is smaller and leads out onto the woods up a slope."

"This is incredible Dor, I really don't know how we can ever thank you for your kindness."

"You don't, I owe you both my life, without you I wouldn't have the life I have had, I will continue to thank you for the rest of my life." All three hugged each other. "Come on let me show you the kitchen." They walked down to a kitchen as bright as the rest of the house, it was very much a country feel to it. "Right, there is food and drink in here. Kitty went to town on it a bit, I hope I remembered properly what you two liked to eat, you can eat with us at the main house or if you are feeling like you want time out then you can stay here. It's your choice. If you need anything just shout. I will leave you both alone now, if you want to come over at dinner time do but you have plenty here if you just want to lay around for the evening."

"Thank you, right now I just want to lay down."

"Agreed, maybe we will skip dinner and just chill out." G winked at Dorian.

"Sounds like a plan, I will see you both in the morning for breakfast then, get lots of rest I will let the others know."

Dorian left heading back to the main house, both G and Moses walked into the lounge. Moses crashed down onto the sofa, G did the same across from him.

"How are you doing Brother? You look knackered."

"I am, trying to keep up the pretence today has been hard work, I'm sorry If I am expecting a lot from you and keeping a lot of it to yourself."

"Fuck off Moses, don't you try and do that shit with me. I'm here for you, I don't care what you need to do to survive, I will keep every damn secret you need if it kills me in the process."

"Sorry, I know and I appreciate that, as I would for you."

"Right now shut your eyes and sleep a while unless you are going to bed?"

"No, I'm okay here, you can still watch the TV though it won't disturb me."

"No need I am going for a stroll outside. I will be back in a while." Moses got comfortable kicking his boots off. He sunk into the sofa. G got up and pulled the blanket off the back of the sofa laying it over him. He went outside and wandered up into the trees. He knew this was a huge garden, well it was an estate, he needed time out too and knew this would give him a great amount of time.

Moses slept for a couple of hours, he woke up hot, it was dusk, he looked over to the other sofa looking for G, he wasn't there, he got up desperate for some water, the house was in darkness, he walked into the kitchen grabbing a glass, he filled it up and headed to his room, he could see some lights outside, he spotted G sat on the sofas with the fire lit. He opened the door.

"What are you doing out here?"

"Just fancied it that's all, had a good walk around the estate, it's beautiful. There is a lake with a waterfall, it's huge, I think it must be where Dor goes fishing."

"Sounds great, look forward to seeing it tomorrow. How long have I been sleeping?"

"A few hours. Are you hungry?"

"I am actually, I really fancy an omlette."

"I can cope with that, do you want cheese or anything in it?" Moses nodded, "let's do it then, it will be good to see you eat something." They both walked into the kitchen, G wasn't a great cook but he could do the basics, he made them both an omelette, they sat in the lounge and ate, Moses was slow but he managed to eat it, G put the TV on for them both, they channel hoped for a while before settling on a film. G had a couple of beers, Moses settled for milk, he said it helped with the feeling of burning inside, which he knew was the radiotherapy. They went to bed early both feeling the effects of the journey and the time difference.

Moses climbed into bed, literally, the mattress was double the normal size he had at home, he sank into it, he was covered in different cushions and pillows, he put a lot onto the floor and sunk his head into a couple of feather ones, within minutes he was asleep. He began dreaming of him and Susan.

They were in the Maldives it was a warm night, the bungalow doors were open, the air coming off the sea was lifting the white thin net hanging over the doors. It was early hours of the morning and the moon was bright, giving some light in the room as it reflected off the water. Moses was hot he moved the sheet from his body pushing it down the bed. He laid on his back, his legs slightly open. He was still sleeping. The breeze was teasing him. His cock was hard standing tall and proud. Susan was awake, she was laid on her side looking at him. She could just make out his features, she pushed the sheet off her. She began to run her hand slowly up and down his body drawing patterns across his chest. Moses moaned gently. Probably dreaming of her doing it. She circled his nipple, which hardened instantly. She moved closer into him, licking it. Flicking her tongue back and forth across it. His cock twitched. She moved down the bed wrapping her hand around his now throbbing cock. His body responding moving into her. His hips getting higher as her hand reached the base of his cock. His legs opened slightly more, she moved to the end of the bed between his legs. She teased the inside from his foot up to his knee, she continued to lick up to his thigh, kissing him leaving tiny kisses until she reached his balls. His legs opened wider, he reached for his cock. His hand moved down to his balls cupping them. His moans becoming louder. Susan gently moved his hand away and started to lick them, she sucked one into her mouth gently. His hand moved to her head. His moans getting louder. He pushed Susan further onto him, filling her mouth with him.

"Babe?" he whispered looking down questioningly. Realising it was real. Susan stopped looking up at him smiling. Moses reached for her beckoning her to him. She crawled up his body. Laying on top of him, she reached his lips, grazing them with her tongue. Her pussy was at the tip of his cock. Moses opened her legs with his, pulling her up so her legs were either side of him. She moved herself, so her clit was laid on his cock. She began to move herself back and forth, the friction bringing her close to orgasm. She was so wet it covered his cock. Moses moved her faster holding tight to her hips, his cock throbbing underneath her. Susan bit her lip trying to be quiet. She didn't want to wake anyone in the next bungalow. She dug her nails into his chest. Her orgasm getting closer. Her clit rubbing the tip as she moved. Moses sensed it, he lifted her, his cock sliding into her easily. He pushed her down onto him, she felt her pussy open for him, he was well endowed, she could feel every part of him. Her body tingled at the feeling. She leant forward getting the pressure where she needed it. Moses pushed up into her holding her down on him. Her body was on fire. She began to ride him faster chasing her orgasm now. Their bodies now erratic trying to find the right pace for them both. Susan felt alive, her body heating up. She began to tingle more, her pussy pulsating on him she knew she was about to explode. She clenched around him. Her eyes fogged over, everything white as her body trembled, her eyes rolled back as her orgasm hit her. Her body jerking against him. She was desperate not to scream out, she bit her lip harder, Moses pushed harder into her, smiling wanting more. She became sensitive to touch but Moses wasn't stopping. He pushed her back laying her down, getting onto his knees, pushing her legs open.

Lifting her bottom as he slid back into her. His thumb rubbed her clit in circles. She clenched around him again, on and off, wanting to make him cum. He fucked her hard, as she screwed up the bedclothes arching her body into him. She couldn't breath, she was exhausted. Moses slowed down, so she could catch her breath, he lifted her legs onto his shoulders, giving her a few seconds rest, he rubbed her clit with his cock, smiling at her. He pushed into her hard, pulling her closer, pounding harder into her. Chasing his own orgasm. Their eyes locked. Moses groaned he was close, his head rocked back. Susan teased him again.

"Cum for me Moses." He whimpered as his cock emptied into her, he was pushing against her, she squeezed her legs as his body trembled. He let her legs go laying them onto the bed, leaning onto her, kissing her nipple biting gently.

"Jesus woman, I thought I was dreaming, wow you can wake me up like that anytime you like. He laid down next to her pulling her into him, kissing her head as they laid together. Drifting off to sleep exhausted.

Moses woke up, his hand on his cock, for a few seconds he forgot where he was, then he remembered. He looked down at himself.

"Wow, well you still work, that's a good sign." He sat up in bed, desperate to pee, but knowing it would be a little difficult with his cock so hard. He went to the bathroom and waited, returning once he had gone, climbed back into bed, he laid thinking about the dream. Before sleep took him again.

Chapter 19

Final Dress preparations

It was dress day for the girls. Gwen was excited to see the dress she was wearing and moreso the dress Jane had picked, she knew pictures didn't do it justice. They also had the big surprise at Dorians, Gwen and Kitty had worked on the menu together and were happy with their choices.

Jasper had asked Jane to visit a client with him, she needed a new dress as he had stressed how important it was. She accepted without question and asked Gwen and Chicca to help her find something to wear. She always had her black dress to fall back on but fancied something nice. The girls arrived early, ready to go, Jane was still getting ready when they arrived. It gave them a great opportunity to chat to Jasper.

"So, did she just accept it?" Gwen asked.

"Yes, no questions at all, she trusts me though, but I'm not sure she will after this wedding is over."

"Will you tell us what you have planned?" Chicca asked.

"Not a chance, you will know the day before, I can't risk anyone slipping up."

"Does she know where the honeymoon is?"

"No Chicca and no I won't tell you either."

"Spoil sport." She pouted, "You know you want to tell us really, she cuddled into him making him laugh.

"No, I promise you I don't, ask all you like, I'm saying nothing."

"Damn, if I do that to James he gives in easily."

"More fool him then", Jasper was laughing as Jane came into the kitchen.

"Hey Belle, can you please take these crazy women out of here."

"Are they badgering you like I do?"

"Yes they are." He smiled.

"You have no chance, I have offered more sex, he still isn't moving on it."

"Okay, how about we pull out the big guns, a threesome with me and Jane?"

"Ummmm, let me think about that for a second." He tapped his bottom lip with his fingers. "It's still a no." he laughed as Jane cuddled into him. "I'm bloody glad you said that." Jane looked shocked and laughed at Chicca.

"You two are no fun, come on let's get out of here, we have shopping to do. See you later JDubz."

"See ya girls, have fun, don't be late back Belle, you know what you are like getting ready." Jane turned and poked her tongue out at him as she walked out of the door making Jasper laugh.

The three of them climbed into Chicca's car and headed into town. The music was on loud and they all began singing and laughing. Chicca turned the music down to talk to the girls.

"So, hen night, we are having two, one with Susan and Alison, it's an open event at Alison's place, you know the one she told us about, anyway it's guests only and of course we are invited, the other is at our club with the rest of the girls. Don't ask me anymore though as I won't be telling you, just have a think about what you want to wear when we go with Alison, it's going to be a hot night so something simple I think would be best."

"A hot night, meaning, don't think I am going to get involved in any of that hanky panky stuff, I don't share." Jane frowned looking at both girls.

Chicca laughed, "Has she always been a prude Gwen?"

"Oi, I'm no prude I just don't share that's all." Both girls laughed at Jane.

"She's teasing you silly. What are you so uptight about?"

"Oh nothing, just silly stuff that's all. Sorry."

"Ummmm, no spill love, talk to us."

Jane harrumphed, slapping her hands down onto her legs like a little girl. "Oh, I don't know. Have you actually looked at Moses, I mean really looked at him? I'm scared to death, I'm scared at how I feel about him, is it because of Susan? I told Jasper, he said it was okay and to be expected, I just can't get my head around it all and I'm supposed to be the bloody counsellor." Jane folded her arms around herself.

Gwen moved between the seats putting her hand on Jane's shoulder. "Right, now listen to me, you love that idiot, Christ knows why, but you do, of course you are allowed to be jealous, but I think this is all because you are scared of losing him, like losing your Dad. Have you spoken to your counsellor about it?"

"No, I haven't, but I will, yes I am scared, I think it's just a shock, you guys have seen the weight come off him, so I suppose it makes it easier a little. I don't mean that you don't feel it too."

"We know what you mean love. Yes it is easier when you are closer, but seeing the dramatic change in him over the weeks has been awful, he swore us to secrecy too. We have been doing his washing, cleaning, cooking. G even does his ironing."

"Bloody hell that's a first, nobody does his ironing."

"Exactly. I'm sure the worst is over and he knows what needs to be done to be well for the wedding. It will be all okay, you mark my words love."

"Thanks Gwen", Jane put her hand on top of Gwen's. "Come on then let's get this show on the road."

"Whoop, whoop." Chicca cheered as they headed into the car park. They climbed out and almost ran into the dress shop. Both ladies were waiting for them smiling watching as the girls composed themselves before walking in.

"Welcome ladies, how excited are we today?" Sasha smiled.

"Very, this is Gwen my maid of honour." Jane motioned behind her.

"Welcome Gwen, let's get you ladies sorted out shall we? This is your final fitting Jane I hope you have been behaving and not starving yourself?"

"I have actually, I just hope I haven't put any on."

"Come on then let's get you sorted out. Ladies, please take a seat, there are drinks on the table for you, enjoy." Jane looked across at the table and spotted Lily sitting there. She had told Jane she couldn't make it, she wanted to surprise her.

"Oh my god! You said you couldn't make it." Lily smiled at her as Jane rushed into her arms.

"I wasn't going to let you down, now was I?"

"You have just made my day, girls this is Lily." All the girls hugged her and went to sit down.

"Oh damn, before I forget Sasha you will need this too." She pulled the tiara box out of her bag and handed it to her.

"How could you forget you had that?" Chicca laughed

"Have you seen the size of her bag, anything could get lost in there, I swear she is Mary Poppins."

Sasha led Jane into the changing room, she closed the curtain as Jane began undressing. Sasha walked up behind her as Jane put her arms up, she slipped the dress over her head, she felt the fabric glide down her body, she helped to smooth it down, as she wriggled, breathing in holding her breath and tummy, ready to be zipped up. Sasha laughed.

"No need Jane, relax darling. Its already zipped up." Jane began to laugh relaxing, her hands gliding across the fabric. She moved her hands around the back to check.

"Are you sure?" she frowned trying to feel the zip.

"Yes, very sure. You look incredible, how does it feel, are you happy with the changes? This is your last chance to do anything else before the big day."

"It looks incredible and feels absolutely amazing to be honest." Jane turned looking at herself trying to see all around it. Twisting from one side to the other. Sasha pulled out the other full-length mirror putting it to one side so Jane could see.

"Right then, Shoes, head dress, veil, then we can open the curtain to your friends.

"Oh my god, I still can't believe this is happening." Jane sat down pulling her dress up so Sasha could put her shoes on. "I love, love, love these. Shame it's a long dress really."

"I'm sure Jasper will enjoy them though." Sasha smiled.

"Oh, I never thought of that, yes he won't have a clue will he. Eeek." Sasha laughed again at Jane's excitement. She finished the shoes helping Jane to stand up. She turned ready for the veil and tiara. She watched as Sasha gently put them both on, the light catching the tiny diamonds in the tiara and on the veil made Jane gasp softly, she covered her eyes with her hands letting out a gentle sob. She opened her fingers a little looking at herself again. Sasha put her hand on her shoulder, squeezing gently. Jane nodded and turned towards the curtain. The girls were sat chatting asking Lily all kinds of questions which she admitted she knew nothing about.

"I swear girls I know nothing, like I said before Chicca, Henry tells me nothing, he knows what I'm like I would have told you everything otherwise." Under her bag she had her fingers crossed. She wasn't a good liar, but she did know a couple of things but promised faithfully she wouldn't say a word.

"I know he is doing something big, I can't wait to see what it is." Chicca fidgeted in her chair as the curtain opened.

All the girls fell quiet, Lily got the tissues out and passed them to the girls either side of her. She gently patted around her eyes, she couldn't believe the difference in the dress in real life. She coughed trying to stifle the sob. She felt so close to Jane in such a short time and couldn't believe how lucky she was to be part of today.

"Oh, my fucking god. Where did our little girl go? look at you all grown up into a beautiful bride."

Gwen jumped up dashing over to Jane, she stopped before she knocked her over, gently touching the fabric, she looked up tears streaming down her face. "Oh bloody hell, that man is going to fall over when he sees you." Jane wiped Gwen's tears laughing at her as she began crying with her, Lily and Chicca came across, they all hugged each other gently.

"Get the tears out of the way now ladies you don't want to do it on the day." Sasha laughed, feeling emotional too, her aunt tutted turning away, wiping her own eyes.

"Oh, the shoes remember, Chicca squealed. She moved back and pulled up the dress gently revealing the shoes to Gwen and Lily."

"Oh, you little strumpet! Jesus, don't tell Jasper, he will be all over you, before you even get down the aisle." The girls laughed. "You can use those in the bedroom. God I need those in my life." Gwen giggled, getting down onto her knees, praying to the shoes, she began stroking them, purring.

Jane cleared her throat. "Ermmmm excuse me, that's my legs you are stroking Gwen." She giggled.

"No, I am stroking these shoes, so hush woman." They all laughed at Gwen as Chicca helped her off the floor.

"Any changes Jane or are you happy?" Jane turned to look at Sasha and her aunt.

"it's perfect, thank you so much. Girls it's your turn now." Jane smiled as Sasha unzipped her getting her out of the dress. She had also been doing her own secret shopping. The girls looked at her confused.

"What are you talking about?" they asked in unison.

"Come with me ladies, you okay now Jane if I leave you?"

"Yes of course." Jane got herself dressed as the girls followed Sasha and her aunt to the other changing area.

"Hi girls how are you?" Jane dialled Linda and Jax before she went into the changing room.

"Hey you, what are you doing, where are the others, I thought you were getting your dress today?" Linda questioned.

"I am, but you two needed to be part of this next bit, come on I will show you." Jane walked through into the changing area, she sat down as the three girls were being sized up. She turned the camera onto the others. They whooped and cheered as they saw Gwen and Chicca.

"Ladies I would like to introduce you to Lily."

"Hi Lily." They waved, smiling.

Sasha took Gwen and Chicca into the first changing area and her aunt took Lily who looked really confused. Jane sat smiling turning the camera back.

"Okay girls, today you will see the dresses I have picked for you, I gave Sasha all your pictures of dresses you have worn since I have known you all and she has come up with an amazing dress that will suit you all. Plus Lily has one the same colour too but different, I wanted her to be a big part of today too." Both girls squealed with excitement. "I hope you don't mind. I know I said we would just grab a dress each when you arrived, but I couldn't do that."

"My god no we don't mind, this is so exciting. Hurry up you two I want to see what we are wearing!" Jax squealed shouting at Chicca and Gwen.

Lily came out first in a taupe dress. The sleeves we long and came in at the wrist. The dress was a high V neck A-line dress, the fabric was soft and floaty. Lily was smiling, she was wearing a pale gold sandal with a small heel and strap around the ankle.

"Jane I am confused, but I have to say this is beautiful."

"You have become a very special part of our lives and we both agreed we wanted you to be in the position of Mother of the Bride, Groom if you don't mind?"

"Oh, Jane are you sure? that is wonderful, of course I would be honoured to do that." She wiped her eyes, trying not to cry too much.

"The big question is do you like the dress? If you don't then please say so. Henry helped us with pictures so Sasha could find the right dress, but you need to be happy in it."

"Happy? I am ecstatic, but I wasn't supposed to be here?"

"We were going to send it to you today after the girls tried theirs on. It was lucky you turned up. We just need to make sure it doesn't need any alternations for you."

"Henry you are in big trouble when I get home." She looked up shaking her fist laughing.

The other curtain opened and outstepped Gwen and Chicca. They were both smiling and grabbed Lily when they saw her. The three stood together.

"Well? Put me out of my misery please?" Jane winced covering her face. Gwen and Chicca nodded at Sasha, swinging their dresses from side to side. They were also taupe, full length, A-Line scoop neck in chiffon. The backs were open, with a gentle diamond shape in the middle of the back. They had the same colour shoes as Lily but theirs were slightly higher.

"Are you kidding me, they are ours?" Linda squeaked.

"Yes love, don't you like it?"

"No I fucking love it! Christ the men will wonder what has happened with us being all scrubbed up for the day, what do you think girls?"

"Bloody beautiful Jane, really lovely. Jax shouted, she was nodding as the girls turned showing the dresses off."

"I feel a million dollars, James is going to collapse in a heap when he gets a look of me."

"Same for me." Gwen giggled. "You have done a wonderful job Sasha."

"it wasn't all me, this lady is the mastermind I have learnt it all from her." She grabbed her aunt around the shoulders kissing her on the cheek. She slapped her hand smiling.

"Oh, stop it you silly girl, people will think I like you." She squeezed Sasha back kissing her cheek.

"Okay girls let's check you over and make sure there are no alternations to be done. I will see you two next week when you arrive, come straight in and we will make sure your dresses fit too."

"Next week? I don't think so?"

Jane grinned. "Ummmm, yeah, she is right, that's my fault, I sorted it with the guys. All arranged."

"Jane, oh my fucking god, this is amazing news", both girls were jumping up and down on their phones. "Are the men coming too?"

"No love, you have a week of freedom." Jane was grinning from ear to ear, so excited to be seeing her friends.

"Even bloody better. I don't get to feel like I am a spare part then." Jax grinned.

"That depends on Billy doesn't it?"

"Oh behave, he's just joking." Jax dismissed it quickly not wanting the others to pick up on it.

"You don't get away that easily lady, spill the beans." Jane teased.

"Billy has the hots for Jax, since you left actually, he flirts all the time and she is pretending not to notice." Gwen spilled quite easily laughing.

"Is Billy the guy that found Helen? He's a hottie girl, don't turn that down!" Jane laughed.

"You have James remember, I think he might have something to say about that."

"Pffttt, he won't mind sharing." She shrugged her shoulders laughing.

"Come on girls, let's get changed and we can talk about this later, I'm sure Sasha and her aunt have more customers to see today?"

"Thanks Gwen, we are intrigued now though, you have to come back and share this."

"Oh we will, if you fancy a night out come and join us. I will text you the information."

"Wonderful thank you so much. Sounds just what I need."

The girls went back into the changing rooms and got changed, Jane turned the camera and told the girls the tickets were ready at the airport and Jasper was emailing them flight times.

Sasha came out of the changing room as Jane was looking through the dresses on the rails.

"You looking for something else Jane?"

"Yes and no, I have a dinner tonight with Jasper, nothing special it's a work thing I just wondered if I could find something simple but nice for the night. He prefers me in dresses so I said I would see if I can find something."

"Okay let's have a look for you. We have plenty of things that can be dressed up if needed. Do you want to stay away from black?"

"Yes, if I can."

"How about this then." Sasha held up a cream sleeveless sheath knee length dress. With a fake wrap at the skirt, closed with 3 large gold buttons.

"Wow love that, can I quickly try it on?"

"Of course you can come on." They walked to the changing area that she went to the first time she went into the shop for her evening dress. She slipped the dress on and loved it. it was simple but business like without being black.

"Jane, it looks perfect, elegant but formal. It does have a little jacket if you need it but to be honest it is warm enough to go without, a pair of black heels will finish the look."

"I love it too. Thank you so much Sasha."

"You're very welcome. Let me pack it for you, would you like to finish your shopping and pop back later for it, so you don't need to carry it?"

"That would be fantastic, thank you." Jane got changed and headed out to meet the girls.

They were all waiting for her as she came out. She was pleased she had found something now the rest of the day was fun shopping.

"Right then ladies, I think it's lunchtime?"

"Sounds like a bloody good idea to me." Chicca grumbled rubbing her stomach.

"Excuse Chicca Lily, she is always hungry, she gets very hangry too."

"Cheeky cow no I don't." she whined.

They replied in unison. "Yes, you bloody do." Chicca huffed folding her arms marching off. They all laughed at her.

"Come on grumpy pants, where do you want to eat?" Jane called after her. She stopped turning to look at the café next to them.

"This one, it's very expensive and Jasper is buying."

"Oh is he now?" Jane laughed at her. Gwen scowled at her. Shaking her head behind Jane.

"I meant you, not him that's the trouble when you both have the same initials." Jane laughed ignoring it as they all walked in.

They sat laughing and joking as plate after plate came out of tasters for them. Jasper had already paid for their meals, he had told the girls where to go, it was a friend of his. He knew they would be well looked after. They spent the next few hours laughing and giggling, Lily had never felt so relaxed in a long time, she was enjoying every minute. She knew Henry was at the house with Jasper and they were meeting Dorian later. She was excited to be meeting him and to meet the rest of her friends, she sat back looking at the girls enjoying seeing the friendship they had, it reminded her of friends she had back in her younger days.

Chapter 20

More surprises

Jane arrived home in plenty of time to get ready for the dinner, she had an amazing day and was thrilled at how great it went with everyone, especially the girls loving their dresses.

She bounded in the door with her shopping bags, walked into the lounge and collapsed in a heap on the sofa with all her bags around her, she slumped down her arms spread out sighing, she had walked her legs off with the girls, spent a huge amount of money which didn't bother her, she had it to spend but always worried after. She knew it was a hangover from her ex, he questioned everything she ever spent and on more than one occasion took a slap or a punch for buying something he felt she didn't deserve.

Jasper came up behind her while she had her eyes closed relaxing, he smiled looking at all of the bags she had surrounding her. He bent over the sofa and kissed her head softly, Jane looked up smiling opening one eye to look at him.
"Hi gorgeous, how was your day?" he kissed her nose, walked around the sofa moving the bags to one side. "Well, it looks like you had a good day?"
"I did thank you it was amazing, oh my god I forgot to tell you too, Lily turned up, it was so lovely to see her, she looked incredible in her dress. Henry will absolutely love it!" Jane was excited and gesticulated so much with excitement.

Jasper smiled knowing full well she was there, they had arranged it all. He wanted the build up to their wedding to be something she would always remember and the days after. Jane turned in her seat lifting her leg onto the sofa leaving her other on the floor, it still gave her pain when she didn't rest it, she needed to be off her feet for a while before the dinner, she didn't want to have to sit down whilst being around people she didn't know. Jasper sat down with her smiling, he was waiting to hear everything and the excitement as she got carried away telling him about her day, he loved how she bounced from one thing to the other. He lifted both her legs putting them onto his lap, he took her shoes off and began rubbing her feet for her while she filled him in on her day.

"So, when do I get to hear about your dress then?"

"Ha, ha, you can't catch me out that easily, you will have to wait. I'm leaving it at the shop so you can't peak."

"Damn, I will wait until you are sleeping then ask, you will tell me then." He teased.

"Well then I will sleep in the spare room then, or gag myself?"

"Ohh, you like gagging you never told me that?" he couldn't help but tease her. She pushed her foot into his leg.

"Stop teasing you know I want this to be a surprise." Japer laughed tickling her feet. Jane began squealing kicking him with her other foot desperate to get away.

"Hey where is Lady she would normally be bouncing all over us by now?"

"Ernie has taken her for a couple of days, well, until tomorrow night, I didn't want her to be on her own too long, she is with Davison anyway."

"What a lovely idea. It's very quiet here without her though."

"Yes, but it gives me more time to tease you." Jasper twisted grabbing her around her waist, Jane squealed louder, shouting for help, giggling. Jasper laughed pulling her up, letting her breath. He pulled her onto his lap. She sat astride him, her hair tousled.

"You get more beautiful everyday Belle. Even when your hair is all over the place." He pulled at some of the strands that were across her face. Jane helped him trying to sort it out. He pulled her into him, his lips brushing hers, his tongue teasing her. She grabbed his face with both hands sucking his tongue into her mouth. Jasper was trying to pull away but couldn't, he was mumbling, Jane couldn't understand him just raised her eyebrows smiling at him. She let go, he sat with his tongue out for a few seconds, Jane slowly slid off his lap knowing she needed to run before she got caught. She backed away as he sat up, she turned and ran towards the bedroom as fast as she could. Jasper was hot on her heels grabbing the door as she tried to close it. she was squealing again, giggling not sure what to do. She ran towards the shower, as she grabbed the door Jasper pulled her down on top of him on the bed.

"Now you will pay for that", Jane continued giggling and squealing, he turned her over, laying on top of her, spanking her bottom, before pulling her top up and blowing raspberries on her bare skin. They tussled for a few minutes until neither could catch their breath, Jasper laid flat out on the bed his arms outstretched, Jane laid in a ball on her side. She was smiling, realising how happy she really was and how easy Jasper made falling in love with him. She turned over leaning on his stomach, his t-shirt was pushed up his chest showing his stomach, Jane smiled looking up at him, circling his belly button with her nail, Jasper squirmed under her. He put his hand under his head so he could watch her. She continued, her touch very light, biting her lip she looked up at him. Jasper groaned watching her. He looked at the clock they needed to get sorted but he didn't want to stop.

Whispering he caught Jane's eye. "If you don't stop, we will be late." Jane smiled, continuing. Jasper growled desperate for her. He grabbed her hand, put his leg over her body and span her over. He sat astride her, his shorts tight across his body showing his already hardening cock. Jane moved her arms so she could reach him, she rubbed his cock through his shorts with her left hand, beckoning him upwards with her right. Jasper smiled, raising his eyebrow questioning her. Jane nodded, he moved himself sitting up on his knees, crawling up further, his legs under her armpits. Jane pushed her hand up the leg of his shorts, she was glad they were soft fabric and stretchy. His cock was now hard, she pulled it towards the leg opening. Jasper groaned, whispering to himself. As she took it in her hand.
"Jesus, fuck. Yes." She moved her head towards him, kissing the tip. Jasper groaned again, she knew he was desperate for more. Gently, she licked the underside, flicking her tongue up and down, then over the tip. Jasper jolted. She slid her tongue down his length keeping eye contact with him, her spare hand slide down the underside, she pushed her finger into the base of his cock between his balls, Jasper pushed forwards again, moaning deeply. Jane smiled. She licked back to the tip covering his head with her mouth and slid down his length, she knew she couldn't take it all, Jasper also knew her limits and pushed gently into her hot mouth, his groans getting louder with each push the deeper he got, the more intense the feeling. Jane cupped his balls squeezing gently, rolling them in her palm. Jasper grunted, pushing further in. Jane wrapped her hand around the base of his cock and began rubbing harder, he tried to stop, she wanted this, she wanted it to be about him, she didn't want him to have to give her anything this is what she wanted. He looked down at her cupping her face, shaking his head. Jane

nodded taking more of his cock in her mouth, Jaspers groaning getting louder, she knew he was going to cum, she wanted it, she wanted him to feel dominant over her. She had never felt so trusting of someone, she was desperate for this. She took his hand placing it on head, pushing herself as much as she could without gagging and pulled back, Jasper understood and began pushing at her, Jane nodded letting him know it was okay.

"Fuuuuuuck!" he whispered as he slid in and out slowly, his head falling backwards. "Oh Jesus Belle, you really don't know how good this feels, I fucking love you so much." Jane smiled as she got faster.

She wanted him to cum now, she knew he was almost there, his legs were opened wide, she pushed her finger into her mouth making it wet then slid her hand between his legs, finding the spot just below his balls, she rubbed getting close to his bottom, He almost stood as she continued.

"Please don't stop, please don't stop, his voice trailing to a whisper as he was losing all control. Jane sucked faster. She felt his balls harden, his cock stiffened as he came, hard.

"Arghhhhhhhh, fucking hell, yes, yes, yes Belle, Oh my goooooodddd." He began panting his body, convulsing, his cock became ultra sensitive as Jane continued sucking swallowing everything he had. He was desperate to pull out but Jane wanted more, he looked down at her laughing, begging her.

"Please stop, Baby please, I can't take it." He laughed. Jane did as he asked. Pulling his cock out of her mouth. Jasper sat back onto his legs, sighing, feeling exhausted and exhilarated. He moved himself laying next to her, pulling her into his arms. He kissed her nose.

"Wow, I didn't expect that, thank you love."

"Don't thank me, I enjoyed it too." He grinned at her like a school boy, hugging her tight.

"Can I just sleep a little now please?" he laughed knowing full well they needed to get ready. Jane pushed up off his chest sitting up.

"No chance come on, you have to wash my hair for me now too, I can't go out looking like I have been dragged through a hedge backwards." Jasper moaned sitting up.

"Okayyyyyyy." He walked around the bed grabbing Jane carrying her into the shower. They were quick to get ready, helping each other in the shower. Jasper dried Jane's hair for her and went to get dressed leaving Jane to do her make up, he walked past her, she followed the smell of him as he walked by.

"Mmmmmmm, you smell yummy tonight."

"Thanks love, Gwen gave me some testers the other day, you know from her friend Laura? she told me my aftershave was out dated, so I thought I would try some." He walked over to her pushing his neck out. "What do you think of this one?"

"Oooohh I like that one. What is it?"

"Not sure I will tell you later when I find the card it's on. Don't choose yet though we have a few to go through." Jane stood back looking him up and down licking her lips, he slipped his hands into his pockets, his left leg cocked out. He had his favourite watch on his left hand, Jane smiled, she loved how masculine his hands were. He had dark blue trousers on and a pale blue shirt, the neck was open, showing the V Jane loved in his throat. Smiling she ushered him away, he hadn't seen her dress yet it was completely different to what she normally wore.

"Go, go, go, I need to dress, you are distracting me." Jasper smiled winking at her as he turned and walked away. He grabbed his phone texting the others letting them know they would be on time.

Jane slipped her white lace bra and thong on, bending over to get her breasts into position she smiled looking down at them. "I do have nice boobs." She grinned standing up. Her thong was tiny but comfortable, the straps sat on her hips. She pulled on her hold ups, they were a natural skin colour, she felt good in them and with the thong she felt sexy. Jasper walked in with her bags as she was bent over the bed adjusting her pull ups.

"That is heaven right there." He slapped her bottom kissed her rose, licking her bottom he stood up hanging her dress on the door. "Do we really need to go?" Jane laughed.

"You set this up remember."

"Damn yes I did, okay, get dressed I will be in the lounge." Jane unzipped her dress taking it off the hanger, she smiled looking at it again, surprised, she would never have looked at it on a hanger. She undid the side zip, putting it over her head. She zipped herself up with ease and smoothed it down, turning side to side looking at herself. She grinned knowing how good she looked, she twisted her hair and brought it over one shoulder, tucking the other side behind her ear.

"Wow girl, you're looking good." She put her hand on her hip pouting in the mirror. She turned away happy with what she saw, grabbed her black heels putting them on, picked up her wrap and clutch bag and headed out. She walked into the lounge where Jasper was sat in the chair waiting. He looked up, his jaw dropping open. He wolf whistled and beckoned her to spin around.

"Wow, wow, wow, we are definitely going to be late, or maybe give it a rain check." He got up moving towards Jane, putting his hand on her hip pulling her into him. Jane smiled kissing him. His hand moved down her bottom to the top of her stockings. He sucked in through his teeth, pulling her dress up slowly. He nuzzled her neck breathing gently, kissing her. Jane stopped him moving away.

"Come on we don't want to be late and upset your client, let's do this then we can get home and enjoy it more." Jasper groaned, looking down at his hardening cock.

"Sorry buddy, the boss says no." Jane laughed slapping him on the arm.

"What? I was just telling him." Jane grabbed her things and walked out into the garage as Jasper set the alarm. He opened the door to the Ferrari, Jane sat down and swang her legs in, he pulled her seatbelt out for her as she strapped herself in.

"Remember Belle, don't get your foot caught getting out this time." Jane poked her tongue out as he walked around the car laughing.

"So where is this place we are going to?"

"Across town, in the posh part. You will see, it won't take long to get there." He put his hand across and took hers. "You look gorgeous Belle, that dress really does suit you."

"Thank you, Sasha picked it for me, I wasn't sure until I tried it on, but now I love it."

"Good I'm glad. Did you enjoy lunch?"

"We did thank you, very naughty of you though, I can pay my way you know."

"I know love, but I enjoy spoiling you, I can't help it." She lifted his hand kissing his knuckles.

"Thank you so much for being you, I am very grateful for everything you do. Just please let me pay for things. I don't want to be a kept woman."

"Belle you are not a kept woman, the house is paid for, as are the cars, all we do is pay household and food, that isn't a lot at all. But if you want to pay towards it then that's ok too, I just don't think about it to be honest. It's not intentional I promise."

"I do, I want to go fifty, fifty, straight down the middle, on everything. Including the wedding."

Jasper scratched his head. Ummmmm, okay, can we do that after the wedding though, we did agree I could sort the venue and food." He was getting hot, he was dreading her asking to see any bills.

"Okay, just promise we can do this?"

"Of course we can love. I promise. We are here almost."

Jane looked out of the window, it was almost dusk, but she could see the houses and the lights that were on already. Jasper pulled into the driveway, stopping at the gate, the guard had already been primed not to mention Dorian. Jasper opened his window.

"Hi, Jasper Mitchell and Jane Kirkpatrick, we are expected."

"Yes sir of course, please follow the road around to the main house, you will be met at the door." He smiled at Jasper as he opened the gate.

"Wow this place is huge, who the heck are we seeing, I thought you said it was a client?"

"It is love. You have met him before. Can you see where the road goes it's getting a bit dark." He was worried now, she was getting suspicious. He was trying to distract her. The road bent round, shrubs were on either side, a bit like the B&B, but on a massive scale, you could just make out the lawn area, leading to outside buildings and the bungalow.

Jaspers hands began to sweat, he knew Jane was going to go nuts at him but love it all the same. They drove past the garages where he knew Dorian kept his bikes and classic cars, he was looking forward to talking to him about those. The house came into view, Jane gasped as they pulled up.

"If I knew we were coming somewhere as posh as this I would have dressed up more. Why didn't you tell me Jasper, I feel really under dressed."

"Belle, listen, you look gorgeous, stop worrying, I told you this is an informal chat with a client, nothing more. Just dinner." He climbed out of the car walking around to Jane's side, he opened the door giving her his hand, she spun in her seat putting her legs out of the door before standing. She was always nervous now in this car after her first ride and making a fool of herself, but it did get her the man she wanted, so not all bad. Jane took a deep breath smoothed down her dress turning to Jasper. "Does my make-up and hair look okay?"

"Yes, you are perfect now come on." He took her hand again leading her to the door. As they approached it opened. Kitty stood there smiling at them both.

"Good evening please come in, you must be Jane and Jasper? I'm Kitty the housekeeper and friend. Follow me."

"Yes, we are, pleased to meet you." They stepped into the house following Kitty to the lounge.

"If you would like to take a seat, make yourself at home I will be back shortly, can I get you anything to drink. Champagne, wine?"

"Oh, thank you, Champagne would be nice but don't open it specially." Jane smiled.

"Oh, it will get drunk there is no fear of that." Kitty smirked as she walked away. Jasper turned to Jane taking her hand kissing it. She was looking around the huge lounge.

"Wow what a place, this is huge, I bet it has an awesome library. I would love to sneak off and have a look, do you think they would mind? Who is it again, sorry I forgot."

Jaspers mind was running over time, he was frantic to think of a name. Jane stood and walked across the room to the huge fireplace, she turned to look at Jasper.

"Mr Dor, Belle." He chocked back the last part of the name not wanting to lie to her. She just nodded not really paying attention.

"Is he married, do they have children, it's a big house, what does he do?" Jane continued to walk around the room. Jasper wiped his head, he was going to be rumbled any minute, he didn't have any answers, he needed bailing out.

"No he isn't married, he does something in entertainment I believe." Jane shrugged continuing to walk around the room.

"Right then, are we ready, let me take you through to the dining room. I hope you are hungry? I have left your drinks in there for you."

"Thank you kitty." She opened the doors, the table was laid out for 12 people. Jane turned to look at Jasper, she looked annoyed frowning at him.

"You better start talking Mr, you told me this was a casual evening with dinner, this doesn't look like a casual dinner!" She growled under her breath, now annoyed with him. Jasper knew time was up, he took a deep breath ready to come clean as the door opened. Dorian stepped in his arms folded across his chest. Jane had her back to him feeling embarrassed.

"Well, well, well, someone has forgotten how to enjoy surprises!" Dorian stood there with a huge smile on his face, Jasper sighed heavily with relief. Jane looked at him frowning, she began to turn slowly, she knew the voice but couldn't believe it could be him. Before she had the chance to turn he grabbed her, spinning her around making her squeal. Giving her a huge kiss.

Jane looked dumb struck, then she slapped him, over and over, Jasper started laughing.

"Thank god it's not just me, I was beginning to think she would storm out for a second."

"You're okay now aren't you Half-pint. I hear we have a lot of catching up to do?" Dorian grinned putting her down.

"Okay? You cheeky sod. You have a lot of questions to answer don't you think?" She slapped him again across the chest. "Where have you been, why the secrecy, what are you doing here in Connecticut. Why haven't you messaged back, who's house is this?" She raised her hands around the room.

"Okay I will answer all those questions in a minute, sit down please."

"Who else is coming? It all looks a bit regal?"

"Well, you are pretty special so we put out the best china didn't we Kitty?" Kitty nodded smiling.

"Yeah, yeah, of course you did." She smiled again and began laughing. "God I hate you Dorian, you made me grumpy and I don't like being grumpy." He looked over her shoulder.

"Jasper is she still a grumpy mare when she doesn't get her own way?" He laughed knowing what the answer was going to be.

"Don't get me involved in your arguments. I'm in enough trouble as it is." Jasper shook his hand at Dorian laughing.

"Okay, I tell you what how about a whistle stop tour of the house while we wait for dinner, so yes in answer to your question this is my house."

Jane nodded. "That would be lovely, but I haven't forgiven you yet." She laughed at Dorian screwing her nose up at him. He took her hand and led her out of the dining room.

"Okay this is the one place I know you would love to spend the rest of your evening in alone, but sadly not, but maybe after dinner, or come back some other time and I will let you enjoy it." He pushed the door open to the library, the door was heavy and creaked, Jane walked in her hand shot to her mouth. "Oh my god Dorian it's beautiful! She stood in the middle of the room turning, to drink it in, the room was quite small, it had bookshelves up to the ceiling with a ladder on rails. In the middle was the biggest sofa she had ever seen with dozens of cushions on.

"Do you like it?" he laughed.

"I think I just fell in love." She turned to look at Jasper. As she sat down on the sofa, her feet didn't touch the floor, she sank into it laughing. "This is heaven, can you smell the books. Oh I need this room in my life, and this sofa, it feels like I am sitting on a cloud." She laughed again. Jasper tutted smiling.

"Sorry to disturb your enjoyment Dorian but dinner is ready." Jane pouted as Jasper and Dorian pulled her out of the sofa.

"You can come back later if you like?" Jane nodded frantically making them both laugh. He took her hand again leading her back to the dining room. He pushed the door open and the table erupted.

"Surprise!!!" they all shouted. Jane jumped in surprise. Her hand going to her mouth.

"Now I am confused, is it my Birthday, did I forget someone's anniversary?" everyone laughed. Jasper walked up behind her kissing her on the cheek.

"No Belle, you didn't forget. We just wanted to surprise you with Dorian being back and everyone getting together. We were going to make you wait until the wedding but we knew you would work out something was wrong when you couldn't see the guys at the apartment." She stood with her mouth open. "oh my god! Lily, Henry!! You knew about this didn't you earlier today?" she laughed at herself for being surprised. Lily nodded. She walked around the table hugging and kissing everyone. She whispered in Moses ear. "You okay love?" Moses nodded kissing her.

"Okay I think you all have a lot of explaining to do." Jasper moved her to her seat next to Moses, he sat next to her taking her hand kissing it.

Dorian picked up his glass, "First of all, a toast to the soon to be Mr and Mrs Jasper Mitchell. Or are you getting all new on us and keeping your name?"

"Hell no, I love the sound of Mrs Jasper Mitchell. We will have the same initials then too." She grinned at everyone, holding her chain with the JJ on it. Everyone raised their glasses. Dorian sat as Kitty and her helpers came in with the starters. Jane looked into the dish and began laughing.

"This is old school Dorian." She looked down at her prawn cocktail picking a prawn out that was covered in sauce.

"It sure is. So where do I start..." he began telling Jane about his conversation with Gwen and then with Moses, how he surprised Moses with a flight in his jet at the airport. They chatted through their starters. Kitty got up to help with the main course. Jane laughed when it came in. Steak chips and onion rings.

"Oh my god, you really have gone back in time, what's for pudding Profiteroles or Baked Alaska?"

"Whichever you prefer we have both. This was the last meal we all had together before I went out on my first tour as warm up for Jermaine."

"Jesus Brother, that is going back a bit, will you quit with the ageing thing, I feel old enough as it is." Moses grumbled, laughing, he was feeling exhausted. Jane took his hand squeezing it, she had watched him eating, he left his prawn cocktail but had attempted some of his steak. She leant into him whispering.

"You ok love? If you need to go and rest, its, okay?" She kissed his cheek as she stopped whispering.

He turned smiling at her shaking his head. "Not missing this time with my girl. I have plenty of time to rest when I die." Jane dug him in the leg. "Don't say that it's not funny." She glared at him with her death stare as they called it.

"Shit Brother you're in trouble, what did you say to her?" G teased him.

"Nothing just a joke that is maybe a bit too early to say." He turned to Jane kissing her cheek.

"Sorry love." He half smiled, he was feeling like hell and desperately trying to keep it together for the evening.

Kitty jumped up seeing the pain in Moses eyes. "Right then who wants pudding?" everyone cheered as she collected plates with her helpers returning to the kitchen.

Moses got up heading to the bathroom. He closed the door slumping against it. He closed his eyes for a few seconds sighing heavily. Moving to the sink he turned the cold tap on, bending over he wet his hands cupping water in them splashing it over his face, leaning on the sink he looked up at himself in the mirror, the dark circles under his eyes had began fading, he still looked gaunt, he knew there was no way he could put enough weight on to look well again before the wedding, but he was trying hard. "Come on Brother you can do this, Jane needs you right now, you can't let her down." A stray tear fell, he wiped it away roughly with his finger. "No time for that shit either." He wiped his face in the towel and left the bathroom returning to the dining room. G stood up as he walked in, he stopped him holding onto his arm. The rest of the table was chatting and catching up.

"You okay Brother?" Moses nodded staring straight at Jane. G nodded understanding, letting him go.

The rest of the evening was filled with laughter and many trips down memory lane, Jasper watched Moses intently, he squeezed Janes knee whispering to her.

"Moses is looking exhausted shall we make a move, give him time to rest, we can come back tomorrow and spend time with him before you go out with the girls?" Jane nodded.

"Guys I hate to break up the party but I am shattered, would you mind if we call it a night?" She looked around at Moses winking. He smiled nodding gently to thank her.

They all stood, Jane went around the table hugging and kissing everyone.

"I hear it's your hen night tomorrow?" Dorian asked.

"Yes it is, we're off down the club, a few of the girls are planning things as well as this lot, I have no idea what is going on but I can imagine it won't be pretty." Jane laughed looking at the others pretending to be innocent.

"Well I will send my limo for you, then nobody has to worry about getting home and the guys can relax too. If you all want to come here guys, we can have a bit of fun if you like, there are plenty of toys here to play with?" All the men looked at each other nodding. Dorian had suggested it then he knew Moses could go and rest if he needed.

"We are travelling home tomorrow, Lily has a few things she needs to sort out, we have some visitors coming to the house next week."

"Are you sure you are both welcome to stay longer?"

"Thank you Dorian, we really do need to go, but thank you so much for allowing us to stay in your beautiful home."

"You are welcome anytime, even if I am out of town and you are visiting you can always stay, Kitty would be glad of the company I'm sure?"

"He's right I would. Please come back soon. But for now, we will let you all get to bed, see you in the morning." Kitty smiled hugging Lily.

"Thank you, we will do that." She turned to Jane and Jasper hugging them both. "We will be leaving early, so won't see you in the morning, but we will see you at the wedding." Jane hugged everyone they all said their goodnights.

They got into the car, Jane sat back in the seat smiling at Jasper as he drove the short journey home.

"Wow, that was a shock, you knew too? I can't believe that. How long have you known?"

"Moses rang me when he heard from him, Dorian then called me and asked if he could help me set up a surprise for you. The guys didn't want to be there without you enjoying time there too, or you wouldn't have known until the wedding."

"I still can't believe it. We haven't seen Dor for years, he has been touring for so long. What are the chances that he is finished for the year and he meets up with us all?"

"It wasn't by chance Belle. I don't know if you remember the guys that came to find you, well they are great friends with Dorian apparently, he rode with them for a while years back before he found his fame, anyway when they heard about Moses, Bullet rang Dorian to let him know. He was supposed to be doing some more work and travelling but he told his media team to cancel everything, he wants to be around for anything Moses needs, you know how Dorian feels about Moses?"

"Yes I do, he has never hidden the fact, he teases Moses now but I know when we were younger he would get angry with himself over Moses, I think that's why he never settled with anyone else, he has had his fair share of men and he plays the field, but he loves Moses. I can imagine what this is doing to him."

"Pretty much the same as how it is affecting you Belle." Jane smiled at Jasper pulling his face to hers kissing him hard. I am so damn lucky that I have you."

"No love, we both are. I am counting the days until you become my wife. I still can't believe it."

"Ohhh, you really do make me melt Mr, do you know that. I still pinch myself some nights watching you laying there sleeping next to me. I love looking at your body, when the light catches it I get horny and want to eat you up."

"Hmmmm, and why haven't you? I am stopping you doing that?" he laughed looking unimpressed.

"I don't want to wake you up." He pulled into the garage dashing round the car to help her out, still chatting as they walked into the lounge.

"Stuff that, wake me up Belle, shit, that's what dreams are made of." He stopped her as she reached the sofa grabbed her kissing her. "Jesus woman you make me hard just looking at you, god help me on our Wedding day, I might need to take something to stop me, or I will be looking stupid stood at the alter with a hard on." They both began giggling. Jasper pulled at his trousers making a tent, pushing his hips out making Jane giggle more.

"Oh my god don't, I will pee myself if you keep making me laugh." She put her hand on his chest, trying to stop herself laughing, they both fell silent, staring at each other. Jasper grabbed Jane pushing his fingers into her hair pulling her roughly towards him, his mouth crashing down onto hers, Jane mewled as she felt their lips touch, his tongue hungrily pushing her mouth open as he searched for hers. Jane moved her hands onto his back, pulling at him, digging her nails into him, longing for more. Jasper pulled off his shirt, smiling at Jane turning her around he unzipped her dress letting it fall to the floor. He groaned just looking at her, catching her hair in his hand he wrapped it around his knuckle bringing it to his nose to smell. He pulled on her bra managing to pop it open as Jane moved her hands letting it fall to the ground, he bent her over the sofa. He groaned. Jane smiled, she loved how he made noises looking at her. She opened her legs feeling wet already, he slid his hand down across her back, moaning, he bent over her kissing her shoulders, sinking his teeth into her. His hand moved lower, one finger slipping inside her thong, he ran it across the lace before pulling them down hard. Jane squealed, excited knowing what was coming next. He spanked her hard on her bottom making her yelp. Her thong now at her feet, she stepped out of them kicking them across the floor.

"Open your legs Belle." Jane smiled biting her bottom lip as she opened her legs wide. Jasper slid his hand between her legs, opening her pussy feeling the wetness of her as his fingers slid deep inside her. "Ohhh, I fuckin love your pussy, always so wet and ready for me. My naughty girl." He slid his fingers slowly in and out of her, Jane put her head down onto the sofa, groaning loudly.

"Jesus Jasper don't stop please", she begged. She pushed her bottom back to him, wanting his fingers deeper inside her. Her body in sync with him, she could feel her pussy pulsating, Jasper pulled his fingers out making Jane groan loudly.

"Fuck no, you can't stop now!" Shocked she turned to look at him, Jasper stood smiling his cock in his hand his trousers around his ankles. "Oh baby I have no intention of stopping." He turned Jane back pushing her head down, he rubbed his cock up and down between her cheeks. Jane groaned impatiently, hitting the cushion.

"Tut, tut Belle you need to learn some patience." He smiled knowing what this was doing to her. He moved his cock down ramming himself into her.

"Oh fuck yes!" Jane yelled as he held her hips fucking her hard. She pushed back into him as he thrust into her, his fingers digging into her hips. Jane was panting as Jasper pushed harder and faster. She gripped the cushions as she grew closer to her orgasm.

"Yes, yes, yesssss." She squealed gripping Jaspers cock as she came hard. She pushed herself back onto him as her body trembled.

"Fuckkkkk, Belle stop please." Jasper begged laughing as Jane continued to clench him hard. "Arghhhh, fuck yes! I'm cumming Belle…." Jasper came, laughing, as he pulled her hips tighter against him as his orgasm slowed, he slumped over her back.

"Jesus that was quick, he slipped out of her pulling her up, he bent to pull his trousers up sinking his teeth into her bottom making her jump. She slapped him as she turned catching him with her nails across his shoulder. She froze as she watched the blood come to the surface. She began to tremble, covering her body with her hands suddenly feeling very vulnerable and scared.

"Ouch, I think I should change your name to Shere khan with those nails, he looked at his shoulder at the scratch she had left. He looked up smiling noticing Jane looked terrified.

"Belle. Baby what's wrong?" he spoke softly as he moved towards her. Jane shook her head grabbing her dress and underwear off the floor. "Baby stop, it's okay. You didn't hurt me." He suddenly remembered why she was backing away, he could see the fear in her eyes. He slowly put his hand out to her, it was like she was in a dream, he moved closer, the house was dark.

"Echo lounge light on." he spoke softly wanting to get some light into the room to help Jane. He moved towards her slowly wrapping his arms around her soothing her constantly.

"It's okay Belle, it's me Jasper. I'm not mad baby, you're safe love." Jane heaved a big sigh and began sobbing, she dropped her clothes onto the floor hugging Jasper tightly like she was trying to stop him leaving her. She shuddered in his arms, He picked her up and headed to the bedroom, he laid her on the bed wrapped her into the duvet and climbed on pulling her into his arms, she cried softly as he soothed her hair. "I got you Belle, it's okay love. Let it go." She openly sobbed, her tears fell for quite some time, her arms moving around his body clenching him. His heart melted, he knew he didn't know everything that had happened to her and he didn't want to know really, it was killing him seeing how she reacted to him. She finally began to relax, her body getting heavier as she drifted off to sleep. She began to mumble, he couldn't understand what she was saying but he had an idea it was her past. He held her tighter wanting her to know she was safe. Her breath became more shallow as she relaxed into a deeper sleep, he didn't want to leave her but he needed to undress. He slid out of bed as slowly as he could trying not to wake her. He crept into the bathroom closing the door behind him, he quickly finished returning to bed, he smiled looking at her, she had sprawled out like a starfish, he knew she was okay, he moved her arm from his pillow climbing into bed before she laid it back across him, he turned her slowly onto her side so he could spoon with her. He snuggled into her shoulder moving her hair out of the way. She purred as he kissed her shoulder. Jasper smiled closing his eyes. Thoughts of her being scared haunting him.

Jasper woke first, Jane was still sleeping, he crept out of bed to make them both a drink. He wasn't sure how she would be feeling when she woke, he felt quite nervous, he knew today was her hen night and he wanted her to enjoy it and let her hair down, he smiled to himself while making the tea imagining her drunk. He didn't hear her creep up behind him. She wrapped her arms around him and kissed his shoulder. He smiled, knowing his girl was good. He turned to look at her.
"How's my girl this morning?" he kissed her gently on the lips.
"I'm good babe thank you, I'm so sorry about last night, I feel really stupid."
"Don't Belle, you have nothing to feel stupid about, that is completely natural, you should know that better than anyone." She nodded agreeing tiptoeing to kiss him back.
"Tea?" He passed her the cup and walked her to the sofa, she had his t-shirt on again, he smiled as it skimmed the top of her legs, it was thin enough to see her nipples through it too which he loved.
They sat cuddled up drinking their tea.

"Big day for you love? Are you looking forward to your hen night?"
"I am, I think I know what to expect but you know what the girls are like."
"God yes, I am glad I won't be there. I think it might get a bit messy."
"Probably, will you be going to Dorians?"
"Yeah, I think so, they boys are on about having a gaming night, Dorian has a snooker table and a huge games room with lots of machines in it,

like pin ball, pool so should be a great night. At least Moses can go and rest when he wants too."

"That's good. It was kind of Dorian to offer us his car too. I've missed that man, he is such a child." She laughed with memories of him.

"We better get sorted then before the girls land on us, do you know what you are wearing?"

Jane laughed. "You are kidding me right, you know what Gwen is like, she will want to dress me."

"Oh lord, maybe I should escape now." He laughed teasing her.

"I don't think so, someone needs to make tea and sort lunch." She grinned up at him. He pinched her bottom making her squeal.

"Come on then." He took their cups leaving them in the kitchen for later. He chased Jane to the bedroom. Making her squeal more as he spanked her making her run.

Chapter 21

Hen night

Gwen and Chicca arrived loudly bursting through the door, arms loaded with dress bags make up and wine.

"Woo hooooo, any body home." Gwen called out.

"Hi honey I'm home." Chicca giggled shouting out. Jasper stood behind the door shaking his head laughing. He pointed to the bedroom, Gwen passed him the holder of wine, kissed him on the cheek leaving a huge red lipstick mark on his face. He screwed his nose up at her. Making her laugh, she grabbed his cheek squeezing it before patting it as she walked away. Chicca waited for Gwen to move, Jasper waited for the impact of Chicca as she ran at him, wrapping her arms and legs around him. She kissed his face over and over making him laugh. Jasper peeled her off him.

"My god I pity any guy who is near you lot tonight."

"Yeah, yeah I know you want to be with us really. You love it."

"That's debatable." He laughed as she walked away waving.

Gwen walked into the bedroom pushing the door wide. Jane was sat on the bed drying her hair.

"I don't think so love, give that to me, tonight you are going wavy, slutty in fact." Jane laughed.

"Have you been drinking already? We have hours yet?"

"I know, it gives me time to prep you, give me your hands, I bet you haven't done your toes in months either?"

"No, I haven't, I don't have time." Chicca came skipping in the door throwing the remaining bags onto the bed.

"What don't you have time for Chick?"

"She said she doesn't have time to do her feet, well I'm sorry every woman has time."

"You know why she doesn't though, have you seen that man she is gonna marry, let's be honest if I had him I wouldn't be wasting time on my toes either unless they were in his mouth." Gwen and Jane laughed as Chicca put her fingers into her mouth.

"Hang on, you have a gorgeous man too, but you do your toes." Gwen said pointing down to her feet.

"Ahhh big difference, I have to keep him interested remember, Jane doesn't have to do that now she won him right from the off."

"Cheeky cow I do try I just don't do my toes, I always do my hands once a week, twice if needed."

"How long have I known you Jane? How long have I drummed it into you, regardless of how comfortable you are with a man there are certain things we need to do, never arrive home looking like the catch dragged you through a bush, always keep your lipstick on, don't let him near you when you need a wax and do your nails!"

Jane shook her head. "If I did that Jasper would think I was having an affair."

"It won't hurt to keep him keen, will it Chicca?" Chicca shook her head.

"She's right babe." Jane huffed shaking her head. Jasper walked in with drinks for the girls, he wasn't opening the wine yet. He knew he could win them over with chocolate and biscuits so he came armed with plenty.

"Hey JDubz do you think it's important for a girl to look her best all the time for her man? How would you feel if toenails are not polished, or the waxing hadn't been done?" Chicca pointed to her pussy making the other two laugh. Jane folded her arms waiting to hear his response.

"To be honest I don't mind either way about the nails, I did love Jane's painted the day we went out to dinner, it was a bit sexy." Gwen looked smug turning to Jane nodding. "However, I would rather my partner was happy and relaxed around me, not thinking she had to make herself up all the time. As for the waxing, I don't care either way, in fact I like a bit of tickle if you know what I mean." He grinned rubbing his beard as he walked away.

"Get out Mr bloody perfect." Gwen shouted after him throwing a cushion off the bed at him.

"I give in with you two. He is too bloody perfect." Jane grinned unfolding her arms. "Howeverrrrr, this doesn't mean you get away with it every day, you will be painting those toes today and on your wedding day, do you hear me?" Jane nodded as did Chicca as she pulled faces behind Gwen making Jane laugh.

"Yes, I have eyes in the back of my head too Chicca." She stopped immediately covering her mouth stopping herself from laughing. "Right then, let's sort this hair out and get the rollers in, then we can sort your hands and toes out. Chicca you can unpack everything please."

"Sure thing. I will do the make up if that's ok with you?"

"Of course, I have everything and more with me, my friend Laura does this makeup called FM, Matt hates it, I spend so much on perfume and make up. he built me a new cupboard to store it all. He knows how to keep me happy."

"Oh I've heard about this stuff, is it really good?"

"Hell yeah. It saves me hundreds to be honest. But let it speak for itself, try it too."

"Thanks Gwen, don't mind if I do."

Gwen got to work on Jane's hair putting in rollers halfway up, Chicca was busy unpacking, sniffing and testing everything she found.

"I'm in heaven right now, I see what you mean. This stuff is awesome. I need this in my life."

"Well, you can always order with her and I will send it across with Jane's parcels we always have something going back and forth. Oh, Jane tell Chicca about your perfume."

"Oh my Baccarat Rouge 540 I love it but it is sooooo expensive, Laura does is for less than £30 for me. The last time I brought some in Harvey Nics it cost me £215."

"Fucking hell woman are you crazy?"

"Have you actually smelt it on me? actually probably not as I ran out." She passed her the new bottle Gwen had given her to smell.

"Wow that's beautiful, I love it. So does it come in the same bottle and everything?"

"No, it just has a number and you don't pay for all the fancy bottles, not that this one does have a fancy bottle, but you know what I mean."

"I'm definitely in then, that will please James, he always complains about how much I have and how expensive it is. Get this girl on the phone!"

"I can do better than that, I have a huge amount of her samples."

"Oh my god give them to me now!" Gwen opened her bag, "I have died and gone to heaven." Chicca began pulling everything out, putting makeup samples on her hand, perfumes in different places. Gwen and Jane sat laughing at her.

"Why are we getting ready this early anyway, when are you two getting sorted? It's barely lunch time. It's only us?" Gwen shrugged her shoulders thinking quickly.

"No reason just an excuse to have some girl time that's all."

"Fair enough." Jane shrugged her shoulders and smiled. Gwen turned her to continue with her hair, she frowned at Chicca whispering to her looking at the time. Gwen slowed down trying to delay time, Chicca went to find Jasper.

"Hey Chicca, everything okay, anything I can do for you ladies?"

"Hi, yeah all good, Jane is asking questions about timing, Gwen is getting slower, any update? I'm too scared to turn my phone on."

"Hang on I haven't looked for a while", he walked over to his phone. "Good news, they are due any time, let's get lunch ready quickly and call Jane and Gwen down." They rushed around getting things ready as the door opened, Linda, Steve and Jax walked in laden down with bags. Jasper put his finger to his lips begging them to be quiet, they all hugged each other and sat down at the table.

"You ready guys?" they all nodded.

"Belle, Gwen are you girls ready to stop for lunch? He called out.

"Give us two minutes Jasper just doing the last curler." They all laughed knowing Jane would go nuts. They sat whispering waiting for her, trying to be quiet.

"Coming." Gwen shouted, they all stayed still waiting for her to come into the room. As she rounded the corner she spotted them and stopped in her tracks.

"Oh my god!!! Where the hell did you come from?" She looked at everyone for answers as they all stood. Jane rushed over to them hugging everyone, wiping her tears away. She turned to look at Jasper. She screwed her nose up, you did this didn't you?" She pointed at him.

"It was a joint effort, we couldn't leave these guys out of tonight, now could we, you were getting the girls over earlier?"

"Ermm, don't forget about me too." Jane froze, she knew who it was and it was the first time she had seen him in a long time. The tears began again as she spun around rushing into Bill's arms. She wrapped herself around him hugging him laughing.

"Please tell me I am dreaming, Is it really you Bill?"

"Certainly is beautiful girl, I wasn't missing this time for anything. However, you could have made an effort." He tugged on her curlers. Jane had forgotten about them in the excitement.

"Oh shit Gwen, you could have made me half decent! Bitch." Jane hugged him tight again. Jax turned smiling at them both. Bill looked over at her winking.

"Not a chance, you would have sniffed it out if I had made you up so early, it was painful taking so much time." Everyone laughed, coming together to hug each other again. Jasper came over to Bill and took his hand to shake it.

"This wouldn't have been possible without your persistence Bill when she was taken, you know I am indebted to you."
"No Brother that was a massive joint effort, without Bullet and the guys it would never have come to an end. I'm just glad I could be here for you both now. It's good to meet you in the flesh. I can see how much you love her and seeing her smile like that tells me how happy she is."
"She completes me Bill, I know that sounds soft hearted but you know she is the best thing to ever happen to me."
"So glad to hear it. I understand what you mean though", he nodded towards Jax smiling.
"Way to go man, that's fantastic news", Jasper patted him on the shoulder grabbing him for a hug.
"Not everyone knows but I think it's about time they do so we will let everyone know before the wedding."
"So happy for you both, she is a great girl, she was an amazing support too. Look after each other."
"Thanks Brother we will, now come on I need time with the little one." They laughed walking back over to Jane. Bill put his hand on her shoulders kissing the top of her head.

"Hey little one, can I borrow you for a little while?" Jane turned to him looking up at the giant in front of her.
"Of course, let's take a walk down the garden." She held Bill's hand and led him outside.
"How are you doing love?" Bill looked down at Jane pulling her into him, his huge arm wrapped around her.
"I'm great, couldn't be happier."
"I can see that. I am so pleased. I just wanted to talk to you, I wanted to make sure there was nothing uncomfortable between us, you know after you were taken?" Jane looked at Bill frowning as they arrived at the rose garden.
"Why would you ever think there was? Without you finding Helen and what you did at the pound I would not be here Bill." She held him tighter as they sat down on her big seat.

"Okay, listen to me, that day was awful, you know you are like a Daughter to me, I was supposed to be here with the others and I let you down. But I suppose I was meant to stay back when it all went wrong. I almost lost Helen, I didn't know what else to do I almost gave up Jane, I have been wracked with guilt since. Thinking about what if I hadn't kept going, If I hadn't gone to the man at the pound or pushed my way into the hospital to see her." He squeezed his eyes with his huge fingers. Jane grabbed his head either side lifting it so she look him in the eye.

"Listen to me, you never gave up, you know we have talked about *what if's* before and we don't talk like that. If we live our lives doing that we will never be happy." Bill nodded sniffing.

"I suppose I needed to tell you, I have struggled with the whole thing for so long. The thought of losing you, I have known you since you were a baby, I am your adopted Dad, we have been through so much together. Watching you destroyed when you lost your parents knowing there was nothing I could do was so painful, you not letting me in with that wanker and never coming to see me, that was hard. Thank god for Moses. When you were taken it was like I failed your parents, I promised your Dad I would always look after you. The thought I could have failed you has been killing me. Since you grew up into the beautiful woman you are, you have been there for me more. I just want to make sure you know how much I love you. How sorry I am and how damn proud I am too." He wrapped his arms around her, squeezing her tight. Jane began sobbing gently into his chest. She hadn't talked to anyone about her parents in such a long time, it hurt too much for her. She pulled away from him looking up into his face.

"You know I thought you were pulling away from me for a while, I thought I hurt you when I moved away."

"Fucking hell child, are you serious?!" He looked hurt and shocked at her. "Tell me you are kidding me."

Jane shook her head. "No, it's true, the last few calls have been brief, when I skype call you never stick around to speak."

"That's because I felt so shit, like I just told you. Little one, you are my family, you are all I have, I know we have the club too, but what we have has never gone away love. I am proud to say I am your other Dad, I helped to bring you up, I changed those damn nappies too remember."

"Enough please, we don't speak about that. Yukkkkkk." Jane screwed up her face making them both laugh. Jane was shaking her hand covering her face in embarrassment.

"So we both got it wrong, very wrong." Jane smiled holding Bills hand.

"Yes we did, we won't make that mistake again will we? Now tell me about this wedding?"

"To be honest I just know about the dresses and the venue, Jasper has done the rest, he asked if he could do it, I said yes."

Bill nodded smiling. "Sounds like you met your match then." Jane grinned.

"Sure have. I have never been so happy, I still struggle at times but he understands."

"That makes me very happy, your Mum and Dad would be too."

"Do you think about them much?" Jane looked up at Bill.

"Yes, all the time, the old gang were inseparable like you Moses and G. We had a lot of fun, partied hard until you came along them our focus changed, you were the be all and end all. Not spoilt by any means but the apple of everyone's eye, like now, with those two big idiots."

Jane laughed through her tears. "I'm scared of losing Moses, he looks so poorly, I know it's because he has lost so much weight. I also feel guilty about it too because he never went home for help because of me, we have talked about it, but I understand you feeling the way you do."

"He would do it all over again love you know that. Regardless of how sick he is. He's also a fighter and he wants to live, don't give up on him."

"Thanks Pappa." Jane grinned like a little girl.

"Jesus now I feel old, you haven't called me that in many years. Come on let's get back in to see the others. Fancy a shoulder carry, your feet are bare?"

"Yay, yes please." Jane clapped in excitement. Bill scooped her up like a child putting her on his shoulders, standing proud walking back to the household her hands in front of his head.

Jasper came to the door as they arrived back. "You're a braver man than I am Bill." He laughed. Jane poked her tongue out at him.

"Cheeky sod, you're just jealous because you can't do this." She poked her tongue out at him.

"Don't you two start a domestic while I'm in the middle please." Bill laughed lifting Jane down, he kissed her head moving past her to the others leaving Jasper and Jane alone.

"You okay Belle?"

She nodded with tears in her eyes. "I am." She walked into his arms, he held her tight, they stood silent for a few minutes, Jane looked up at him.

"You are incredible, you never stop giving."

"No Belle, I didn't do this, your friends did that, I just kept quiet."

"You're still part of it. Thank you for loving me the way you do."

"You make it easy love. You may want to go in though. You have more visitors." Jane looked shocked again, she walked into the house, Moses, G Matt and James had joined them.

"Gwen, look at the state of me, all of my favourite people together and I can't even do a decent picture because of these damn rollers."

"Well Dorian isn't here so you will have to wait until the wedding." Gwen teased her. Jane grabbed her phone beckoning Jasper to stand with the men.

"Come on you lot get together, damn these rollers, I don't care." They all moved about mumbling and laughing, as they crowded together so Jane could get her picture.

"Time to eat I think." Jasper said as Gwen and Chicca stood up moving into the kitchen to help out. Jane went over to Moses hugging him. "Hi love, you okay?"

"I'm feeling better today, thanks love. Had a good night sleep."

"Oh good, what can I get you to eat then?"

"Let's both look shall we, I'm not on my last legs yet." Jane spun frowning at him. "Figure of speech, sorry."

"Don't bloody scare me", she hit him on the chest as they walked over to the worktop to see what Jasper and the girls had laid out. Everyone chatted for a couple of hours enjoying time together before Gwen spoke.

"Right sorry to break up this party but we have to get the Belle of the ball ready for tonight." She grinned. "Did you see what I did there? Belle of the ball?" Everyone groaned at her.

"Come on girls let's go." Chicca laughed. "It made us laugh Gwen love, don't worry."

Jax and Linda grabbed the wine bottles and glasses before running off to the bedroom to join the others. Bill followed with all the bags.

"Thanks Bill, you're my hero", Gwen blew him kisses.

"Bugger off, you cheeky mare." He smiled as he left them to it.

The girls went to work on Jane and each other, it was getting late and Dorians car was due back to collect the guys, Jane wanted to see Jasper before he left.

"okay now what dress am I wearing tonight then?" Gwen grinned.

"Well, it has to be slutty so we have something special for you. Close your eyes." She opened the dress bag and pulled it out. Her hair hung in soft big curls around her shoulders, Gwen pinned one side up showing her ear, they put long earrings on, as Chicca slipped on her strappy red heels, moving her into the mirror.

They all giggled in excitement holding their breath. Jane opened her eyes, she was reminded of her goodbye party so knew what kind of thing to expect, but she wasn't expecting what she saw. It was a one shoulder plunge mini dress in red. With a chain that held the other side of the dress up which went across the other shoulder, it had long sleeves on each arm, it hugged every curve, and reached the middle of her thigh. The front plunge was low to the waist. The girls all nodded grinning. It was tight enough not to let her breast fall out, but Gwen had brought tape with her to put either side to ensure it stayed in place. Janes mouth fell open, she didn't recognise herself again, she turned to look at herself from behind, the dress was tight across her bottom, she wasn't sure what Jasper would think, she laughed covering her face.

"Oh, good God! You really have excelled yourself Gwen. I'm not sure if I am this confident though."

"Of course you are, we are all going in similar short tight dresses, so you are not alone. Go and see Jasper while we finish up." Jane went to the dining room where the men were all sat talking. As Jane approached the door looking sheepish. Bill stood up first.

"Nope sorry, you are not going out looking like that, I don't know who is going to be there. I'm standing firm as your other Dad." He was shaking his finger at her. "you can go right back to the bedroom and change young lady." The others laughed at him. Jasper walked over to her. His mouth wide open, his eyes all over her.

"Heaven has just walked into the room", he sighed taking Jane in his arms. He laughed turning her walking her into the lounge.

He nuzzled her ear. "I don't think I can go back in there now, someone woke up as soon as you walked into the room. My God Belle you look delicious in that, I am jealous though, all the guys are going to be looking at you. Just don't take it off tonight will you? I want too." Jane laughed shaking her head.

"As you wish."

"Oh I wish we were staying in on our own, me and that dress could be having some fun tonight." He wrapped himself around her body rubbing himself on her bottom.

"You and the dress, do you mean you want to wear it?"

"Cheeky, you know what I meant. In all seriousness Belle please be careful, don't leave your drink unattended and don't go anywhere alone, I know the guys will look out for you all, but you also get some odd ones in too."

"I know love, we are very careful, don't worry, you should know girls never go to the loo alone."

"Yeah true, I suppose." He spanked her hard. "Grrrrrrr, I want you right now."

"Thank you for making me feel like a million dollars, you may need to calm Bill down though, he does get quite protective."

"So I see, was your Dad the same?" Jane smiled reminiscing.

"Yes, Bill was always at ours, they would both say it unison if my skirt was too short. At least I know they cared but being a teenager I didn't think so." He kissed Jane on the nose. She hadn't shared much about her parents with him and just having snippets made him feel closer to her. The noise of the other girls arriving in the dining room made them laugh as the men gave them the same lecture as Bill had given Jane.

"Come on let's go and see what's going on." Jasper took Janes hand leading her into the dining room. All the men were on their feet complaining about how the girls were dressed. Jane and Jasper stood laughing in the doorway.

"Quiet!!" Moses shouted. "the girls will be okay as long as they stick to the rules, we know Animal is with Shadow tonight they will be keeping an eye on everyone. We have to allow them to let their hair down, they deserve it as well as we do." Steve went to comment. Moses put his hand up. "I know you are all jealous of the guys seeing our girls and worried about them, but I promise you this is in hand. They will be safe. Right girls are you are ready you take the car first it can come back for us later. Have an awesome time if you get drunk please look out for each other." In turn the girls went to Moses kissing him, leaving him covered in lipstick.

"Bugger off the lot of you." he laughed as Gwen spat on a tissue trying to rub it off his face. The doorbell sounded letting them know the car had arrived. Jasper went to the door to let the driver know the changes before the girls marched out singing loudly as they got into the car.

Chapter 22

Bring on the night

The girls arrived at the club, the live band was in full swing, they stepped out of the car to wolf whistles from the guys and girls. Jane felt very self-conscious, she was trying to pull her dress down.

"Time to party girls. Woo hoooooo", Gwen squealed, the girls joined in with her as the they walked to the bar. Shadow came over to them smiling.

"Well, well, who is this sweet sugar honey thing stood in front of me?" He laughed deeply looking straight at Jane, she walked into his arms as he knelt down to hug her.

"Wow, you look gorgeous, I'm surprised you were let out of the house dressed like this. I'm not complaining though because we get to enjoy you all." He laughed his deep laugh again. "Right then, we have cornered off an area for you all, you don't need to come to the bar, Animal will be keeping an eye on you all so just wave him over and drinks are on the house."

"No Shadow that's not fair. We have to pay our way." Jane complained pouting.

"Sorry it's not up for discussion, just go and enjoy your night." Jane kissed him on the cheek before joining the others as Animal walked them over to their own area. It had been dressed up with balloons, banners and anything pink the guys could get their hands on." Jane felt overwhelmed by it all. It was all very different this time round for her.

They all sat, Animal took the order and went off to the bar. Susan, Alison, Violet and Sasha arrived to huge screams from the girls, they all hugged as 6 bottles of champagne were brought to the table. Animal and Shadow opened them pouring the first glass for them. Gwen kicked her shoes off climbing onto the table.

"Shhh, shhhh, okay, I would like to make a toast to our beautiful girl Jane. We have been friends for many years now, you are an inspiration to us all, we miss you like crazy, but I can't tell you how good it is to see you looking so radiant and happy. Finally, you are definitely the Belle of the Ball, sorry had to say that again, here's to many years of happiness and sex. Cheers." Everyone shouted at the same time, turning heads from the crowd listening to the band.

"Let's get this party started!!!" Chicca squealed. She pulled out a box from under the table, it was full of paper items Jane couldn't make out. She pulled out a sash passing it to Jax to put over Janes head. It was white with Bride to be on it. Then a plastic crown and a short veil. Jane laughed, feeling silly. Everyone took a seat as Chicca pulled out different styles of knickers for everyone to embellish.

"Right then the best one voted for by the crowd Jane you have to wear for the rest of the night and home later." Jane blushed, nodding her head. "We also need proof of this by you giving us your own knickers." Jane put her head in her hands laughing. They passed the knickers around as the flowers diamantes glitter, paints, pens feathers and more were unpacked.

"The clock starts in 2 minutes get ready girls you have 15 minutes to make these the best ever." Linda started the countdown, as the girls grabbed at everything on the table. The timer started, they all frantically stuck things to the knickers and thongs, grabbing at anything else on the table they could find. Shadow sounded the alarm to make them stop, they all held up their knickers laughing at each other. Jane was shaking her head. Animal grabbed the microphone and quietened everyone down.

"Right then lads and ladies, we need your help. Whichever knickers you make the loudest noise for Jane our Bride to be has to wear for the rest of the night and home tonight to Jasper. So, are you ready to vote?" The crowd erupted. Shadow held the first one up, it was a thong with toilet paper hanging from the back embezzled with lipstick kisses and fur. The crowd laughed and cheered. The second was a high leg pair, across the front was *Soon to be Mrs Mitchell*. With condoms hanging off and glitter inside. The crowd again laughed and roared. They got through all pairs and the cheers were about the same, Jane turned to look at Shadow raising her hands as she heard the crowd erupt, the cheering was louder than before she turned to see the biggest knickers she had ever seen with tinsel, glitter, lipstick, feathers and love hearts. Jane was in a fit of the giggles with the rest of the girls. There was no way she could keep them on.

"Ladies please join us on the stage we would like to see this happen." The girls walked down to the stage helped up by Shadow and Animal.

"So, you have to wear these for the rest of the night I hear? well to be honest there is no way you could do it alone. Come on ladies climb in too. Animal laid the knickers down on the ground helping the girls to stand inside each leg, they were all laughing at each other as the crowd joined in cheering. "Are we ready to pull these up?" He asked the crowd. They all cheered as Shadow and Animal pulled the knickers up, the girls held onto them laughing at themselves as flashes went off in the crowd. "I would say you can walk off the stage together but to be honest I don't think with those killer heels on anyone of you could make it. Let's give a big cheer to the girls." The crowd erupted as the girls were helped out of the knickers, Shadow folded them up passing them to Jane. They were all helped down off the stage by the guys and returned back to the table, they were all laughing at themselves as Shadow poured more champagne.

"You may want to check your phone", he laughed walking away. Jane got her phone out to see a video had been sent by Shadow. She opened it leaving it on the table, he had someone record them on stage, they all began giggling and squealing watching themselves.

Chicca had arranged cupcakes to be brought out she had a huge amount of icing. She handed out two cakes to each girl. "Right then ladies, as naughty as you like, use these icing pens to draw onto to cake, the best one wins a prize. The girls squealed cheering loudly as Chicca held up the prize it was a My Viv, a small palm held vibrator.

"Gwen I need to pee, will you come with me please?" Jane tapped Gwen on the shoulder.
"Sure love, come on." They headed inside laughing and giggling entering the toilet, they stopped at the sink to check their make-up.
"How you doing love?" Gwen asked fussing with Janes hair.
"I'm wonderful, I think I might have had a little too much champagne though. She giggled as she walked into the cubicle.
"That's good to hear. Christ, I think I am peeing for England, how much have we drank tonight for God's sake?"
"I have no idea. Oh bugger, I'm out of paper can you pass some under please." Jane giggled. Gwen rolled the paper under the partition, Jane caught it with her shoe kicking into the next cubicle.
"Shit I kicked it away, you got anymore in there?"
"No love, that was the last. Shake it off."

"You must be joking, I don't do drip dry." They both began snorting laughing. Jane tried to stand up, but fell against the door. She started giggling again.

"Fuck it." She stepped out of her knickers, folded them up and wiped herself.

"What are you doing in there are you okay love?"

"Well, what is it they say, if you can't beat them join them."

"Sorry love you lost me?"

"I just used my knickers as paper, I'm going commando, go me, go me!!"

"Christ woman you are going to get me in trouble", Gwen giggled.

"Why it's me who is doing it? Ohhhh that feels good, letting the air get to my girl. I think I should do this more often, ooohhhh shame Jasper isn't here."

"I'm supposed to be looking after you that's why."

"Don't you worry about that pussycat, I will sweet talk him with a good suck of his cock!" Jane tumbled out of the door towards the sink.

"Now I know you have had a lot to drink, I love it when you are drunk, come on hold onto me." Gwen held Jane under the arm trying to walk out of the toilets properly in a straight line, Jane wandering though, they both kept giggling.

"Gwen you're supposed to be looking after me, stop swaying." She giggled again losing her balance.

They walked outside of the building as three guys approached them out of the dark. Gwen stopped the hair on the back of her neck standing on end. She couldn't see their faces.

"Jane stop love, come on walk properly." She kept walking turning towards the crowd of people, feeling nervous.

"Excuse me ladies can we help?"

"Nope thanks we're okay." Gwen answered abruptly. Trying to walk faster.

"Are you sure, you look like you could both do with a helping hand back to your table."

"I said no thanks we are fine." She snapped again, her whole body prickling nervously.

"Don't be rude Gwen, they are being helpful." Jane giggled. Gwen felt a hand on her shoulder, she stopped walking, fear ripping through her, she felt her blood run cold.

"Gwen, that's not a nice way to speak to your friends."

"Let go or I will scream, the guys are just there." She was getting mad, she screwed her fists up tight ready to swing at him.

"You obviously don't know who you are talking too."

"I really don't care, just please leave us alone." The other two men came out of the dark and stood in front of Gwen, she was more concerned about Jane than herself, she was ready to fight.

"Gwen, look at me." He began to laugh. Gwen looked up slowly to see Bullet, Axel and Jock stood in front of her.

"Oh, my fucking god, you bastards!" She laughed lunging at Jock smashing into his chest with her fists. "You scared the fucking crap out of me."

"Sorry love I thought you would recognise the voice at least, but then by the look of the pair of you I would say you have had plenty to drink tonight, good job we arrived when we did."

"What do you mean arrived when you did?" she frowned, Jane was completely oblivious.

"Moses told us you were here for Jane's night and we were local said we would come and look after you all. There are some dodgy guys out there."

"Well they could have fucking told us. Jesus Mother of God. I almost shit myself."

"Are you always so potty mouthed Gwen?" Axel asked laughing.

"Fuck off Axel, you would be if you were scared shitless like we were."

"Sorry love, we didn't mean too. Now can we help you back to your table?" Axel scooped Gwen up making her squeal. Jock did the same with Jane.

"Oh Hello, have we met? Jane giggled.

"Kind of yes. We are friends of Moses." Jane screwed her eyes up trying to focus.

"What did you say your name was?" She put her finger onto his nose.

"Jock, that one carrying Gwen is Axel and this is Bullet. Ace had some personal stuff to do tonight so couldn't join us." Jane pushed herself back in his arms.

"Hang on a cotton picking minute, you're the guys that……, you did the….., you…….." Jock and Bullet laughed.

"Yeah, that's us, it's a pleasure to meet you under better circumstances Jane, it's good to see you looking so well."

"Oh my God, Oh my God." She threw her arms around his neck hugging him tight. "Thank you, thank you, thank you for finding me and doing what you did…., I think….I don't know what you did to him and I don't want to know, but thank you so much."

"Any friend of Moses is a friend of ours, we were pleased to help." He stood her up steadying her. "Now enjoy the rest of your evening Jane, we're here if you need us, we will follow you back to Dorians when you're ready."

"Why is something wrong? Do I need to be worried?" Bullet laughed.

"Not with us around love, nothing is wrong, Moses just wanted you girls looked after that's all." Jane kissed them all on the cheek.

"Well, you can have a dance with us later then, can't they ladies?" Jane shouted to the others. They all cheered in response.

"Bullet shook his head laughing, "sorry love I don't dance, not my thing."

"Oh come on, loosen up, it's fun, come on."

She grabbed his hand leading him to the stage. Chicca grabbed Jock and Gwen Axel. They all complained as they were dragged down to the stage. The other girls followed with other men. The band began singing Fat bottom girl, everyone cheered, Jane kicked off her shoes and began jumping up and down singing loudly with the others. Gwen began slapping Jane's bottom, as she air guitared. The men stood watching laughing. Chicca jumped into the arms of Jock head banging backwards. Jock was spinning them both around enjoying the music with her. The music slowed, each girl swapped men. Bullet was the youngest, she had heard Moses talk about him before.

"Come on my turn." She pulled him towards her, he raised his eyes huffing.

"Relax Bullet for Gods sake, show the lady some love." Jock shouted laughing at Bullet standing stiff.

"Sorry love, I don't dance, not my thing either."

"Well tonight we are letting our hair down so at least try for me?" Jane looked at him with her big eyes and pouted making him smile.

"Oh wow I nearly got a laugh out of you." She wrapped her arms around his neck, Bullet held her waist not wanting to touch her anywhere else. The guys laughed at him as they joined in with the girls. Jane had enough to drink to give her the confidence to push things with Bullet, she grabbed his hips making him move, he half smiled at her, she kicked his boot getting him to open his legs.

"You know if you were any other woman doing this, I would put you over my knee and spank your arse."

"Damn, well it seems I'm unlucky tonight then doesn't it?" She bent over spanking her own bottom. Bullet began laughing.

"Cheeky bitch, I can see why Moses and G like you. Sassy lady."

"Oh no sweetheart they don't like me, they love me, well tolerate me at times. Come on limber up. Show me you can shake those hips." He huffed again giving in, grabbing her around the waist, lifting her up, she wrapped her legs around him, forgetting she had no knickers on. They began to move to the music, Jane laid back letting her hair fall looking upside down at everyone else as Bullet moved them around. She began feeling dizzy so sat up.

"Maybe I shouldn't have done that." She laughed wrapping her arms around his neck again, as they swayed to the music which changed up again in speed. He looked into her eyes, his heart softened, she reminded him of his Mum.

"Come on let's get you back to your friends." He stopped abruptly taking her back to the table sitting her down. "Good to meet you Jane, see you later." Jane frowned, he walked off quickly to the bar. Jane wasn't focused properly but found it odd still. She raised her shoulders turned to the table picking up a bottle of champagne and began drinking from the bottle as the girls arrived back giggling and panting.

"Oi save some for us cheeky girl." Jane stopped, gasping for air as she finished drinking. Passing the bottle to Chicca.

"Well, I have never been a girl for champagne before but I kinda like that one." She burped loudly bubbles going up her nose. They all began laughing at her. As she rubbed her nose trying to get rid of the tickle. "Right then, I want to win that prize so come on girls get decorating."

Jane grabbed the icing pens and began drawing a cock on her cupcake, she added balls and hair, attempting to add a pussy at the top but she didn't have enough room, she grabbed the other one and decided on a cock head. Her attempt was a mess, but you could make out what it was supposed to be. They all began looking at each others. The giggling started again. Chicca picked up Jax's.

"Wow I love this one!" she exclaimed showing everyone else.

"Oh, beautiful, I love that, such a pretty rose, can I have it please Jax, I love roses?" She slurred.

"Ummmm, it's not a rose love." Jax laughed.

"Yes it is." Jane screwed her face up. "Let me smell the pretty rose please?" The girls burst into a fit of the giggles as the cake was passed to Jane, Chicca nudged Linda to get her camera ready. Jane took the cake and began sniffing it.

"It doesn't smell of roses." she pouted, showing it to everyone else.

"What does it smell of Jane?" Linda giggled filming her.

"Funny lemon I think."

"Taste it Jane, see what you think, right there look in the middle." The girls were beside themselves as Linda continued to film. Jane stuck her tongue into the middle lifting some of the cream onto her tongue.

"I never thought I would see the day you would lick a pussy, but I suppose there is time for anything," Gwen giggled holding her side. Jane looked up confused.

"It's a pussy Jane, not a rose", Susan couldn't breath watching her. Trying to explain it to her. The penny finally dropped and Jane began giggling with them. She was holding her face.

"Stop please my face hurts from laughing."

"You better finish that now, nobody else wants a second hand clit." Susan spat her champagne out across the table, Chicca was patting her on the back trying to get her to breath.

"Who's next Jax shouted holding Jane's cock head up. Who wants this one?" As she spoke Animal came back to the table. They all thought the same thing as he spoke.

"Anything I can do for you ladies?" each one in turn began roaring with laughter.

"Would you close your eyes for me please Animal and put your tongue out?" the girls couldn't breath with laughing.

"Why what are you going to do to me?", he looked quizzically at them all.

"Nothing hun, honestly." Chicca giggled. She turned and nodded at Linda to be ready. She moved towards Animal as he closed his eyes.

"I think I might regret this. But what the hell, what harm can a bunch of women do?" Chicca stood next to me, angled the cake so the cock head was level with his tongue.

"Animal have you ever licked another mans cock?" He screwed his face up.

"No, I haven't why? Not my thing, but I don't have anything against gays."

"Just wondered, you can lick now." He pushed his tongue out licking, not sure what he was doing, he tasted the first part and went back for more, making the girls uncontrollable with giggling and snorting. He licked up a lot of the cream.

"Mmmmm that's nice, can I bite it? Is it supposed to taste bad or something?" Linda was bashing the table uncontrollable.

"Fuck it I think I just peed my pants." She took her shoes off dashing for the toilet passing her phone to Gwen. The girls we beside themselves as Chicca fed the cake to Animal.

"You can open your eyes now." He looked at the girls wondering what they were laughing about as Gwen stopped filming.

"That was nice can I have another please?" he set the girls off again, Shadow came out to see what was going on.

"What are you naughty ladies up too, I hope you're not abusing him?" Gwen showed him the video. His laugh was deep from the pit of his stomach, like a roar of a lion. "You poor bastard, you fell for it didn't you. Never trust a drunk woman." He continued laughing with the girls as Animal looked confused looking around at them. Gwen showed him the video holding tight to the phone so he couldn't delete it.

"Fucking hell, you little bitches." He laughed at himself. "I will never fucking live that down." He rubbed his head.

"You sure won't, it has now been sent to all the guys."

"Oh fuck, oh well it wasn't the real thing thank fuck." He laughed along with the girls not believing he had been conned by them.

"Ladies I think we have a winner, the prize goes to the lovely Animal!!! Thanks for being a good sport, now you can go and enjoy this." She passed him the vibrator. He looked at the box confused again.

"Yeah right what is a My Viv?"

"Open it and find out." Gwen laughed. He opened the box taking the tiny vibrator out, he turned it in his hands confused.

"Turn it on." He felt around it pressing the button, it began vibrating in his hand.

"You are fucking kidding me, what would I want one of these for?" Gwen grabbed it holding against his nose.

"How does that feel? If it feels nice it means it's the right one for you." He pushed it away as he felt a tingle in his body, he huffed putting it back in it's box walking away with it muttering under his breath.

"He didn't leave it then did he, I think someone is going to have a play later." Gwen teased. They all began giggling again. They stopped laughing as Shadow brought some food out for them placing it on the table.

"Thank you Shadow, this looks awesome, I am soooooo hungry. Jane groaned digging into the pile of cheesy nachos with her fork. They all began eating and chatting. The drinks flowed Jane was feeling very drunk but happy, she looked around at her friends smiling feeling emotional.

"Hey Janie you okay love?" Jax looked across at her.

"I'm ok, just super happy you are all here with me, feeling a little emotional about it all." She sniffed wiping a tear from her eye. The girls moved around her cuddling as Jane laughed and cried.

"Woooo wooo, no panda eyes tonight love please or we all will have." Gwen laughed wiping another tear from Jane's face.

"Come on let's go and have a last dance before we head home to the men." Alison shouted. "Then I can abuse the old man for a while." They all got up supporting each other, they left their shoes behind and ran down to the stage. The band nodded and changed the music to something slower. *I'll be there for you* was sung loud. The girls held onto each other in a circle. Singing at the top of their voices. The chorus they sang loud pointing at Jane. Nodding their heads at her. She was crying and smiling again. She felt arms wrap around her waist, she swung her hand around to slap whoever it was but found Jasper stood behind her.

"Oh my god, you're here. Awwww I love you Jasper Mitchell. She slurred. Jasper smiled hugging her moving her back from the crowd as the rest of the men arrived. "What are you all doing here? I don't mind its lovely."

"We decided it was time to rock with you, Dorian fancies a song or two so we came down, You're not disappointed are you?"

"Oh my God never, this is the perfect night." She kissed Jasper hard as he lifted her, she wrapped her legs around him as he swayed to the music.

Moses walked up to Susan, kissing her openly in front of everyone. She pulled back looking shocked.

"Are you sure about this Moses? Your friends are watching."

"I don't care Susan. You make me happy, I don't know where this is going but right now this feels good." He kissed her again grabbing her around the waist dancing with her. Susan looked over at Jane nervously, Jane smiled and gave her the thumbs up.

Dorian jumped onto the stage with the band, the gang erupted. He was on his home turf where it all began. He looked down to see his oldest friends in front of him, Bullet saluted him. He nodded down at him smiling.

"Evening all, I'm sorry to disrupt the night but my good friends are here from the UK and if you didn't know already Jane and Jasper are getting hitched soon, so I thought we would gate crash the ladies night and I would sing a few songs." Everyone cheered as he walked back to the band talking about what they could sing.

"I know my kind of stuff isn't all your kind of thing but suck it up and join in anyway." The crowd cheered waiting to hear him. He did three songs and left the band to continue. He was met by Bullet Axel and Jock. They all hugged and spoke at once.

"How long has it been since we rode out last? It's about time you got your leathers on Brother and joined us again, this new found fame has gone to your head." Jock patted him on the back laughing.

"It's good to see you all, I'm home now for quite some time, I have been travelling too long, you must come up to the house, plenty of room for you all, kick back and have some down time. I could do with putting a few miles under me on the bike though."

"Let's do it after the wedding then? It would be good to spend some old-fashioned time with you Brother." Axel slapped him on the back.

"Where is Ace?"

"Personal stuff, he didn't say but must be important for him to go off-line for a while."

"Hope he's okay. Seems we have a lot of catching up to do, I've been hearing lots of things. Any way I think the girls are ready to leave."

"Hop on with me, we are following them back anyway."

"Cheers Brother I will." They walked back to the car and bikes.

James had driven to collect Chicca as he knew she would be drunk. There was just enough room for everyone else in the car. Dorian jumped on the back of Bullet, he smiled being close to him.

They arrived back at the Dorians, everyone except Jasper and Jane got out, everyone hugged each other before the car pulled away. Jane was still very light-headed after all the champagne she had drunk. The driver closed the partition between them leaving them alone.

Jane snuggled into Jasper stroking his beard. "I would really love to feel that right now." Jasper smiled.

"You are Belle."

"Oh, no, no, no, no, no, I don't mean like this." She pulled on it running her fingers through it.

She wiggled her finger at him from left to right. "Would you like to know a secret?" she whispered giggling, beckoning him closer to her.

"Sure I do." He smiled, rubbing noses with her.

"Shhhhhhh." She giggled putting her finger on her lips. He put his ear down to her lips.

"I'm going commando." She laughed, "and I want to feel your beard right now." Jasper looked at her shocked.

"You mean you went out without any pants on? You didn't tell me that. I definitely wouldn't have let you out of my sight." She giggled again.

"Shhhhhhh, no I needed to pee." She kept giggling and whispering Jasper was struggling to understand a word she was saying.

"You can have my beard when we get home Belle." She climbed onto his knee, her dress riding up her legs. Holding his face she began peppering him with kisses.

"Do you promise?"

"He laughed "Yes Belle I promise." She laid her head on his chest, he held on tight to her, until they got home. He scooped her up carrying her to the door, she was giggling as he opened the door and put her down.

"Right lady bed for you I think." Jane pouted.

"You promised me."

"And I keep my promises, but before that, you need plenty of water." Jane stumbled towards the kitchen, Jasper was watching her laughing, she had her shoes in her hand, she was swaying back and forth, she slumped on the counter.

"Oh please tell the floor to stop moving it's making me wobble."

"Okay, floor stop moving Belle is feeling wobbly."

She looked up at him slurring, one eye open the other shut talking from the side of her mouth.

"Thank you captain." She saluted him. Jasper laughed, her veil was hanging off the back of her head, her mascara had run under her eyes, her sash was the wrong way round, he frowned laughing wondering what on earth they had been doing all night. He shook his head.

"I don't think I want to know. What happens at the club with these ladies stays at the club."

Jane drank almost a glass of water before Jasper filled it up.

"Hold tight Belle." He scooped her up again carrying her to the bedroom. He was so relieved he had been at the house after the girls had left, he walked into the bedroom to grab his jacket and was met with total chaos, he had called on G to help him pack it away, the bedding was stained with different colours from all the products and different smelling perfumes. They had to change the bed to get rid of some of the smell. He told Moses when they went back to the dining room, he laughed and told him he hadn't seen anything, to wait until he went to their club and saw the ladies room, he said it smelt like a brothel. They packed all of Gwens things up and dropped them back at Dorians, G and Moses had laughed about Gwen without her make-up in the morning was not worth anyone's life.

As they walked into the bedroom Jane began to giggle.
"Hi bed, I have missed you today, are you okay?" Jasper laid her on the bed. He was smiling listening to her, he had never seen her drunk before.
"Oh you feel sooooo good", she pushed her head into the duvet snorting at the smell. "I love that smell, I need that in a bottle. Jasper please can you buy me that smell I love it, come and smell please." She beckoned him onto the bed, he sat down trying desperately not to laugh.
"Sniff like this." She put her head back into the duvet snorting at it again. Jasper laid down, sniffed a bit, he could smell fresh air.
"No, you're doing it wrong, like this look", she pushed his head back onto the bed, sniff now. Jasper did as he was told, he started laughing.
"Belle that is fresh air smell."
"Nooooooo, definitely not, that is something realllllly special, I have to have it." She went back down snorting the bedding.
"Belle, we need to get you ready for bed, you can sniff all you like in a while come on love." Jane sat up looking disgusted. Like a naughty little girl. Jasper stood pulling Jane to stand, he turned her unzipping her dress.
"Arms up." She did, Jasper slipped the dress off over her head, he looked down and noticed she was in fact knickerless. He went to ask and decided not to, it would be too much like hard work to get the right answer out of her. He walked her into the bathroom sitting her onto the toilet, he grabbed her make-up wipes and began cleaning her face off. She screwed it up like a child making him laugh again, he now wished he had taken a picture of her. He pulled out her veil and hung it over the shower cubicle. She finished and wiped herself, she tried to pull her knickers up.
"Oh my God, you stole my knickers, where are they, did you want to keep them in your pocket to sniff later?"
"Oh lord, what have I let myself in for, I didn't see a Jane manual anywhere." Jasper laughed as he picked her up.

"Yes Belle I took your knickers off."

"Phew." She wiped her brow dramatically as she stood at the sink. "I thought you had stolen them, I know what you men are like for wanting our knickers." Jasper shook his head putting her hands under the water to help her wash them.

"Moses you and I need a chat tomorrow, there must be instructions somewhere?" he looked up to the ceiling laughing, talking to himself. He picked up Jane's toothbrush to give to her looked down at her as she started to move like a robot. He looked back at the toothbrush and put it back down.

"I think not." Jane was now walking like a robot around the bathroom muttering to herself. Jasper slapped his head, grabbed her in his arms and laid her in bed. He quickly pulled his clothes off before she had chance to wander off again climbing in next to her, as he pulled her into his chest he heard her snoring. He turned onto his back laughing.

"Thank god for that. I love you Belle but I'm so glad you are asleep." He kissed her head cuddling into her smiling.

Jane woke up feeling groggy, opened one eye and quickly closed it again feeling very hung over. Jasper was already up making lots of noise. Jane covered her head with the duvet groaning.

"Good Morning my love, how are you today?" Jasper laughed walking in with a cup of tea. "There are pain killers and water on the side."

"Please don't shout I have a headache." She mumbled from under the duvet.

"Do you have tiny hammers in your head love?"

"Shhhhhh please it's too early."

"Sorry Belle, it's 11.30am."

"Oh my God what?" she screamed jumping out of bed stumbling towards the bathroom. Brushing her hair out of her eyes with both hands, it had matted at the back with the hairspray Gwen had used. "You know we are all getting together today? come on, come on, we need to get sorted." She was pulling on her hair trying to put it up but failing. Jasper walked in behind her laughing.

"It's not funny!" she snapped holding her head. She got onto her knees retching, Jasper held her hair up while she vomited and groaned hugging the toilet.

"Feeling any better?" he asked passing her a wet face cloth.

"I bet you think it's funny don't you?" She looked up at him mascara spread across her face her hair stiff and in clumps. Jasper tried desperately not to laugh knowing he couldn't speak he just shook his head walking away to get her water.

"I can hear you sniggering." She shouted holding her head in pain. Jasper composed himself turning walking in with her water and painkillers. She took them putting her hand out to him to help her up.

He pulled her into his arms. "Belle I wasn't being cruel love, you are just so funny. Oh and by the way it is only 9.30." She smacked him hard on the chest.

"You shit bag, how could you do that to me?" She pouted looking down.

"I'm sorry love, I didn't expect you to get up, I thought you would turn over and not bother, come on lay down, get some more sleep until the painkillers work." He guided her back to bed sitting her down, she put her hand out to him to join her, he climbed on with her pulling her into his chest.

Chapter 23

Thank you Susan

Moses was laid awake looking at Susan, a piece of her wavy auburn hair had fallen over her face, he moved it away gently with his finger. He sighed to himself, tucking both his hands under his head as he laid on his side. The sun caught the gold in her hair, he could see rainbows in the different colours of it. He smiled.

"You have brought so much unexpected joy into my life, thank you so much for being here, for listening and not complaining." He brushed his finger down her temple, another hair fell loose, he tucked it behind her ear gently. Susan moved moaning softly. Moses smiled leaning down kissing her ear.

"Are you awake gorgeous. Would you like a drink?" He smiled as she sighed screwing her eyes closed.

"Is it morning already?" She groaned.

"Sadly yes, I could lay here all day watching you."

"Oh god no, I must look bloody awful." She laughed covering her face.

"Sorry I beg to differ. You look gorgeous." He pulled her hand away from her face, she was laughing trying to pull it back turning her head burying it in the pillow.

"Oh god, did I really stay last night, I am so sorry."

"Why are you sorry? I wanted it too."

"I didn't want you to feel pressured." Moses laughed.

"Isn't it me that's supposed to say that to you?"

"I know how you feel about Jane, you are going through a lot too I didn't want to get in the way."

"Susan listen to me", he pulled her closer to him looking straight into her eyes. "There is nothing sexual between Jane and I, yes I love her and I always will but that love is different. I know that now. Yes, I did want her years ago, but look how happy she is now, I would never do anything to destroy that, I did think about it when she left for here but what would that have done to our relationship if she didn't want me? Yes, my cancer sucks and I don't know what is going to happen, shit you probably know better than I do, but don't we deserve a chance?" he took her face in his staring into her big brown eyes. Desperate to hear her answer. She turned her face into his cupped hand and kissed it.

"Yes, we do, it scares me though, what happens when you go back to the UK, having you here for a few weeks then you leave is going to be hard." He sighed relieved that she had said yes.

"Let's not think about that, we can enjoy the time we have and then think about that later." He moved his arm around her head pulling her into him. Their lips touching, he pulled softly on her bottom lip as she moved closer to find his. Their mouths opened, both catching their breath as their lips crashed together, Moses got up on his knees pushing Susan onto her back never leaving her lips, he moved her hands above her head.

"Don't move them." He demanded in a whisper. She nodded. He moved down her body, his lips leaving hers, moving across to her neck, she moved her head to feel his lips against her.

"Please Moses." She begged He bit gently making her catch her breath as he worked down her body to her small breast, he took the right into his mouth sucking hard, his tongue finding the nipple ring, he teased it making her laugh and groan. Her nipple hardened the more he teased her, she squirmed under him, he sucked hard letting it pop as he let go, he moved further down her body, his tongue tasting her, his lips stroking down her stomach. He reached the top of her pussy, he kissed it gently, she sucked in air biting her lip.

"You don't have to do this." She whispered.

"I know, I want to, so be quiet and hopefully you will enjoy it." He smiled as he poked his tongue out licking her across the top, he felt her tiny hairs stand on end as he licked her again. He smiled catching her eyes, he moved his tongue further down spreading her legs, never looking away from her, she strained to watch him as his head moved further down between her legs, he blew on her, Susan groaned opening her legs wider. He frowned noticing her piercing, moving his hand down he opened her lips wide so he could see the ring, his mouth watered to devour her. But he wanted to take his time. He flicked her ring, making her mewl, he smiled doing it again.

"Do these really work?" Susan nodded flushing red.

"Yes, they do, the little balls would help you too or another woman especially if two pussies are together they both benefit, you would feel it too on the shaft. Those beads bounce onto my clit making it more sensitive. Moses moved his tongue flicking the ring making Susan groan at him, she moved her arms to grab him.

"No, no, arms back." He shook his head smiling. Moving back to her clit. "What can I call it? Does it have a name?"

"It's called a Venus." she laughed.

"Oh like fly trap you mean, does that mean it is going to eat my tongue?" Susan smacked her head with her hand laughing at him. Moses flicked it again making Susan groan again, he moved his tongue down further, her juices glistening in the sun light, he pushed the covers off them both completely spreading out down the bed so he could get lower, he lifted her legs up tilting her towards his face. He moved towards her again his nose touching the hood catching the ring. He circled it as his tongue licked at her juices. Susan grabbed the pillow squeezing it around her face trying not to scream, Moses continued moving further down, licking up from the bottom drinking her. He sucked his middle finger pushing it inside her, she began moaning louder, he pushed deeper, she panted hard, biting her lip, grabbing the pillow almost covering her face. Moses pushed another finger inside his tongue flicking back and forth over her clit, Susan pushed up into his face, he stopped licking just fucking her with his finger, she turned onto her side squeezing her legs together, Moses grabbed her hips putting her on her knees.

"That's how you want it is it?" he whispered. Susan moaned in response, her pussy on show as her head touched the pillow. He ran his finger up and down, sliding it in and out slowly, she pushed back on him, he looked down at his cock, he was hard, he wasn't sure if he should try but he ached to be inside her, he pulled her to the edge of the bed and stood up. She turned to watch, as he got closer she sat up on her knees taking his cock in her hand, bending slighty, she rubbed it up and down her pussy. She looked at Moses and nodded bending over. He rubbed himself over her again making his cock wet before he opened her up sliding slowly inside her. Susan grabbed the bedding pulling the sheets up in her hands as Moses filled her with his hard long cock. He held her hips as he slid in and out slowly enjoying the feeling of her hot pussy tight around him, her juices making it slip in and out easily.

"You okay love?" he whispered.

"Oh God yes", she giggled, mewling as he pushed deeper again. Her knuckles going white as he began to get a little faster. Moses was exhausted already but his cock wanted this and so did he. He kept going harder into her.

"Stop love, please." Susan begged. She sat up.

"What's wrong, did I do something?" he frowned looking worried.

"Nothing at all, laydown I want to ride you." Moses grinned climbing onto the bed panting, he didn't argue, Susan straddled him, his cock standing to attention, she took hold of him teasing her pussy before sliding down slowly into him, she whimpered as she felt the full length of him fill her, she leaned back, his hands now on her breasts. He teased her nipples with his thumbs circling them, she bent back again as she slid up and down his cock. Her ring rubbing up and down the length of him. He felt himself almost cum the sensation was intense.

"Slowly Susan please or I will cum so damn fast, that ring of yours is teasing the fuck out of my cock." She grinned getting faster, leaning into him further, the ring teasing them both, Moses moved his hand onto her clit, rubbing faster, if he was going to cum he was damn sure she was too. He pushed up into her teasing her more as Susan turned up the pace, her head fell back as the shock of her orgasm overwhelmed her suddenly. Her body began to tremble, she pushed harder onto his cock, her pussy pulsating as she came hard. Moses joined her his body heating up, his balls tightening as he felt himself cum hard. He covered his mouth as he yelled. His body on fire. He was exhausted. Susan slumped over him her hair covering his face, he laughed he couldn't catch his breath, he pulled her down into his side, they both laid exhausted laughing.

"Wow now that's the best morning alarm I ever had." Moses laughed kissing Susan gently. Her arm was hanging off the bed the other tucked under her.

"Please tell me I can stay like this all day? I don't have the energy to get up." she giggled. "Well I didn't expect that this morning. He's working again then?"

"Looks that way, I didn't think he was, but you must have done something to him. I'm not complaining either. That was incredible, ready for round 2?" Susan scoffed.

"Please tell me you are kidding, I am definitely out of shape."

"Oh, I'm kidding, I don't think I'm quite up to that yet."

"Thank god."

"I beg your pardon, are you telling me that was no good?" he teased her pinning her down with his body nose to nose.

Susan began laughing. "No, no honest, I am out of shape, I meant I'm too tired."

"Hmmmm, I believe you this time." He kissed her again and laid flat on his back.

"Anything you would like to do today?" Susan asked leaning on her arm turning onto her side.

"If I get to spend the day with you then anything you like."

"Sounds perfect, I have a week off including the wedding, so my time is yours, use me as you wish."

"Well in that case…." He grabbed her laying her down covering her in tiny kisses. She squealed laughing trying to push him off. They both laughed kissing each other before laying down wrapped in each other.

"Would you like to go for a walk around the estate, apparently is has some amazing things."

"That would be nice but promise me if you get tired you tell me so we can rest."

"I will I promise, I don't want to ruin the time for us or the wedding." Susan felt her heart squeeze and her heart sank at the thought of Jane.

She shook it off sitting up in bed, "First things first I need coffee, you?"

"Sounds good to me." She pulled on his t-shirt and her skirt heading out into the kitchen. G came in at the same time in his boxer shorts.

"Shit sorry Susan I didn't think."

"Oh don't be silly, nothing I haven't seen before."

"I beg to differ, you haven't seen this before." Susan laughed looking him up and down.

"Now that's true, but when you've seen one you've seen them all."

"Cheeky mare." G laughed as Moses walked in dressed in his boxer shorts. "Get a grip of your woman will ya, she thinks I'm just like any other man, I am insulted. These holes and scars took me years to perfect."

"He likes to show his scars and bullet holes off Susan, just ignore him." G gave Moses the middle finger, as he turned back towards his room to get some clothes on.

Moses wrapped his arms around Susan as she made the drinks. "You look good in that t-shirt, you can keep it if you like. I think you would look good on the back of my bike too."

"Not so sure about the bike, never been on one."

Well, there is no time like the present. Dorian has plenty I can take you out on one, or we can ask Jane if we can borrow the trike if you prefer."

"Yes, I think the trike might suit me better."

"Sorted then, I will get the keys and we can go out later this week." He spanked her bottom moving away as she carried the drinks to the bedroom.

"You do realise you are going to leave me with a huge bruise if you keep spanking me."

"Oh, sorry don't you like it?"

"I didn't say that, but there is plenty of it, spread it out a bit." She teased putting the drinks down. She took his hand leading him to the shower.

"You want me again already?" he grinned following her.

"No I'm being your carer and washing you." she teased him.

"Damn woman you got an old mans hopes up then." He pouted putting his head down stopping in the bathroom as she turned on the shower. She pushed her skirt off folding it up and pulled his t-shirt off. Moses gently took her breasts into his hands pushing them together kissing from one to the next. Susan laughed watching him.

"Can I do that with your balls too?"

"Help yourself, I will never say no." She spanked him on the arm as he continued sucking and kissing."

"Come on don't waste the water. They climbed in together. Susan wet her hair then his head, Moses looked at her.

"What made you decide to have piercings?"

"I had always loved them as a child they fascinated me, I had my ears done when I was young and it kind of went from there. I had more when I started nursing but had to remove them for the job, it didn't look right with blue plasters over my face. If you look closely you can see the holes still." She leaned forward showing him.

"Amazing." He traced a line on her face from one to the other. "What did your parents think?"

"My Dad hated them, but he also hated the multi colour hair I had too."

"Wow, now that I would love to see, but why would you cover this colour, it's amazing, or is this coloured? you didn't have any on your pussy so I couldn't compare."

"This is natural, I hated it as a child, it was much brighter and I was teased because of it. Carrot top, copper knob, you name it I got called it, so I kind of rebelled at 16 and put all kinds in it. What about your tattoos?"

"When I joined up with G on my first tour I had one, it went from there too. Then I joined the club, the bike club and had this one." He pointed to the skull and roses. "We all have one, even the guys out here."

"Oh that's great. I didn't realise you were the same club I thought you just knew each other."

"No this club goes back years, they all knew each other from the military and started it, over the years more people, not military have joined which is nice. It's an incredible group of men and woman, we have the guys you met last night that are outlaws, they come and go as they please."

"Why outlaws?" She frowned.

"Okay there are things you don't know about that happened when Jane was taken, you might not want to know though, so you need to think about it before I tell you about them. If I do tell you I am putting my trust in you completely."

"Oh, maybe I don't want to know then. Forget I asked." She waved her hand in front of her then covered her face. Moses laughed.

"You can ask anything you like but if I'm not sure about telling you then I will say so, but only to protect you."

She gulped hard. "Can I just ask have you done anything bad, you know killed anyone since you were out of the military?"

"If I said yes would it matter?"

"It depends on why."

"Okay, well no I haven't but if I had got to Mark before anyone else then I would have pulled the trigger."

"Who's Mark?"

"Jane's ex-husband. The one who put her in hospital."

"Oh, sorry it seems I have a lot to learn. I don't think I really know much about it. We don't get involved in our patients lives. She was hardly ever alone anyway you guys were always with her. I just know about her injuries and how much she is loved by you all."

"Sorry I assumed you did, well we can talk about it some other time. Come on we better get out of here before we turn into prunes." He looked down at his hands all wrinkled. He turned the shower off brushing himself down and turned Susan to wring her hair out. They wrapped up in the towels and headed into the bedroom.

"Come with me." He opened the door to the private patio taking Susan's hand leading her out to the sofas under the canopy. They sat cuddled up listening to the birds in the trees.

"I could get used to this."

"What's that love?"

"Relaxing like this on my days off, this is perfect."

"I couldn't agree more but it's more about you being here than where I am."

"Are you getting soft in your old age, I thought you were a tough biker. Have I been robbed of that?"

"Ha, ha, very funny, I thought you might like the soft side of me, or does the dirty biker thing do more for you?"

"I wouldn't say no to a dirty biker." Moses spanked her hard on her bottom.

"I will remember that." Susan grinned kissing his chest tracing one of his tattoo's.

"We better get dressed and find something to eat." He sat up as Susan moved away from him.

"Good idea, I am a bit hungry, how about you?"

"Starving actually." Susan clapped her hands together.

"Do you know how pleased I am to hear you say that?" She was grinning at him.

"I can tell by that daft grin on your face. Come on woman." He pulled her up leading her back inside. Susan grabbed her clothes from the night before pulling them on, tying her hair up out of the way.

They walked up to the main house to be met by Kitty.

"I wondered when you two would surface, did you sleep well? What can I cook for you?"

"Hi Kitty, don't go to any trouble we can do it."

"Not in my kitchen young man and not while I am here. Sit down and tell me what you fancy."

"I'm not sure I just know I am really hungry today. What about you love?" He turned to Susan, whatever he's having."

"Right then, leave it with me, I will be back shortly." They both looked at each other and smiled. Moses looked around the room and saw the others outside with Dorian, he smiled to himself, he couldn't believe they were here.

"Who's out there."

"Just the gang, did you meet everyone last time?"

"Yes I think so, I don't know those guys though.? She pointed to Bill and the Outlaws.

"That's Bill, he's an old friend of Jane's he's like a Father to her. That's the guys you saw last night the Outlaws."

"Oh that's them, yes they were following us last night. This house must be huge then, how do you know Dorian?"

"He's an old friend we met on tour, he's a great guy, come along away from singing to us. We haven't seen him in a few years, so it was a shock to hear from him a few weeks back."

"It's nice that you can pick up like that though isn't it."

"Yes, it is to us he is still Dorian, his success will never change him."

"Come on you two, don't let it get cold. I have done you both poached eggs on toast I didn't want to overload you with bacon as you haven't eaten much in a while. There is also juice there I will bring some coffee in shortly."

"Wow haven't had that in years. One of Dorians favourites." Moses smiled feeling his stomach grumble.

"Yes they are, nothing changes with him does it?"

"No never has. It's a good thing though Kitty." They both tucked into their food. Chatting to each other.

"It's so good to see you eat. How are you feeling?"

"I feel great, the rest and company has done me the world of good. I couldn't have got through this without G and you of course."

"Just don't over do it please, reserve your energy until the wedding."

"I will, don't worry." He leaned across kissing her. "Thank you for being here Susan." She smiled blushing slightly. Kissing him back before finishing her meal.

They decided to go on a quiet walk into the grounds and get to know each other a little more. Moses knew the week was going to be hectic and once Jasper gave them the heads up on the wedding plans they could help to get them organized. They spent a couple of hours exploring before going back to the cottage and sitting on the patio curled up together. Susan was feeling happier than she had in a long time but still something wasn't sitting right with her and she couldn't put her finger on it.

Moses phone rang, he checked to see who it was, got up and went into another room. Susan could hear him but couldn't make out what was being said. She got closer to the door.

"I understand, thank you for telling me, no it's fine honestly I will call you in a week. Thanks again." Susan dashed back to the sofa. Moses stayed in the room for a while thinking then came out with a smile.

"Everything okay love?"

"Yes, just a bit of business that's all."

"Okay great." He sat back down pulling Susan in close to him.

Chapter 24

Wedding preparations

It was three days before the wedding, Jasper had taken some time out to finish off a few things while Jane was out of the way. They hadn't seen much of each other all week, both trying to get things done before the wedding as they were going to be away for 4 weeks.

He had arranged to stay at Dorians with the guys the night before and the girls were staying with Jane. She had called Susan and asked her if she would like to come over too, she wanted to make sure she didn't feel left out or the odd one of the group. Susan had agreed after talking to Moses about it. She was still troubled by his phone call, but she didn't want to know if it was anything with the club, she wasn't sure she needed to know. Or if it would change the way she felt about him.

It was the last day at work for them both, Jane was up earlier than Jasper, she had been working a couple of hours before he woke. He put his hand out to find it empty. He groaned realising she wasn't there, he sat up in bed pushing the heels of his hands in his eyes rubbing them. His alarm went off, he hit the off button throwing back the bed cloths to go in search of Jane.

She was sat at the dining table he could hear her fingers going across the keys on her laptop, he knew she was doing something from memory by the speed she typed, he crept up behind her wrapping his arms around her neck.
"Good Morning my lady." He kissed her on the head. She bent her head backwards to look at him.
"Hi gorgeous, did you sleep ok?"
"I did, it seems you didn't, how long have you been up?"
"A couple of hours, I just wanted to clear everything up then I can concentrate on wedding things."
"Don't burn yourself out love. I don't want you to be tired."
"I'm ok love honest." She smiled turning to get off the stool. "I will make some tea."

"No stay there, keep going if you are in the flow. I can do the tea. Have you showered yet?"

"No love I wanted to wait for you, I'm not starting that."

"What do you mean?"

"I only got up early to finish working and didn't want to be tapping on my laptop in bed. I won't be doing it regularly, that's when we start to drive a wedge between us when we don't shower and get up together, I want to start every day with you unless one of us is away." He wrapped his arms around her squeezing her tight.

"I'm glad you said that Belle." He walked away to make tea for them both.

"So, when do the girls take over the house? I don't mind when I got to Dorians but I know it's going to be hard being away from you. But then I get you to myself for 4 weeks and I can't wait." He grabbed her under her bottom lifting her up. "God I love you Belle. I get butterflies thinking about our wedding and having you all to myself for such a long time, I don't think I will want to come home."

"Awww you are such a big softie, I really love that. Promise you won't make me cry at the wedding, I don't want to spoil my look that early. She wrapped her arms around his neck as he span her around.

"I feel like a child, the excitement is killing me. I can't promise you that Belle, but I will carry a tissue just in case." He laughed kissing her. "Come on let's make this tea and go and shower or we will be late." He put her down and turned to make the tea, she cuddled him from behind, kissing his bare back. She moved her hand down across his back sighing. She kissed further reaching his bottom, he clenched his cheeks making her laugh, she spanked him making him release his cheeks. She dug her fingernails in grabbing a handful. Making him yelp.

"Are you trying to mark my body or do me an injury before the wedding?"

"Just claiming my stake that's all."

"Well unless you want the same you better run little lady." He moved to grab her, she ran off to the bedroom giggling, he left the tea running after her, she locked herself in the bathroom.

"You know I am a big bad wolf and I will blow this door down Belle, you can't hide from me."

He heard her squealing. "Come out and I promise I won't do anything, he crossed his fingers behind his back.

"Do you promise?"

"Yes love, we need to get ready for work." He grinned waiting. He heard the door lock turn, she opened the door slightly, poking her head out.

"Come on silly it's okay." She opened the door further stepping out, she was still unsure, as she reached the bed Jasper grabbed her, she began squealing loudly, he spanked her sitting down with her over his lap, he bent down to her bottom taking a mouthful of her. She squealed more trying to get away. She was panting.

"You promised." She giggled.

"It doesn't count when you cross your fingers."

"Noooo, you rat bag, I will never believe you again." He sat her up, pulling her into him.

"I'm sorry, no, not sorry, cheeky madam you started it, I just finished it. Now come on time is getting late", he stood up putting his hand out to her, she took it standing up and walked into the bathroom with her. They showered quickly and dressed giving themselves enough time to eat before leaving for the office.

Jasper had a lot to finalise and knew he would be in and out. He dropped Jane at her office, as she walked in it was covered in balloons, flowers and banners, she turned to look at him. He shrugged his shoulders, smiling stepping in to look at what they had done. Jane wiped a tear when she spotted a card next to the gifts.

To the perfect couple, we wish you both the happiest day and send you so much love for your life together, may it be filled with happiness love and laughter.

"oh my god that's beautiful, who did this?"

"I don't know Belle, but I'm sure Chicca had something to do with it." He kissed her. "I have to go love, I will see you at lunch time, I will be in and out so will grab lunch. Be back around 1pm."

"Okay, see you then. I love you." she called out after him, he ran back in.

"Love you too Belle." He kissed her again and walked out leaving her to look around the office in awe of what had been done.

"Knock, knock, can I come in?" Chicca sang out. She stood with a huge grin on her face.

"Hey you, come on in." Jane grabbed her giving her a huge hug. "Are you trying to make me cry all day?"

"Would I?" She grinned squeezing her hard.

"Yes, you would."

"To be fair it wasn't just me, the guys had a lot to do with it too. Ohhh I am so excited about the wedding, I hope this mascara Gwen is giving us is waterproof or we are going to look like bloody pandas. I keep getting emotional James just tuts at me." Jane pulled her in for a hug.

"If you cry then I will and I cannot ruin my make-up. Talking of that are you coming over for the make-up test?"

"Oh yeah, not missing anything, I have had my orders, Gwen wants us all the same."

"Why am I not surprised. Any way I better get on if I can find somewhere to work. I will catch up with you in a while." She kissed Chicca's cheek as she left.

"See you later chick."

Jasper parked his car and walked into the jeweler. He was excited about the gifts he was collecting.

"Jasper, Good Morning, is it really that time already, this wedding has certainly come around quick. I have everything ready for you."

"It's good to see you too, I know I really don't know where the time has gone, three days and counting."

"Right then here are the rings, as long as neither of you have put on or lost weight then they will be perfect. But if you want any alterations doing come back and see me. Now this little thing was a little harder, but I think she will love it. He opened the box, Jasper stood speechless for a few seconds.

"Wow that is more beautiful than I could have ever imagined it could be. You are a master. Thank you so much."

"Jasper it has been a pleasure, it's not often these days you find someone as romantic. I would love to see a picture of her with it."

"I will frame it I promise, you can put it up there then." He pointed behind him.

"Great idea. Right then I know you have a lot to do today so I won't keep you, have a wonderful day and I look forward to meeting Mrs Mitchell when you get back from your honeymoon." They shook hands, Jasper took the bag and left the shop, he was grinning.

"Oh Belle I can't wait to see your face. It's just perfect. Right then next stop....." He walked across town keeping the bag close to his body. He picked up the last of the items he had ordered and went back to the car.

He headed back to site with lunch to see Jane. He was desperate to show her what he had but it would spoil the surprise. He locked everything in the car boot and walked into the site. He knocked on the door as Jane called to come in. She stood when he entered coming around the desk to meet him.

"Hi love, you okay?" She moved things from the table so they could sit down with lunch.

"All good thank you just a few loose ends now and I am ready to relax."

"Perfect. I know we only have tomorrow together, should we check on the venue and see if everything is okay?"

"All sorted love, everything is ready, why don't we go for a ride out instead and have lunch somewhere before I say goodnight and leave you?"

"God it sounds so final. I like the sound of a ride out. Moses asked if he could borrow Red Robin while we were away, he wants to take Susan out. I said yes. She hasn't been on a bike before, so she wants to try mine first."

"That's a good idea, I understand that, I was nervous too."

"But look at you now."

"I don't think Susan would be buying a bike though do you?"

"I don't think so but who knows. They seem to be getting on really well which is nice."

"Are you sure about that Belle. I know how close you two are, especially now you are more protective."

"I promise, I am more than happy Susan is lovely and good for him. If she hurts him then that would be different, but I don't believe for one minute she will. But if he hurts her I will kick his arse too."

"You are funny. Kiss me please, I want to taste you." He puckered his lips, Jane did the same and kissed him making silly noises.

"I love you so much you silly man." She wiped her lipstick from his face with her finger.

"Good job someone does. You drew the short straw."

"Oh no I didn't, I definitely won the star prize." Jasper kissed her properly.

"Promise me this will never change, the way we are, we must always be honest and talk to each other." He looked at her seriously.

"I promise, no secrets, no silly thoughts. I just want you and me forever."

"Good, now I have something to tell you that might hurt but I have to be honest."

"Oh? Jane froze for a second not sure what she was going to hear."
"Can you please move that piece of lettuce from your nostril. It doesn't suit you." she wiped her face with her cloth and smacked him.
"Bloody hell you had me worried then." He laughed grabbing her kissing her hard.
"Come her I want a cuddle, it's going to be hard leaving you for two days, well two nights anyway. I just want to hold my girl. Jane sat on his lap and curled up into him. She laid her head on his shoulder. She was twisting his shirt in her fingers.

"You okay love?" she nodded. He lifted her head with his finger. "Talk to me love."
"I was just thinking about my parents, I wish they were here."
Belle they will always be with you, the same as mine will be."
She nodded. "I know, I just feel a bit lost without them sometimes."
"Then tell me love, I don't want you to hide anything, or feel you can't talk about them, it's important. I want to know everything, if you don't tell me I will ask Bill and I guarantee he will have some funny stories to tell me."
"Oh lord no don't do that, he will love embarrassing me." She laughed remembering Bill from her childhood. "He was everything to me, with him and Dad I was so happy, I knew I was protected."
"Can I ask why he isn't giving you away?"
"Moses and G are like Brothers, it felt right for them to do it. Bill has had his problems over the years and I didn't want to add the extra stress. He went away for a while a couple of years ago, he closed himself off from the world when his wife died."
"Oh Belle, I'm sorry I didn't know."
"He still blames himself, she was on her bike, he was behind her, they had found the perfect home, she was decorating it out while he was away, friends and family helped too, she had found out she was pregnant. He didn't know, she wanted to wait. He was away at the time, he had come back and she was going to surprise him at the house when they walked into the room."
"Oh no. that's awful."
"She rode out to meet him, she took him to the garage to collect his bike and he followed her home. They were on the motorway, a car came across from the slip road into the outside lane and didn't see her, the driver crushed her against the central reservation. They took her into surgery but she died from internal bleeding, that's when Bill was

told she was pregnant. He went back to the house to see what she had done and found the babies room. He spiraled after that, went on a drinking spree bounced from one woman to the next, until he came back and finally spoke to me, we got him into a specialist unit for a few months and now he's good but has a wobble from time to time, she was his world. I know him and Jax are getting close I just hope they take their time."

"Jesus that's awful, how does any man recover from that?"

"I don't think you do, it's like any death it stays with you."

"Why does he blame himself?"

"She was going to take the car, he said no he wanted them to have a ride home together. He hadn't had his bike out for 6 months the weather was bad before he went."

"Wow, that's not his fault, but I can see why he blamed himself, I would too. So did you ask him to give you away?"

"We spoke about it, I told him I wanted to ask Moses and G, that I loved him and it didn't change anything, I just knew how he would struggle. He agreed with me. He is still part of it, he will be my witness."

"That's nice, I'm sorry if I upset you by asking Belle." He pulled her closer kissing her head.

"You didn't love, I suppose I never thought about telling you before."

"That's ok, we have the rest of our lives to catch up." He patted her bottom.

"Right then, back to work, I have to earn lots of money now to keep my woman happy and in the life she has grown accustomed too."

"Oh really, well I hope she is grateful for that. Don't tell her our secret though will you?" Jasper laughed. Gritting his teeth.

"God I bloody love you Jane." I am going to eat you up tonight."

"Oooooh, I can't wait, now get out of my office I am a busy girl." Jasper left with the rubbish smiling, he headed back to the car, he knew he had just enough time to do what was needed and get back to collect her.

Chapter 25

The night before the wedding

The girls arrived like a whirlwind, Jasper stood back as they marched in the door, he thought there had been a lot for their hen night but this was nothing in comparison. Jane came to meet them taking bags and cases from the girls, Jasper kissed her and left, he sighed in relief knowing he got out just in time. He had taken Jane shopping for provisions of ice cream snacks, drinks and chocolate. They were ordering in for the night and that's all he needed to know. His phone rang as he got to the car.

"Hi Henry, you okay?"

"Yes, all good, just checking on tomorrow, are we set?"

"Absolutley, I am going to let the guys know tonight, then it's just Jane and the girls who won't know so if Lily calls Jane remind her Mum's the word."

"Okay Son, no problem at all, we will see you bright and early. Safe journey."

"Thank you, see you both tomorrow." He got in the car happy with all the arrangements. He had primed Gwen she had her orders for the morning.

Gwen walked around the house leaving bags and cases in different places everyone had their bed sorted, they decided to leave Jane on her own unless she wanted someone in there.

"Right then lady, did you shower already?

Jane lifted her arm and sniffed her arm pit, she pushed it towards Gwen.

"Well what do you think?"

"I was only asking, I am going to wax your arms, legs and do your toes that's all. The girls will do each other so I have set up areas around here for us all."

"Sounds great. Just tell me where you want me."

"Well for starters have you done your pussy wax yet, I will do it if I have to?"

"Yesssss, I did it last week."

"Did I not teach you anything, you will have stubble now, come on, we will have to do a full body, you cannot go to your wedding with any stubble, get to your bedroom I will let the girls know."

Jane shrugged her shoulders and walked off. Gwen went into the lounge the girls were unpacking the make-up.

"Right, I need to do an all over for Jane she has stubble, I will use her room to get it done, can you all start on yourselves we will be down soon." She went back to Jane. As she walked in Jane was sat on the bed inspecting herself.

"What are you doing?"

"Look Gwen, it's fine, it's just a bit of fluff, I don't think I need it."

"You don't need it, you are marrying the most handsome creature I have ever seen, do you think he wants a face full of fluff on his wedding night?"

"We've been through this he doesn't mind."

"Well, I do, I'm sorry Jane but this is different if you want to go back to fluff after that's up to you but as I am in charge of getting you ready then it's coming off."

Jane looked down again straining her head to see herself. "It looks like Auntie Gwen isn't a fan of you guys so I would run and hide if I were you, this isn't going to be pretty."

Gwen stood shaking her head at her. "You would never make a princess would you, I can see you now with your boots on under your skirt." Jane giggled.

"Yep that's me."

"Right knickers off lady and spread those legs, let's get that done first."

"Why can't I use the cream? You know I don't like the wax."

"The cream is as bad as the razor. No." Jane sighed kicking her knickers off and opening her legs.

"You do know I don't trust anyone else to do this don't you?"

"Well I hope there are not many others you would want to open your legs to either?"

"Ummmm, no!"

"Right, this will be a little warm."

"Just don't tell me please just do it." Jane picked up her book and began reading, trying to take her mind of what Gwen was doing.

"Whatever you say", Gwen got down on her knees and began to apply the wax, Jane was wincing, Gwen shook her head impatiently at Jane. Continuing to apply the warm wax. She waited until it was ready to come off and as requested she didn't tell Jane. She moved down to get closer to her pussy and find the starting point, Jane winced but still wasn't aware of what was about to happen. Gwen counted to 3 to give Jane a second to be ready still nothing. She continued and pulled at the wax.

"Arggggggghhhhhhh, what the fucking hell is that, Jesus Mother of God are you trying to rip my VJ from my body?" she jumped off the bed and began hopping around the bedroom holding her pussy.

"Owww, owww, fuck that hurts, it's throbbing and not in a good way." She ran out of the room as the girls came running in. She stood on the spot jumping up and down.

"Jesus what happened?" Chicca looked worried.

"She didn't want to know when I was pulling the wax off, I even gave her a countdown." She burst into a fit of giggles making the others laugh with her. "She hasn't realised that's the first part, there is another bit left."

"Oh Jane, you may want to come back, let us take a look, I'm sure it's not as bad as you think it is?"

"Oh, you think do you?" she spat as she hobbled back to the bedroom. "Let me rip your VJ out and see how you like it." They were all sniggering. Jane had a face like thunder but trying not to laugh herself. "Go on get it over with, laugh all you like." She folded her arms in front of her.

"Jane come and lay down let me see. I promise the next bit won't be so bad."

"I don't really have an option do I, when Jasper looks at me tomorrow walking down the aisle and sees I'm walking like someone who just got off a 200 mile horse ride you can tell him why. Then when he wants to lick me and wonders why my VJ looks like it's had botox you can explain."

"Move, move, I need the loo I'm going to piss myself." Chicca pushed everyone out of the way.

All the girls we laughing hard, Chicca sat on the toilet with the door open as Jane laid back on the bed and opened her legs. She huffed.

"Well?" Gwen got closer. "Susan as a nurse what do you think. Any damage?" Susan was holding back her laughter as she bent and looked.

"It's a bit red but that's normal. We just need to get the rest off, you can hold my hand if you like while she does it. Don't tense though it will be worse, as she says 3 breath out and squeeze my hand." Jane looked up confused but nodded. Susan gave Jane her hand. Gwen got ready.

"Right on 3, are you ready?" Jane nodded. "Okay 1, 2."

"Wait stop, I'm not ready." She panted getting herself ready, "okay. I'm ready."

"Okay on 3, 1, 2,3." She pulled as gently as possible, Jane breathed out and screamed again squeezing Susan's hand, Susan screamed begging Jane to let go of her hand before she broke her fingers.

"Did I ever tell you I hate you Gwen? Well, I do now. That fucking stings."

"Here put some of this on, its Aloe Vera it will sooth it, I promise it will be worth it. You don't hate me, you just need to take care of yourself a little more."

"Up yours." Jane spat then laughed putting her hand between her legs, "Linda give me the ice from your drink please, I need to stop this ache." Linda spat out her drink laughing.

"I will go and get you some ice, this has alcohol in it that will make matters worse. hang on." She came back with ice wrapped in a towel, Jane put it against herself sighing with relief.

"Are you ready for your under arms and legs?" Jane scowled at her.

"It can't get any worse just do it quick." The girls left going back to get themselves ready.

"Once it's done you are sorted for weeks." She warmed up the wax again and began applying to Janes legs.

"You must love torturing yourself doing this all the time."

"It's not so bad love when you get used to it. Matt helps me sometimes too."

"Well your husband is a bloody sadist."

"That's true. How is it feeling?"

"It's cooling down now thank god."

"I promise later you will thank me, it feels so nice and for a good long while too. Jasper will thank me too."

"I will let you know."

"Right get ready, 1,2,3." Jane held her breath as Gwen ripped it from her legs. "And the next, I'm not stopping so grin and bear it love." Gwen continued, Jane felt like her body had been punished when they finished.

"Just the nice bits now, you need to choose your nail colour and make-up, I have a few suggestions though so let's go and see the girls." They went back to the living room they all cheered as Jane walked in and began singing like a Virgin." Jane poked her tongue out as she sat down in the chair.

"Make-up time girls, I have got all Laura's kit with me and I told her we will all be sending her an order. I suggest we keep it natural, Jane I have foundation for you, I know you don't like it, but I promise you will love this, it has a blur affect so the camera doesn't see any lines or imperfections and it dries like a powder, so you won't look like a doll, here let me show you." She grabbed her scalf and put Janes hair out of the way and began applying it on one side, on the other she put Jane's powder. She handed her the mirror.

"What do you think?"

"Wow I like that, you can't even see it, it won't come off on his jacket though will it?"

"No it won't, here", she passed Jane another scalf, she wiped it across her face and it came away clean.

"I like this, thank you. okay what next, please don't give me huge eyebrows." Gwen put her hands on her hips.

"Have I ever?"

"No, I'm just saying that's all." Gwen tutted pulling out the rest of the make-up, she went to work within 20 minutes she was done, she passed the mirror to Jane.

"I know your hair isn't done but we will do that tomorrow the same as you had it the other night. What do you think?"

Jane's eyes glassed over. "OMG Gwen I love it. I don't know how you do it but it's perfect." She got up out of the chair squeezing Gwen tight. The others cooed watching them. "However for me to look this good on my honeymoon you have to come with me." She giggled.

"Let me think about that for a minute, do I want to be around while you two have sex every minute of the day? Do I want to stop you mid orgasm to touch up your make-up? definitely not, you're on your own kiddo, I will show you how to put it on, the foundation is so easy. The mascara is waterproof too. That goes for all of you." She turned to everyone pointing it at them all. "Okay now here are all the colours of the nail polish, I don't think red is right, I know you love it but to be honest it would look wrong. I know you don't like a French Polish and it would ruin your nails they are fine without it, so I think this would be nice it's a really pale pink, but not pink if that makes sense. It will show your nails perfectly and won't look silly through your shoes."

"I like that, okay go for it. I trust you Gwen even though you tried to pull my VJ off so I will do whatever you say."

"Sit let's get these nails done so we can relax." Jane sat down putting her feet up.

"I still can't believe this is happening you know, just look at him." Jane pointed to a picture of them both on the side from the restaurant.

"A beautiful couple is what I see girl, don't do yourself down, he is lucky to have you." Chicca blew her a kiss.

"What are we eating tonight? You girls can choose, it's on Jasper. He has put some bubbly in the garage fridge too." Linda and Chicca jumped up pushing each other out of the way to get to it. They came back arms full of bottles.

"Pizza goes well with bubbles don't you think?" Linda grinned.

"I'm game, but I want ice cream too", Jax piped up.

"That's in the freezer, you may want to check out the fridge and cupboards first Jasper went shopping for us." They all stampeded into the kitchen, pushing and shoving each other knowing full well what Jaspers shopping trips were like. They were squealing and cheering as they pulled food out of the fridge and cupboards.

"Jane order pizzas we have everything else here we need, are you sure you want to marry this man? I would happily take him off your hands." Jax laughed pulling out more food and chocolate ice cream.

"I don't think so sweet cheeks he is mine if Jane is having second thoughts." Gwen slurred.

"Hang on, no I saw him first remember?" Chicca chipped in laughing. They all began arguing who was having Jasper.

"SHUT UP!!" Jane shouted, "Stop arguing. Nobody but me is having Jasper. Gwen you are married, happily I might add, Jax you have Bill and you better look after him, Chicca I am disappointed in you James is a lovely man. I think you all need to go and play with your toys tonight and get rid of that pent up sexual tension."

"I'm not doing that sharing a room with this bunch! You never know we might end up having an orgy" Gwen giggled.

"In your dreams love." Chicca laughed. "I thought I was bisexual once, then I tried a pussy, nah not for me, I am a cock girl through and through."

"You mean if the most beautiful girl stood in front of you that you felt drawn too you wouldn't do it? Hell I would." Matt would love that!"

"Are you serious Gwen?" Jane asked looking shocked.

"Damn right, I watch girlie porn with him a lot, we both get off on it. We use it as playtime he will tell me about a girl he wants to try and we pretend. You need to try it." Jane sat with her mouth wide open looking at Gwen.

"Do you all do that? I think I must be a prude."

"Yep, we do it too, a little different to that." Jane looked at Linda.

"Wow, how am I only just hearing this now?"

"You never asked." Chicca laughed with the others. "You need to ask Jasper, I bet he would do it too."

"What if he doesn't is that a bad thing?" Jane looked worried.

"Of course not, but if you are always truthful with each other its worth exploring these ideas." Susan laughed, "Look at the sex clubs Alison goes too, she loves it, they share too."

"I'm in shock, my god I really do sound like a prude."

"Well why don't you call Jasper tonight and have a bit of video sex, tease yourself and see what he does, I promise you he will love it." Jane covered her eyes laughing.

"oh god, okay, I will." The girls squealed making Jane blush.

"Right enough sex, I need food, get those pizzas ordered Jane before I start eating one of you." Jane grabbed her phone looking for the app.

"Okay what do you want." They all bombarded her with their choices, Jane ordered it getting up and going into the kitchen to get the plates and cutlery sorted. Jax followed her out.

"Hi love, you okay?" Jane looked up at Jax.

"Yes love, how did you know about Bill and I? Do you think I am making a mistake, I know he has a lot of history and he is a lot older than me."

"You know I love that man to bits. I think it's fantastic if I'm honest, just look after each other, who cares about age, it's just a number and if you are happy and he is then who cares. I saw the way he looked at you, the secret touch of the hand and the knowing smile. It's beautiful."

"Thanks Jane, that means a lot, you know better than anyone what he has been through, my life hasn't been perfect either, but I know he cares a lot, that's all I want."

"Then don't let anyone stop you. Bill must think you are pretty special, no woman has turned his head in years."

"That's a compliment, I know he could have far better than me, some of the club girls are gorgeous."

"Listen Jax, you are beautiful, I know you have been treated badly and told a lot of lies but this is real, Bill is real, believe him when he says nice things because he doesn't say nice things easily." Jax sniffed and wiped her eyes. Before Jane could open her mouth Gwen appeared by her side with an empty glass.

"There is no room for panda eyes tonight love, come on time to party get that food out and get the music on." She pulled Jax into her side kissing her on the head. Jane came into them both and had a group hug. "Right then pizza coming up. it's in the oven." They went back to the fridge to get everything else out ready. The girls all came dashing in, they moved around each other giggling pushing and shoving to get the rest of the food prepared. The kitchen that Jasper loved was now a bomb site. Jane stood laughing, all her friends together who loved their homes had turned hers into a playground. Within a half an hour the pizzas arrived, they were marched ceremonially into the lounge with all the other food. The room fell silent as they began to eat. All that was left in the pizza boxes were crusts from the pizza. They cleared the boxes leaving the accompaniments out to feast on through the evening.

"Let's play a game." Gwen picked up the packs of chopsticks and passed them around, she emptied the packets of fruit rings into a separate bowl for each girl. "Right the sticks in your mouth, hands behind your back. You each have a saucer, the one who gets the most fruit rings out wins." They all gathered together with one chopstick in their mouths. "Okay you have 2 minutes. 3,2,1. Go." They all began pushing the sweets up into the bowl scrabbling to get them on the end of the sticks and not drop them before they got them to the plate, the giggling began, they each started pushing one another to win. Jax was in the lead with 4 the time was slipping away, Chicca grabbed her bowl emptying it on her plate, everyone began laughing as she picked up Gwen's bowl and emptying it on hers too.

The door knocked, Jane looked around at the girls, "We expecting anyone?" They all shook their heads following her to the door. Jane opened the door a courier stood their loaded with boxes.
"Jane Kirkpatrick?" Jane nodded.
"Yes, that's me."
"These are for you then. Please sign here." He put the boxes down inside the door and handed her his hand-held device while he pulled another box out of the van, he stood it up against the door. Jane signed for it all as he walked off. They carried the boxes in piling them up for Jane, she began to unpack them looking confused.

"Who did this?" They all shrugged. All boxes were numbered so she opened box number 1 , a note was laid on top.

Belle, I love you. Have a wonderful evening.
Xxx

Jane looked around at the girls holding the note with tears in her eyes. Chicca took it from her.
"I bloody love this man! come on then open what have we got?"
"Hang on", Jane giggled, she pulled out the first of the pure silk dressing gowns, across the back in pink was Belle, she pulled out the next, Gwen, they continued to pull them out until everyone had their own, everyone squealed putting them on straight away. Linda grabbed the next box which was huge.
"Open it quick what we got next?" The box was long, narrow and wide. She opened the top, Gwen and Susan were at one end the others pulling from the top. They slowly pulled out a huge picture frame mirror, they put it down onto the ground, finding a cable to plug it in, Jane was even more confused.
"Oh my god, this is one of those mirror camera things, look!" Linda squealed. The mirror switched on across the screen it lit up *Belle's hen night*. They all began squealing, standing in front of it to take their pictures.
"Now what? come on Jane open it." Jane opened number 3. Inside were selfie sticks, blow up champagne bottles, Giant rings, signs, glasses, feather boa's, wigs and a pink hydrangea flower wall. The squealing began again as they pushed and jostled in front of the mirror giggling like children.

Open together was written on 4 and 5, Jane opened them, tears running down her face. Inside were individual boxes with the girls names on. She gave them out, they waited for each other before opening them, Jane nodded as they opened their boxes. Each box contained a glass vase with a candle with the girls names on and a pamper bag, complete with face masks, chocolate, hair and body masks, puffs and scrubs bath oils and a miniature of each girls favourite drink. Jane stood and cried as she opened her own bag. Inside was a long velvet box inside was a note.
I am missing my girl like crazy, you have made me the happiest man in the world.

This is for your bouquet tomorrow, to remind you of our first day as a couple. xxx

The girls cooed as Jane pulled out the gold rose bud and stem, Jane wiped her eyes again, she held the rose to her chest falling silent as the girls came together to hug her.

"What a beautiful gift Jane, what does it mean your first day as a couple?" Susan asked.

"Our first day Jasper helped me move into my new apartment and sent ahead 24 yellow and red roses to mark the hours we had known each other, the red one was his choice as he knew I loved yellow ones." She sniffed again remembering him carrying her into the apartment and seeing them for the first time.

"Oh, what a romantic man, I knew how much he loved you after seeing everything he did at the hospital, but this is just incredible love." She hugged Jane again. Feeling more relaxed about her and Moses, angry too that she could feel that way about Jane.

"Oi Mrs, come on we have pictures to take." Jax called Jane over, Susan smiled pulling Jane with her. They used everything they could find taking hundreds of pictures from serious to silly to half undressed. They were exhausted from the giggling and all crashed out onto the sofa. Gwen grabbed a fresh bottle of champagne topping everyone's glasses up.

"Steady on Gwen we have to be up early tomorrow, I don't want to be hung over on my wedding day......OH MY GOD, did I just say my wedding day!!!" She jumped up out of her seat and began dancing around the room, everyone else got up and joined her. Champagne was being spilt, the girls began to giggle again. Jane put the music channel on turning it up loud, they bounced around the room together to a few songs, Jane was squealing and shouting.

"I'm getting married tomorrow!! She squealed, the girls cheered. She ran around the house screaming waving her arms shouting into every room, the girls watched laughing at her as she came back onto the lounge and crashed down onto the sofa, she was puffing and panting.

"Pinch me please, I need to know this is real." The girls jumped her, all pinching her together making her scream louder. "okay, okay, it's real." she laughed sighing heavily.

"Movie time I think to quieten us down. Any requests?"

"Runaway bride?" Gwen laughed, Jane slapped her hard. "Oww, what was that for?"

"You saying that cheeky cow."

"Well, you never know." She laughed to herself.

"Yes, you do I will not be running anywhere. Just into him." Jane poked her tongue out at her. Making Gwen laugh. "Sorry love just teasing."

"I know. Come on then what do we want, an old favourite or a new one?"

"The Notebook. It's a love story and it makes you cry." Jax shouted. Susan smiled turning away, lost in her own thoughts about Moses.

"No, no, Me before you." Linda squealed.

"Oh my god yes, that's beautiful I love her."

"She reminds me of you Jane." Chicca smiled

"Is that a compliment? It better be."

"yes it is, she is just like you in the films."

"Awww thanks Chicca." She blew her a kiss and laughed. They settled down all grabbing the snacks snuggling up to each other as the film started. They sighed and cooed throughout, wiped each others tears and cuddled each other. Jane looked around at each one thinking how lucky she was to have each one in her life.

"Susan, have you decided how you are getting to the wedding tomorrow?" Jane asked.

"I was going to drive over by following one of the cars if that's okay?"

"No, you are part of us, you can travel with the girls." Everyone clapped agreeing.

"Are you sure Jane?" Susan was looking shocked.

"Yes, I am sure, I won't have it any other way."

"That's lovely thank you so much", she got up moving towards Jane kissing her on the cheek. "You don't know how much that means to me." She whispered to Jane hugging her tightly.

"I know how much you mean to Moses in such a short time, so it's important to me." Jane kissed her cheek, Susan moved away sitting back down with Chicca and Gwen, they both hugged her tight.

"Well ladies I don't know about you, but I need my beauty sleep. If you don't mind, I am going to go to bed?" Jane stretched and yawned pushing herself up.

"Sounds like a plan", Gwen agreed, standing up. "We better tidy in here first though girls or we won't be organized tomorrow morning. Jane, go to bed we will sort this lot out."

"No, I can't do that." She grabbed some glasses turning towards the kitchen, Chicca took the glasses out of her hands as Susan turned her to face the direction of the bedroom. She huffed turning to hug them all.

"I love you all, thank you for being her." She walked to her room leaving the girls clearing up.

She was exhausted and excited, she was missing Jasper and wasn't relishing her second night alone, she went and showered removing her make-up and climbed into bed. She picked up her phone putting her earphones in and video called him.

"Hi beautiful, you okay?" She saw his face appear on the screen. She smiled feeling the butterflies in her stomach.

"I am now I can see you." She blew him a kiss. "I miss you so much."

"I miss you too Belle, it's been great fun with the guys but there is nothing better than being with you, how has your evening been?"

"Well, we have 3 drunk bridesmaids, my pussy and body has been pounded to death and I have only the hair on my head left. It has been fantastic, my tummy aches from laughing."

"That's good to hear love. Why does your pussy hurt?" he frowned looking concerned.

"Gwen waxed it." Jasper began laughing, trying desperately not to.

"You're not supposed to laugh."

"Sorry love I can't help it, would you like me to kiss it better?" She pouted lowering her eyes.

"Yes please." She opened her legs tilting the camera to show him, he got close to the screen kissing her. She began to giggle. "I wish you were here. You could see how smooth it is."

"You could show me?" She felt her cheeks flush.

"You're naughty."

"It's fun though. don't you think?" She nodded, putting her finger between her lips. She opened her legs wide propped the camera up close to her pussy so Jasper could see clearly.

"Show me Belle." He whispered. She licked her fingers and slid them down the outside of her lips, squeezing them together.

"Mmmmmm, don't stop baby. She looks beautiful." Jasper got closer to his phone. Jane continued rubbing up and down her lips, her middle finger slipping inside, she caught her breath moaning softly.

"That's it Belle, open up for me." Jane spread her lips wide, Jasper groaned looking at her. She pushed two fingers deep inside, she began mewling pushing harder into herself, Jasper watched as her pussy became wet. Her fingers teasing the outside again, spreading the wetness around, rubbing circles around her clit. Jaspers mouth went dry his cock rock hard.

"Jesus Belle this is so fucking horny." He began rubbing himself watching her. She picked up her new toy from the bedside cabinet and turned it on, Jasper frowned as she held it in her palm placing it in her pussy. she arched immediately as the vibration teased her, she took it out panting. Jasper could see her juices covering it.

"Do that again Belle, that was so hot." She did but opened her lips so he could see, she pushed it up into the hood holding it.

"Fuck I want you so bad." He was rubbing himself harder watching her. Jane continued feeling hornier. She dropped the toy on the bed, it slid towards her catching her bottom, she jumped as it vibrated, she pushed it closer feeling alive and naughty, she could feel the sensation now it was driving her mad. She slipped two fingers inside herself, her thumb strumming her clit, back and forth getting faster as she fucked herself, she pushed the toy further against her bottom, her whole body trembled with pleasure.

"Oh my god I need you Jasper." She pulled on her nipples, making them harder. She was biting her lip pushing her fingers in deeper. Jasper could see her juices seeping out of her, he licked his lips desperate to touch her. He could feel himself ready to cum. Jane rubbed herself faster, moaning louder, Jasper knew she was getting close, this was turning him on so much. He squeezed his balls tightening his grip around the base of his cock. Jane pushed her fingers deeper, opening her legs as wide as she could. Her other hand rubbing her clit and holding her pussy open.

"Tell me to cum baby please?" Jane cooed.

"Come for me Belle, let me see your beautiful juices."

"Oh yes, baby, yessssss." She pushed harder with her fingers pushing her toy to her bottom. Her cheeks clenching with the sensation.

"Belle I'm going to cum baby, fuuuuuck ."

"Oh my god, oh my god, yes, yes, yes, she cried out, her body trembled, her legs jerking as she came, Jasper watched as he felt his balls tighten.

"Fuck Belle I'm cumming", He pumped harder, faster as he teased the tip with his finger as his cum seeped out, his head rocked back as he emptied himself into his t-shirt. He laughed looking down at himself and Jane, they were both panting. Jane moved the toy away. Closing her legs, throbbing her finger still inside her, the sensation of the toy making her body tingle.

"Oh my god, that was amazing and so naughty." she panted laughing looking at Jasper.

"Wow that was, at least I will sleep better now. I want to use that toy on your bottom too now."

"As long as I can do it to you?"

"Of course." He grinned looking forward to exploring more with her. Before you go to sleep Belle please open my bedside drawer." Jane frowned. She laid across the bed and opened it, a box with a ribbon on it was laid inside, the label said simply *My Belle, my wife to be.* Jane took the box out bringing it back to the phone.

"Open it love." She pulled on the ribbon, taking the lid off, another card. *La Vie Est Belle, perfume 413. Please wear me tomorrow. My Belle.*

"Oh, Jasper this is beautiful, how did you find it?" She took the lid off spraying it on her wrist. "Mmmmm smells lovely."

"As you are Belle. My beautiful lady. It was Gwen who helped me, the name was just perfect, she got it from her friend Laura."

"Oh of course the lady who does the perfume and makeup. How lovely. Thank you, of course I will wear it tomorrow. I love you Jasper."

I love you too Belle. Can't wait to see you tomorrow. Sleep well love. He put his phone down on the pillow next to him, Jane did the same as she slipped down into bed. They both laid on their sides looking at each other.

"Remember no video call in the morning. But text me if you need anything. I'm not going though until you are asleep. I want to see you sleep as Jane Kirkpatrick for the last time."

"You still feel like a dream Jasper, I really don't know how I got so lucky."

"We both did love. Now close your eyes and sleep my love." Jane nodded closing her eyes, Jasper laid watching her as she drifted off to sleep peacefully, his heart ached to be close to her. He hung up and rolled onto his back leaving his phone where it was closing his eyes, smiling happy that all his plans had come together.

Chapter 26

The Big day arrives

Jasper woke earlier than the others, he went down to the kitchen and sat quietly with a cup of tea. He heard the door, he turned to see Moses behind him.

"Hi Brother, how are you feeling?" Moses patted him on the back.

"Nervous, excited, lucky, sick." He laughed at himself.

"Sounds about right, another tea?" he pointed to Jaspers cup.

"Thanks yes please." He passed his cup across the table.

"How are you Moses, honestly?"

"You know me Jay, I bounce back."

"No, I don't know Moses, that's why I want you to be honest."

"Listen Brother it is your wedding day, we are not discussing me today, so get that tea down you so we can get this day started." He passed Jasper his tea smiling.

"Not going to win, am I?"

"Not today no. I promise we will talk about it though."

"Now you got me worrying Moses, talk to me."

"Nothing to worry about honest, come on, tell me the details now."

"All I will say is get yourself sorted early, we need to make a move an hour or so earlier than needed."

"Jesus, you really are keeping this under wraps."

Jasper laughed. "Sure am."

"Right then we better get breakfast sorted so we can get organised." Moses turned to the cupboard and opened the door to get some dishes out.

"Oh no, not in my kitchen you don't. Sit down please." Moses smiled turning to see Kitty in the doorway.

"Oops that was close Moses." Jasper laughed as he sat down next to him.

"I understand you are setting off earlier so let's get this breakfast sorted for you. Cooked breakfast all round coming up."

"Wow are you sure Kitty, there are a lot of us?"

"Of course I am, I have had many more to feed, this is easy, you might want to go and wake your friends up though, I think there might be a few sore heads this morning."

Jasper and Moses left the kitchen to wake everyone up, Moses went to Dorians room, he banged on the door, no answer, he knew he was a nightmare to wake, he walked in, Dorian was spread out across the bed naked, his partner laid on his stomach his bottom bare. Moses shook his head it wasn't the first time he had seen this. He had seen much worse. He walked over to the window pulling back the curtains, still no movement.
"You playing hard to get this morning Dorian, we will see about that." He walked into the bathroom filled a glass with water, walked out to the bed pouring it over Dorian. He moved back as it hit him.
"Oh my fucking god, who the fuck...." He wiped his face brushing the water from it, his partner now awake looking up at him rubbing his face.
"What the fuck was that for Moses?"
"I was told to wake you so here I am." He laughed walking towards the door.
"Kitty is making breakfast get your arses up and not for that! I mean downstairs sharpish, we have to leave earlier than planned." Dorian threw a pillow across the room at Moses as he walked out and shut the door. He went back down to the kitchen as G walked in.
"Morning Brother, how you feeling?"
"Been better but keep it to yourself, I am not spoiling today. I don't want Susan to know either."
"Whatever you say. Anything I can do?"
"Just make excuses if you have too. We need to be at Half-pints a bit earlier to get moving apparently, so we will go once breakfast is done. The girls can get sorted a bit quicker."
"Ha, ha, ha, you are kidding me right. You do realise this is the wedding of the century for them."
"That's ok, I have already texted Gwen and told her, she's in charge."
"This will be fun to witness then, come on then let's get breakfast."

The men sat around the table chatting about the night before, they teased each other about who was cheating and how they would have a rematch. Moses sat quietly listening, he had sat out of most of the evening, he was feeling tired and knew he needed a lot of energy to get him through the wedding. He had missed Susan which surprised him. He was scared of getting close to her.

"Right then I need to head off, Dorian has the details, he has organised the cars for us, I will see you all in a couple of hours.

"Well, I would rather not know so I don't get into trouble if I say something to Half-pint."

I'm glad I won't be seeing them, Gwen would beat it out of me, I feel for you two." Matt laughed pointing at Moses and G.

"If you want to know I'm cool with it?"

"No, no, don't, you have no idea how manipulative these women are, keep it to yourself." Steve shook his hand not wanting to know anything.

"See you in a couple of hours then guys, thank you for last night, I really appreciate it."

"Get out of here, before you have us all as soft as you." Bill laughed.

Jasper left jumping into the Range Rover heading out of town to the venue. He checked the time, he was earlier than needed to sat back trying to relax for the journey.

His phone rang. "Hi, Jasper here."

"Hi Mr Mitchell, I just wanted to confirm that the flowers have been delivered and are currently being set up, did you still want them in the same places?"

"Yes please, did you manage to bring the other one with you?"

"Yes, we did, it looks great and there is a small yellow and pink bud on it too."

"That's perfect, thank you so much, I can't thank you enough, I am on my way now, I will see you in a couple of hours."

"Great look forward to it." Jasper hung up, smiling happily, he hit the steering wheel cheering to himself, happy that things were coming together.

He dialed Henry. "Hello Son, are you ok?"

"Hi, yes all good, on my way now, should be a couple of hours. I just spoke to the rose supplier everything is ready he has begun to set up."

"Fantastic that's great, we will see him when we arrive, we will keep an eye on things until you arrive."

"Thanks Henry. See you both later."

"Drive carefully Son."

"Will do." He hung up and dialed Jane.

"Hey you, I didn't think I would hear from you."

"I needed to hear your voice I miss you like crazy."

"I miss you too, especially after we played, how was your evening with the boys?"

"It was fun, we played every game I think Dorian has, I was kicked out on the first round on Call of Duty, I told them I don't play, but I'm sure they just wanted to whoop my arse."

"Well, you were up against mostly military men." Jane laughed.

"How is your pussy now, you do realise it won't get any rest once I get my hands on you."

"She's fine thank you, waiting to be touched, she's misses you too."

"Glad to hear it." The door knocked.

"Jane sorry love this came for you." Gwen stuck her head into the bathroom door.

"You okay Belle?"

"Yes, Gwen just brought a small parcel in for me."

"Okay, I will leave you to get ready. Can't wait to see you later."

"Me either, I love you Jasper."

"Love you too Belle." They blew each other kisses hanging up.

Jane put her package on the side as she left the bathroom, she showered and went down with the girls who were sat in their robes. The flowers had arrived, the lounge and dining room had been transformed into a salon, dresses were hung everywhere, the door didn't stop with well wishes flowers and cards.

Jane sat in the chair, Gwen came in and hugged her. "How are you chick?"

"Good love thank you. How long were you up last night doing all this?"

"Not long, the dishwasher helps to get the dishes done, it was just food to clear then and get everything unpacked. How did you sleep?"

"Good thanks, I rang Jasper before I went to sleep."

"Oh, did you show him your smooth pussy, did he like it?"

"Gwen!"

"oh come on love, I know what it's like to be away from the hubster, Matt and I still have a great sex life, we played together last night."

Jane blushed. "No way?"

"Hell yeah, come on you did too, you can tell me?" Jane nodded putting her hands over her face.

"I am so embarrassed. We have never spoke about things like this Gwen, probably because I was single."

"It is love, so now you can, what's on your mind?" She pinned parts of Jane's hair up and combed oil through it to stop the frizz.

"This is silly, but I know you two have a great sex life, we spoke about this when I was in hospital but how did you get to bums, I mean we have touched each others, but never gone further, just a slight finger inside." Jane covered her face again. She felt her skin burning as she blushed.

"This isn't silly love, it's all about trust for you both, you say you have tried slightly and how did it feel for you?"

"It was a shock, but I liked the feeling it gave me. I was desperate to go further with Jasper too but didn't want to spoil the fun we were having. I'm not a prude Gwen, we have been really naughty, sex on the bike, in the ladies at the black tie event, I also wore eggs all night, but this seems one step further, I don't know how to ask about it."

"Wow I am impressed, to be honest it sounds like it is your next natural step, if Jasper has played around there then tell him it's okay. Just be honest with each other."

"Thanks Gwen, did you do that with Matt?"

"Yes, we had been smoking it was a lot of years ago before the kids came along. He slipped with his cock, it sort of helped with the situation, we both looked shocked and he asked what I thought, I suppose being a bit high made it easier, like I said before, once you try it you will never look back. Try your small toy on his first, plenty of lube, slide it in gently but listen to him, be guided by him, it will give him an amazing orgasm with that and you sucking his cock. Right now we better stop this or I will be dragging Matt off when I see him for a good fuck during the wedding." Jane giggled.

"Sorry Gwen, I know what you mean though." They hugged each other again as Gwen got to work on drying her hair.

Moses and G arrived as the girls were almost ready, Matt had also called Gwen and told her something was going on but to keep it shut. She told the girls who moved quicker. They were all in their robes still, hair and make-up done. Susan opened the door as they arrived. Moses wrapped his arms around her waist kissing her hard. He spanked her bottom grabbing it.

"Mmmmm, do we have time for me to take you somewhere so I can rip this lot off?"

Susan laughed. "No, we don't."

"Damn, you turn a man on and then turn him down."

"Behave." She smiled slapping his chest. He swung his clothes bag off his shoulder.

"Well, if you are not going to let me devour you then you better show me where I can get changed."

"Come on, you can use the bedroom", she led him off into the spare room she had shared with the girls. "I may as well get dressed now too, then the girls are free to do what they need to do."

"Now you're teasing me again." He grabbed her head as they walked into the bedroom and shut the door. He span her around, her hair had been put up so her neck was showing. He began licking and biting gently, down to her shoulder. He pushed her over bending her onto the bed getting onto his knees, he pushed the robe up over her bottom pulling her knickers to one side pulling her cheeks apart, she spread her legs as he pushed his tongue between her cheeks. Susan bit her hand to stop herself from screaming, her legs weak with pleasure, he pulled her cheeks further apart, licking lower towards her pussy. Susan groaned into the bed, covering her face.

"You taste so fucking good." He moaned sliding his finger inside her. Susan's legs began to tremble, she could feel her wetness as his fingers slid in and out of her.

"Keep still love, stay there." He moved himself sitting on the floor his back to the bed. He laid his head onto the bed pulling her pussy down onto his face.

"Oooh fuck…." She whispered into the bedding. Moses pushed his tongue inside her, her lips naturally opening as she moved her tiny knickers from her pussy. She pushed herself down onto his face, his beard teasing her, she moved back and forth his tongue catching her clit as she moved, Moses sank his fingers into her bottom, his cock rock hard, he wanted her but knew it would wipe him out. He pulled her further onto his face, his nose now on her clit, he rubbed her, feeling her legs begin to buckle. Her face now buried in the bedding, she was desperate to scream out. She couldn't wait anymore, she moved faster on his face, his tongue inside her, draining her. He sucked and licked groaning wanting more, Susan went rigid as her orgasm hit her, her body trembled as she came hard, Moses sucked, gulping as she filled his mouth, sucking hard, he wanted more, Susan was out of her mind, her sensitivity making her move away. Moses pulled her harder onto him not letting her go. He continued to tease her. Susan was squealing into the bed, feeling like she was going to pass out. Moses continued his tongue darting in and out of her. She punched the bed as she sank her teeth into it, her pussy contracting as she came harder, Moses was moaning louder trying to capture it all, his face wet with her. Susan slumped onto the bed, exhausted. Moses smiled as he finished licking her, he moved away sitting up as Susan crawled onto the bed. She turned to look at him heaving to catch her breath.

"Wow, that was incredible, you taste fucking amazing, I just had to have more." He moved towards her on his knees, kissing her.

"I wish my tongue was longer I would lick my face to taste more of you." He grinned at her.

"I don't think I have the energy now to get ready." She laughed. "I swear you're going to kill me."

"Not a chance, I just need to eat you all the time." She grabbed his face kissing him again.

"What about you, I want you too."

"We don't have time now love, later I promise. As much as I want to taste you for the rest of the day I better wash my face." He grinned licking his lips again getting up off the bed heading into the bathroom. He closed the door slumping onto the sink, looking at himself in the mirror. He washed his face, he sighed going back out into the bedroom. Susan was pulling her knickers off.

"I need to wash myself too or everyone will smell me."

"Shame, it would be nice to know you are still wet and sticky all day because of me."

"Not today." She grinned as she headed into the bathroom. Moses pulled his suit out of the bag. It had been a long time since he had worn it, he smiled as he pulled it out remembering events he and G had taken Jane too. He pulled off his jeans and began getting dressed. Susan came out of the bathroom naked, her clothes in her hands. Moses was bent over, she spanked him hard, making him jump.

"Lady you will pay for that later!"

"I hope so", she grinned, walking past him sexily, teasing him. He stopped her pulling her into him. Bending down he took her nipple in his mouth sucking it hard. Flicking it with his tongue, He let it go with a pop kissing the other as he moved up her chest to her lips.

"Such a tease." He spanked her letting her go. Pulling his trousers on and shirt. Susan left her knickers off without telling Moses, she pulled her dress on, sitting on the bed she slipped her strappy heels on standing in front of the mirror applying her lipstick again.

"Wow! Shit you look beautiful." His eyes were up and down her body taking it all in. She stood with her hand on her hip. Her dress was sleeveless, it was dark blue with huge lilies. The neckline plunged showing the cleavage, she had no underwear on, the dress fell onto her hips and wrapped around into a waterfall at the back, the split at the front came just above the knee. She felt good which gave her more confidence. Moses was licking his lips making her laugh. He turned doing his shirt up before putting his jacket on, Jane didn't want anyone in ties, it was a relaxed wedding. He turned to look at Susan, she stood with her mouth open staring at him.

"Jesus, you look..... wow!" She moved towards him turning him to see more of him, she lifted the back of his jacket to see his bottom, she spanked him laughing.

"You're in trouble tonight. Grey looks good on you." She winked at him making him laugh.

"Ready?"

"Yes, are you?"

"Yes, let's go and see what the girls are doing. G should be ready too."

They walked out into the lounge together, Chicca whistled at them both.

"Wit woo, look at you two, what a handsome couple." Susan blushed holding Moses hand, he squeezed it hard letting her know it was okay. G came out of the other room, Chicca span around to look at him.

"My God!! Where have you two been hiding this gorgeousness." She walked up to G, walking around him checking him out.

"I'm not a toy Chicca, you make me feel like a slut." he laughed, "I'm not for sale."

"Damn shame, I could have fun with you."

"I am sure James would have an issue with that too."

"Don't you worry about that pussy cat." She teased walking away. The doorbell rang, Linda was closest, she opened the door, Graham and the girls were stood smiling. The girls were in their flower girl dresses grinning."

"Wow, look how beautiful you look come on in. Jane! the girls and Graham are here." She called out.

"Thanks, I will be out soon. Make yourself at home."

"Thanks love, Graham shouted moving the girls into the house."

"Right ladies we better get our dresses on now." Chicca pushed all the girls out of the room into the bedroom, they stripped off within seconds pulling their dresses and sandals on. They lined up, Chicca went down the line doing everyone up, ensuring they all were ready. She turned for Linda to do her up. "Okay ladies we are ready, let's sort the flowers out and hopefully Jane and Gwen will be dressed."

They walked back into the lounge to wolf whistles from the men. They all grinned standing like models showing off their dresses.

"You look gorgeous girls." G spoke first.

"Yes, you do." Susan echoed.

"Thank you." The doorbell went again. Graham answered the drivers had arrived. They sorted who was going in which car as Jane's white Rolls Royce pulled in. She didn't know what car she was going in. They all walked outside to see the three cars adorned in ribbon on the bonnets and door handles, the drivers were dressed in suits and hats.

Jane was ready, she looked in the mirror, her small veil across her face, her mum's tiara on her head. Her hair cascading across her shoulders in soft curls.

"You okay love?" Gwen asked noticing the tears in her eyes.

Jane nodded. "Yes love, I just can't believe this is really happening. It's like a magical dream."

"No tears honey." She squeezed her tight. "Are you ready for your guests?" Jane nodded as Gwen opened the door. They walked into the lounge as everyone was outside talking and having pictures taken. Moses turned as if he sensed her behind him. His smile grew across his face, he stood looking at her in awe. He walked towards her G following her, the others stood back watching.

"Wow, when did our girl grow up into such a beautiful princess. Half-pint you look mesmerizing, absolutely stunning." Moses wiped his eye. He took her hand kissing the back of it.

G took the other. "Jesus Doc, you have floored me, I really don't know what to say. Just perfect." He kissed her other hand turned to stand next to her as the others came in. the girls squealed making the younger ones join in, they were all jumping up and down, Jane was fighting the tears, G wrapped his arm around her waist leaning into her.

"You got this love, no panda eyes today. Jasper is going to be blown off his feet." Jane turned blowing a kiss at G. Moses moved her veil.

"I can see that is annoying you so for the journey we will leave it off, the photographer wants you outside too. So we may have to put it back down just for pictures." Jane nodded going outside with them all. Graham came to Jane.

"Hey cupcake, you look stunning, so angelic." He kissed her forehead. "Forget Jasper I saw you first, marry me instead?" He teased her, she dug him in the ribs making him laugh. "A man has to try."

Jane turned to see her car, she suddenly realised there were three cars. "Where did these come from?"

"Jasper of course, you put him in charge."

"Wow, look at these cars they are beautiful. That man is crazy, he never stops surprising me." G and Moses looked at each other raising their eyebrows knowingly.

Jane went off with the photographer, they spent 30 minutes together having different pictures together before all getting into the cars. Moses grabbed Janes bags loading them into the boot with the other girls things before helping Jane in. Both G and Moses sat either side of her. Jane gave Moses her bouquet, it was white roses and white gypsophelia.

"Are you ready beautiful, any last minute regrets or doubts?" Jane shook her head.

"None at all." Moses pressed the button to tell the driver to leave.

"Wait, wait, in the bathroom there is a small parcel, please I need it, I don't know what it is but I have to have it."

"Jesus woman, you trying to kill us?" G jumped out of the car trying to unlock the door as fast as he could, dashing to the bathroom, he returned minutes later panting holding the box.

"Is this it?" Jane nodded taking the box.

"Are we ready now?"

"Yes definitely." Jane sat back turning the box in her hands, not sure if she should open it. Moses took her hand.

"You don't need to open it." She smiled nodding.

"I know, I just feel it's important so I want too." She played with the tape, looked around at both men looking down at it and ripped it open. Inside was a small leather box, with two openings, Jane pulled on the little handles, a card sat on the top. Jane picked it up. The front was pale blue, a yellow rose laid across it. She turned it over.

Hi beautiful, I know you are really missing your Mum and Dad today,

So I hope having this with you helps a little to feel like they are still with you.
I can't wait to see you. I love you so much Belle. Xxx

Jane struggled not to cry, G put his finger under her eye making her laugh as he caught a stray tear. She took the last cover out of the box, laid inside was a bracelet. She lifted it out frowning not understanding the link, she saw something on one of the tiny hearts, she recognised instantly her Dads writing and the curly kisses he always put in her card. She looked around at the other two, she moved the chain through her fingers to the next heart. Her Mum's writing and her kisses on the next. Her jaw went tight as she tried desperately not to break down, she sighed heavily moving the bracelet, a rose was next. Jane knew the relevance. Her hands flopped into her lap. She sighed again, looking at them both.

"How does he do this? Where does he get the ideas from?"

"It's love Half-pint, that man couldn't love you anymore than he does." She nodded as another tear escaped, Moses caught it with a tissue gently touching her face he dried it up.

"Which wrist love?" G asked taking the bracelet from her. She put her left hand up. He put it on her, it fit perfectly, she twisted it in her fingers. Smiling sadly.

"They are with you love, always." Moses squeezed her arm. She nodded sitting quietly. Moses took the box putting it into his jacket pocket for later.

They had been driving for more than an hour, Jane suddenly realised she couldn't see outside.

"Why are the windows so dark, why can't we see anything?"

"I have no idea, but don't open them we don't want to lose your veil do we." Both men looked at each other nodding. G mouthed. *Good save* over Janes head. She wasn't taking much notice just accepted it sitting back in her seat.

Jasper was sat in his room, he could hear the guys chatting in the living room and kitchen, more guests arrived. Lily knocked on the door.

"Hello sweetheart are you okay?"

"Yes, thank you, just having a few minutes alone before the day starts."

"You may want to open this then in peace and quiet." She handed him an envelope and a small box. He looked up at her frowning.

"Thank you Lily, where did this come from? Moses gave it to me when we were with you having dinner as he was going to be with Jane."
He smiled up at her, she kissed his head leaving him to his thoughts. He opened the envelope to a card. It was pale blue which made him smile. At the bottom were two pictures of him and Jane. Across the middle.
Jasper you are my happy ever after.
Love always your Belle xxx

He ran his finger down the card and across her face smiling. He opened the cover.

On this day our wedding day, I can never describe how happy you have made me,
My life has changed completely since I met you.
Thank you for finding me and making me the happiest girl in the world.

He wiped his eye catching a tear. He sighed heavily putting the card down looking at the box. He pulled the ribbon off, undoing the bow, lifting the lid he found a tiny bag. Inside was a tiny silver heart. Engraved, *Forever with you.* He gulped, looking at it, desperate to see her, to touch her. He slipped it into his pocket. Holding onto it, he put the card on the bedside table, picking up his jacket from the back of the chair and walked out of the room.

The driver opened the intercom. "Miss Kirkpatrick could I please ask you to close your eyes now."
"Is something wrong then?"
"Nothing at all, just my instructions."
"Okay thank you. I can't see anything any way, but I will." She looked at G and Moses, they took her hands, squeezing gently.
"This is it love", G kissed Jane's hand gently.
"All these years you have been with us, today it feels like we are losing you a little, I know that sounds silly, it's like parents handing their child over to someone else to care for. You know how much we love you, how much you mean to us and regardless of where we are, we will always feel the same, call and we will be there for you." Moses kissed her other hand. Before wiping another stray tear way. They both helped to pull her veil over her face as the car came to a stop.
"Keep your eyes closed love." Jane smiled nervously. The door opened Moses got out first followed by G, they took her hands and guided her

out of the car. Holding onto her dress for her. She stood still for a few minutes until the car pulled away.

"Open your eyes Jane." Jane squinted into the sun, she was a little confused at first looking at the trees, suddenly realising where she was. The girls came dashing over to her. Jane looked around, confused.
"Why are we here, where is everyone?" Moses smiled. Taking her arm, G the other side. The girls walked on ahead. Graham took Susan with him. They stood waiting for a few minutes until they heard the music.

Grahams girls walked down the aisle first scattering rose petals, everyone turned smiling watching them, the reached the bottom running into Jaspers arms, he kissed them both as they stood to the side with Susan and Lily. The girls followed, Jasper was holding his chest, his heart pounding, his girl only a few minutes away. Both men began walking with Jane, they went to the side of the building which opened up onto the small wood by the water. Jane gasped, in front of her white chairs were in rows filled with all their friends. Hanging from the trees were white lights, there were two doors positioned open with planters full of roses and gypsophilia, which led down the aisle. The trees gave a beautiful canopy and had white net panels hanging from them making an arch, at the end was a huge wooden arch, covered in roses, vines, lights and more net panels. Everywhere Jane looked were roses. Her heart was beating out of her chest, she was struggling not to cry, she thought it looked like something out of a movie, it was so romantic. At the end of each outside chair were more flowers and candles in hurricane glasses.

Jane stopped for a second to catch her breath, she looked at the sea of faces looking at her. She couldn't see Jasper anywhere. Her heart sank. She looked at Moses for answers.
He turned her to the side, walking her to a small wooden doorway, stand there love and put your hand out. She frowned but did as she was told as the men moved back. She felt Jasper take her hand from the other side of the door, she caught her breath.
"Jasper, what's wrong?"
"Hi Belle, I just wanted a moment with you before the wedding started. I needed to touch you for the last time as my fiancée. My heart is beating out of my chest, I am overwhelmed with love and joy. I'm fit to burst."

Jane sniffed, tightening her jaw again, knowing she couldn't cry. "I have missed you so much. I thought you had changed your mind."

"Never my love." He looked down and saw her bracelet, knelt and kissed her hand before letting it go. "Now I'm ready are you?"

"Yes, more than ever." They both moved away from the door, Gwen appeared by Jane's side.

"You okay Chick, let me check those eyes, we have all been crying already. Yep, you are good to go, see you there love." Jane grinned as Gwen moved away towards the start of the aisle with the others. She looked up at the boys and nodded.

The music began, and they continued to walk down towards the aisle, Jane caught sight of a marquee, tables and chairs in the field, she stopped looking and shook her head smiling, amazed at what she was seeing. She walked down the aisle, Moses and G looking prouder than ever. Her friends snapping pictures, blowing kisses and wiping tears. She looked up to see Jasper turn, she caught her breath seeing him stood there looking at her. She could see the tears in his eyes. The music suddenly silent, she felt like she had been transported and only the two of them were here. His mouth dropped open as she got closer. Her legs went to jelly, their eyes not leaving each other's. *I love you,* Jasper mouthed as she took her last steps to him. He took her hand kissing the back of her knuckles. She looked up as the Officiator cleared his throat.

She looked into Bills eyes and began laughing, he winked at her. Smiling.

"Friends, we have been invited here today to share with Jasper and Jane a very important moment in their lives. In the short time they have been together, their love and understanding of each other has grown. They have now decided to take the final step and live their lives together as husband and wife. Please could I ask you both to turn and face each other."

Jane turned to look at Jasper, her mouth growing dry, she couldn't stop looking at him in his dark suit and pink shirt. Her heart caught, like the first day she set eyes on him.

"Who gives this woman to be wedded to this man?"

"We do." Moses and G spoke in unison smiling, stepping forward. Jane looked back at them smiling, they both winked at her.

"Are you Jasper Mitchell free to lawfully marry Jane Leah Kirkpatrick?"
"I am."
"And are you Jane Leah Kirkpatrick free to lawfully marry Jasper Mitchell?
"I am."

Bill continued with the wedding ring blessing.

"I understand you have your own vows, as you place the ring onto each others fingers please say your own words."
Jasper took the ring from Bill. Jane put her hand out as Jasper slipped the ring on. Her hands were trembling, it matched her engagement ring perfectly.

Belle, you have become my best friend, mentor, playmate and confidant, not forgetting my greatest challenge. But most importantly you are the love of my life and you make me happier than I could ever have imagined. I could lose possessions, money and I could live, but I look at you and know I could never live without you. I feel lost in time. You take my breath away and bring magic to my life, I am honored to call you My Belle." Jane wiped a tear from her eye laughing as Jasper pushed her ring onto her finger.

Jane took the ring from Bill, placing it onto Jaspers finger, she looked him in the eyes.
"Jasper, you came into my life like a whirlwind and a grumpy sod." Everyone laughed his friends nodded. "You have made me a better person, your love makes me strong, you are my once in a lifetime love. One that I could never imagine I could have. As our love for one another grows I will always know in the deepest part of my soul that no matter what challenges might carry us apart we will always find our way back to each other. You are my soul mate, my one true love." She pushed the ring onto his finger. They could hear people sniffing, they grinned at each other, Jasper took Jane's veil tucking it out of her eyes, he placed one hand on her right cheek taking her left hand in his he bent down taking her soft bottom lip between his, as he kissed her so softly. His tongue gently running along her lip line.
"I love you Belle." He whispered.

"I love you too Jasper." They looked back up at Bill as the crowd erupted into cheers and claps. Bill waved his hand to quieten the crowd.

"I have great pleasure in presenting to you Mr and Mrs. Mitchell. You may now kiss your bride." Everyone stood and laughed as they kissed again officially. The girls huddled together wiping one anothers tears. Jasper took Jane's hand turning to their friends and cheered. They stepped away from the alter and walked slowly down the aisle to the waiting photographer. They stopped at the end and turned to their friends. Jasper picked Jane up and spun her around, as everyone cheered again.

The photographer spent a lot of time taking pictures of everyone, when they were finally done they moved onto the field, Henry had set up a marquee and dance floor, tables and chairs around the outside, the place was filled with flowers. Janes face lit up when they walked in to see what had been done.
"How did you do this? Why here?" She looked at him frowning.
"Don't you like it?"
"I couldn't think of a nicer place to be honest, you know how much I love it here. I just can't believe you did all this without me knowing."
"Nobody knew Belle, well apart from Henry and Lily, at the last minute I let Dorian in on it and Kitty as they helped a lot too." He pointed to Kitty and Lily who were waving at them.
"Oh my god, that's incredible, I am amazed."

"There is one more thing Belle, come with me." He took her hand, they walked down to the cottage, as he reached the stairs he scooped her up into his arms carrying her to the door.
"Open it Belle." Jasper took her over the threshold standing her on her feet. "Come with me, he took her hand leading her down the hallway past the bedrooms to another door. "Open it."
Jane frowned and turned the handle. She pushed the door open and gasped. She span to look back at Jasper, he nodded beckoning her to step in. Her hand shot up to her mouth, tears in her eyes, still confused she turned back to Jasper. "It's your little nook. Your reading room."
Jane looked around her, the room was brick and wood built with a small fire, with a huge seat similar to Lilys, there were blankets on the side and a huge sofa for two. The shelves were filled with books that Jane had read and others that she had in her wish list.

"I don't understand Jasper, why is this here?" She felt silly for asking but was so confused. Jasper handed her a box.

"Open it. she took the lid off to see a key. She turned the fob, *welcome home* was inscribed . She smiled looking at Jasper not convinced what she was reading was true, she looked up to him, he was grinning smiling at her.

"Am I understanding this right, am I being a bit thick?"

"No Belle you are not being thick, welcome home darling. This is ours. He held up his arms. The whole house is ours." Jane stood motionless in shock.

"This house……is ours……yours and mine?"

Jasper laughed. "Yes Belle."

"How….when….why, what about Henry and Lily?" He took her hand leading her to the sofa. He pulled her down to sit with him.

"When we left here you never stopped talking about it, you were so relaxed and said you wouldn't want to be anywhere else, every weekend you asked if we could come back, that's when I decided to buy it. Henry had already offered it to me, so we came to an agreement on the price. I couldn't bring you here because he was working on this room for you, he wants to know what other changes we want too, he had a great lad working for him who he is training."

Jane's mouth dropped open, Jasper put his finger under her chin closing her mouth.

"Catching flies with your mouth open is not a good look on you." He laughed teasing her. "Now you might want to go back out and look around properly. Jane got up frowning again and walked out of the room, he turned her around and pointed to the top of the door. An engraved wooden plaque read *Jane's den.* She began to sniff. Trying to stop her tears.

"No, no, no Belle, please don't cry." She walked back into the lounge and stopped, on all the walls were pictures of them both and their friends. Their parents were in the middle of a collage.

"You are one sneaky sod! I don't think I can ever trust you again." She laughed slapping him.

"I'm sorry I just wanted it to be perfect, I promise I will never do anything as sneaky again. Well maybe little things anyway. Oh except, one last thing. He took her head leading her outside. They walked along the balcony stopping outside of the bedroom window, he sat her down on the swing.

"I know how much you love the roses that we brought for the children and wanted to do something for you. I got in touch with the rose garden and explained it to their top man, this is what he did." He pointed to the rose. This is part of all the roses we brought and put into the garden, including the one I gave you in gold, that was the first rose of this bush. I had it named for you, it's called. *For the love of Jane."* Tears prickled her eyes. Jasper pulled her into his chest.

"Belle there are no words to express my love for you, I know you are not materialistic, but I just want to buy you the moon, to show you."

Jane sniffed. "I have never ever felt as loved, you don't need to do all this to show me, I already know, but you have really blown my socks off, I have no words Jasper, I just want to kiss you forever." She laughed at herself for her silly words. He tilted her head up wiping the few stray tears he found. He bent down kissing her softly again.

"Mrs Mitchell, can I escort you to our wedding reception?" She nodded throwing herself at him hugging him tight. Jasper laughed scooping her up and carrying her down the steps and into the field, everyone was sat chatting as they walked in, Jasper didn't put her down, just continued to walk through with her to everyone cheering. They stood clapping as they arrived. He walked her around to their table sitting her down. The room quietened, Jasper stood.

This wedding is not an ordinary wedding as you all know, we did it our way. Well, I must admit I did a lot without Belle knowing", she looked up scowling pretending she was annoyed. "But it looks like we got away with it. We are not going to go through lots of speeches, neither of us wanted that. We just want you all to have a great time. I do have some thank you's to say of course. Th first is to my beautiful wife, who I haven't told yet how gorgeous she looks today, Belle you took my breath away." The girls all cooed. "In no particular order I would like to thank you both, Henry and Lily for everything you have done here, I know it was no mean feat, allowing us to buy this place is the icing on the cake so to speak and all the changes you have made Henry are incredible, you were right Lily she didn't even notice the pictures or the name above the den door. I would like to thank each and everyone of you for being here, for everything you do for us, we are closing the door on what happened and looking forward to our lives going forward. We want you all to come and go here as you please. We want to share it with you all. Dorian and Kitty, thank you for all of your help with getting these guys out here, the cars and assisting Lily and her team with the food we are about to eat, when I shut up. The amazing decorations, you read my mind Lily by the way." Jane stood covering his mouth.

"What my husband is trying to say is, get off your bottoms and get over there and sample some of the amazing food that has been put together by these lovely people. Then get on that dance floor and dance the night away." Everyone laughed as Jasper pouted sitting down, Jane grabbed his face making a fishy face before she kissed him making him laugh.

"Now can we eat I am starving." Jane rubbed her stomach.
"Well then we better eat." Jane filled her plate making Jasper laugh. They sat and ate together, their friends stopped by to chat and hug them. Jane was overwhelmed with the day, Jasper was smiling as Dorian got onto the stage.

At last – Etta James

"Good evening folks, Dancing is obligatory. But first I would like to invite Jasper and Jane to the dance floor for their first dance."
Jasper took Jane by the hand leading her to the floor. Taking her in his arms, he guided her around the floor, he looked down at her and rubbed noses, before kissing the end.
"I never imagined this day would come, I meant everything I said Belle in my vows, you are my everything you complete me. I have never been so sure of anything in my life as I am with you, that moment I set eyes on you properly on site I knew you were going to be my girl."
Jane smiled. "I thought I was the mushy one in this marriage. You never fail to make me smile, every day waking up next to you is the happiest day of my life. I am the happiest girl in the world." Jasper grabbed her face with force, their lips met crashing together, they panted as they kissed wanting everyone else to be gone, to be alone for a moment locked in time.

Jasper felt a tap on his shoulder, Moses stood looking at her.
"May I?" Jasper smiled. Nodding, he handed Jane to him and turned towards Susan.

"Hi beautiful, are you okay?" He smiled kissing her head. Jane nodded.

"I couldn't be happier Moses. It's like a dream come true. It is a fairytale, who would have thought this would happen."

"I'm so pleased love, you deserve to be happy, now I know you will be looked after and treated as you should always have been. I don't need to worry anymore."

"I will always need you though Moses, you will always be my best friend."

"I know that love, as you are mine. But life moves on love. Things change."

"No, this will never change, just because I'm married." Jane scowled at him.

"I didn't mean that love, nothing in this world can change the way I feel about you." Jane nodded happier. Moses felt a tap on his shoulder he looked back to see G stood there.

"My turn." Moses smiled kissing her again before handing her to G. He swept her into his arms and marched her around the dancefloor making her laugh.

"You're crazy do you know that?" she laughed.

"Yep, one of us has to be, that old sod is too serious."

"Is everything okay G?"

"Of course it is Half-pint, you know what he can be like all emotional at times." Jane nodded as G moved them around the dance floor again. She began to giggle as she saw Moses sit down with Susan, she was frowning at him. He nodded to her. G moved her head back to him.

"Right then little one. Just because you are married it doesn't mean we are not here for you, you ever need anything you pick up the phone, you hear me?"

"I hear you."

"We love you little lady, don't ever forget that, you can come home as often as you like I will move into the club and you can use my house."

"The same goes love, my home is yours too, please don't be a stranger."

"Fat chance of that." A tap came to his shoulder. Bill stood towering over him. G tipped his imaginary hat and passed Jane his hand, he kissed her on the head and walked off to find someone else to dance with.

"Hey gorgeous girl, how are you doing?"

"Hi Bill, I'm overwhelmed if I'm honest, all of this is down to Jasper. Seeing you stood at the alter was a shock but a beautiful shock."

"I wanted to do something for you both, it seemed perfect to marry you. I asked Jasper who agreed very quickly, he said you would love it. I know you have probably been thinking of your Mum and Dad a lot today?" Jane nodded. "Me too, Jasper showed me the bracelet, its beautiful that guy really loves you, we had a man to man chat too."
"Oh no, what did you say?"
"Nothing for you to be concerned about it's between us." Jane nodded again. "Any way before your Dad died, the other one", he laughed he gave me something and I promised I would keep it for you until the right moment, today is that moment. Let's sit down." He took her hand and led her to the outside sitting with her on a bench.

Bill handed Jane a small dictaphone. Jasper came out to see if she was okay. She took his hand sitting him down next to her.
"This is from my Dad. He asked Bill to give it to me at the right time."
Janes hands were shaking, she pressed play, and closed her eyes.
"Hi little lady, it's Dad." Jane caught her breath. "I assume Bill has given this to you, I don't know how long he has had it, we both made a pact to do this in case anything ever happened to either of us. I assume now it has." She opened her eyes staring at Bill he nodded. "I was going to write you a letter, but this felt more personal. I don't know how old you are love, but I wanted to tell you some special moments in my life, the first is the day your Mum told me we were pregnant, that big old sod sat next to you will remember it. He was like a big kid crying." Bill nodded.
"Anyway, I talked to you every day while you were growing, I sang to you too, much to your mum's disgust. The day your mum went into labour was the craziest day, if you ever saw the three stooges running around like lemmings, you will know what I mean when I say Bill and I were doing that. When they handed you to me, I cried buckets, you were wrapped up in this pink blanket, your big blue eyes looked up at me, I knew I would never love anyone the way I loved you. You were my little girl, I swore to protect you every second of your life. I know maybe sometimes I was a bit hard on you, but it was only because I was scared something would happen to you. You grew up with your Mum's attitude for life and your love for others. She is so proud of you, we both are love. I wonder sometimes what you will be doing when you are older, I know whatever it is it involves people, you love everyone and in return you are loved too. I hope you find someone that treats you like a princess but doesn't spoil you, who accepts you for you and never steps out of line. I love you my darling, never forget that, no matter where

you go in life we will always be watching over you, keeping you safe. I love you sweet pea. I am going into your room now and will give you the biggest hug you ever had and kiss you goodnight, never forget your old man, I will never forget you."

Jane turned the dictaphone off and sat with her head down quietly crying, Jasper wrapped his arms around her. She turned into him crying softly.

"Jane I am so sorry, I didn't want to upset today of all days." He rubbed her back as he spoke.

Jane turned to look at him. "it's…, it's okay", she sniffed wiping her eyes. "It's a shock to hear his voice after all these years. Why did you wait so long?"

"We talked about it, he mentioned the day you got married but then there was no guarantee you would, then when you were with…..him, there was no way I was going to give it to you, he would have destroyed it. Today seemed perfect." Jane nodded wiping her nose with her hands. Jasper pulled out a new hankie out of his pocket and handed it to her.

"Here Belle, I thought you might need this today, she looked down into her hand to see a pretty cotton and lace hankie with her new initials on it. "I know what you are like, so I thought it would be nice." She laughed wiping her eyes into it. She moved towards Bill wrapping her arms around him. He sighed. "For a minute I thought you would kick me out." Jane looked up shaking her head.

"No Bill, you are my family. It was just a huge shock, that's all. So do I get to hear yours?"

Bill blushed. "No love, not until I go, then you can have it." She nodded smiling at him.

"Well, I need to put it somewhere safe now, then I am going to dance my heart out. Are you too coming too?"

"Let me take care of it while you two go and dance you can have it later when you go to bed." Jane nodded passing it back to him but reluctant to let go of it. "I won't lose it I promise." She let go kissing him on the cheek, she took Jaspers hand and went back into the tent dragging him on the floor.

Dorian was up on the stage giving the DJ a break, he had everyone on the floor, he saw them come back in and announced their arrival.

"Let's get this party started properly shall we?" the music started, Barry White sang out. You're the First, the last, my everything. Jane and Jasper began dancing around the floor singing to each other. Moving across to those who were sat down pulling them up out of their chairs. The music continued every one was up dancing, singing and dancing, Jane and Jasper smiled at each other as they bounced around the floor.

It was almost 11pm Jasper nodded to the DJ, as he led Jane outside. He turned the music down and asked everyone to go outside. It was time for the Bride and Groom to end the evening. The girls stood outside with buckets of sparklers, everyone took two and made an archway down the path out of the field. The DJ played a piece of music that Jaspers friend Tempo O'Neil had written for them called Brighter Day. Jasper smiled he loved it when he heard it the first time, he said the title was perfect. He looked over to his friend nodding. They began their walk through the sparkler archway. Stopping at each person on their own side kissing and hugging as they left.

They reached the end, Jasper scooped Jane up running out of the field with her, as they reached the door he stopped, panting.
"Welcome home Belle." Kissing her softly he opened the door carrying her in. He slowed down so she could see all the pictures and trinkets they had already added to the house.
"How on earth did you do this, I can't believe you did all this without me even wondering what was going on. You really are spoiling me. It's quite overwhelming. All I gave you was a small heart."
"No Belle you have given me much more than that, you gave me who I really am, you showed me what true love is, you showed me what it was like to truly love someone. This is just things, you gave me much more."
Jane was shaking her head as they both became emotional.
"No love, that's not true, I feel safe, loved, wanted, do you know how that feels knowing I can say or do what I like and know it won't be questioned, I don't get scared about talking to you when you are busy, I don't fear you in bed, I can sleep properly, I am in love for the first time in my life, you are my world, my life, my everything." Jane took his face in her hands, kissing him, they both allowed their tears to fall. He sat them both down on the sofa still with her in his arms.
"You are amazing, I would never hurt you, I would rather die than think I ever hurt you. My life started the day I met you." In unison they wiped each others tears away with their thumbs laughing at each other. Jasper

brought Jane's face closer to his, rubbing noses he smiled before rubbing his thumb across her lip gently. He pulled them open slightly, he could feel her heart rate rise as their lips crashed together. The hurt, pain and loss dissolving as their lips joined.

"I want to take my wife to bed for the first time." Jasper stood up with Jane in his arms again, walking fast towards their room making Jane laugh.

"Wait. Please, I need to take this off." she pulled gently at her veil and laid it over the back of the chair before he continued to the bedroom.

He pushed the door open Jane gasped. A bottle of champagne sat next to the bed on ice, balloons covered the room, laying on the pillows were a red and yellow rose. Sprinkled across the duvet were red rose petals and a heart in the centre.

Jane grabbed his head kissing him.

"I know it's tacky but I wanted to do it. However, I don't fancy making love on those petals in case there are any thorns in there, I don't want my arse poked or anything else for that matter."

"I love it, thank you so much." She peppered his face in tiny kisses, he screwed his face up laughing.

Putting Jane down, she stood in front of him looking up into his eyes. He slipped his jacket off hanging it over the back of the chair, Jane ran her hands up and down his chest through his shirt smiling at him, she pinched one of his nipples to tease him, he sucked in hard as her hands travelled down his body to his waist, she pulled at his belt undoing it slowly, biting her lip smiling at him, his eyes locked onto hers. He smiled rubbing his hands over her shoulders, as her hand moved down to his zip. He groaned quietly as she undid it pushing his trousers down, he stepped out of them kicking them behind him. He stood in his shirt and white tight boxer shorts, Janes hand moved slowly down to his hardening cock, she over exaggerated licking her lips, Jasper smiled stopping her hand. He span her around bending her over pulling her wedding dress up over her bottom.

"Fuck, I have been imagining this all fucking day, just looking at you in this dress has made me hard so many times, you never disappoint." He grinned bending, pushing her legs apart. Her delicate lace knickers sat in the crack of her bottom, he eased them out with his finger, continuing down to her pussy moving them to one side. His hand now between her legs rubbing her lips. Jane whimpered softly, he slipped his finger in as he moved back and forth, Jane caught her breath, he growled at her getting onto his knees. He pulled her cheeks apart licking at her pussy, Jane crouched further wanting his tongue deeper, Jasper smiled giving her what she wanted. He flicked it back and forth teasing her clit, lifting her leg putting it onto the bed, opening her pussy further for him. He pushed his finger deeper inside. Jane bucked on him, groaning louder, pushing back as his tongue moved closer to her bottom.

"Yessss, Jasper please, I want it." She mewled. He stopped.

"Are you sure Belle?"

"Yes." she whispered, groaning, as he opened her again circling her hole, Jane pulled away not sure how she was feeling, he pulled her back to him, pushing his tongue onto her more, she relaxed she felt his wet finger pushing slightly against her, she blushed feeling more turned on than she thought she would. He stopped waiting for her conformation. She pushed back against him, he knew she was ready, he pushed his finger into her pussy covering it in her juices, her pussy now soaking wet, circling her hole he pushed again gently, the tip of his fingers sliding inside.

"Ohhhhh", Jane purred as he pushed a little further in, she felt like she was losing her mind, her whole body was on fire. Her legs grew weak as she felt herself fall further onto the bed. Jasper stopped, moving both her legs onto the bed, she kneeled at the edge opening her legs wide for him, he came back to her, his hands on either cheek as he opened her again, his tongue now teasing her hole, Jane moved back and forth gripping the bed, her eyes closed as the sensation grew, her pussy fluttering, needing him. He brought her so close without touching her, Jane could feel her body heating up. He stopped, Jane turned getting off the bed standing in front of him her back to him, he undid her dress pushing it over her hips as it fell to the floor, he picked it up putting it onto the chair, she stood looking at him in her lace shoes, stockings and suspenders, her breasts pert, her nipples hard, she cupped them, biting her lip pushing them in together, leaning down flicking her nipple, Jasper groaned watching her. His hand moving to his cock, he cupped himself squeezing watching the show in front of him, Jane squeezed both together again teasing her nipples with her thumbs, pulling gently with her fingers making them harder.

"Sit please." she whispered walking towards him, her breasts still in her hands, Jasper pushed his pants down kicking them away, he sat down his legs open, his hand still on his cock, he was now rock hard, he rubbed himself slowly watching her, she walked between his legs offering one breast to him.

"No hands." She ordered. Jasper bent towards her taking her nipple between his lips, continuing to rub himself, He sucked harder, groaning as he took more of her breast in, he moved across to the other licking it, flicking the nipple. She pushed him back onto the bed. His cock standing to attention. She brushed his hands away straddling one of his legs, taking his cock in her hand, she licked her lips looking at him as she lowered her head towards him, her hair falling onto his leg and stomach. her lips brushed the tip as she blew gently, Jasper growled softly, her tongue circling the head, she squeezed it at the bottom, she lowered her lips over the head sucking him. Jasper pushed towards her wanting her to take more, she teased him concentrating on the tip a little longer before tightening her grip with her lips and sucking him in deep as far as she could go without gagging. Jasper screwed the bedding up in his fists.

"Fuuuuuck", he groaned as she sucked him harder, her hand moving to his balls, she rolled them gently, as she sucked a little faster. Jasper gripped the bed, feeling like he was losing control. Jane sucked harder, stopping and starting as she brought him closer to cumming, she felt his balls tighten so she stopped, moving down she raised his legs to get to his balls. She licked and teased them taking them each in her mouth sucking gently, Jasper was out of his mind. She opened her legs dipping her finger in making it wet before teasing his hole with her juices, Jasper tensed his bottom as Jane continued to rub, he pushed back as she pushed her finger in just a little as he had done to her.

"Ohhhh yessss, ohhh Belleeee." He whispered as she eased in a tiny bit more. His cock back in her mouth, sucking from top to bottom faster than she had before, his cock tightened, he was desperate to cum. Jane stopped again, taking him out of her mouth she climbed onto the bed to straddle him, she flattened his cock with her pussy rubbing herself up and down almost bringing herself to orgasm. She trembled stopping herself. Jasper grabbed her rolling her onto the bed taking control. He pulled her leg up leaving the other flat pushing his cock into her.

"My dearest wife you are such a fucking tease you have me going out of my mind." Jane grinned as he rammed into her, taking her breath away, Jasper smiled bending to kiss her, licking her lip and biting softly, he kneeled pulling her into him pushing harder into her, Jane moaned loudly as he pushed into her again.

"Fuuuuck yes, please don't stop, I need you now." She panted.

"My baby wants to be fucked hard, does she?" Jasper asked gritting his teeth.

"Yes please." She begged. He grabbed both her legs pulling her closer to him, putting them both over one shoulder laying Jane her on her side. He rammed harder. Jane screamed, he continued harder than ever, feeling like he was punishing her the way she wanted. He spanked her, she pushed into him, his cock feeling deeper as he did it again. He dropped her legs.

"Sit up." He pulled her up climbing on the bed turning her onto her knees, "head down" he wrapped her hair around his hand, his other pushing her legs open, taking his cock he pushed hard into her holding her to him, Jane pushed back meeting his thrusts with her own, her pussy was being pounded, she could feel the tingle, he pulled her head up gently. Jane continued to moan at every thrust as his cock rammed in and out. Moving her hand to her pussy she felt his cock sliding in and out, she rubbed it feeling Jasper push harder. She moved her fingers feeling her juices all over his cock and balls, she was desperate to cum.

"Cum for me Jasper, please baby." She purred, his bottom tensed as he picked up speed, moaning at every thrust as she gripped his cock as he entered her.

"Yesss, Belle, oh yes, don't stop now, I'm going to cum Belleeeee........Arghhhhhhh." he panted thrusting harder his hand going white as he sank his fingers into her hip, tightening the grip on her hair pulling her head up. Jane rubbed her clit faster as she clenched around him draining him, her body tingled, her pussy pulsed as she went rigid, her fingers rubbing faster, she felt the warmth of her orgasm flood her, Jasper pushed feeling her juices cover his cock. Jane panted not wanting it to stop as it subsided, she became sensitive, she stopped as Jasper stayed inside her laying down gently on her. They rolled over laying on their backs. He kissed her lips softly, taking her lip in his, her tongue darting in and out to meet his. He took her head in his hand looking into her eyes.

"That was intense." He smiled, Jane nodded kissing his nose.

"Now I'm ready to sleep." she laughed.

"Not until we get out of these clothes", he looked down at them both smiling. Sitting up. "Come on, let's get you underdressed and make up off and get you back to bed." He pulled her up kissing her again, pulling her off the bed to help her get sorted. Jane groaned she was so tired.

They went into the bathroom, Jane looked around at all her things, even her hair grip. He smiled watching her.

"Did you empty the house?"

"No love, just doubled up on everything in here, then you never have to pack apart from a few clothes, I didn't go that mad. We can come here as often as you like, you have the trailer for Lady so she can come too of course, then we can leave the car at home."

"I love you Jasper. I am lost for words. Thank you for everything, for the most incredible day, for bringing our friends together and making it the happiest day of my life. She tiptoed kissing him on the nose. He wiggled it kissing her back.

"There is nothing I wouldn't do for you Belle."

"That makes me the luckiest girl in the world and happiest."

"Me too, no looking back, from here on in it's about us and our future." Jane nodded.

"Most definitely." They cuddled, Jane felt tearful, this was finally her time to let go of the past, all that was in front of them was new to be discovered.

She grabbed her comb passing it to Jasper, he began to gently comb her hair as she removed her make up, He moved closer smelling it, rubbing it on his face.

"Did I tell you how beautiful you smell today?" Jane grinned.

"No, you didn't, but thank you, I have to say it is a beautiful smell I will have to alternate them now. You have good taste", she teased, "but I should have known that as you married me." He spanked her with her comb making her squeal.

"Come on you, bedtime, did you want any shorts and t-shirt?"

"Are you?"

"No love."

"Me either, I want to feel your skin on mine. He smiled taking her to bed, they climbed in together, he pulled her into him, as she laid on his chest, he lifted her chin up kissing her.

"Goodnight Mrs Mitchell. Sweet dreams."

"Goodnight husband", she grinned "Sweet dreams of me." He squeezed her kissing her head as they settled down to sleep, he felt Jane's breathing slow down and her body get heavier, he smiled kissing her head again, before closing his eyes.

Chapter 27

Don't go.

Susan woke up to moaning noises from Moses, he was laid on his side holding his stomach, she could see his eyes were closed but wasn't sure if he was awake. She knew he had eaten quite a bit the day before and they had also had rough sex too. She had noticed how tired he became after and how quickly he had fallen asleep, she thought then he had done it to please her.

She was a little concerned but didn't wake him. He hadn't received the results of his tests that she knew of, but she was worried. She got out of bed quietly pulling on his shirt and shorts before going out to the kitchen to make a drink. G was already up when she walked into the kitchen.
"Morning Susan, drink?" He held up a cup.
"Coffee please if you don't mind."
"Something on your mind, you're frowning." He asked concerned.
"Moses is in pain, I left him sleeping, I just wonder if it is eating too much or something else, has he called for his results yet?"
"Not that I know of, I hope to god it's just food though. Can you think of any other reason?"
"Sadly yes. But let's not think about that now. Let's see how he is the next couple of days." G nodded turning away to make the drink. He screwed his fists up in temper, his jaw tightening. He knew things weren't good he just didn't want to think about it.

Susan took her drink back to bed, she climbed in grabbing her phone. Moses was still sleeping, she sat back looking across at him, he was still grimacing, she felt worry building in her chest, she had pushed it away the past couple of days, she knew he wanted to be on form for Jane, now he was exhausted. She scrolled through her social media trying to distract herself but it wasn't working. She finished her coffee, put her phone down and headed to the shower. She closed the door turning on the water. As she stepped in her emotions won, she began to cry, she had been around Cancer long enough to know the signs and she had seen Moses trying to hide it from her. She just needed to know what was going on. She didn't want to scare him in case she was over reacting. She sobbed into the water, hugging herself, she was gulping for air as the sobs got bigger. She sniffed hard under the water that was beating down on her. She heard the door, she turned facing away so he couldn't see.

"Morning love, how did you sleep?" She asked calling out.

"Great how about you gorgeous?"

"Good love, thank you, I didn't want to wake you, I hope I didn't?"

"No love, I needed to pee." He stood watching her. "You are a sight for sore eyes, I'm too knackered after last night or I would come in there and take you right now."

"Me too, you definitely wore me out." Susan smiled, gulping back the tears. Lying to him.

"I will grab you a coffee when I get out of here give me a few minutes."

Moses nodded sitting down on the toilet to watch her, she caught sight of him when he thought she wasn't looking. She could see he was in a lot of pain. She finished up quickly leaving him alone in the bathroom as she grabbed her towel heading into the bedroom.

Moses stayed sat on the toilet his head in his hands. The pain in his stomach was getting worse, he knew he needed to make the call. He picked himself up put a smile on his face and went out to the bedroom. Susan was dressed and sat with the door open on the patio. He walked out to see her, kissing her on the head and sat down.

"Hi love, you ok?"

"All good love thanks, what are your plans today?" Moses smiled.

"I need to go home at some stage, I wanted to talk to you first though."

"Okay, what's up?"

"G and I know something is wrong, we didn't talk about it, but please don't keep us in the dark, we are far from stupid, I know you wanted to be well for Jane and Jasper, but you have to think of yourself first. When are you planning on going home?"

"I don't have any plans to dash back not now we are together, I am not keeping anything from you love, I just haven't made the call yet, I wanted to enjoy the wedding first." He put his hand out to her, she took it squeezing it.

"I'm not going to lie to you Moses, I care a great deal about you, getting to know you this last couple of months and being with you now has been pretty special, I don't want to lose you, so please do something and talk to the Doctor."

"I care about you too Susan, I didn't plan to feel the way I do, I just thought we could have some fun, but having you around this last few months has been pretty special, I can tell you anything, so why would I hide it from you, let's be honest you have more knowledge of it than I do anyway, so how could I?"

"I just want to know how you are feeling. I know you're not right." He squeezed her hand moving onto his knees in front of her.

"No, I'm not, I think it's going to be bad news, but I am going to fight this. You're the first person I have got close to like this since I was a teenager and that wasn't real. I don't want to lose this now."

"Good, keep telling yourself that then, but please let me in, let me be there when you call the Doctor instead of trying to remember everything, I can then explain things to you." She put her hand on his face cupping it.

"Okay I will, we can do it tomorrow. 9am sharp. When are you back to work?"

"Thank you love, not back for another few days then I'm on nights, so won't see you for a week, so depending on when you go home is if I see you again before then."

"There is no way we won't see each other, I am not rushing away, I want time with you before I make a decision to go back and that all depends on the Doctor. The gang are going back in a few days. G and I have no return date yet." She pushed herself onto the floor with Moses, grabbing his face in her hands.

"If this is all we have from here on in that's ok with me, after last night my pussy needs a break anyway." She kissed him.

"I am not dead yet love." He teased kissing her back. "Come on let's go and eat." He stood pulling her up as they went back into the bedroom.

"Don't you think you need a shower first?"

"Ahhh, yes, well you could be my nurse maid and help me?"

"You're not that sick, get in there now."

"I think I've changed my mind, I might trade you in, you're too hard on me." Susan smacked his bottom as he walked into the shower naked, he wiggled his bottom as he walked making her laugh. She joined him in the bathroom just to enjoy the time with him and watch him shower. Every time she saw him touch himself she gasped. Her body tingling, he was oblivious to her, he just continued washing himself, she stood licking her lips as he smothered his body in soap, he turned so she could see his bottom, she groaned when he bent over. She laughed at herself for getting in such a state. He stepped out dripping wet grabbing a towel, Susan wiped the dribble from her mouth. He looked up at her.

"You okay love?" She blushed.

"Yes, just watching you that's all, I meant I stayed in here in case you needed anything."

Moses laughed. "Oh? watching were you? See anything you fancy?" She felt her face burn.

"Ummm well, yeah of course, but I wasn't watching for that reason." She got herself flustered, Moses walked over to her smiling dropping his towel. She caught her breath again, this time Moses saw.

"You know you can take what you like, if I'm not up to it you can still help yourself?" Susan didn't know what to do, she was so embarrassed, she felt like a teenager around him. He wasn't the normal kind of guy she went for, so for her the honesty and sex were very different.

"I'll remember that", she smiled turning away, her body hot, her pussy tingling. She walked out back into the bedroom wafting her face with her hand trying to cool down laughing at herself.

Moses came out a few minutes later, towel around his waist. Still wet from his shower, Susan was beside herself, she stood up.

"I will go and make a drink, I'm quite thirsty, do you want one?"

"Yes please." Moses laughed pulling his towel off standing naked in the room. "I take it you don't want this then?" He held his cock rubbing it from top to bottom.

"Well, it's not that I don't want it, but I am still recovering from last night and you need to rest a bit."

"Suit yourself", he laughed walking away wiggling his bottom again to tease her. Susan left the room going to make them both a drink. She sat in the kitchen waiting for the kettle, trying to cool herself down, she knew she wanted Moses, she wasn't recovering at all but she didn't want to spoil his day, she still felt coy in front of him too, he was a dream come true to her, not only ex-military but a biker too.

G came in, "Isn't he up yet? How is he?"

"He's okay, he's going to call Monday, so fingers crossed. What are you doing today?"

"Nothing much, I think recovering from yesterday is a good shout. We won't see Jasper and Jane now for a few days but will try and catch them before we go."

"Good idea, I need to pop home for a while need to do a few things then I will come back."

"You know where to find us. I think Dorian is heading off for a few days once we leave too with the Nomads, he fancies some time out. If you are still up for going out on the bike we can go and collect Jane's?"

"I would love that yes please." Susan was grinning from ear to ear.

"Bring some jeans back with you, Jane's jacket and lid will fit but you will need some jeans and boots."

"Will do, I can't wait now, thanks G."

"You're welcome, get you used to it then we can get you on two wheels."

"Oh, I'm not sure about that."

"Don't be daft, you are very safe with us. It's easy I promise. Jasper did it for Jane."

"He's a man."

G laughed, what difference does that make, look at Jane, she only rides a trike because she is so damn short and it's easier."

"We will see." She smiled as Moses came out of the room, she pushed his coffee across the table at him.

"We will see what?" He asked them both.

"We were talking about bikes, I said if Susan brings some jeans and boots back she can get on Janes trike with you or me, then maybe she can go on two wheels. She's not so sure."

Moses laughed. "Ignore him, you do what you want love. Never get on with him though, he's a crazy arse."

"Speak for yourself!"

"Right before you two start arguing I'm going home, I will be back later." She walked towards Moses putting her hand on his chest, kissing him softly. She grabbed her things and left.

"You've got feelings for her haven't you?" G quizzed Moses.

"I like her yes."

"No Moses, I know you, I can see it all over your face."

"Yeah, well keep your mouth shut please. I don't need anyone knowing."

"Hey Brother, your secret is safe with me. Just be careful is all I'm saying."

"I'm not a fucking child!"

"I didn't say you were, but I know how you feel about Half-pint being married, that's all. The fact you haven't spoken about it says it all."

"Fucking drop it, it was never going anywhere."

"You never knew that, I love that girl too but was never in love with her like you. How do you know it would never work, well you lost your chance now. That's all I'm saying I just don't want Susan getting hurt."

"Thanks for the fucking vote of confidence, I may be fucking dying but I do know my own feelings."

"What??"

"Forget it." Moses went to storm out of the room.

"Back up Brother, you better sit your fucking arse down there now and talk to me. I'm not giving this up." He was angry now.

"It's nothing, just a throw away comment, drop it."

"I don't believe you, talk to me."

"Nothing to talk about."

"Don't make me fucking force you to sit."

"Fucks sake!" Moses slumped down in the bar stool. "I know this cancer hasn't gone, the pain has got worse, I'm losing weight again, I don't want to eat, I'm tired all the time and trying to be well for the wedding has knocked me for six. I'm bleeding again. Happy now?"

G put his head in his hands, his jaw went tight, he felt sick. He looked back up at Moses properly, he could see for himself he wasn't good again. He just didn't want to look to hard, he was scared, he didn't want to lose his best friend.

"I need to get out of here, can we go for a ride?"

"Sure thing, are you up to it?" Moses turned scowling at him. G put his hands up in defeat. "Sorry."

They both grabbed their gear and headed out to the garage. There were enough bikes to choose from. They took the front two, neither wanted to take one of his prized possessions. They headed out of town, Moses began to relax a bit, G called ahead and let the boys at the club know they were going out Animal and Shadow rode out to meet them. They stopped for coffee at the old café to catch up on things. Shadow pulled Moses to one side.

"What's going on Brother, you're looking pretty crap today?"

"Just a rough day yesterday trying to keep going, that's all."

"Hmm, if you say so."

"I'm ok damn it Shadow."

"Listen Brother, we would have to be blind not to notice how sick you are looking. Don't go at us for caring." Moses put his head down. Shadow put his hand on his shoulder.

"Let us care about you for once. Come on, let's get your pathetic arse back on the bike so we can get some air in your lungs." Moses nodded walking back to the others.

"Ready lads?" Shadow asked, Animal put his cigarette out as they climbed back on their bikes.

They pulled out onto the open road, it was a beautiful sunny day, the road was clear, Moses was smiling feeling alive without a care in the world. He was up front where he preferred to be, he was enjoying the bends of the road it was one of his favorites. The road narrowed just before it opened up again, as they went into a corner, on the opposite side of the road was a truck coming from the other direction, he was all over the road, Moses pulled across to the inside of the road and slowed to get out of his path. The driver missed the bend, accelerated, came across their path colliding with Moses, the bike hit the truck on the outside, it careered down the side trapping Moses, the bike came to a stop with the truck embedding itself underneath the truck rear wheels, Moses rolled back like a lifeless rag laying motionless on the ground. G yelled to Moses as he saw the impact, almost jumping off his bike he ran to him as Shadow and Animal stopped the traffic. G skidded onto his knees, for a second he just sat looking at him, he gently turned him onto his back, his arm was buckled, his jacket ripped open as he was caught by the truck, he opened Moses crash helmet visor to see his face, he was bleeding from his mouth, blood was spilling onto the floor from his arm. G bent over him trying to hear him breathing. He was still alive, but barely breathing. G sat back on his heels looking around, everything had gone quiet, his heart was pounding, he didn't know what to do. He knew he couldn't move Moses, time just stopped. He heard a deep guttural scream, he turned to look but nobody was there, he realised it was him. He began to cry, talking to Moses.

"Brother please hang on, don't you dare leave me now, I'm not ready, none of us are ready, keep breathing. The Emergency services are on their way, hang on Moses brother please." He wiped his eyes with the back of his hand, bending back down to listen to Moses, he was still breathing, he sighed heavily, his nose was running tears were stinging his eyes.

"Where the fuck is the ambulance, come on man for fucks sake my buddy is dying here", he screamed out, looking up to the sky, he began punching the ground in frustration. Shadow appeared by his side.

"Come on G the medics are here let them get to him."

"Fucking leave it, he's my Brother", the medics were trying to assess Moses and move G out of the way, he was pushing their hands to leave him alone. Shadow grabbed him picking him up moving him from Moses.

"Listen to me G, let them do what they have to do, he needs their help now if he has any chance of surviving." G fought to be let go, Shadow wasn't letting that happen, he could see it wasn't looking good and G getting in the way with all best intentions wasn't going to help Moses.

The Police came to talk to them all, Shadow and Animal explained the situation and were asked to give statements later. The driver was being pulled out of his truck by the Police. The other ambulance crew pushed through to get to the driver, he was crying barely able to stand up. He kept repeating he fell asleep.

The medics gently lifted Moses onto the stretcher running with him to the ambulance, G didn't take no for an answer jumping in with him. Shadow nodded as the doors closed grabbing his phone to get the recovery truck out. G looked terrified, his face was grey his eyes prominent. The crew continued to check Moses over as they traveled to the hospital at full speed.

Shadow rang Jasper, "Hi Shadow, nice to hear from you buddy, everything okay? Jasper smiled.

"Not really Brother, there has been a crash, Moses is in a bad way, they are taking him to the hospital now, you may want to get down here. It doesn't look good, but don't tell Jane until you see the Doctor."

"Jesus Christ, okay will see you then shortly, thanks for calling, where is G?"

"He's in the ambulance with him, he's a mess."

"Okay thanks." Jasper brushed his hand through his hair not wanting this conversation. He walked out onto the patio, Jane was sat on her swing with a book.

"Belle, we need to go out, can you get your shoes on love."

"Hi love, sure", she put her book down standing up walking towards Jasper. What's up love, where we going, no more surprises please?"

"No Belle, there has been an accident, Moses is being taken to the hospital now, we need to get down there." Jane stopped walking her legs buckling, Jasper grabbed her holding her up. She began to cry frantically, she pushed her way out of Jaspers arms running inside, she didn't know which way to run, she crumbled onto the floor crying, Jasper grabbed her sandals bringing them to her with her phone. He picked her up sitting on the sofa.

"Belle come on love, breath", he rubbed her back as Jane sobbed, she used her arm to wipe her face and nose, Jasper half smiled. Grabbing the tissues off the side.

"We need to go love. He picked her up and headed out of the door, he put her in the car running to his side, he wheel span on the drive before driving out onto the main road. He took Jane's hand squeezing it.

"Who....who...told.....told.......you....?" she heaved trying to catch her breath.

"Shadow called me, he never said much just to get us to go down there."

"Where was G?" She sniffed again.

"He's with Moses in the ambulance." She nodded squeezing Jaspers hand, she turned to look out of the window, her shoulders shaking as she continued to cry.

Chapter 28

Please stay

The ambulance crew pushed through the doors and were met by the Doctors. They spoke fast G was lost listening to them, he held onto Moses good hand until the nurse forced his hand away.

"Please let him go, we need to treat him, the longer you delay us the longer you will wait for an answer. Go to the check in desk and give them as much information as you can to help us." G nodded walking in the direction she pointed. He checked him in with the receptionist, she told him to take a seat in the relative's area until someone came to see him, instead he paced the floor.

Inside the emergency room they began to cut off Moses jacket and jeans to get to his body, they needed to find out what was going on, his arm was hanging loose, the wound was open, they were trying to stem the bleeding again. They connected him up to the machines. The Doctors continued to check him. The lead stood back.

"Is the family here?"

"Yes Doctor his Brother is outside." He wiped his hands removing his apron and gloves and went out to reception, G was pacing up and down the corridor as Shadow and Animal arrived.

"Brother of Christian?" G dashed back to the Doctor.

"Yes me. How is he?"

"Let's take a seat, shall we?", the others sat with them. "Christian has sustained some life- threatening injuries, the next hour for him is critical, if he can get through that then his chances are better but not by much. He is a very sick man, I understand he also has cancer?"

"Yes he does, he's not long had Radiotherapy and another scan to see if it has helped." The Doctor nodded.

"Can I ask who is his next of kin?"

G looked around at the others as Jane arrived. "We both are."

"And you are? He frowned at Jane." He's my Brother."

"I was just telling your Brother, Christian is a very sick man and has life threatening injuries, the next hour is crucial, I can let you see him for a few seconds, but just the two of you, I mean seconds too." He was being firm but fair. They nodded following him, Jasper squeezed Janes hand as she walked away holding onto G.

They walked into the room the Doctors and nurses were still working on him, the floor was covered in blood, swabs were covering a lot of the floor near his bed, as they saw G and Jane walk in, they backed away. He was on a ventilator, his clothes cut off him, his arm was being held on until they stabilised him. Jane felt her legs give way as they got closer to him. She hid her face into G's shoulder, he gripped her hard trying to stop the tears.
"You can touch him, but be very gentle." A nurse spoke softly to them. They moved closer, Jane kissed his head.
"Don't you dare give up, do you hear me? we haven't come this far to let you go now. Please fight Moses." She sniffed fighting her tears. She backed up for G to get close, he bent down kissing his head.
"You heard Half-pint, you got to pull through this, we are trying to reach Susan for you too, please Brother, don't let go. We have too many more miles to cover. We need you here with us."

"I'm sorry I need to ask you to leave", the alarm sounded as Moses stopped breathing, the nurse pushed them both back as the crash team took over. Jane and G stood motionless looking over at the bed, the defibrillator was charging as they put the pads onto his chest, Jane gasped as his body thrust, nothing....., they charged again. Still nothing. Susan came running through the doors, she was stopped by the nurses.
Jane interrupted. "That's his fiancée, please leave her." Susan stood holding onto Jane, as they tried again. The Doctors continued for 40 minutes with no luck. The room fell silent. The Doctor spoke.
"Time of death. 15.31 hours. Jane wailed, trying to push her way through to Moses, Susan began to sob as G stood motionless. The Doctors came towards them.
"I'm so very sorry for your loss. His injuries were too much for his body to take. Please let us clean him up and you can come back in and spend time with him." The nurse came over trying to guide them away. Jane screamed buckling to her knees.

Jasper heard her, he knew it was her, he ran down the corridor calling her, Shadow was behind him, he burst through the doors, he was on her knees, he crouched down to pick her up, she began to punch his chest, screaming and crying. G held onto Susan he picked her up, Shadow supported him as they walked out of the room to the visitors area. They sat the girls down, Jasper kept Jane on his lap, she was sobbing into his neck. He had no words to say. He buried his head into her shoulder. G began pacing around the room, he had no idea what to do. The door opened as the others arrived. They all looked at Jane and G, he shook his head, he pushed past them almost running outside. Bill followed him.

"G, stop. Where are you going?"

"I have no fucking idea, I don't know what to do, I just couldn't stay in there." Bill put his hand on his shoulder.

"I just watched him die Bill, he just gave up, I told him not too, how the fuck am I going to cope?"

"I don't have all the answers Brother, we just need to take one day at a time and be there for you."

"How the fuck do I look at Half-pint? You didn't hear her, she was like an injured animal, we were inseparable. This wasn't supposed to happen, he just started a new life with Susan, this is so fucking unfair." Bill put both hands on each shoulder.

"Listen one thing at a time, you are raw with emotion, your head isn't straight yet, which is normal. We have a lot to do but for now just be with your friends. Come on, let the guys help you." He turned G around walking him back into the hospital, the Doctor was heading towards him.

"We have moved Christian to another area somewhere quiet where you can all see him. I am so sorry."

"His name is Moses." G barked at the Doctor.

"I'm sorry, Moses. If you would like to follow me, I will show you where he is." G followed with Bill, they had moved him into a side room, he was undressed under a sheet, just his head showing. He had been washed down, his cuts and bruises showing. G took a huge breath before going in. He looked back at Bill, he nodded and closed the door to give G time alone.

G pulled a chair across and sat next to him, he laid his head against Moses. His hand on his shoulder.

"I'm lost Brother, you have only been gone a few minutes, I have no idea how I am going to deal with this. I never imagined I would say goodbye like this, I never believed your cancer would take you either, or was I just fooling myself." He sniffed hard his tears coming fast. He punched the bed.

"Fuck you Moses, fuck you!" He put his head back down crying like a child, his hand on his friends shoulder. "You can keep all your fucking houses and shit, I just want you back Brother, please jump up and tell me this was a bad joke, I will beat the crap out of you then laugh. I can't do this alone."

Jealous of the Angels — Donna Taggart

Jane walked up the corridor holding Jaspers hand and arm. Susan was behind her with Bill and the others. Jane looked back at everyone. She had never seen any of them look so lost. They reached the room as G came out, he walked straight to Jane grabbing her, hugging her into him, they both began to cry again.

"I'm sorry I don't know what to say this time, I don't know what to do." His voice broke as he sobbed. Jane buried her face into his chest. Jasper held them both.

"Neither do I. He sorted everything."

"Go in and see him love." He stammered. Jane nodded moving away from him wiping her eyes, she grabbed Jaspers hand taking him with her. She faltered at the door, took a deep breath and walked in. She squeezed Jaspers hand as he moved her closer sitting her in the chair. She looked up at Jasper pulling him down with her.

"This is your time Belle, it's okay love." She shook her head pulling him closer. He walked into her arm as she held onto him.

"He looks so well, like he's going to wake up", she stroked his face, his body only just starting to get cold. She laid her head against his kissing him. "You were not supposed to die, there are too many things left unsaid, how can I live without you, you're my best friend.....my, my guide." She began to cry softly, her tears falling on his face. "Please wake up Moses, please, don't leave us, we need you. I need you. I love you, please Moses." She begged, choking on her tears, Jasper hugged her tightly, his heart being ripped apart watching her. He just wanted to pick her up and take her home.

"He will always be those things Belle, he will still be around you every day, we won't ever forget him." Jane nodded leaning her head against Jaspers stomach. He bent to kiss her and moved around to Moses. "I promise I will look after her, she will want for nothing except you, I will keep her safe until you see each other again." Jasper choked on his own tears, he kissed his head and stood up taking Janes hand.

"Ready?" She nodded. Jasper opened the door leading Jane out first.

Bill guided Susan in and closed the door. They all stood together hugging and crying, not saying much to each other.

"I need some air love", Jane looked up at Jasper. He half smiled taking her hand leading her outside. They walked towards the benches, Dorian was sat with his head in his hands, his hoodie up and a baseball cap on. They say down either side of him. Jane took his hand. He turned to look at her grabbing her, openly crying.

"I really loved that man, I know I teased the fuck out of him, but he was my first crush, I held a candle for him all this time. He never once complained, he took it in good spirit, I wish I had been honest with him." He wiped his face. Looking at Jane, his eyes full of sadness and deep loss.

"He knew Dorian, you didn't need to tell him, I don't know anyone else that would do what you did for him. You may not have been around much in the last couple of years but that didn't change anything. She wiped his tears away as he cried, he nodded listening to her. "We just need to be together now to help one another. I don't know what his wishes were G does, we will have to pull together now for each other." He nodded again taking her head in his hands kissing her on the forehead.

"Thank you love, have you seen him yet?" Jane nodded. "I don't know if I can."

"There is no pressure, think about it, we can come back can't we Jasper?" Jane questioned.

"Yes love, they will need to move him to a funeral home, depending on what you and G want is if we arrange transport back to the UK for him."

"Nobody is touching him, he goes in my plane, I won't have anyone else doing that, it's the last thing I can do for him." Jasper nodded, Jane squeezed his hand in thanks.

"We don't need to do this today. It's too raw." She pulled him in closer hugging him hard, he coughed through his tears, as Jane consoled him.

The others came out, hugging each other as they walked towards them. Dorian stood up walking into G, they hugged each other tightly.

"Don't try and talk Dor, it's okay." Dorian cried again openly. G let him cry, he knew how he felt about Moses. Dorian pulled away wiping his face roughly.

"Come on, let's go home." His car had waited for him.

"Come with us G?" Jasper asked. He nodded taking Janes hand as they walked towards the car.

"Susan?" Jane asked.

"I have my car, I don't belong with you now he's gone, it's okay I will go home."

"No Susan, you are family now, regardless of Moses, we look after each other, come back with us please?" She nodded wiping her eyes.

They travelled in convoy back to Dorians, they congregated in the lounge together drinking quietly, in their own thoughts, there was anger in the room, everyone had questions, they were waiting on news from the Police about the driver.

"Probably not the right time to ask, but I know we are all thinking the same, do we know what Moses wanted?" Steve asked.

"Yes, we do, I was with him when he wrote his Will. Jane and I need to talk about it first though." Jane looked around shocked. "We are executors of the Will love. We will need to contact his solicitor tomorrow morning and get the documents sent across. Can we talk about it then?" Jane nodded looking back at Jasper. He nodded.

"If you need a solicitor here I will contact mine G." Jasper offered.

"Thanks Brother, it seemed quite straight forward but as he is here and not in the UK, I don't know what we have to do. Once I get the documents it would be good to talk to him about it."

"No problem I will get him to come over." G nodded.

"Thanks, appreciate that."

Kitty came into the room. "I don't know if anyone is hungry, but I have laid the table with finger food, please come and eat." Everyone smiled at her nodding in thanks.

The girls got up following her in they stood in the dining room hugging in a group. Jane began to cry again with the others, they all looked up at each other, Gwen began wiping their faces making them all laugh.

"I don't know what to say to anyone, I'm sorry." Jane wiped her face screwing her fists into her eyes.

"Why are you apologising, I don't think anyone of us does. It's a shock."

"Jane, can I borrow you for a moment?" Kitty came to Jane. She turned and nodded. "I wondered if you and Jasper would like to stay here tonight? I have a room ready if you want it, but I don't want you to feel pressured."

"Thank you Kitty, that's really kind, I think we will, I know our place isn't far away but I think we all need to be together tonight. I'm sure the girls will give me some things if needed."

"That's sorted then I will go and air the room for you." Kitty hugged her making Jane cough again as she fought her tears.

The girls sat quietly picking at the food talking about Moses when the men came in, they all sat quietly eating. Kitty brought more beers and wine out. Dorian had drank himself into a stupor, he was swaying from side to side talking gibberish. Kitty was trying to get him to bed, she was speaking softly to him with no success. Shadow walked over.

"Leave it to me Kitty, show me the way." Shadow picked him up, following Kitty to his bedroom. They laid him on the bed, pulling his boots and jeans off before covering him, they turned the light out and closed the door before returning to the others.

The alcohol had relaxed everyone, they were sharing memories of Moses. Susan was sat with the girls listening. She felt like she didn't belong with them, this was their time to mourn their friend. Jane saw she was looking uncomfortable.

"Susan, tell us about the moment you met Moses?" Susan smiled. Jasper began smiling he knew what was coming.

"Oh god, you mean the time when you moved a finger or when you opened your eyes, he was running around the room, grabbed me as I walked in and kissed me, I nearly fell over."

"Jesus anyone would fall over after being kissed by him." Matt teased.

"Every time he came near me after that I blushed. I felt so stupid, then out of the blue he texted me a few months back."

"Wow." Gwen looked shocked. "Is that how you got together?"

"Yes, we spoke every day, it was when he found out about the cancer, he just wanted to talk to someone who he wasn't close too. He felt like he had put so much pressure on your shoulders G, he hated that. I know you were sworn to secrecy for a while." G gulped, nodding. "I never thought for one-minute things would go as far as they did, but it felt natural when you all arrived." She put her head down and began playing with her fingers.

"He had fallen for you Susan, it was written all over his face, I asked him this morning when you went home. He got all defensive. He was scared to tell you because he was convinced the cancer had spread." Susan wiped a tear away at the side of her eye, Jane squeezed her hand.

"I'm sorry love I didn't mean to upset you, just thought you should know."

"I appreciate it G, thank you. It means a lot to be honest." She smiled through her tears.

"Let's be honest someone had to want him." Steve teased making everyone laugh to lighten the moment.

The girls began to yawn, "I think I'm ready for bed." Gwen announced, everyone began to agree standing and hugging each other.

Kitty stood up. "Shadow, Animal come with me, we have another room for you to use. James you and Chicca can use the one you had the other night the bed is fresh again."

"Thank you Kitty, you don't have to do all this."

"Yes, I do. It's important you are all together."

Susan stayed in the lounge, she didn't know what to do, G stopped and turned.

"Do you want to stay in the bungalow? It's your bed too if you want it, if you don't you can have mine, I will take the sofa?"

"If I'm honest I don't know what to do, part of me wants to curl up in that bed and never get up, I know that sounds silly as we didn't know each other for long."

"No, it doesn't, you got close to each other over the months on the phone, being together the last few weeks just completed it for you both. Don't ever think you don't deserve to be hurting Susan, you do."

"Thank you G, can I come with you?" He nodded waiting for her, she grabbed her bag following him.

They walked into the bungalow, Susan felt sick, she held her stomach as they walked into the kitchen.

"Would you like a glass of water before you go to bed?" She nodded.

"Yes, please G, it suddenly feels very real." He nodded not saying a word, forcing his own tears back.

"If you need me at all just wake me up."

"Thank you I will. the same goes for you too G, we all need to go through this together."

Susan walked into the bedroom, she could smell Moses, her legs gave way as she reached the bed, she laid on his side, burying her face in his pillow, the smell of him more intense, she began to sob quietly. She pulled the duvet around cocooning herself in it, her heart was broken, the pit of her stomach was heavy, 'what if's' going around in her mind. Her eyes were becoming sore from the tears, her head was thumping, she sat up in bed to have some water. She noticed his t-shirt on the chair, she took her clothes off putting it on, wrapping herself back up laying down again. She was exhausted, she fell into an unsettled sleep.

G couldn't sleep, he was angry, he got up and paced the bungalow, he felt like a leashed dog, he walked out of the bungalow grabbing his jacket and began walking, he didn't know where he was going he didn't know this end of town, he had been gone some time when he walked into the town, it was early hours of the morning, he walked into a park area and sat on a bench. His chest was tight, he felt unsettled, he couldn't believe only 12 hours previous they were talking and now he was gone. The anger was building inside him again, he felt like he needed to hit someone or something. He grabbed his head in his hands and screamed.

"Nooooo, this is not real. Please Brother come back." He begged punching his legs with his fists, he began to cry hysterically. A woman was walking through the park, she looked at him with pity sitting down with him.

"Are you okay?"

"What does it look like?" he snapped, sniffing wiping his face.

"I was only asking, anything I can do to help?"

"If you want to be used as a punchbag then yes, if not go away." He put his head down again, the heels of his hands in his eyes.

"Well, I'm not into that kind of thing, but I sure can make you forget if you want to for a while?"

G looked up at her out of the corner of his eye. "I beg your pardon?"

"Well, I do love and English accent, this time of night I come cheap, but I don't like that weird stuff, we can go to my room if you like?" She sidled up closer to him her hand on his knee stroking him.

"You mean you want to fuck and I pay for the pleasure?" She nodded smiling at him, biting the corner of her red lips. "Where?" She stood up taking his hand, he followed her.

They crossed the road entering a dark alley, she led him to the bottom, he could smell urine, beer and food, he didn't care. He continued with her, she stopped at a beaten door opening it leading him up the dark stairs into a room that smelt as bad as the alley way. The old sofa in the corner had seen better days the arms were torn and the stuffing was showing, a thin scalf had been put over the top of the lamp shade putting a dim light in the room. He looked around at the mess, the dirty clothes on the floor, she pushed him onto the half-covered mattress. He stood up grabbing her. Pushing her over the bed, her short skirt rising up over her bottom. He could see she was naked, he slapped her hard.

"Open your legs", he growled. She did as he asked her head on the mattress, he pulled out his wallet fishing out a condom, tearing the corner off he pulled it out, he was already hard, he knew it was out of anger and loss, he pushed the condom over his cock spat on his fingers pushing them between her legs, she was dry, as he expected, he spat down onto his cock rubbing it over the condom, pulled her hips close ramming his cock hard into her. She gasped in pain, he was larger than most. Thrusting into her was giving him the release he needed, he spanked her again hard, leaving a red mark on her, he didn't care about this woman. He pushed her down onto the bed she was flat, he got on kneeling above her.

"Turn over." He demanded, she did, he grabbed her hair pulling her up to sitting position pulling his condom off.

"Your pussy is not doing anything for me, suck it good if you want paying." He pushed his cock into her mouth, she wrapped her hands around it, twisting it sucking the tip, he pulled her hand away in temper.

"I said fucking suck it!" He pulled her head closer pushing his cock deeper into her mouth, she was gasping for air, her mouth spread wide over him, he pushed himself deeper, she began to gag, he pulled out of her letting her catch her breath before pushing back in again hard. He forced her head back and forth.

"Easy isn't it?" he growled. She nodded gagging, her spit coming out of the side of her mouth, he pushed her back and forth until he felt his orgasm build, he looked down at her with no pity, he didn't care anything about her. She was a means to an end. He forced her harder onto him pushing himself faster but not as deep. He stopped, his cock deep in her mouth as he shot into her, she was gagging on it trying to swallow, he pushed harder as she tried to pull away, he screamed as he came like an injured animal. Letting go of her head she sank onto the bed coughing on his cum, her face red and tear stained, she was gasping. He grabbed the edge of the bedding wiped his cock clean and redressed himself, pulling out his wallet he threw two hundred dollars at her. Without a word he walked out leaving her laid on the bed crying.

He walked out into the alley as two men came towards him, he was still angry and wanted to take on the world. One of the men knocked his mate and laughed as they approached him. He knew trouble was heading his way. The two men drew knives as he reached them. He stopped.

"Empty your pockets if you want to live." The tallest one shouted. G shook his head.
"I don't think so gentlemen."
"Do as he fucking say's or you will be sorry."
Like I said, I don't fucking think so." The first came at him with a lunge aiming for his stomach, he moved his arm to cover him, it caught is jacket ripping the arm.
"Want that again Mr? if not do as you are told." G shook his jacket off throwing it onto the ground.
"You want to play boys, well come on then show me what you have." He grinned at them both, waiting. The first came back at him, he was taller than G but skinny, he missed him completely.
"You have one more go then it's my turn." He grinned again. The second began to circle him, pushing the blade at him, G laughed.
"Times up boys." He moved quick at the biggest, grabbing his arm as he went for him, the blade caught his arm cutting down the forearm, he shook it off, gripped the guys arm twisting it, grabbing the blade with his other hand. He pushed the blade up to the guys throat.
"If you want to go home on your feet tonight then you better run home now to Mummy or you will be going in a body bag", he pushed the blade into his neck drawing blood, his friend ran off leaving the guy alone.
"You don't fucking scare me." The guy screamed at him. G dropped the knife turning the guy to face him. He spat at G, it caught him across his cheek, he pulled the guy by the shoulders towards him head butting him, he felt him go limp in his hands, he pushed him back, punching him in the face, catching his nose, he heard the crack, it instantly bled. He didn't stop, he continued punching him, he could feel the pressure of the day releasing, he began to cry as the guy slumped to the floor. He

was bleeding badly, his eyes swollen his lip was split. G pulled out his wallet throwing money at him.

"You need that to get to the hospital, next time someone tells you to walk away I suggest you do it." He wiped his face with the back of his hands, they were covered in blood. The guy spat at G, enraging him, he screwed his fist up ready to hit him again, he didn't care if he killed him. He knew it wasn't the answer, he grabbed his jacket and walked away. He was covered in the mans blood, he stopped, pulling his t-shirt off putting it in the bin in the park, he pulled his jacket back on walking to the water fountain to rinse his hands and clean his face. He was exhausted, he wanted to sleep, he walked back to Dorians slowly, walking into the bungalow he kicked his boots off and headed to the shower, he wrapped another t-shirt around his arm to stop the blood leaking on the bedding before collapsing in bed.

Chapter 29

Making arrangements

G put the phone down to the Solicitor, he sighed heavily standing up rubbing his head. Heading to the dining room. James met him as he walked in hugging him.

"Hey Brother, anything we can do to help?"

"No nothing, the Will is being sent across by email now, Jasper we will need your guy as soon as he can get here. We need to talk about the plans for Moses." He choked as he said his name.

"I will call him now and see if he is free today to come over." G nodded.

Jane put her hand out to him to sit with her, he kissed her head as he sat down.

"None of my business but the knuckles, who or what was it?"

"You're right Half-pint none of your business, but he came off worse than I did."

"At least let us look at your arm!"

"No need it will heal up."

"G, it has a dirty t-shirt wrapped around it, I'm sure Kitty has a decent first aid kit", she pushed herself up out of the chair going into the kitchen. She came out with the kit and sat cleaning his arm up, he wasn't bothered, it was still bleeding and quite a deep gash, he looked down at it smiling, it had been a long time since he had tasted blood from another, it was just what he needed, he knew Moses would be proud. Jane finished bandaging it up. He smiled at her.

"Thanks Doc, as good as new. Now eat up we need to talk." Jane grabbed her tea following him into the lounge, he sat down with his coffee opening the email on his phone.

"Right then, don't speak until I have read this out, no arguing, I just want this done as soon as."

"Oi don't go off at me we are all hurting, I don't like this anymore than you do."

"Sorry Half-pint, I'm struggling with this."

"Give me the phone then you know what's in it so don't read it out." He huffed handing her the phone, she took a deep breath and began reading. The tears welling up in her eyes, Jasper came in and sat with her while she read it. She grabbed his hand desperate not to cry. She handed the phone back to G, he shook his head pointing to Jasper.

"Read it please Brother this involves you now." Jasper took the phone and began reading. Jane put her head in her hands pushing her fingers into her hair, rubbing her eyes, she was trying her hardest not too.

Jasper finished reading it, he sighed. "Well he needs to go home for sure, regardless of not being buried, he will be repatriated, the Solicitor will be here a little later, he has all the contacts apparently. What do you want us to do G?"

"Fucked if I know, I know I need to go back to his place and get everything sorted."

"We will come with you, it's both of you who need to do this, our honeymoon can wait, can't it Belle?"

Jane nodded. Her tears spilling over, Jasper pulled her into his arms kissing her on the head.

"I'm so sorry Belle."

"It wasn't you, it's okay. Of course we can go home with you, I wouldn't have it any other way. We can have a service here for him so the guys can pay their respects if they want it? I know there is a Pastor in the club."

"That's a good idea, I will speak to Shadow when he get's back."

"Someone call me?" Shadow walked into the room. "What can I do for you?"

"We were just saying we need to take Moses home but wondered if the guys here would appreciate a chance to pay their respects, you know have a service for him?"

"Of course we would, I will speak to the Pastor, he will organise it." Jane half smiled. "The bike is back at the garage, the Police are coming in later to take it away, it sounds like the driver will be prosecuted.

"I should fucking hope so, he was out of the way, that crazy fucker came right at him, he didn't stand a chance." Shadow put his hand onto G's shoulder.

"I know Brother, we will make sure our statements are water tight with every detail, that mother fucker is going down, my boys on the inside will sort him out." Jane covered her head she didn't want to hear it.

"Sorry Half-pint, didn't want you hearing that. We're just angry and blowing off steam." Shadow got down on his knees in front of her opening his arms. Jane went to him, he wrapped his arms around her like a giant teddy, she wept into his chest, as he rubbed her back soothing her like a child.

The Solicitor arrived, everyone gathered around as he read the Will. He handed the papers back to G, "well that's all sorted which makes it easier, there is a lot of paperwork we need to do to get your friend home, we do have a company we work with that can help us do that. He will need to go to the funeral directors for preparation purposes to enable him to travel home." Jane frowned at him, unsure of what he meant. Jasper bent down to her ear.

"I will tell you later love." She nodded as the Solicitor continued.

"I assume the Police are involved in this case, if you need help from us let me know, I would imagine it will be an open and shut case but to be honest you never know. Anyway you have my number call me if there is anything else I can do. I will get in touch with my colleagues to arrange for Moses to be moved to the funeral directors, then speak to the local Embassy and start the paperwork."

"I would like him to travel home on my plane if that's possible?" Dorian stood up.

"We can certainly sort that out, I will ask the question for you."

"Thank you, I appreciate that. We just don't want him in the hold of a plane with a bunch of holiday makers."

"I understand, I will call you tomorrow with an update. In the meantime call if I can help at all." Jasper stood walking with him to the door. He shook his hand as he opened the door.

"Thank you for coming, I do appreciate it, any costs please let me know and I will settle them."

"As you wish Jasper. I will call you tomorrow."

Jasper went back into the room, everyone was sat chatting about what was going to happen.

"We can have him home within the week?" Gwen asked wiping her fresh tears.

"Yes love, better for him too, it's not fair to keep this hanging on."

"We will travel home together, Dorian is going to travel with Moses if he's able too, we can then get everything arranged. There will be a memorial service here after his funeral for the club. I will come back with these guys and Dorian. Susan you are welcome to stay in England as long as you like or travel back with us. It's your choice or not at all. I'm sorry I am assuming now." She nodded.

"I would like to be at the funeral please."

"Jane hugged her, of course you can. It's important for us all to be there, Shadow you are welcome too and you Animal, anyone is." They nodded in thanks.

"I will arrange a place to stay for a few weeks then close by, can you give me an idea of where is best Matt, Steve?"

"Of course Brother, you are welcome to stay with any of us but I appreciate you both want time alone too."

"Thank you it's appreciated."

"I would like to go home and get changed now, half of our things are at the cottage that we will need, can we go back Jasper and sort things out?" He nodded hugging her.

"Sure we can", he stood up with Jane, everyone else stood and began hugging each other.

"We will see you tomorrow, by the time we get to the cottage and back it will be late so we will stay there tonight and come back here tomorrow. Hopefully by then we will have had an update."

They drove in silence back to the cottage, Jane was looking out of the window remembering the last time she did the journey on their wedding day with Moses and G, Jasper had hold of her hand, his thumb rubbing across her fingers. She wiped her tears away with her hand.

"I'm sorry Jasper."

"What for love?"

"For being like this, I just can't help it." Jasper pulled over to the side of the road popped his seat belt off and turned to face Jane.

"Listen love, if you didn't react the way you are I would worry. You need to let it out, you tell others enough not to bottle it up. Moses is your best friend, he has been the main part of your life for many years, it's expected. I just ask that you don't push me away, I am here for you love."

"I know, I'm sorry. I just feel lost without him, he was like my big brother, now he's gone. I don't know how I will manage without him."

"One day at a time Belle. There is no rush, you will always miss him, he will always be with you, with us." She nodded, her tears falling silently. Jasper pulled back out onto the road. Jane took his hand laying on her side watching him as they continued to the cottage.

Chapter 30

Time to say Goodbye

Jane was sat in the garden of the house Jasper had rented for them, they had been home for two weeks, they had sorted Moses house out and as per the Will it was to be sold. They had it with a local agent and due to the location it already had a lot of interest, G had given Jane her memory stick that he found from Moses, he had written on the envelope not to be seen until after the funeral. They both had one, Jane had almost crushed it in her hands not wanting to let go of it. It was 4am the birds were waking up and the sun was shining. Jasper came out of the house with a drink for them, he quietly sat down beside her kissing her head.

"Morning Belle, how are you love? you had a bad night again."

"I'm sorry if I woke you, I am just so restless, not sure why."

"It's to be expected love, this is the last time you will see Moses, are you sure you want to go in and see him." She nodded. "Okay, well we have plenty of time." Jane picked up her phone, she was scanning through the pictures of Moses, she knew she was hurting herself doing it, but she was scared of forgetting what he looked like. She finished her tea and stood up.

"Can we go back to bed please?"

"Of course love." Jasper stood up taking the cup from her. He put them on the sink in the kitchen and walked her upstairs, she climbed into bed with him curling into him. She looked up at him.

"I love you Jasper, promise me you will never leave."

"I love you too Belle, I promise you, I am yours forever, as you are mine." He took her hand kissing her wedding ring. "You are the single best thing that has ever happened to me." He half smiled.

"Can I ask a question?" She stared up at him her eyes wide. He melted looking down at her, she looked like a doll.

"Of course, anything."

"Why haven't we made love since Moses went?" Jasper looked down at her shocked.

"The only reason I haven't Belle is out of respect for you, I thought the last thing you would want is me pawing you." Jane pushed herself up on her elbow looking at Jasper.

"Darling I need you all the time, it isn't wrong for us to be doing it. My Mum said people need that for the closeness especially men in times like this. I'm telling you I need you Jasper." He looked down at her smiling.

"I need you too Belle, I'm sorry, I should have said something."

"No, we both should, I suppose it's another thing we will learn as we go on really. We always promised we would talk about things and right now this is important. I want to feel you touch me, I want to feel you inside me, to lose my mind the only way you make me."

Jasper gently laid Jane down onto her back, putting his finger over her lips.

"Shhh, enough talking." He whispered moving his finger, his lips brushing the top of hers, Jane sighed her body responding, her arms enveloping him pulling him to her, her right hand moving into the back of his hair. Jasper moaned as he parted her lips with his hot tongue, Jane mewled, her tongue meeting his dualling slowly, his hand moved down her body, caressing his fingertips up and down her side catching her breast, Jane gasped at the sensation. Her left hand moving down to his bottom squeezing his cheek with her fingernails. Jasper pushed into her, she could feel his hardening erection, she opened her legs letting him know she wanted him. His hand moving between as he laid on his side, he crossed over her soft tummy edging closer to her pussy. Jane was gasping in anticipation as his fingers moved further down, he caressed the top of her pussy teasing her, she lifted her body up the bed forcing his fingers down, Jasper smiled licking her lips. His fingers walking down to her outer lips, he slid them down either side. Closing her pussy, Jane groaned opening her legs more, her wetness showing, Jasper slid his fingers down the centre collecting her juices bringing his finger up rubbing them along her lips before licking it off her. He got onto his knees pushing her legs open further, his cock hard, slowly he moved himself between her legs sliding his cock inside. Jane arched pulling him in, her pussy wet and welcoming. They slowly came together, their bodies in synch with each other. Jasper didn't take his eyes from Janes as he continued slowly sliding in and out of her, his cock plunging deeper each time. Jane was moaning, her pussy was pulsing around him, she was desperate for the release, Jasper got up on his hands, just his cock touching her, their bodies hot with want and lust. Jane moved her hand down to her clit, Jasper watched as she pleasured herself, he began moving in and out faster, she was teasing him now licking her fingers of her juices, Jasper opened his mouth asking for some, Jane slid her fingers in, he sucked them hard moaning, Jane teased herself more, she wanted to cum.

"Come for me Belle, I want to watch you", he slid out sitting back on his heels. Jane continued, her fingers sliding inside, her other hand opening her pussy so he could see her. She glistened, her juices making his mouth water to taste. He bent down to her pussy laying on his stomach watching her closer, Jane played faster, her legs pushing her up off the bed, her body went rigid as she rode her orgasm, Jasper dove between her legs as she came, claiming her juices, sucking hard, his tongue thrusting at her clit for more, Jane began to squeal pushing his head away, he didn't stop he kept going, he wanted more. He sat back pulling her to him, she sat astride him, his cock now teasing her clit as she rode him, she bent backwards her arms on the bed as he thrust into her, his own orgasm hitting him, his cock like a rod of steel, pumping harder into her as she felt another orgasm arrive, she grabbed him around the neck riding him hard clenching her pussy around his cock wanting every last drop. They were both panting hard as they slowed down coming to a stop, Jaspers hand was around her waist holding her on his lap. He pulled her into him kissing her.

"I love you Mrs Mitchell, now will you sleep please." Jane laughed swatting him on the arm.

"I think I love you too, but not sure after that." She grinned. He spanked her hard sitting her on the bed.

"Ouch!" she moaned smoothing her bottom.

"You deserve that for being so cheeky, now get into that bathroom and let's clean up so we can have another couple of hours sleep." Jane poked her tongue out him running into the bedroom, he ran after her making her squeal. She stopped turning around to him.

"Thank you love, for listening and for being you. Today is going to be hard, but I know with you I can get through it." He didn't speak just held her for a few seconds kissing her on the head. They went back to bed. Jasper set the alarm for 7.30am giving them plenty of time to get ready.

They woke just before the alarm, the sun was already high and the house was warming up. Jasper looked across at Jane.

"You ok love?" She nodded smiling.

"Yes, I am thank you, let's get today over." She pushed herself out of bed heading to the shower. Within an hour they were ready to leave, they were going to see Moses at the funeral directors before the funeral.

They arrived at 9am prompt, they walked into a quiet office, the lady at the desk stood.
"Good morning, you must be Jane and Jasper?" Jane nodded. "He is all ready for you, would you like to come with me?" Jane nodded again, her heart in her mouth, her stomach doing somersaults. She could feel the tears building. The receptionist opened the door, gentle music played quietly in the background, candles had been lit around the soft yellow room. Moses coffin was in the middle. She let them in nodded and walked away closing the door behind her. Jane took a deep breath grabbing Jaspers hand. They took the last few steps over to him. He was laid in his suit with his regimental badge on his pocket. His hands crossed in front of him. His leather waistcoat at his feet. Jane let out a sob. The tears spilling over, Jasper put his arm around her as she reached in to touch him. She kissed the yellow rose before putting into his hand.
"He's so cold. But he looks so beautiful and at peace." She smoothed his beard down, touching his lips, "his beard was normally unruly, but he hated long bits in the way when he was eating." Jasper smiled. She stroked his temple. "Oh Moses, this is so unfair, just as you found happiness this happens. Promise me you will watch over us from time to time, I don't know how we will live without you, you were my saviour, you gave me back my life. I can never thank you enough for that. I love you so much." She bent into the coffin to kiss his head, her lips staying on him for a few seconds. "Please wake up, we need you." She whispered, her heart breaking into a million pieces. Jasper held her as she sobbed openly, moving her away from Moses. He held her tight letting her cry, he stood looking into the coffin.
"Thank you Moses, for everything. Goodbye Brother. Sleep tight. Rest in peace." He choked on his own tears as he led Jane to the chairs, they sat and hugged for a few minutes until Jane was ready to leave.

Jasper took them to the coffee shop next door, they had an hour to wait before the funeral cars left, they had arranged to meet there with the guys from the club who were leading him to the crematorium. They sat drinking coffee as G, Susan and Dorian arrived, they stood hugging each other before Jasper went to get more coffee. Jane and Susan sat holding hands. The rest of the gang arrived taking over the coffee shop. It wasn't long until the funeral directors pulled the cars around ready to leave. They all stepped outside bowing their heads. His coffin had the club flag on it, his crash helmet and gloves on top. Flowers filled the inside. Jane squeezed Jaspers hand hard. As the cars stopped they all prepared themselves. G led on Moses bike, he had spent the night polishing it. The others fell in behind, it was a sea of bikes. Jane, Susan and the girls got into the family car all holding hands as they drove slowly to the crematorium. The noise of the bikes was loud as they rumbled through the town, passers by stopped hanging their heads as they passed. Jane turned to look out of the back window. Bill nodded from behind leading the other bikes, Jasper was by his side. She half smiled sitting back down. They arrived at the crematorium, the bikes parked first as the cars waited for them to be ready as they lined up outside the doorway, the cars moved stopping at the doors, Jane and the girls got out standing with the men as the coffin was pulled out. G, Jasper, Dorian, Matt, Steve and Bill stepped forward to take their friend. Shadow being so tall led them in as Jane followed with Susan, they held onto each other as they walked down to the front. They sat together as the coffin was positioned. Jasper and G came and sat with them both. The room filled quickly, others stood around the walls and outside, they left the door open so others could hear.

The priest stood and began talking, Jane stared at the coffin lost in thought. Tears streaming down her face.

"Jane and G would you like to read your piece?" She looked at Jasper he nodded, moving back for her to step out. G took her hand walking with her. They stood together at the front holding hands.

"As most of you know Moses was my best mate, we go into trouble a lot especially on tour, but as the saying goes, what happens on tour stays on tour. We fought often but never held a grudge, he was there for me as often as I was there for him. He was my Brother. When he was diagnosed with Cancer the pain inside was immense, it felt like my heart was being ripped out, but nothing prepared me for this. For him to be taken so quickly is harder than watching him die. I never wanted him to suffer but at least I could say the things I needed to say." Mumbles went around the crowd. "Neither of us were emotional kinds, until this little lady came into our lives", he squeezed Jane's hand looking down at her. "She sure changed that. I couldn't be closer to two people more than I am, with these two. Moses being taken from us is probably the hardest thing I have ever had to deal with." He let go of Janes hand walking towards the coffin.

"Goodbye Brother, you will never be forgotten as long as we all have breath in our bodies. Stand down soldier your duty is over." He coughed trying to stop himself crying as he kissed his fingers and placed them on the coffin. He walked back to Jane kissing her on the head taking her hand. Jane looked up at the crowd.

"I know he would be mad with us all being here sad, but for once I don't care. Moses was an incredible man, he gave me back my life, cared for me, treated me like a doll with G, without their love and support I couldn't be the person I am today. If any man or woman can be half the person he was then they are pretty damn special. He had a lot of love to give, finally he found someone to make him happy in Susan, that short time they were together she made him happier than we have seen in many years. Thank you Susan. He told me off for putting him on a pedestal but he belonged there and always will. He was a pain in the backside but he was my pain. My hero, my true friend."

The room fell quiet, the sea of people stood in front of them in leather and black suits bowed their eyes wiping their eyes as Jane began to read the poem he loved.

"Stop all the clocks, cut off the telephone,
Prevent the dog from barking with a juicy bone,
Silence the pianos and with muffled drum,
Bring out the coffin, let the mourners come.

Let aeroplanes circle moaning overhead,
Scribbling on the sky the message, He Is Dead,
Put crepe bows round the white necks of the public doves,
Let the traffic policemen wear black cotton gloves.

He was my North, my South, my East and West,
My working week and my Sunday rest,
My noon, my midnight, my talk, my song;
I thought that love would last for ever: I was wrong.

The stars are not wanted now: put out every one;
Pack up the moon and dismantle the sun;
Pour away the ocean and sweep up the wood;

For nothing now can ever come to any good."

I love you Moses. Goodnight love. You are loved more than you could ever imagine. Sleep tight until we meet again." Jane wiped her tears away looking up at the crowd, they lifted their heads and began to clap. The priest came to the front as Jane and G walked away, standing with Susan and Jasper.
"Would you please stand for the committal. To everything there is a season and a time to every purpose on earth, a time to be born and a time to die. Here in this last act, in sorrow, but without fear, in love and appreciation, we commit Moses to his natural end.

Goodbye, from Kenny Rogers began to play as the heavy green curtains closed around his coffin.

Jane felt her legs go beneath her as she caught sight of his coffin for the final time. The man that had given her everything, his life, his love and his heart. She knew her life would never be the same again, but he had left her at a good time. She knew he would love her for eternity as she did him, now it was her time to live her life with Jasper.

The End.

About

Grace Williams

I am a new Indie Author, my books are from a few genres including Contemporary Romance, Erotic Romance.

When not writing and researching I enjoy learning more about Mental Health and how to help others. Spending time with my friends and family.

Spending time with my followers on Social Media

Links

Facebook – https://www.facebook.com/gracewilliamsauthor

Instagram – Grac.e2609

gracewilliamsauthor@gmail.com

THANK YOU

Thank you for reading Moses. Gaining exposure as an independent author relies mostly on word-of-mouth, please consider leaving a review.

Printed in Great Britain
by Amazon

23982290R00162